THE HORIZON

Praise for *The Wall*

'A deeply intelligent and thoughtful intellectual adventure that raises some fundamental questions in a strikingly original and provocative way.'

—Gary K. Wolfe, *Locus*

'A significant Indian debut in science fiction on the theme of freedom.'

—Pratap Bhanu Mehta, *Open*

'An exciting new direction for Indian sci-fi.'

—*The Hindu*

'A fast-paced, gripping read, it is an important addition to Indian and world speculative fiction.'

—*The Hindustan Times*

'By rebuking static, formulaic utopias in favour of dynamic, complex societies, *The Wall* asserts itself a descendant of Ursula K. Le Guin's *The Dispossessed* ... an unforgettable story and a fantastic addition to contemporary Indian (English) SFF.'

—*Strange Horizons*

'It would be hard to put the book aside, even for a bit, for the last part. *The Wall* comes across as a deeply imagined, stylish and confident debut of an author who has introduced one new world to us, and will hopefully introduce many more.'

—*The Wire*

'The novel pulls in readers with its thoughtful and detailed world-building.'

—*Scroll*

THE HORIZON

BEING THE SECOND BOOK OF

THE CHRONICLES OF SUMER

GAUTAM
BHATIA

HarperCollins *Publishers* India

First published in India by
HarperCollins *Publishers* 2021
HarperCollins *Publishers* India, Cyber City, Building 10-A, Gurugram, Haryana-122002, India
www.harpercollins.co.in

2 4 6 8 10 9 7 5 3 1

P-ISBN: 978-93-5422-763-9
E-ISBN: 978-93-5422-788-2

Typeset in 11/14.2 Adobe Garamond at
Manipal Technologies Limited, Manipal

Printed and bound at
Repro India Ltd.

HarperCollins *Publishers* , Macken House, 39/40 Mayor Street Upper, Dublin 1, D01 C9W8, Ireland

To Strange Horizons—
My anarchic collective
and my sanctuary

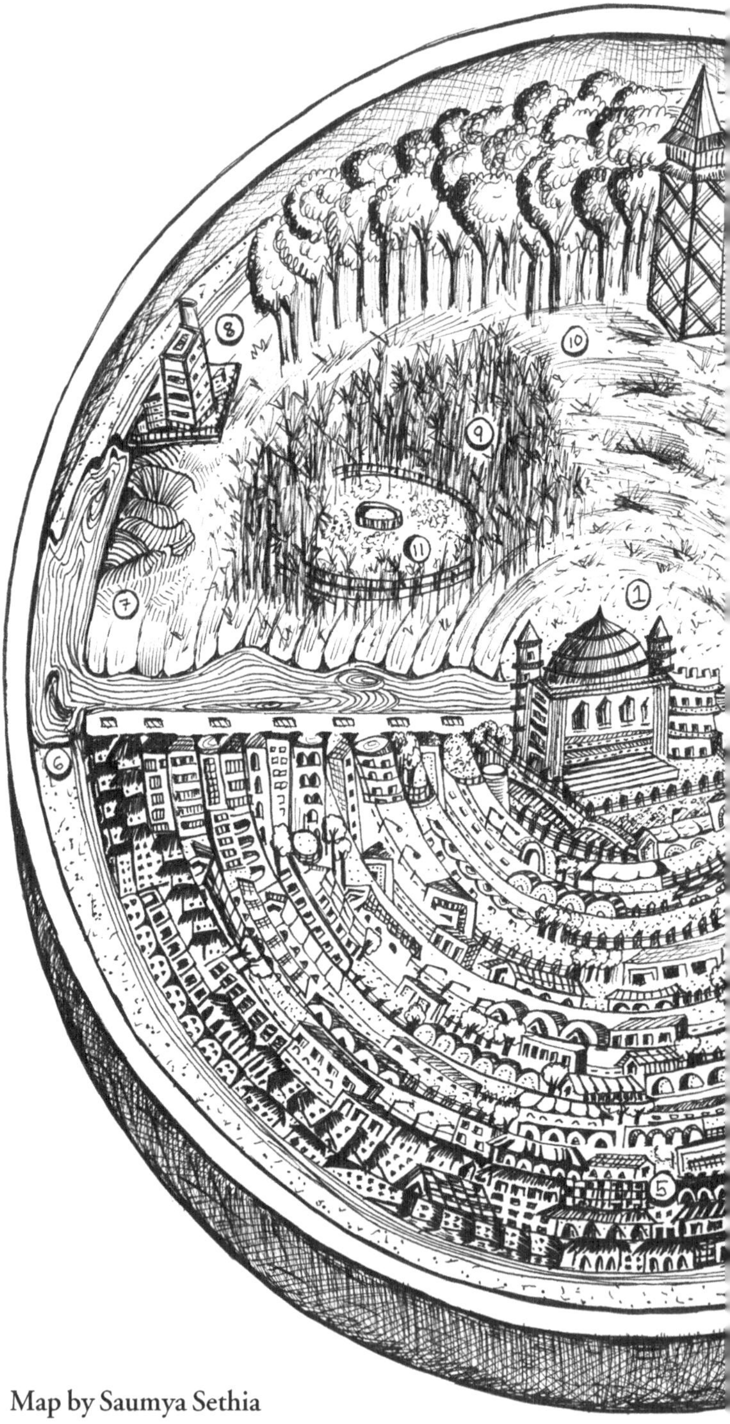

Map by Saumya Sethia

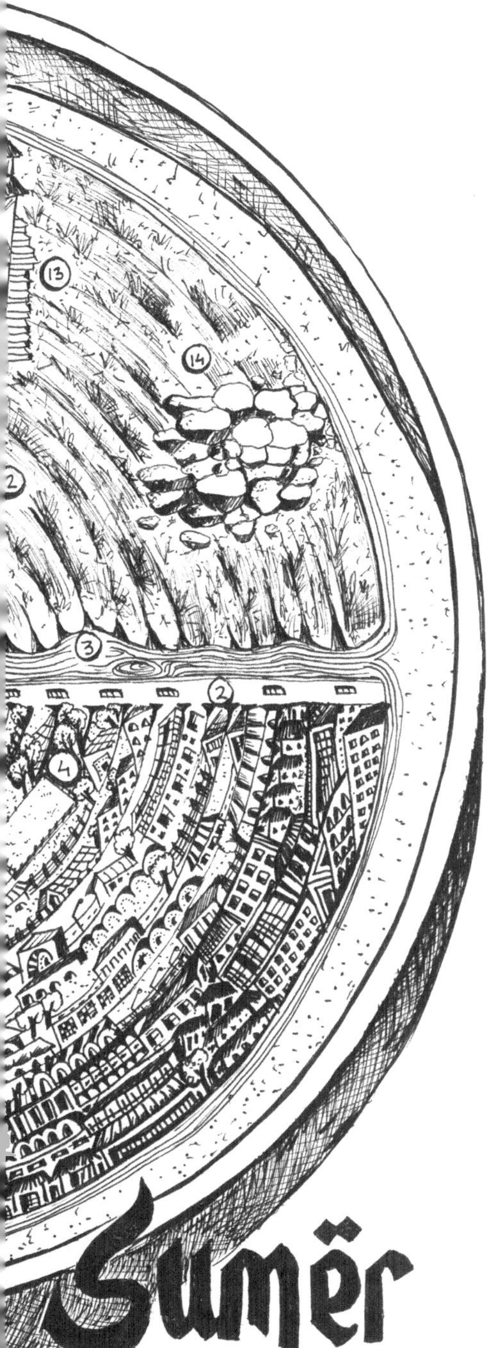

1. The Forum
2. The Maliot Road
3. The Rasa
4. The Maidan
5. The Dooma
6. The Lake
7. The Iron Swamp
8. The Furnaces
9. The Bamboo Grove
10. The Woodlands
11. The Woad Garden
12. The Farms
13. The Towers of Rebirth
14. The Stone Quarries

Contents

PART THREE: MIDDLEGAME

PART FOUR: ENDGAME

Characters

The Elders

Hansa, President of the Council
Raja, Officer of the Public Peace
Varsha, Farmland Administrator
Paras, a senior Councillor
Malati, a member of the Progressive Faction
Rama, Speaker for the Eleventh

The Shoortan Priesthood

Minakshi, the Matriarch
Rastogi, the High Priest
Tefnakth, leader of the Coterie (now expelled)
The Acolytes

The Scientists (the 'Select')

Marwana, leader of the Select
Kanu, a scientist

The Young Tarafians

Mithila (Seventh Mandala)
Alvar (Ninth Mandala)
Lamon (Eighth Mandala)
Mankala (Eleventh Mandala)

The POUM

Prana, representative of the Farmers' Union
Meghana, representative of the Farmers' Union

The Unforgiven

Maji, the leader of the Unforgiven
Carina, a singer

Others

Elmandar, leader of the Hedonists
Ananta/Savarian, Mithila's father
Kodali, Head of the Carers' Circle
Bhavi (Eleventh Mandala), a farmer
Aashna (Eleventh Mandala), a farmer, and Bhavi's wife
Sekri (Ninth Mandala), a weaver, and one of Alvar's fathers

PART ONE

COMPOSITION

Prologue

Twenty-seven years ago...

'Come back when you've saved the Revolution.'

Maji remembers Upar's last words—only half-joking—just before she'd drawn him into a kiss and stopped his mouth. 'The Revolution doesn't need us to save it,' she'd murmured into his ear. Then she'd torn herself free, and run to join the others.

Moonlight glimmers on an iron blade. The sky is the colour of lampblack. His laughter rings inside her, holds her body together, even as her heart threatens to explode.

She moves in silence through the *rahi* fields, at the rear of their ten-person expedition. The farmlands are deserted. Far to the South, an orange light glimmers. Cries carry over the air. The Circles burn tonight, like a dying blaze that flares up one last time before dwindling into ash.

Ahead of a dark knot of trees, their leader raises an arm, halting them.

'One final time,' Rahul-Eleven says. 'We go in—we get her—we get out. We're back before Wallrise. Any questions?'

There is no sound but their breathing, ragged after the wide loop they took through the farmlands.

Rahul signals. They run into the bamboo grove.

Far from the Dooma, the grove is forbidden to all but the Elders. Maji has never been here before. The bamboo stalks loom above her. They blot out the sky for a deeper darkness. As she runs on uneven ground, she feels the fronds brush against her skin, fleeting little touches.

The only sound they make is when they cross the wooden bridge that spans the Rasa tributary, running through the grove. Then the sky opens again, the trees thin out, and Maji sees a scattering of starlight.

They burst into the clearing that houses the woad garden. It is larger than she thought. There is a wall in the middle, surrounded by a labyrinth of hedges. In the shadow of the outer hedge, a young woman looks calmly back at them.

'Get the President!' Rahul shouts.

Hansa turns and ducks into the labyrinth. Savarian's soldiers leap after her—but Maji stops for a split second, because she has seen the President's blue gloves in the moonlight, the gloves of battle, and something gives her pause.

Beneath their running feet, the ground opens. With horrible yells, four of their men plunge through, upon the bamboo spikes ten feet below.

The others pull up short. The screams of their fallen comrades rend the night. Shouts of *'Council!'* join their cries. The Watch rushes upon them from the grove.

Maji spins, her blade out. Instantly, she is fighting for her life. Iron meets iron; a parry, a duck; she sticks her leg out, tripping her assailant as they go past her, sending them headlong. The spikes do not discriminate between rebels and the Watch.

'*Formation!*' Rahul calls.

The six of them move together, a tight unit, blades covering all angles. The Watch presses, outnumbering them by two to one. The rebels dig their feet in, backs to the treacherous ground. They fight at close quarters. Maji's blade is a blur, anything to maintain a sliver of space, to avoid letting them catch her sword and heave her on to the waiting spikes.

Out of nowhere, there's an arrow sticking out of someone's back.

It is her companion on the left. As if in a dream, Maji sees his eyes widen in surprise. His head jerks back. He drops his blade and pitches back, into the pit.

Hansa has reappeared in the clearing. There is a bow in her hands.

The President takes aim again.

'*Break!*' Rahul shouts in the night.

Maji attacks. She takes wounds on her shoulder and her side, but fights her way to the edge of the clearing, helped by the Watch choosing to focus their energies on her remaining companions—hardened veterans. And then she's in the grove once more, sprinting back through those narrow, twisting paths.

She sobs as she runs. She sobs because Upar was wrong. The Revolution was already lost. All that is left is for the dream to die, the dream of a City without Circles.

Outside, in the fields, she realizes that she no longer wants to run. She stops, grits her teeth, and turns to face the grove. Already, she can hear scrabbling, and the sound of quick feet. She crouches and grips her blade, ready.

Rahul bursts out from the grove. 'What the fuck are you waiting for? Move!' He runs past. Maji turns and follows, numb.

They race South, towards burning Sumer. The wind is in their hair. An arrow whistles past her ear. There are shouts from the edge of the grove.

A part of her wonders why they are running straight into the Upper Circles, where the fight is on, instead of North to the empty farms.

But Rahul seems to know where he's going. The Rasa appears before them, a dark line bisecting Sumer. Rahul sprints across the thin wooden bridge, and into the First Mandala. Maji hesitates, then follows.

The stone mansions of the First Mandala surround them. Another place that Maji has never been to, in her twenty-three years within the Wall. As they run, she takes in the clean-cut flagstoned roads, the rows of lit flame lamps, the two-storied houses set apart from one another with their gardens and porches, all in darkness.

Rahul takes two quick turns and stops outside one of those houses. He raps on the door.

A face appears in the first-floor window.

'Who is it?' a woman's voice calls out.

'We beg for sanctuary,' Rahul pants. Maji's hands are on her knees, and she takes deep, juddering breaths to deal with the crick in her stomach. 'We're rebels,' Rahul continues, 'we're trapped—they'll kill us if they find us.'

The head pops back in. Silence takes back the night. After a thousand eternities, they hear footsteps from close within. They grow louder.

The woman opens the door. 'Inside.' She jerks her thumb. 'First floor. Crawl under the bed if you need to.'

'Councillor Malati—thank you.'

'Go!'

Maji sees her lighting a lamp in the hallway as they rush through the passage and take the stairs, up into the Councillor's bedroom.

Every limb in her body aches, but Maji doesn't dare go and collapse upon the bed. She stumbles to a corner of the room, next to the window, and slumps to the floor, her back against the wall. Her right shoulder—where she'd taken a blade—has begun to sting, sending out little ripples of pain. Maji winces.

Rahul walks past her to stand by the window.

'What was the point of running?' she says.

'Don't you care to live?' Rahul asks mildly.

'We failed….' Maji trails off.

'Why did you join the Revolution, Maji-Fifteen?'

The question throws her. She is back in the Fifteenth Mandala. It is a summer day. They crowd the terraces, flush in the sun. Sweat mingles with anticipation. The Wall looms in the distance.

She shades her kajal-limned eyes with her palms—wouldn't *you* deck yourself up for the day the world will change, with lampblack you can't afford?—and looks at the man who stands before them. He is perched precariously on a parapet, dressed in rebel blue that she knows *he* can't afford. His arms are spread, his body taut, his eyes dancing.

'*Can you see it?*' he calls.

The vision fades.

'Just for a moment,' says Maji, 'Savarian showed me a City without Circles. It was enough for a lifetime.'

'And dying in the *rahi* fields will help you?'

'What is left to live for, Captain?' She adds as an afterthought: 'What has my life been for?'

'You won't know unless you live—' he stops, putting a finger to his lips.

Maji's eyes struggle to adjust to the dark, even though moonlight is streaming in through the window. She can hear herself breathe.

Below them, there is a rapping at the front door.

A creak. 'Yes?' Malati's voice floats up to them.

'Councillor Malati—sorry for disturbing you so late—'

'—or early.'

'Yes—there are rebels on the loose in the Mandala.'

'I thought we were winning?'

'We are, but they've come in from the North, the farmlands.'

Rahul stands rigid at the window.

'Bit lax of you, Madeesh,' Malati says, after a pause. 'Good luck with your search.'

'Councillor—'

'Yes?' Iron enters Malati's voice.

'We're doing a house-to-house search.'

'No, Madeesh-Six,' Malati says. 'You're searching *empty* houses in case they've crept into a garden or a study. I am very much in my house.'

'But they might have climbed up through a window—'

'Do you want to try climbing, to test that theory?'

Beneath the window, there is muttering.

'Councillor,' Madeesh speaks again, 'President Hansa specifically told us to—'

'*I* will answer to the President, Six,' Malati snaps. 'Now stop wasting my time and find those rebels—isn't there a barricade that needs tearing down?'

More muttering. Maji can hardly move—her body is hurting too much—but Rahul is crouched by the window, blade in hand. A few minutes pass in silence. Rahul relaxes.

'Safe.'

Maji breathes. Rahul allows himself to slump, sliding down against the wall, dropping his blade. Maji hears it clatter. For a while, neither of them says anything.

'Dooma,' Rahul whispers at last.

'Mm, captain?'

'Is it really true what they say—about the Unforgiven?'

Maji laughs in her throat. 'What, you think I'm mad?'

'No, not you, no. You know.'

'I know what?'

'Don't make me say it.'

She looks at him in the dark. 'How long have you been waiting to ask?'

'Ever since Savarian assigned you to my company,' Rahul says, ruefully.

'Never spoken to someone from the Dooma before?'

He rubs his neck.'Not as a companion. Not until the Revolution.'

'Only as labour. I'm not surprised.'

'I know, I know. Could be that Savarian has the right idea, with his whole integration thing.'

Maji smiles.

'Alora,' she says.

'What?'

'Alora the Builder, captain. The only Builder we of the Dooma acknowledge, who stood against the Wall and was punished for it; who asked us to have faith, because *light will come from light.* Alora.' She lets her voice deepen. '*We will carry the memory of your name like hot iron beneath the tongue.*'

He turns to her. 'There is so much I don't know about my own City, this side of the Wall. Things I've begun to see, to touch—ever since I joined the Revolution, because the Sumer Savarian dreamt of felt more real than the one we live in. Will you take me to the Dooma, once this is over? And tell me how you live? That is not an order,' he adds hurriedly.

She is touched, in spite of herself. They both know it is never going to happen.

'Yes, captain. You can come.'

'Thank you.'

To fill the silence, she says: 'I have a question too.'

'Ask.'

'You of the Eleventh—I've heard you talk among yourselves upon the barricades. You have your own name for Savarian: garuda. Why's that?'

It is his turn to laugh. 'We have our stories too.'

'Go on.'

He thinks for a while. 'Listen, then,' he says at last, as if he's been waiting to tell. 'Season after season, in the long afternoons, when the sun shines golden upon the *rahi* fields, we have seen the garudas fly.' Rahul's voice changes, growing soft like dew. 'They come from beyond the Wall, and there they return. From the sky they look upon us while we toil, as if language is a memory that has been taken from them, and they would speak to us if they could remember. But in the fields, we remember.'

His voice quickens. 'Two brothers, there were. They flew together. Garuda flew too high, too close to the Sun. But before she could burn him in her rage, Samati interceded. He took upon himself the bolt meant for Garuda. His wings were charred and he was hurled down to the ground.

'Garuda escaped. But in punishment, words dried up in his throat forever, turning to ashes, like Samati's wings. And to separate the two brothers, the Wall of Sumer came to be. This side we dwell, the daughters and sons of Samati, doomed only to gaze upon our sky-faring cousins, who come back to us from beyond the Wall, but can neither speak nor stay.'

'I've never heard this story,' Maji whispers.

'A story spun in the forever hours upon the *rahi* fields, watching the sky in the shadow of the Wall. And we call Savarian garuda because that is how he came to us, on the wings of a dream, to show us what we might have been—and what we might be again.'

Maji smiles. 'Don't think me rude, Captain. But I'm from the Dooma. We're on the side of the lost. So I can't help seeing this from Samati's point of view.'

'What?'

'That if you want to fly, someone must sacrifice themselves for you.'

'Oh—'

The door swings open. Rahul leaps to his feet, but it is only Malati at the threshold.

'Wallrise. You need to get out of here.'

'We will,' Rahul says. 'Do you know the lay of the Upper Circles?'

'They are only guarding the bridges,' Malati says. 'If you go carefully, you'll be able to get as far as the Seventh without meeting the Watch. Then it's up to you.'

Maji blurts out: 'But why are *you* helping us, Councillor?'

Rahul winces, but Malati does not appear to take offence.

'You've lost your revolution,' she says. 'I can afford to save two lives.'

In the cold light of Wallrise, they creep through the Upper Circles.

Rahul leads. Shadows of patrols pass them in the distance, murmured voices and footsteps along adjoining streets. They stay away from the bridges and swim across the Rasa tributaries to cross the Circles. By the time they reach the Sixth, the sun has appeared over the Wall. There is mild autumn warmth in the air. Their clothes are soaking.

Rahul walks slowly now, almost crouching. He pokes his head around corners before turning, and stops every other moment. Maji's calves begin to hurt.

Then she sees sunlight glint off the flagstones of the Maliot, and hears the gurgling of the river.

In the shadow of the last row of houses, Rahul halts, motioning to her to stay behind. He peeks around the corner—and pulls his head back.

'What is it, captain?' she whispers.

Rahul looks up at the brightening sky. Then he turns to her and grasps her shoulders. 'Will you do as I say?'

'Wha—yes of course,' she says. 'Your orders?'

Gently, he nudges her forward until they've exchanged positions. She stands in front of him, sheltered by the wall.

'When I say "go"', he says, 'Run. Into the river. Don't come up until you've crossed the barricade.'

'And you?'

She feels him smile at her back.

'Remember Samati. Remember me.'

'But—'

'*Go!*'

Maji sprints. In the two seconds that she is upon the Maliot, she sees many things.

To her right, Savarian's huge barricade across the Maliot, battered but still standing, rising into the sky, higher than the roofs of the Sixth.

To her left, out of range of the rebels' arrows, the Council's forces, massed together.

The sun, hanging in the sky.

The *rahi* fields, glistening.

The Rasa, rolling to the Wall.

Rahul emerges at her heels, his body a shield. From the roofs of the Sixth, arrows whistle through the air. They strike him in the legs, in the back, and the neck.

As she leaps into the Rasa, she hears him sigh. She hears him fall.

The river takes her.

The cold. Her wounds are on fire. Maji gasps, swallows water, and strikes out with the current. She hears arrows slap the surface.

She swims until her breath gives out.

She clears the barricade—just about.

As she comes to the surface, there are shouts around her. She lets herself float to the bank. Hands reach into the river and haul her out upon the Maliot, wet and shaking. She sees someone, stark against the sun, bending over her.

'Upar,' she whispers.

He holds her in his arms. She clings to him. 'You're back,' he murmurs into her ear.

'I couldn't save the Revolution.' Her words break against each other.

Other voices around them and other hands, taking over. They strip her of her sopping clothes and drape her in a swaddling of dry linen. She stands uncertainly, dripping beads of water.

In front of her is a man, tall and straight-backed. His black hair falls to his shoulders, framing a sharp face, a laughing mouth, and eyes that seem never to rest.

'So it didn't work,' Savarian says.

She stares at the ground. 'It was an ambush.'

Savarian nods. 'What we feared. Not that we had a choice.'

He doesn't ask about the others. He doesn't need to. The guilt that begins at the soles of her feet and rips through her body needs no Savarian to speak it into a lifelong cramp in her heart.

Savarian turns away. Maji grows aware of her surroundings. There is a knot of people around the leader of the Blue Revolution, and further away, little scattered groups of fighters upon the Maliot.

What a change from two nights ago, when they'd marched alongside the people, when none could tell the difference between rebel and citizen. Perhaps there had been none.

'Is there anything left?'

Savarian turns to the man who has spoken, but his words are for them all. 'Nothing. This was our last chance, Maran. But we should have known. When the Revolution came down to one last heroic act, we were lost already. And now it's over.'

Maji feels tears at the back of her throat.

'You've known this for a while,' Maran says.

'I knew it when the people melted away after our first defeat. I knew then that they came with us not because they believed, but because they thought we'd win. When we were no longer winning—'

'I don't believe it!' It's Upar now. Maji's heart leaps. 'The way you spoke in every Circle, the way they answered …'

'No more illusions, dear Upar.' Savarian sounds tired. 'Our Revolution's failed—not just on the barricade. We couldn't give them a Sumer so very different from the City they knew, different enough for them to stick with us until the end. A Sumer without Circles. But perhaps Circles weren't—*aren't* as bad for them as we thought.'

'*You* are doubting?'

'Never!' Savarian says lightly. 'I never doubted. But I couldn't stop the people from doubting.'

'That can't be,' says Upar.

'Oh?' Savarian laughs. He leaps upon the barricade, deftly climbing until he is at a height, looking down upon the Seventh.

'Citizens!' his voice cuts through the air, the voice that they have loved and followed for so long.

'Citizens. It is I, Savarian, who calls. Will you stand with me? One last time, I ask you. For a City without Circles. For the Blue Revolution!'

His voice dies away. Nobody answers.

Savarian descends from the barricade with the same unhurried calm. 'You see?'

'What do we do?' Upar says.

'Now?' Savarian bares his teeth. 'Now we make them bleed before we go.' He raises an eyebrow. 'But before that—is there anything any of you really want to do—or say? It's your last chance.'

Maji remembers, that thing at the back of her mind ever since Upar had hauled her up from the Rasa, that thing that may never happen now, unless …

She pounces on Upar. Before he can react, she has a grip around his elbow, and is half-pulling, half-dragging him towards Savarian.

'What?' Savarian says.

'Marry us.'

'*What?*'

'Your first act was to free us of the Marriage License Laws,' she says. '*No license for lovers.* You just said it. You said all that was needed would be a witness, to read the Promise. Well, here we are. And here *you* are—witness us.'

Laughter rises around them. Savarian doesn't join in.

'We didn't win, you know,' he says. 'The Marriage License Law is still law.'

'I don't care,' Maji says. 'This is still the Revolution. We are still in Liberated Sumer, because that's what *you* call it. You can do this for us.'

Savarian turns to Upar. 'You want this too?'

Upar has recovered. He steals a glance at her. She sees his lips quirk in the way that she has always loved. 'Shortest marriage ever,' he says, 'but that only makes it all the more—'

Boom!

The first stone from the trebuchet strikes the barricade, sending debris flying. People duck. Shouts rise around them.

'Very well,' says Savarian. 'The first—and last—Marriage of Truth. He unties the cloth around his waist holding his blade. 'We'll have to make do with this. There is no time. Give me your hands.'

Maji and Upar reach out. He deftly winds the tattered sash around their wrists.

'Quickly, say after me. In coming together, we break our Circles. If my Mandala has filled my hands, let them now be empty. No Mandala's hold has joined us, nor now can it do us part. This day on, my hands are filled with yours. By these hands, the Circles will fall.'

They repeat the words. Then the second boulder blows a hole in the barricade. Dust rises in the air, pricking her eyes, choking her.

'*Fuck!*' People mill around them, calling to each other. From the Maliot and the Seventh, the remaining fighters hurry towards the barricade.

Savarian takes control, cracking out swift orders, getting his forces into formation. In moments they are ready.

Behind them, the Seventh Mandala is silent, but Maji can feel the people watching. Upar is standing next to her. His presence fills her mind.

Savarian turns to the small circle around him. 'It was beautiful,' he says softly. 'But it's over. And I'm not going to bore you with a bloody farewell speech. No more orders. We fight. All of us.'

A rustling of readiness.

'Except Maji-Fifteen.'

'*What?*'

Savarian holds her gaze. 'You,' he says, 'are the only face, out of the Executive Committee of the Revolution, that is not known to the Council. They will not look for Maji-Fifteen when the day is done.'

'But—but—I am ready to die.'

'This is not about you.'

'No, but—'

Savarian holds up a hand. 'After they kill the Blue Revolution, they will try to kill its memory. You will keep it alive. From Dooma to the Forum, in every Mandala, you will tell our story. You will see to it that there is a next time. And *that's* an order.'

She looks at Upar. His eyes are set, his lips drawn together. He is ready. He has always been ready. Glimpses pass before her eyes: from the afternoon they first met, at the protest against the banning of the *Sumer Dawn,* and fled from the Watch, together into the rain-soaked mud-paths of the Dooma, to her home; through all their days upon the barricades, and all their nights without a past or a future. He has prepared for this moment.

She has not.

'I don't need a forever,' she whispers. 'Only a little more time. We had a world to discover.'

But before she can finish, Savarian has turned to one of the men by his side. 'Vibhu.'

'Yes, Savarian?'

'The prisoners from last night's battle?'

'Yes, Savarian?'

'Kill them.'

A shifting of feet. But nobody objects.

Vibhu slips away, his blade shining in the sun.

Savarian looks to her once more. 'After the day is done,' he says, 'send a Messenger to Amrit. Tell him it's from me. Tell him not to celebrate his victory too loud or too long. I will drag him down with me, from the Towers of Rebirth if I must.' He turns away, back to his people. 'For the Blue Revolution!'

They stand, swords drawn, one final time. Her words have run out. She kisses Upar.

'See you on the other side,' he says.

The last of the rebels run through the gap in the barricade, upon the Maliot, at the ranks of the waiting Watch.

Maji's courage leaves her. She cannot watch. She turns and runs the other way, Downcircle, towards the temporary safety of the Dooma.

Her eyes are blinded by tears.

Zero

Dhara

One year ago ...

In the hour before Wallrise, Sumer slept.

Dhara closed the door behind her and stepped into the lane. Clutching a sheaf of papers, she hurried along the clean-cut streets of the Sixth Mandala. The lamps were out. Rows of mud-brick houses glimmered in half-light.

She took the Maliot Road westward, to the Forum. The Rasa ran grey beneath an iron sky.

This had always been her favourite time of day. Before Wallrise, she could almost believe that the Wall was as temporary as the changing, unsettled light.

As she entered the Forum, Dhara grew aware of her beating heart.

She looked down at the papers, at the diagrams, the figures, and the calculations. For a moment, she stood still. Then she advanced to the Citadel of the Select.

The first light of Wallrise struck the Citadel. White stone gleamed gold. At the threshold, Dhara reached into her pocket and withdrew an iron key. The door sprung open.

She stepped into a hall of pillars. They glowed with a throbbing blue light. Dhara slipped off her sandals and crept between the columns.

She reached the end of the hall and took a passage that sloped downwards. Two turns, two empty rooms—*yes*. Dhara stood on the threshold of the third room. She slowed her breathing.

She tiptoed to the cages. The garudas were asleep, drugged. She rifled through her papers one more time, looking at her diagrams.

She walked back to the door and peeked out. The way was clear. She went and stretched out a hand to the first of the cages—

'What are you doing here?'

She swung around at the voice, just as the speaker pulled down the hood that covered their face.

'You?' she whispered.

'Yes.'

'How are you here?'

'Come with me and I'll show you. There is more underneath this City than in the worlds beyond the Wall.'

Dhara laughed. 'Convenient timing, no?'

'Don't you trust me?'

'Why should I? Aren't you here to stop me?' She ran a hand over the knife strapped to her thigh.

'Never. But maybe I can persuade you to stay.'

'Stay?' She laughed again, raw. 'Twenty years, every day a forever, and now—*now*—you ask me to stay?'

'Give me a chance. We haven't even begun to know Sumer. Just let me show you before you decide.'

She closed her eyes, counted to five, and steadied her trembling hands.

'If I was to believe you—then all this?'

'You can do it whenever you want. All I'm asking is, do it after you know, after you see what lies beneath Sumer. And if, after that, you still choose …'

'And you won't tell anyone?'

'I came here alone, Dhara. I chose to come to you alone.'

The words hung in the air. Dhara chewed her lip.

'All your life, you've only wanted to know, haven't you? What the Wall keeps out—*and what it keeps in.*'

Dhara raised her head.

'Show me,' she said.

'Come. You can leave your diagrams here. Oh, by the way—all your calculations are correct.'

'I know.' She put the papers on top of the cage. 'And they're in my head.'

At the end of an empty chamber was a passageway that sloped downwards. As they descended, Dhara touched her knife again. She thought of Mithila, who would be walking to the Forum for an appointment that would not now be kept. *We'll still chase the sun.*

'Mithila knows you came to the Citadel, of course.' Her guide seemed to read her mind.

'You knew I would tell her,' Dhara lied.

'Yes.'

They walked. Dhara looked back once. Darkness enveloped them. And then she heard it: a dull, muffled roar that beat against the uneven walls of the passage.

'What's that?'

'The heartbeat of Sumer. Alora the Builder who was cast down into the City, and from whom the Rasa issues—'

She stopped. Her guide walked on for a few moments, before her absent footsteps forced them to halt and turn.

'I did not come down here to be played with,' Dhara said softly. 'Try this on the Shoortans. I know it's the source of the Rasa. And I want to know where it's coming from.'

'I don't know, Dhara! You know what they say about the Select—science and magic, it's the same thing when you don't know how it works. That's the Rasa—or its source—but nobody knows the mechanics. And we don't want to tear down these walls to find out.'

They walked on. Dhara emptied her mind. She listened to the rhythmic sound, noted the moisture on the walls—the shining crystals that glistened upon them—and the bumpy ground, strewn with little pebbles. She looked for turnings, branched passageways, the corridors they didn't take—but found nothing.

'I promise you,' her guide said, 'this is no more than a straight passage.'

'Sorry for checking,' she said, 'but I'm sure you understand.'

The sound ceased. The floor became smoother. In the distance, she saw a light. It was blue.

'Tell me, Dhara, do you actually not believe in the Builders?'

Dhara searched for the trap in the question, as the light grew brighter. 'Why do you ask when you know I don't?'

'Well then.'

Dhara stopped dead.

They had entered a space filled with blue throbbing light. It wove itself around containers that floated in the air. In each of those containers rested human figures, except she knew instantly that they were not human beings of Sumer. The women and men were too tall. They wore faces that were less Sumerian, and more something Sumer's sculptors would have carved if they were imagining Builders.

'Changing your mind, Dhara?'

'I—*they're floating*. Where's—where's gravity?'

'You're the engineer. The one who's always liked to build things.' Her heart clenched at the words. 'Think you might work it out if we gave you all the time in the world?'

Dhara wandered around the chamber—careful never to turn her back—until she stood in the centre, before three containers. She looked at the two men and one woman. No pallor here, no *finality*. Only life, interrupted.

'Who are they?'

'The ones who were before. Builders, if you want to call them that. They knew how to preserve themselves for eternity. Or—what counts as eternity?'

'How can you be sure?'

A pause, and her guide's voice sank to a whisper. 'If you wait here a little longer, you will see. Two of them—they enter the room and talk to each other. Always the same scene, that finishes with the same moment, circular like the Rasa.'

'What do they speak of?'

'Of a great battle overground, of what was lost, of how this chamber was to save them. And other words, new words: '*There was so much I wanted to show you. Red sprites over the troposphere in Tannor. I wanted to show you the Aurora, dancing in the sky, beyond the Reinmar Gate. There was a galaxy...*''

'Other worlds,' said Dhara. 'Other worlds among the stars, that they could reach?'

'Yes.'

'*Galaxy*.' She rolled the word on her tongue, tasting it. She stole another look at the containers. 'They're lovers aren't they?'

'How did you guess?'

She smiled. 'They're turned towards each other. Just the slightest. As if for a last look.'

'Ghada and Samir. They're the two who play out that scene for all time.'

From somewhere in the distance she heard footsteps approach the chamber. The sound cut through the dull disbelief that had been clouding her mind. 'You've known this? And this has been a secret? For two thousand years?'

'Some things must be, Dhara. Imagine if Rastogi learnt of this. Think of what he would do?'

'But the people! This is our history, right here!'

'A history we can't even begin to understand. You know how the Shoortans manipulate this City. *You* know, better than most. They will turn this into a weapon, just like everything else we can't understand about Sumer.'

'Who's we?'

'You know what I'm saying is true.'

Dhara pursed her lips. 'At least Mithila needs to know.'

'If she finds a way beyond the Wall. Not a moment before.'

She almost walked away, then. But all her life, she had only longed to know. To take the world apart, grasp its design, and make it whole again. Now, unasked, a part of that world was before her, a glimpse of infinite space beyond the ken of those who passed their lives above ground, in a finite Sumer.

Dhara decided to stay.

'You haven't told me,' she said, as the footsteps grew louder, 'the first bit of what you actually know. You think stories will keep me here any longer?'

'Very well,' the voice was resigned. 'I should have known you're too sharp. You see the woman? Ghada. I'll tell you her story. Can you see what she's holding in her hand?

Dhara turned back to the woman, to the face that had drawn her from the moment she had first seen it. And she realized her mistake as she did so, an instant before she heard those three words, spoken quietly behind her:

'I'm sorry, Dhara.'

Dhara swung around, snatching at her knife. Out of the corner of her eye, she glimpsed a woman and a man walk into the chamber. Then her head exploded in a blaze of pain.

Dhara sank to the floor. She heard one last thing.

'*Nobody leaves just yet.*'

The darkness was absolute.

PART TWO

OPENING

Present day

When Rama awakens that morning, the world has changed.

She had known the moment it happened. Minutes before Wallrise, when she was drifting in that space that was not quite sleep and not quite wakening. Like the touch of a falling leaf, soft upon the skin, the slightest sense that the shape of the world was altered.

Rama rises. She goes to the window. Wallrise is sharp and clear. Sumer is as it has always been. Only a little emptier.

Mithila is gone.

She places her palms upon the windowsill and raises her eyes to the sky. A garuda circles the top of the Council Hall. Once, in a world that had been, she had told Mithila that it would not matter if she missed the moment. Wherever she was in Sumer, she would know. They had laughed. Mithila had looked at her with that smile, loving and mischievous.

'You think I'd ever leave without you knowing?'

Rama smiles now, even though Sumer feels smaller and emptier.

The morning stillness fills her. The stone mansions gleam in the slanting sunlight, the empty streets newly washed. The Rasa tinkles in the distance. She steps away from the window. Below her, the house is quiet. Her mother is asleep. And father—he'd sent a Messenger late last night: 'Regular operation in the Dooma.'

But now, if this morning brings with it the news that the Wall has been crossed …

Rama paces, her hands behind her back. Amrit would need to know. The Elders would need to know.

She asks herself if it is still her story to tell.

When she wanders back to the window, she notices a stream of people on the Maliot, walking towards the Forum.

Two files, marching in good order. Upon their shoulders, they carry a bier.

Rama turns her eyes past the awakening City, Wallwards. She cannot see the Wall from her window, but it glimmers in her mind, almost floating. There is a fragility to it, as though someone could blow it down with a breath.

When she looks again, the marchers have turned away from the Forum.

Coming from Downcircle, coming to the First Mandala. For the first time, Rama feels a tingle of disquiet. They are walking deliberately, stepping to a beat, the bier steady upon their shoulders. They reach the edge of the First Mandala, by the house of the President.

Rama almost forgets to breathe. For a moment, it seems that the column has halted. It is an illusion. They are still walking, deeper into the Mandala. She can see their colours: plain linen, brown sashes.

The Watch.

They turn into her street.

Rama waits no longer. She slips on her sandals and runs downstairs. Through the darkened living room, through the hallway, out onto the porch.

As she steps into the street, the column comes to a halt outside her house.

She is breathing hard, her face flushed. Her heart leaps in her ribcage like a stone tossed by a skilled hand into the Rasa, bouncing on the water before it sinks.

Arjun-Six, leader of the Watch, steps forward. Behind him, they lower the bier onto the ground.

'Rama-One.'

She nods.

'Your father did so much …' he trails off.

Rama screws her eyes shut. When she opens them again, to free herself of those dancing red spots, Sumer still exists.

Even emptier.

She walks to the bier. Nobody stops her. She kneels and stills her trembling hand.

She draws back the white sheet.

The Councillor Amrit lies there, his eyes closed, his chest unmoving. Her eyes travel down. Her father's blue sash is stained dark red.

For the second time that morning, Rama feels the world change.

One

The Judgment of the Council

The sky poured in upon Mithila.

She cried out. The world swallowed up her voice.

Her eyes squeezed shut. Wind pounded her skin. The wing-beat of the garudas drummed in her ears. Her body swung like a leaf in the wind, high above the ground.

She lurched.

Across the Wall, the garudas could carry her no more. Two more jerks. Her stomach contracted. The rope around her waist tightened, making her gasp.

She opened her eyes a crack. The world rushed in through the curtain of her eyelids. They were plummeting towards a vast, green carpet. Her head spun.

The wind whipped her hair into her face. A dull roaring filled her ears. Mithila braced.

The world turned dark. Something cracked across her body, slapped her face, making her shield her eyes with her hands, then a brief respite, before—

She hit the ground with a *thump* that knocked the breath from her. Her right elbow and side took the first impact. Still shielding her face, Mithila hit the ground again and rolled twice, before coming to a halt.

She lay there, dazed and aching. Her face was buried in soft, muddy ground. Leaves were tangled in her hair. Dirt was in her mouth, splattered upon her skin and clothes. She gulped for air. The scent of soil rushed into her, the smell of the woodlands of Sumer, but richer, sharper, deeper.

She heard a garuda screech. The birds were pecking at the ropes. Mithila struggled to her feet, spitting out dirt. The garudas looked at her. One of them screeched again.

Mithila limped over. She undid the rope around the first, and then the second. She watched their wings spread, watched them leap again—this time without her—and fly.

She held out a hand as they disappeared through the canopy forever, leaving her wingless in the world, and alone.

'*Thank you*,' she whispered.

Mithila looked around. Trees surrounded her. They formed corridors and passages, twining paths and doorways, clusters and darkling groves. A cool breeze rustled the leaves and played upon her skin. Dappled, cloudy light filtered through the canopy. Beneath her feet, the ground was soft and uneven.

She spread out her arms, lifted her face, and let the world wash over her. The weight that had always been lodged in the cavity of her chest was gone, leaving a strange lightness behind.

The end of *smara*.

When she opened her eyes, something was pricking at the corners of her vision. Mithila blinked, her throat tight. The world was blurry. She dabbed at her eyelids with her sleeve, but only got more dirt on her face. She pressed her eyes shut again, and felt a trickle of tears trail down her cheeks, soft as a breath.

She sank to her knees. Her fingernails dug into the ground. She breathed, letting the cool air fill her lungs, soften the tightness in her throat, beat back her tears.

Mithila stood and shook her head. Hazy colours began to come back into focus.

She was the first in all the world.

There was a moment, when Mithila had drawn level with the Wall-top, that Alvar had felt Minakshi's hand tighten around his. He had turned to her, their fingers interlacing for an instant. Then his gaze was torn back to the sky, to see Mithila cross. In that moment, their hands had parted.

He turned back to her now.

'And so it ends,' he said.

She looked back at him. He thought he saw a light in her eyes.

'And so it begins, doesn't it?' Minakshi said.

Suddenly Sumer felt smaller than ever. There were pins and needles in his blood. He wanted to jump, to jump higher than he ever had, to run, to keep running, to sing until the Wall crumbled and fell, until the last Wallset of circular Time.

He searched for words instead.

'Yes,' he said. 'It begins. A new world.'

'The world Mithila made.'

Out of the corner of his eye, Alvar saw two figures hurrying across the fields. He reached for her hand. 'You've come back.'

This time she snatched it away. 'Back *where*, Alvar?'

'To—us?' Confusion washed over him. He spoke quickly. 'Mithila wanted to give up but I—I knew you weren't gone forever. And we've killed the Circles!'

She gave him the ghost of a smile. 'So, now? What now, that you've done it?'

Alvar laughed, feeling his chest unclench. 'We'll make it up as we go along!'

'I see.' She looked away.

'We can start the world over, Minakshi,' he whispered.

'Alvar!'

It was Mankala and Lamon, running. Minakshi reached across and touched his sleeve. 'I'll see you again soon, Alvar,' she said. And then she was gone, walking swiftly by the Wall, towards South Sumer.

'ALVAR!'

They ran at him.

Alvar spread out his arms. They reached him together, shouting, and almost took him off his feet.

'We saw it,' Lamon whispered, as they locked him in the tightest of hugs. 'Why didn't you tell us?'

'I couldn't … Mithila … someone found out … had to change …' he gasped, the breath squeezed out of him.

They swayed together. Then Lamon leapt over to the Wall, and with a whoop, began to beat his fists against it.

'*Fuck the Builders*!'

Mankala grinned. Looking at her, Alvar felt something swell in his stomach, something that rushed up to swirl in his throat, and finally escaped him in a torrent, a laughter that wouldn't stop. And he heard it echo—or was that Lamon and Mankala laughing with him—as he dropped, gasping, to his knees, a crick in his side.

'Okay, that's enough,' Mankala said after a while. 'Let's get serious, we have to—'

'*Uff!*' Lamon grunted, and swooped on Mankala. He swung her around. 'Let it out for once—we just changed the world! The Young Tarafians? We lived up to our name!'

'Put me down, Lamon, you big lump!' Mankala protested, but she was laughing too—and then she stopped suddenly, as her face turned towards the City, and her eyes widened.

'Wait!' she pointed.

Lamon put her down. They followed her arm. Walking towards them, all in black, his face a mask of stone, was Tefnakth of the Coterie.

Alvar took a shuddering breath. 'Can't you fucking Shoortans give us a moment?'

Mankala fell in beside him. Lamon came up from behind. They stood together, side by side, facing Tefnakth.

He stopped before them. His eyes shifted to the Wall, and back to them again.

'What have you done?' His voice was a whisper, uneven like frayed cloth.

'What we said we would,' said Mankala.

Tefnakth's mouth opened and shut.

'Why, Tefnakth,' said Alvar, light-headed, 'don't you like the new world?'

'It is not yet time!' Tefnakth cried out. His voice seemed to hit the Wall and bounce back.

'What do you mean, *not yet time*?' Alvar laughed. 'When would it ever have been time for the Shoortans, you and your Malan and your *raika*?'

'That's not—'

'And didn't you tell us the world is ending in a month?' Mankala added.

'Yes—yes, but—'

'Time to get out of here before that happens, no?'

'*Not like this!*' The words escaped him in a squeal. He raised an arm, palm out, almost as if he was trying to ward off a blow. 'You—' he rasped, 'you don't know what you've done.'

'And what are *you* going to do about it?' Mankala taunted. 'Ostracize us, like you did to Taraf, six hundred years ago? Try it and find out. But oh, wait, I forgot—*you* can't Ostracize anyone, the Shoortans threw you out, Tefnakth!'

Tefnakth's nostrils flared. Without another word, he turned on his heel and strode away from them, back towards the City.

'Is it just me, or was he acting even stranger than usual?' said Mankala.

'It's not the last we'll see of him.' Alvar shook his head. 'Doesn't matter. It's over.'

'Mankala, Alvar?' Lamon said, his voice suddenly hesitant. '*He* can't ostracize anyone, but the Shoortans can?'

Alvar felt a chill in his bones. As the Young Tarafians, it had never been possible to think about Taraf without remembering his end: Ostracized, friendless, cast out from the life of the Circles, not a touch or a glance dared thrown his way, until at last, in the shadow of the Wall that he'd fought with his words, his songs, and his dreams, he had ended it all by his own hand.

'They can't, can they?' Alvar whispered.

They turned their faces to the Wall, as if under the force of their gaze, under the force of what Mithila had done, it would crumble, fall, reveal the horizon.

Nothing happened.

Above them, a bounded sky remained.

Heaviness crept back into Alvar's chest.

'Only for her, then, the horizon,' Mankala said, softly.

'Her.' Lamon swallowed. 'How is she going to come back?'

Mankala turned from the Wall. 'She's not coming back.'

'She is!' Alvar broke in, his words colliding with hers. 'She'll find a way. She always does.'

Mankala only gestured at the Wall.

'But if she doesn't?' Lamon's voice rose. 'What will all this have been for? She's gone. The Wall's here. We're here. We can't all just fly out.'

One of Mankala's feet was making little circles upon the red earth, turning up small clods of soil. 'If she can't come back to us,' she said, 'we have to go to her.'

'*How!*' Lamon's voice quieted. 'The Shoortans are still around, even if they can't do anything like Ostracism anymore—and if she's gone forever—what if everything here just stays the same?'

'But it doesn't have to,' Alvar said. 'Now it's possible. Now there's actually someone who went beyond, and look—no punishment by the Builders, no Builders at all! What does that mean, Lamon? The myth of Malan—gone. *Praya*—gone. Circular Time—gone. Gone, gone, all gone. The *Shoortans* are gone. And without them, we'll find a way.'

'You think it's going to be that easy?'

'Oh *Builders*, Lamon.' Mankala walked up to him. 'Was *this* easy? Look. Hold on to this. Imagine. Imagine that the world is starting again today. All over again. Here's the Wall. We're still the Young Tarafians. Only, Mithila's on the other side. We have to get to her.'

'Okay, okay!' Lamon held up his hands. 'And when do we start?'

'Now.'

He stared. Alvar did too. 'What?'

'You don't remember? The Council's judgment. In our trial. Today.'

'Builders, yes, I forgot!' Alvar said.

'But—but—' Lamon said, 'you know they're going to ban us. After what happened at the trial. That Shoortan mob, remember? The Young Tarafians won't even exist after today.'

'Exactly, Lamon!' Mankala swung around to him. 'They're going to ban us from something *we've already done*. And then we're going to tell them. Can you see it? The Forum, the crowd, the President reading out their decision, they think that's the end of us, they don't know—and *boom*! In front of Sumer. We change it all.'

'Yes!' Alvar breathed. '*Yes*.'

'Come on!' said Mankala, her eyes glinting. 'Let's get moving, Young Tarafians. There's a world to make.'

They set out back across the fields. The sun climbed into the sky behind them. Everything was clearer today, thought Alvar. From the Rasa, the outlines of the Dooma looked sharper, as though all these years he had been seeing the City through blurry eyes.

Carina ran across the fields. The sun came up behind her, striking the red earth near the Wall, making it glow. Into the Fifteenth Mandala, she passed under the shadows of hanging ladders, stepped through dark tunnels, and ducked under clotheslines that blocked the narrow streets. There was a stirring from the cramped mud-brick houses around her, as the last of the Circles began to wake.

She reached the tall, three-storeyed house and hurried up to a circular room, where sunlight streamed in from arched windows.

Maji was leaning over the table. Her palms were pressed against its wooden surface, her grey head bent.

When she raised her eyes, Carina saw that they were streaked with tears.

She pulled up short, breathing hard. 'What happened?'

Maji straightened and wiped her face with the back of her palm. The sunlight cast a halo around her head.

'He left last night.'

'Savarian? He was always going to leave,' Carina replied, uselessly.

Maji turned and walked to the window. She stood in the sunlight, her back to Carina.

'Did you really think it was going to happen?' Carina said. 'That he would begin the Blue Revolution all over again?'

'Maybe I let myself believe,' Maji said, 'that it was possible. Twenty-seven years of waiting. I've been so alone.'

Carina noticed the little piece of cloth wrapped around her wrist, its colours long faded. 'What did he say?'

'The same thing he said that last day on the barricade. "*Maji, the people do not want a City without Circles badly enough to die for it.*" I argued with him. I told him how close we got last time. Then he just started to theorize at me. Quoted Noiker. Said that Sumer had already achieved its most advanced form of "social relations"—you know, his favourite phrase—this side of the Wall, and—'

'This side of the Wall, yes.' Carina couldn't resist. She advanced into the room. 'But *that*?'

Maji stared at her.

'Maji. They've done it. They've gone beyond the Wall.'

'*What?*'

'Garudas. Mithila-Seven flew. I saw it.'

'Flew?' Maji gaped. 'But then—but then she can't ever come back.'

'Maybe,' Carina said softly, 'she is our Samati.'

Something changed in Maji's eyes. They all knew the story, in the Dooma: of Savarian's commander, Rahul-Eleven, who had given up his life for Maji's. A man of the Eleventh, for a woman of the Fifteenth, for a dream of a City without Circles.

If you want to fly, someone will have to sacrifice themselves for you.

'Why did he leave?' Maji said. 'Now we're going to miss him even more ...'

Carina crossed the room, and seized Maji by the shoulders. She shook her. For once the older woman felt fragile in her hands.

'Maji, listen to me. Savarian's time is done. The Blue Revolution is not coming back. *He's* not coming back. No one is. Not Rahul. Not Maran. Not—I'm sorry—Upar. This time, it's you.'

'I can't—'

'You can. The Wall is breached. The world is changed. We're not bound by the limits of the Blue Revolution. We can imagine more. Maji. Maybe it's *time*.'

'Time?'

'Alora,' Carina murmured in her ear. 'We will carry the memory of your name like hot iron beneath the tongue. Alora, your breath is the river, and the stars are constellations of you. In a time before the Circles, you said to us: *everything will be remembered.* Alora, we remember. With your name, we will shatter the Circles.'

She stepped back from Maji, and watched the first sign of a smile curve at the corner of her lips.

They paddled up the Rasa. By the First Mandala, where they stepped onto the Maliot, there was a massed crowd already, moving towards the Forum. It parted instantly. Once again, Alvar felt the eyes of Sumer upon them, as they walked to the Council.

Just as they stepped into the Plaza, the doors of the Council Hall swung open. Hansa walked out, flanked by two Councilors. 'Shit, we're late,' Alvar muttered.

'Don't break stride,' Mankala said.

As they crossed the Plaza, a phalanx emerged from the Council Hall, fanning out around the three Councillors. 'What's this?' asked Lamon. Mankala narrowed her eyes. 'Brown patch—the Watch.'

Alvar counted around twenty-five of them, standing with their backs to the Council Hall, in a loose semi-circle around the three Councillors.

And in their hands—

'Those aren't staves!'

'No,' Mankala muttered. 'They're swords.'

Alvar's knees buckled. 'Swords!' Lamon stammered. 'But they *never* …'

'Something must've happened last night,' Mankala's voice remained low. 'There's protocol for this—an attack on an Elder. May not have to do with us. Just keep walking.'

'Easy for you to say,' Alvar grunted. Beneath the noonday sun, the blades glistened with a liquid light, as if they had been forged that morning: wrought of iron, reinforced with bone, keen-edged and clean. They caught his eyes, making him aware of the veins that carried his blood and the sinews that bound his bones.

Behind them the crowd gathered, quiet.

Hansa looked up when they stopped, ten metres from her.

'Where is Mithila-Seven?'

Alvar felt a bead of sweat trickle down his back. 'She's not here, President Hansa.'

'We can't wait for her,' said Hansa, sounding annoyed. She looked beyond them, her eyes widening at the size of the crowd. Alvar's skin prickled. He did not turn.

'The Council met this morning, and voted on the question before it,' Hansa said, her voice pitched to carry to the ends of the Plaza. 'As President, here in the open Forum, I must tell you our decision, and our reasons.

'We have been asked to ban a group of Citizens called the Young Tarafians, and order them to end their activities against the Wall of Sumer. To decide this question, we must begin with the Six Freedoms, the legacy of our Democratic Revolution. These include the freedom to believe and not to believe, the freedom to speak and to remain silent, the freedom to go where one wills in Sumer. These are precious. They are our inheritance from Maliot and all those who died fighting the tyranny of Dichio. We have never—and will not ever—betray them.'

'Now watch them find reasons to,' Mankala said.

Behind them, stillness.

'The Council,' Hansa continued, 'knows well the importance of this case. Ordinarily, we would never ban anyone from speaking as they like, doing as they like. I say *ordinarily*, because you all accept that this side of the Wall, freedom is not absolute. There are exceptions. The Council has looked to our history to understand what they are. It found one.'

Her voice resounded across the Forum. 'Thirty-one years ago, we banned the *Sumer Dawn* newspaper. The only time in the history of our Democratic Age that such a thing was done. Why? Because the *Sumer Dawn* agitated for a City without Circles. It called for a destruction of the Order that has kept balance and peace for two centuries ...'

'Oh, fuck this,' Lamon whispered. 'This is Shoortan language!'

'... and to disrupt the harmony under which we all survive, this side of the Wall. That was unacceptable. The Six Freedoms are important, but for the Six Freedoms to exist, Sumer must survive. What use is freedom if Sumer falls?'

'That's what Amrit argued at the trial,' said Alvar, his voice dead.

Behind them, muttering filled the air. Alvar smelled sweat, a metallic smell, glistening and eager, pressing down on them; a smell made flesh.

Hansa stared at the crowd, stony faced. The muttering passed through the people like a ripple on Rasa in an unexpected breeze—and was gone. The smell lingered.

'So we asked ourselves,' Hansa went on, 'if the Wall was so integral to Sumer, as integral as the Circles. On this point, the Prosecutor Amrit was persuasive. To go beyond the Wall would be to alter everything. Our precedent in the *Sumer Dawn* case indicates that we must, with all reluctance for the sacrifice of freedom, answer "yes: the Wall is integral. It cannot change."'

The crowd was silent, watchful. Alvar suddenly wondered how many of the people at his back had marched to the Council Hall three days ago, calling for Mithila's blood. His stomach knotted.

'Is it time? Are you going to say it?' he muttered.

Mankala nodded. She opened her mouth, but at that moment, Hansa resumed.

'Then one of us reminded the Council of something else.

'Three years after the *Sumer Dawn* was banned, Sumer was bathed in the blood of Savarian's Mutiny. A Mutiny that pretended to call for a City without Circles, but aimed to raise another tyrant in blood and death—you remember. But do you remember that Savarian once used to work with the *Sumer Dawn*?'

'Wait—what?' Lamon said.

'Did that ban work? It did not. Savarian found another way. A more violent way. Because it wasn't about the *Sumer Dawn*. It was about who *he* was.'

The Watchmen had not moved. Alvar's eyes strayed to their blades—fresh, unused, polished, whetted—gleaming in the sun.

'It was put to us that the Young Tarafians are no second Savarian, to impose their will upon Sumer by violence. But that is not the point. No one knew what Savarian would become either.'

Alvar gave in and turned his head a crack. The crowd had drawn closer, almost upon them, a mass bunched together like a single body.

Where would you run, when all roads end by the Wall?

'But here is what we do know,' dimly, he heard the President's words. 'There is no straight road between our actions and our consequences. The paths are many, and to say that we know all ends is to assume the arrogance of the Builders. And it was put to us that to deny the Six Freedoms on mere speculations about what might happen would be unworthy of our Democracy.

'We agree. A long time ago we banned the *Sumer Dawn*. History showed us we made a mistake. Thirty-one years later, we will not repeat that mistake.'

'Wait—*what!*' Lamon said again.

'Those who oppose the Young Tarafians may do so,' said Hansa. 'But the Council will not enter this fray. Thus we answer the question: "No. We will not ban the Young Tarafians. And we will not ban the idea of going beyond the Wall."'

A din broke out in the Forum Plaza. 'The Council has spoken,' Hansa finished. She turned and strode back into the Council Hall. The Watch trooped in behind her. The doors closed.

'What just happened?' Lamon shouted over the noise behind them. 'Did we … *win*?'

'Sounds like it,' Alvar yelled back, numb. 'But what about—'

'*Congratulations!*' a voice was at their back. Alvar turned. It was Kodali, from the Tenth Mandala, beaming at them. He came up, seized Alvar in a tight hug, and thumped him on the back. 'Never in doubt! We all heard about Mithila's speech at your trial—hey, where *is* Mithila?'

'She couldn't make it today,' said Mankala.

A shadow passed across Kodali's face, but cleared swiftly. 'Come down to the Tenth sometime, eh? I've been hoarding some of the Select's Drink—what better time! They'll be talking about it for months—they'll be talking about *you* for months—oh wow—I see there's a full line behind me. Won't take up more of your time!'

Alvar smiled unsteadily. 'We'll see you.'

After Kodali, others came to greet them, shook their hands, grinned and laughed, said things he barely heard. But there were still others who kept their distance and whispered from afar. He did not know how long it was before the crowd melted, leaving the three of them alone in the Forum.

'Well,' breathed Mankala. 'The President has a sense of humour.'

Alvar let out a long sigh. 'Too much for one day. I honestly thought those swords were for us. But hey—the Council, acting on *principle*? Who'd have guessed?'

'Why didn't you tell Kodali?' Lamon said.

'I—there was no time to think. This wasn't what was supposed to happen,' Mankala said. 'We need to work this out.' She paused. 'I guess this really is the first day of the rest of our lives.'

The Forum was quiet.

'What do we do now?' said Alvar.

Mankala opened her mouth, but it was Lamon who spoke. 'I have to tell you something. I'm done.'

Alvar stared. 'What?'

'We did it. We crossed the Wall—'

'*We* didn't, Mithila did—'

'The Young Tarafians. Same thing. This is what we existed for, and now—'

'We existed—exist—to destroy the Wall,' Alvar's voice rose. 'It's only just beginning. What good will it do if we stop now?'

'The Wall's been crossed,' Lamon said, toneless. 'And I—I've given you all I could, Alvar. Yesterday, I threw the Race for Mithila, I gave up my marriage license, I gave up my whole world. What more can I do?'

Alvar flinched. He lowered his gaze. 'I know.'

'I told Mithila,' Lamon said, 'The horizon, maybe it's not for me. I'd like to get to it some day.'

Mankala smiled. 'Maybe you already have. Good luck with Eraina, Lamon.'

'Thanks. Need to do some thinking now.'

'It'll work out—the marriage license,' said Mankala. 'We'll see you around sometimes, eh Lamon?'

'Oh yes—yes, of course—for that drink with Kodali?'

'Yes,' said Alvar, 'I'll send a Messenger.'

They watched him turn and walk away across the Plaza, into the stone complex of the First Mandala, heading South, leaving them alone, in the shadow of the Forum's towers.

'Just the two of us then, this side of the Wall,' said Alvar.

'Aren't you forgetting someone?'

'Who—oh,' Alvar shook his head. 'Not Rama, Mankala. I don't know what happened, but Mithila—'

'Mithila's gone. The Wall's still here. We need to make our own path. Did you know, Alvar, that Mithila thought one of the Young Tarafians is a traitor?'

'*What!*'

'Or at least, that's what Garuda believed. It was all written down in some journal of Dhara's that she found.'

'Oh!' Alvar said, uncertain. 'I guess if there was a traitor—they're feeling pretty stupid right now. So you're going to talk to Rama?'

'Let me see. I spend my days in the First Mandala anyway. I think—'

The sound of the Sumer harp cut her off.

They heard the familiar-unfamiliar threnody, soft and low, coming from the Maliot, and then the words, swirling with the breeze in the empty Forum like fallen leaves seeking a home.

When power by power confronted
In nameless struggle by the Wall
And councils shaken by revolt
Even though the war was lost
It is never lost …

'Carina!' Alvar said.

She entered the Forum Plaza from the West and walked towards them. 'Once more,' she said, in her melodious voice, as she came up to them, '*a crossing of paths foretold.*'

'What are you doing in the Forum?' said Alvar.

'*For in the shadow of the Wall/ we look for sap to grow/ we thirst for sunlight*. Why? Can't I come to walk in the Forum? Perhaps I'm here to see how you broke the shape of things.'

'I don't know what—'

'Alvar-Seven, do you think everyone sleeps till Wallrise? Or do you think the sky is a place to hide?'

'I …' Alvar's voice died away.

'May her luck never leave her, that side of the Wall.'

'She was with you,' Mankala said slowly, 'the night before she left. Wasn't she? What did you do with her?'

'We showed her the beginning,' said Carina. 'We showed her Alora.'

Alvar and Mankala looked at each other.

'Who are you really, Carina?' Mankala said at last.

Carina smiled. 'We are the wick they cut so that the fire would never burn again. We are the ones who were asked to remember. The dreams you have as children, the dreams about the Wall that fade as you grow older, the thing they call *praya*, the penance—your dreams are our memories, and for that Sumer calls us mad. And what is madness but the memory of what you cannot see with your waking eyes?'

'Who's *we*?'

'You will find out,' said Carina. 'I only came here to tell you: *have care*. You think that now you've changed the world, you can remake it to your heart's desire. But dreams can take strange forms, once you force them from the sleeper's eyes. We'll see you, Young Tarafians.'

She turned to go.

'Wait,' called Mankala. Carina paused.

'Where's Savarian? Just in case we need some … revolutionary help.'

'This is no longer his revolution,' said Carina, without turning. 'He's gone to silence. This time for good.'

'The Builders have no need of him yet.'

So says the doctor when she steps out of the bedroom. Rama stands. Her hands tremble. 'May I go inside?'

'Yes.'

The room is cool and dark. Councillor Amrit lies upon the bed. His chest is bandaged, his breathing laboured. His eyes remain closed.

Rama kneels at her father's bedside. Behind her, the doctor says, 'The wound wasn't lethal. But the shock—his heart gave out.'

'His heart?'

'He has lived a full life, Rama-One. Thirty years in Council and a revolution. No heart could bear that with ease.'

Rama takes her father's right hand from beneath the sheet that covers him. The Councillor's pulse is irregular.

'He may live,' says the doctor.

'But will he come back?' she strokes the palm.

'The Builders decide.' The voice is flat, warning her against hope. In the same tone, the Doctor of the Tenth recites instructions. 'If he opens his eyes,' she finishes, 'send for me.' Then she is gone.

Alone, Rama buries her face in the sheet, beside her father's chest. Somewhere in the house, her mother is dealing with it in her own way, staying far away from the bedroom. Rama lets herself breathe. Tears flow freely, the tears she has held back through the morning.

For a moment, Councillor Amrit seems to stir. Rama looks up. It is an illusion.

She draws his hand to her. Closing her eyes, she feels its warm—too warm—touch upon her skin.

'Please stay,' she murmurs into his ear.

Rama lets her head sink once more to the bed, where—touching Councillor Amrit's side—she can sense the faint movement of breath in his body. She remains like that, she does not know how long, until the sound of footsteps.

'Rama-One.'

The voice clears the fog from her mind. Rama stands. 'My President!'

'Be at ease. How does he fare?'

'As you see him.'

President Hansa looks at Councillor Amrit and makes the sign of the Circle, a blessing.

'They told me how you responded when he was brought here this morning,' she says. 'He would have been very proud of you.'

There is a ball in Rama's throat, tightly wound. It aches. She swallows, and gulps. As the tears rise into her eyes and mouth again, she blinks them back, and clenches her fists until her nails dig into her skin. Hansa notices. She takes a half-step forward, but stops herself.

'There is something you must know.'

Rama smiles wanly. 'It wasn't a routine operation at the Dooma, was it?'

Hansa starts. 'Sharp as a blade,' she whispers. 'No. He wasn't in the Dooma.'

'I'm listening.'

'Last night, intelligence told him that Savarian was heading towards the Towers of Rebirth to claim sanctuary. There was no time. So he decided to go himself and head Savarian off by the Towers.'

'Go on.'

'He must have taken the boat and then run like the wind. A farmer saw it. He says they arrived together. Your father challenged Savarian as if they were once again across a barricade. But Savarian, he'd always been more skilled with a blade …'

Hansa's words sink upon her. When Rama speaks again, her voice is even. 'Savarian did this—to my father?'

Hansa nods. 'He'd sworn revenge, those twenty-seven years ago, for their duel upon the barricade. We never thought—but anyway, he's in the Tower of the Third now, under sanctuary. We can't go in. But men are stationed outside, and will remain there. Savarian will never come out.'

'I see.' She looks back at her father. Her mind is clear and empty, as though every sensation this day on will be a new one.

'That wasn't all that you came to tell me, was it?' she says.

'No.' Hansa stands stiff-backed. 'I don't need to soften you for this. There is very little chance the Councillor will recover. That means there's a vacancy in the Council.'

She has known it. Known it since she first set eyes upon her father that morning. Only, she did not expect it so soon.

'I am four years underage,' she whispers.

'Discretion of the President.' Shadows chase each other around Hansa's face. 'We've been waiting for you for a while now, Rama. And given what's happened, we thought it would be … fit. You don't have to decide now of course,' she adds quickly. 'Take your time, be with your father, come back to us when—'

'No need,' Rama cuts her off. 'If this is the Council's will, why postpone it? If you think I'm ready—'

'We know you are.'

'Well then, my President.' She takes one last look behind at the bed. 'When do I start?'

Hansa smiles at last. 'I told them this is what you would say. You start now, Councillor-Elect Rama. Come.'

Rama follows the President out of the room. 'I'll be back soon,' she tells her father. Then she closes the door and steps into her new life.

Two

Tree and River

Mithila walked in the world.

Leaves crunched beneath her feet. Leaves yellow, brown, and green, in shapes she had never seen, dancing in the breeze before they came to rest on the ground. There was so much *colour*.

At first she kept the Wall in her sights. But before long the only path forced her away. The Wall was lost behind the trees. With it, Sumer was gone, a memory of circles, the sound of the Rasa, and the lingering taste of bamboo soup upon her tongue.

The sun rose with the morning. The colours began to turn lighter shades. Here and there, through gaps in the canopy, curtains of light showered down on her.

There was a ceaseless rustling sound in the air, the sound of many trees in the breeze, a sound familiar and unfamiliar. It swirled and wrapped around her. And in answer, from a dream half-remembered, she found herself singing as she walked:

Upon the map, an empty place
A blank, a white deserted space
Unseen, unknown to one or all
The World that lies beyond the Wall ...

Her voice pierced the listening air. She was no longer alone. The trees around her glimmered, moved, and transformed into human figures. It was an evening in Sumer, beside the river, on the edge of the Forum Plaza. Garuda played the harp, teasing the light of Wallset with his music. Mithila sat with her hand in Rama's, her head upon her shoulder. Alvar lay on his back, looking at the sky, mouthing poetry. Lamon stared into the river. Dhara was beside them, her dark head bent over a scroll, the scratching of her pen a counterpoint to Garuda.

So stark, so desolate, so bland
The map that shows a faceless land
Without remembrance or recall
The World that lies beyond the Wall ...

Dhara leapt to her feet with a cry that scattered Garuda's notes in the air. '*Done it!*' Mithila lifted her head from Rama's shoulder. Garuda looked at Dhara. 'Done what?' 'Digging! The way to measure depth—I've worked it out!' Garuda rose to his feet. 'What do we need?' 'Bamboo,' Dhara breathed. 'Wood. Iron. Nothing more.' And Garuda turned to them all, the light of the world in his eyes. '*It's time.*'

A world, unbound and infinite
Beyond this map, beyond this sight
Of Wall-bound gaze; and endless sky
Beyond the grasp of chasing eye

But it wasn't time. Not yet. They were in the Pit, where the last words of the song, meant to herald the new world, had only yielded to the darkness of the Wall. Lamplight glancing off the tumblers. Garuda and Dhara's fingers brushing each other as he handed her a drink. The two who had brought them so far, the leader and the builder. Did they know that within the year, they would both be gone, but the Wall still remain?

Beyond the Wall, the sunrise swift
Dispels the iron dawn to lift

The shards of mist, and sunbeams fall
Upon the World without the Wall …

They were falling now, curtains of light, illumining her path. The song ended. Garuda and Dhara winked out of existence.

'I asked you to trust me with your dream, Garuda, brother,' Mithila said to the trees, '*and we've only just begun.*'

A sound answered her. A sound in the distance, churning and periodic.

It was something known. Her mind strove to place it within a new system of coordinates. She walked on. The sound grew louder, a rolling and a tumbling, many voices together.

She came upon it suddenly. The canopy had given no sign of breaking, but she found herself stepping out of the line of trees and into daylight. Before her a wide channel of water tossed and rushed towards an unknown destination.

A river, like the Rasa, if the Rasa had a loud, unruly elder brother. There were no clean-cut banks, no ordered flow to the Forum, no *symmetry*, but an upheaval of water, many currents that twisted and turned upon each other. The whole was travelling … Mithila tried to orient herself, but was lost. In Sumer she would have turned her back to the Rasa, faced the fields, and known North. Now there was no Rasa, no fields, and no North any more.

She felt momentary dizziness, and realized how thirsty she was. By the shore she went down on her knees and drank from cupped hands. The water was unfamiliarly, deliciously cold. Mithila washed her face, feeling weariness dissolve.

She sat back on the bank, slipped off her sandals, and opened her pack. Mankala had been sensible. The dried *rahi* was rationed into sets, designed to last her three days. Mithila unwrapped the first bundle and chewed it carefully, letting her feet hang in the water as she ate, watching the current take the crumbs when they fell in. Across the river, the line of trees waved at her in the breeze.

For the first time since last night, the world slowed down around her. Knotted muscles relaxed, tensions dissolved. Mithila leaned back with a sigh. Alone, and with time to think at last, her mind turned to all the questions Sumer had thrown at her in those last days of madness, before she had abandoned her City for the world: the night the sky had turned red, and she'd almost been attacked in the Maidan; *smara*, that was memory, not yearning; the chamber deep beneath the Council Hall, and the two sightless men she had followed there; Ghada and Samir, in that chamber, speaking to each other of war and of love, unaware of whoever watched them down the centuries, because *there was a galaxy*; her strange dream in the Dooma, where a Builder called Alora had protested the raising of the Wall, and had been cast down for it, as Sumer burned around him.

So much that would now remain forever unanswered, unless the answers were here, in the world beyond the Wall.

She finished eating, stood, and measured the current with her eyes. There would be no fording, not here. Mithila came to a quick decision, and set off in the direction of the flow, walking beside the river. There were times when the line of trees descended almost to the water, where she had to temporarily wade in to make a path for herself. Her sandals were soon soaking wet, until at last she removed them, and felt her bare feet touch the cool, moist ground.

The hours slipped by. She had long lost sense of time, for time itself was now standing still, waiting for her. Long streaks of pink spread like meteors in the dusky sky. The sun had passed out of sight, hidden beyond the trees; but sometimes through a gap in the canopy, she saw it hanging in the sky, a pale red that she had never seen in Sumer.

We'll still chase the sun.

Dhara's last words to her, words made real. And then as she walked, a new scent came to her over the evening air, a scent that was not of the trees. It beat upon the doors of memory, struggling for a name that was lost.

The stars appeared. They came out in numbers, filling the night, reminding her of the three kings in the underground chamber, of Ghada and Samir, of the words they had spoken to each other: the *aurora*, the *troposphere*, the *galaxy*.

There was a world to discover.

The scent remained, a little sharper. But her limbs were aching now. She looked at the trees around her, tall and forbidding. But before she could consider climbing them, she came upon a small clearing, just a little way from the river.

There was a faint, autumnal chill in the air. Mithila lay on her back, feeling tufts of springy grass beneath her. She stared up at the sky. Her thoughts turned to Sumer. Early night, and the City would be coming alive beside the Rasa: the traffic of the returning Citizens filling the Maliot, the wicks trimmed by the Fifteenth and the lamps lit, the food stalls abuzz: *rahi,* peanuts, bamboo and sometimes—just sometimes—sweet sugarcane.

All those people within a City of Circles, and her, alone. In an unbounded world. A world that began to spin.

She felt her heartbeat quicken, a fluttering against her ribs. The clearing pressed upon her, the trees suddenly closer. Her breath shortened. Mithila closed her eyes. A tingling spread across her body, a thousand tiny needles jabbing into her skin. A dim part of her *felt* her nails dig into the ground, trying to hold on to the earth, but there was no sensation at all. And then it felt like that part of her had detached, and was floating mid-air in the clearing, looking back down upon Mithila, another Mithila, who lay on the ground. The Mithila on the ground was flailing, thrashing, while Mithila-in-the-air regarded her with cold curiosity.

From somewhere in the depths of her mind, she twisted into shape the remnants of a memory, a memory that she pulled into the present: Wallset in Sumer, a lamplit room in the Academy, faces around a round table. She willed herself to imagine them *now*, meeting, not too far away from her, only a Wall between them: Alvar, Mankala, Lamon …

… and Rama.

I want to see the stars with you one day, in a world without the Wall.

Her eyes flew open.

The stars were around her.

Her throat felt sour, as if she had thrown up inside it. Her nails were caked with dirt.

By degrees, her heartbeat slowed and her breathing lengthened. The world began to knit itself back together.

She checked herself and sat upright, wondering what had happened. Sleep was far away. To keep her mind busy, she opened her pack again and began to rummage through it, going over what Mankala had kept aside for her. The food—the water—the cotton pads—and then her fingers brushed against … *paper*?

Mithila pulled out a sheaf of paper, bound together by twine: a makeshift journal. She screwed her eyes, but the starlight was too faint. Surely Mankala would have … she felt around in the bag, and—yes, there it was. Mithila drew out a fire-striker, a flint and a char cloth.

By the light of the small, makeshift flame, she read the cleanly-formed letters on the first page:

To Mithila, beyond the Wall
Write it, for us
The Young Tarafians

Mithila laughed. She reached into the pack, and soon found it: a bottle of lampblack ink and a reed pen. All for her.

'Don't know whom I'm writing for, if I'm never going to see you again,' she muttered to the clearing. But then she lay on her stomach, opened the journal, and, resting her chin upon one hand, began to write:

When they used to tell us the story of Malan, I'd wonder why he never said anything about what he saw beyond the raika. *I didn't believe the story, because who could see the world and say nothing?*

I had to become Malan to understand.

I feel like someone who once knew how to speak, and now all I have is the memory of words. Dhara had asked me what it would be like, the moment when we saw true at last. I compared it to someone who had never seen the Forum before, standing in the Plaza, wreathed in mist, and then seeing it all as the mist vanished. That is what I thought it would be: clarity, clarity, clarity. Sunlight for shadow, like Taraf said.

But today, it's been more shadow. Yes, smara is gone. But I've been walking through mist, the mist that should have vanished. The things I've seen today—I feel like there are words for all these things, a language for these things, that I knew it once, that we all knew it, and then it was taken from us, so now we speak in sounds that remember words.

The trees around me—like Sumer's woodland, but endless. It's like the Builders made it to measure. Am I in the world of the Builders?

I know, maybe it was foolish to think that the moment the Wall was crossed, everything would be remembered, who we were, who we are, why the Wall …

But now it feels like smara *is gone, and what has taken its place is loss.*

And I don't even know what it is that we have lost.

I've remembered Garuda today, and Dhara—I know we lost them. Garuda would have found the words—when did he not?—but it's Dhara of whom I've thought the most. We'll still chase the sun. There was a world to discover. No more orality.

All her words, coming back to me, as if she was here somewhere in this forest, taking notes, like she always said she would.

But it's just me now. I have to find those words. Maybe I'll even find the Builders soon—or they'll find me.

We'll know. I'll know.

As she snapped the diary shut, Mithila felt thirsty again. The sound of the river was close, and her water wasn't for wasting. She stood, shouldered her pack, and walked out of the clearing.

In the trees, a star appeared—and vanished.

Then another. And another.

Mithila stopped, her mouth open.

Above and around her, the stars were there—and then they weren't. Like sparks from a fire that died in the air, only to be reborn.

Then, as if in answer, there were stars on the ground, in the bush, and by her knees, moments of light that meshed around her.

All these years she had longed for the stars, and now the stars had come to her.

She wandered, her arms out, reaching for the light. They were all around her, speckling the trees, dappling the night, a net of glimmerings. One floated—and almost settled—on her palm, but inches away, it flickered out of existence.

Mithila gasped, in surprise and in longing; but like water through her fingers, these stars were not for keeping.

She found herself running after them anyway, and running with them she knew not where, laughter in her throat and wetness on her cheeks. It was as if the forest had come alive in the night, in still motion with the dancing light.

And then, just like they came, the netted stars were gone.

One by one, the lights winked out and did not return. Mithila stopped. Darkness crept back into the world.

'Please wait,' she whispered.

The last of the stars went out forever.

They had chosen not to stay.

Her heart ached, and she did not know why.

From somewhere in the distance, she heard once more the sound of the river.

Through the corridors of the Council Hall, Rama does not speak. Only when they have descended the ramp, and their sightless guides have been left above, does she ask: 'Who are they, that brought us here?'

'They are the prayas,*' says Hansa.*

'Praya—*penance?'*

'Yes.'

'Why?'

'Because what you're about to see,' says Hansa, dodging her question, 'is too dangerous to leave unguarded. None but they know the secret of the entrance, and none but the President can command them. And they, you see, cannot betray.'

'Even you can't come down here on your own?'

'Nobody can. But it is the President's duty to bring every new Council member here, so that they know.'

They step into the hall of pillars. Rama staggers. Hansa smiles. 'Impressive, isn't it?'

'How many people know of this?'

'The Elders. And some of the senior members of the Select.'

'Why is it a secret?'

'You'll see.'

Hansa takes her through the pillars, through light and shadow, and into the chamber. Rama shivers as they enter, and shivers again as she takes in the circular room, the blue light, the cold, and the containers arrayed all around her.

'What ...?'

'Take your time, Councillor.'

She wanders around the room, pausing at last before the three in the centre. Hansa comes to stand behind her.

'Who are they?' Rama asks.

They hear footsteps.

'They're coming to tell you.'

The footsteps grow louder and seem to come from everywhere. Rama peers around, but Hansa gently puts a hand on her shoulder, and steers her to stand beside the three containers in the middle. 'Don't worry,' she says, 'they cannot see or hear us.'

They walk into the room and Rama cries out, clapping a hand over her mouth a moment too late. They do not hear. They come up close, speak to each other, the same words that Mithila had heard two days ago—if Rama but knew—strange new words that echo in her head, that remain long after they have gone.

Red sprites. Aurora. There was a galaxy.

'Well,' says Hansa, when they have gone.

'Here they were …' Rama replies, dumbly, 'and there … they are?'

'Nobody understands what they've done to time and to space. All we can tell is that there was a fight. They came down here to save themselves. Here they sleep—but the two of them, Ghada and Samir, here they live, in a circle of time that has been turning for two thousand years.'

'And if they came escaping a battle they had lost,' Rama says slowly, 'then the winners …'

Hansa nods. 'Even more powerful than these, who can bend time and space to their will. They were out there. Would you bet against them still being there—somewhere?'

Rama stares at the floor.

'The City does not need to carry this burden, Councillor,' says the President. 'But now you know. There were Builders, once. Some of them left—but some stayed. And those who sleep…'

'… are waiting to be woken,' Rama completes, in a whisper.

'You've seen the depths. Now let's climb to the sky.'

The President takes her back, through the Hall of a Thousand Pillars, and up the spiral stairway to the to balcony, the balcony that Rama had broken into with Mithila, a week and a world ago. There is no moon this time, just bright light, like a shard, over Sumer.

'Always remember,' says Hansa. 'The Sixth protects. The Seventh dreams. The Eighth builds. The Ninth crafts. The Tenth cares. The Eleventh grows, the Twelfth harvests. The Thirteenth to the Fifteenth labour.'

Rama turns to her. 'Why are the last three always grouped together?'

Hansa knits her brows. 'You want to go into differences? Let me remember from their banners—the Fifteenth is the candlewick, for the trimming of our lamps every night. The Fourteenth bears the sign of the sandals, for the messengers. The Thirteenth has the broom, for cleaning. But there are so many more tasks, they keep switching, so it's just easier this way, and anyway—' Hansa grimaces, 'at the end of the day, they are all controlled by the Dooma.'

'You all keep saying Dooma, Dooma,' says Rama. 'What really is the Dooma?'

'The neighbourhood that covers parts of the Fourteenth and the Fifteenth, we can't go there and they exercise this—this strange sway over the last Three.'

'You think it's because how we've treated them?' says Rama dryly.

Hansa puts her hands behind her back. 'In the history of our City, mistakes have been made, yes.'

'Like saying that the inhabitants of the Dooma suffer from hereditary madness?'

'That wasn't us,' Hansa says quickly. 'This hereditary madness thing—it's complicated, Rama. Now you're in Council, I guess you should know—it's—it goes a long way back. There was a time when the Shoortans were not the only ones who told stories about the Wall. There were—there were many stories, and what we call the Dooma had their own.'

'What were they?'

'Lost. I don't know if even they remember. But the question of where we come from, this side of the Wall, tells us also where we are going—and where we cannot go. So they fought, the Shoortans and the Dooma. The Shoortans won. The myth of Malan, the story of the transgression and of praya, *the penance, became the story of us.*

'And with that the Dooma was banished to the shadow of the Wall, the Dooma became the Dooma. And to corrupt their story for all time, the Shoortans told the City that they were mad. We—the Elders—we're just two hundred years old, Rama. The City is so much older. We can't fight everything.'

'But because you didn't even try,' says Rama, 'that's where Savarian got all his support—didn't he?'

'That's right. I can't deny that.'

'And if it happens again? You keep people in Wallshadow forever, won't they fight to come into the light—whenever they get the chance?'

'I know. Trust me, I do.' Hansa grasps the bars of the balcony. 'But this is the balance that my predecessors chose. This is the balance I have chosen. Something has to be sacrificed.'

'No balance lasts forever,' says Rama.

Hansa smiles, suddenly tired. 'Let whoever comes after me decide if they want to change it.'

Three

The Matriarch and the Councillor

A single shaft of sunlight streamed in through the slit window, high up on the wall. She knelt in the pool that it made, her palms on her knees, watching the motes dance. In the silence, she heard herself breathe.

Behind her, the door opened.

'It's time.'

'Already?' She rose. A white cloak, adorned with two woad-blue circles on each shoulder, and made to measure by Prasanna, master-weaver of the Ninth, reached her feet. She stretched out her arms, watching the sleeves fall to her elbows.

'Lead on.' She walked to the door held open for her, and into the hall.

'This way first,' said Priest Baku.

Minakshi followed him through the pillars, reaching a passageway that ended in a curtain. 'You know what to do,' he said.

Minakshi parted the curtain.

The Heartstone floated before her, glowing gently, its light filling the room. For a moment, she stood still. Then she stepped forward and placed her hands around it.

Light radiated into her brain.

Minakshi staggered.

Starburst behind her eyes. She was arrowing through uncontained space, circling around many suns that winked in and out of existence.

The Heartstone drew her into its beating heart, a wild moment of flight in whiteness, and—

Minakshi cried out. Her eyes flew open.

She was alone in the room. The Heartstone was in her hands, light like a bushel, smooth like a stone, pulsing like a heartbeat.

The hair on her arms were standing up.

It was exactly how Matriarch Soma had told her it would be. And it was over.

She steadied her tingling body, cradled the Heartstone against her chest, and walked back out through the curtain. 'Ready?' Baku asked.

'Ready,' she said. 'Let's go.'

They walked back up the hall, and to the doors of the Temple. Baku threw them open. She stepped past him and into the Forum, bathed in late-afternoon light.

The breeze rocked against her, a cold breeze from beyond the Wall. She stood there, framed by the Temple, its single spire reaching into the sky. Sunlight struck her face and her eyes.

The Circles had come.

The people were a blanket of colour, a blanket that shifted before her, the fifteen shades of dye known to Sumer, woad blue to ochre red, and everything in between. They stood in their Circle uniforms, in ordered columns that separated one colour—one Circle—from another, behind their several banners that waved in the breeze, waiting.

A festive buzz greeted her arrival, the expectation of a familiar ceremony. Minakshi took slow steps into the Plaza, looking straight ahead of her, the Heartstone in her palms.

Rastogi detached himself from the line of Temple priests and came forward. He bore a crown in his hands, the crown that had been impossible to imagine on anyone but Soma.

Minakshi knelt.

Standing over her, Rastogi spoke.

'Time, like the world, is a Circle. Matriarch Soma led us for thirty-nine years. She saw much: from the Mutiny of Savarian, to those who clamour for a world beyond the Wall. We took sanctuary in her wisdom, her gentleness, her steady hand. Now she has gone to the Builders, leaving us bereft.

'But Time, like the world, is a Circle. A Matriarch passes. Another takes her place. Matriarch Soma named her successor before the shadows took her. Here we stand today, to pass on the light, the Stone—and the crown.'

Minakshi felt a weight upon her head.

'Matriarch Minakshi,' said Rastogi. 'Duly consecrated. Rise. And lead us.'

Minakshi rose. Rastogi knelt in turn.

Hansa took two steps forward. 'The Council's greetings to the new Matriarch,' she said. 'May we live in balance.' She placed her right fist upon her heart, the greeting of the Council.

Marwana stepped out to join her. 'The Select acknowledge you, Matriarch Minakshi,' her voice was the same lazy, half-amused drawl they all knew. 'We stand ready to assist, as we always have, should our services be needed.'

Minakshi made the Shoortan sign of the Circle. 'I see you. And I thank you.'

She stood erect, faced the crowd, and inhaled. 'For the first time,' she said, drawing her voice from deep, 'I greet you as Matriarch.'

'This side of the Wall, we live in balance. To the Elders-in-Council is given the governance of Sumer. To us, the Shoortans, guardianship of the Wall. We remember Malan who, at the beginning of all things, crossed the *raika* and brought Time and the Wall into the world. We remember his transgression, for which we must all live in *praya* until the end of Circular Time. We remember so that you may not forget.'

'This is the balance that has brought us peace—a peace that we will always defend against those who would destroy it.'

She sensed Rastogi relax. The transition was done, and she had spoken by the book. Now life could go on.

Inside, she laughed. *Not yet.*

'Until last night,' she said, 'I thought I would speak about how the balance must be kept when some ask to go beyond the Wall. But now I must tell you: it is too late. The balance is broken. Forever.'

Rastogi stiffened. Minakshi did not turn, not towards him, not towards Hansa or Marwana. Before her she saw sudden confusion, faces jerked out of placidity.

'This morning the Wall was crossed.'

Rastogi gasped.

'I do not know how,' she continued, 'and I do not know by whom—yet. I shall find out soon. But hear me: the world has changed. The Compact lies broken. The Time calls for us, the Shoortans—and we will answer. When have we not? We answered six hundred years ago, when the City faced another great peril, and that peril was called Taraf. As we did then, so shall we do now—we *will* restore the balance. With gentleness if we can. But without mercy if we must.

'How do I know all this?' She raised the Heartstone to her forehead, and held it out towards the people. 'The Heartstone, the light of the world, the beacon of the Builders. To us, the Matriarchs, it is given—and with it the way of seeing. We use it, always, for the City. It is the Heartstone that I looked into before I came to you, and there I saw the compact destroyed.'

Out of the corner of her eye, she saw Rastogi staring at her, uncomprehending. She permitted herself a moment of vicious satisfaction at the thought that the man who hoped to become the power behind the crown was seeing his dream go up in smoke.

'Citizens, one who was lately among you has vanished. You now know why. But *we* cannot—we *will not* vanish, this side of the Wall: we are for each other, and we will always be so. We do not flee. *We do not leave.*'

She bowed her head once, and lowered the Heartstone. In the Plaza, the silence was absolute. Minakshi looked to the crowd. 'I thank you, Citizens,' her voice softened. 'I shall see you again soon.' Without a pause, she turned and walked back to the Temple. She heard the first murmurs break out—to her right and to her left—heard them swell, and the sound of footsteps as Rastogi leapt after her, the line of Temple authorities following. Then she was inside, the doors of the Temple closing behind her, shutting out the world.

Sunlight glinted on the tributary between the Tenth and the Eleventh Mandalas. It caught the old wood of the bridge, making it glisten. It shone on the dark hair of the woman who walked along the bank and stopped by a three-storeyed building that stood a little apart.

She pushed open the door and entered a rectangular hall, lit by sunlight that struggled through high, arched windows. At the end of the hall there was a long table. Around the table sat five women and men. There was one unoccupied chair.

'You're late, Meghana,' the man at the head of the table said. 'We've already passed three resolutions.'

'I was at the consecration, Prana.'

'The—what?' Prana frowned.

'The new Matriarch's consecration,' one of the women at the table said. 'It was today.'

'I see,' Prana said, as Meghana slipped into the empty chair. 'And what's Shoortan succession got to do with us?'

'It's a good thing,' Meghana said, 'that at least someone in the Farmers' Union is bothered about what's going on in this City. Because you will not believe what happened.'

Prana leaned forward. 'Something that—'

'—affects us. Yes.'

'What is it?'

'The Wall. It's been breached.'

'*What?*' Prana started, to gasps around the table.

'Yes. That's what the Matriarch said.'

'Who did it?'

'Who knows. Maybe one of those people who go around talking of the horizon—the Young Tarafians? But that doesn't matter.'

And as Meghana looked around the table, she saw their faces alter and turn. It reminded her of the first time she had seen a garuda fly, and known that something lived that was not *her;* not human; it was a feeling that tilted the axis of her sight, that the world was asking for a new way of seeing.

And now all she needed were the words.

'This is what we were waiting for,' she said, 'and we didn't even know it.'

She walked around the table, pausing as she went past each sitting figure, measuring each word like a harvest gathering. 'All these long years, generations of us lived and died on the fields, dreaming of a bushel more of *rahi*, or a few coins more for our work. Our mothers and fathers, to the turn of the seasons, always here, always bound. We burned out our dreams like a charred lampwick, and nothing ever changed. Because whoever it was that we toiled for, tyrant or democrat, would say, "*Farmers, there must be a quota, there must be limits, you cannot fight the laws of the world, you cannot fight the Wall.*" That was the beginning and the end of all we could imagine.'

'That's what the President said just last week when we asked for a third share,' said Prana.

'And that's what we had to accept. Because of the Wall.'

'Are you saying,' Prana whispered, 'that *we* must go beyond?'

'Not now. Not yet. But now we know it can be done. Now *they* know it can be done. And with that knowledge we can change things, *this* side of the Wall.'

'I understand,' Prana said. 'But what can we, the Union, do about this?'

'I,' said Meghana, 'have an idea, O charismatic leader of ours.'

There were chuckles around the table. Prana frowned again. 'Go on.'

'Do you know of a new Councillor called Rama-One?'

'The Committee—shall have—equal representation of—'

Mankala stopped writing and looked up. Malati had broken off mid-sentence. She was leaning upon the desk, her head bent.

'What happened, Councillor?'

Malati lifted her head. The lamplight cast half her face in shadow.

'I miss Sanchika.'

Her hand clenched the edge of the desk. Across the space between them, Mankala extended her own hand and let it fall lightly upon Malati's.

'There was life before him, wasn't there?' she said softly.

'There were years of loneliness.' Malati looked into the distance. 'A lonely vote on the Franchise Bill. A lonely campaign for clemency to Savarian's aides. So many lonely fights in Council, just to make this City of Circles a little more just. Then Sanchika came, and we were the Progressive Faction, and it wasn't so lonely anymore. We even began to win some votes in the last year, you remember. But then …' She tailed off, shaking her head.

'You've never talked about it.'

Malati's hand tightened around the table. 'There is nothing to talk about.'

'No?'

Mankala let the question linger in the air. Malati stared straight ahead of her. Lamplight flickered around them.

'I feel like Time has really become a Circle,' Malati whispered. 'I'm in the Council Hall once more. We're all there. Waiting for Sanchika. Waiting for the Social Law, that's going to change everything. He's late. Of course, he's late. That's the way he likes it. Keep the Council waiting.

'The President's at her seat. Amrit's staring at the dome. They're quiet. Everything's normal. But no, wait. On the floor below me, I see the Three—Varsha, Paras, Raja—and two of the younger ones, Raja's acolytes.Why are they on the floor after the Council's been called to order? I look at the President. She's staring at her own fingers. I look at Amrit. He's gazing up at the dome.'

'I know something's wrong. I stand. I'm going to ask Hansa what these five are doing there. But the door opens. He's here.

'Sanchika stops at the threshold. He sees the five. He looks up, looks for me. Our eyes meet. Something's locked my throat. I can't speak. He gives me a nod, as if my presence has comforted him. He enters the Hall.

'They surround him. Someone's speaking. I see lips move, shoulders shake, but I can't hear anything. I lean forward, over the drop. His arms are out, like he's asking them a question. Raja is kneeling. And then I hear Sanchika's voice, cracking through the Hall.

'*No*,' he says. 'No, no, no.'

Malati paused. Her knuckles had turned white and her eyes were closed.

'There is blood.

'Blood, so much of it. Oh, Builders. Blood on the floor, flowing around the feet of Maliot's statue. Blood on white clothes. All that blood, so deep, so red, so close, as if—' she shook off Mankala's grip, her hands in front of her—'it's on *my* hands.'

Mankala stood. She stepped around the table, to where the Councillor's chair stood empty. She pulled it back behind Malati. Gently, Mankala pressed down on the Councillor's shoulders, lowering her into the chair. Malati, still staring at her hands, did not resist.

'I scream.

'It's like everyone's been sleeping. *Now* they're on their feet. *Now* they're shouting. *Now* Hansa is calling for order. And I—' Malati broke off.

Mankala rested a hand upon Malati's shoulder. 'And you?'

Malati continued to stare ahead. 'And I, I want to run down, I want to save him even though it's too late, I want to kill Raja, I don't know what I want—and then I see Amrit. He's shocked, his eyes are telling me, *I had nothing to do with this*, but they're also pleading, *the Council could fall right now, Malati, this City could fall*, and I remember Savarian and the last time I saw blood, and I … I …'

Malati's shoulders slumped.

'I sit back down,' she finished. 'Hansa calls order, Raja invokes the *Law Felon* to justify what they've done. Hansa moves to vote. I can't speak, it's like all breath has left me. I vote against, of course, my vote—' she finished in a whisper, 'one out of ten.

'And each time when I can't sleep, when it all comes back to me, I think of everything I could have done differently. Challenged them the moment I saw them on the floor. Called out to Sanchika, told him to get out. Run down when they surrounded him. Or just … not stopped screaming. All that was left to me. All I could not do.'

'It's not—' began Mankala, but Malati cut her short.

'*Not your fault*—I know what you're going to say. Yes, not my fault. That's right. But I've always been a coward, and I couldn't stop being one that day. Oh well.' She smiled, without warmth. 'I volunteered to lead Sanchika's journey to the Towers of Rebirth. Hansa, so magnanimous, allowed me. I carried the bier on my shoulders, along with Thanu, to the Towers …' she broke off suddenly. 'Never do that, Mankala. You don't want to see a person for the last time, disappearing into those decomposition boxes. That's not how you say goodbye. That's not how I want to remember him.'

'How do you want to remember him?'

'Sitting with me in the conferral room. Plotting how we were going to outwit Varsha and Raja in the next round. The thousand versions of the Social Law that we worked on, each one so beautiful, like a dream. That's how I want to remember him. But all I can think of is the ending I can never change.'

Malati took a breath that seemed to move through every part of her body. Mankala bent and encircled the Councilor in her arms. Malati leaned back with a sigh, her head on Mankala's chest, hands clasped upon her wrists. Her body felt like paper, the paper of the Encyclopaedia that had burned so easily.

For a while, neither spoke.

'Do you remember,' Mankala murmured, 'the day they voted down the Progressive Tax Bill in the Council?'

'I do, I do,' Malati whispered. 'We were sure we were going to win. We'd spent weeks—spoken to so many—even Amrit supported it—and Sanchika's speech—but then we lost.'

'And do you remember that night, when you and he sat here, and –'

'And I said we'd never win.'

'And he said—'

'He said, *Malati, we have no time for a counsel of despair.*'

'Then he said—'

'*There is no defeat we can't undo, just as there is no victory that we can't squander.*'

'And then—'

'And then we wrote the Social Law that night,' Malati breathed. Mankala felt her grip tighten. She smiled. 'There, you said it yourself.'

'But I can't do it alone.' Malati's voice rose, but it was stronger, more solid than before.

'Thanu is—'

'No! He makes all the promises—then compromises. *Pragmatism*, he says. They knew exactly what they were doing when they brought him to replace Sanchika.'

Mankala straightened. She walked back to her place, and picked up her pen. Malati was slumped upon her chair. 'I'll just have to get used to it,' the Councillor said. 'I'm alone.'

For a while, Mankala didn't reply, only fiddling the pen between her fingers. Finally, she said: 'maybe not as much as you think.'

'What?'

Even though Malati's study held only the two of them, Mankala walked across to her and whispered a name in her ear. Malati started.

'*Her*? In Council?'

Mankala smiled faintly and nodded.

'You think?'

'You'll see, Councillor.'

'Hmmm.' Malati pursed her lips, calculating. Mankala stood beside her, her mind wandering to the afternoon's events when, amidst the crowd, she had seen Minakshi take something from them again, and make their victory meaningless. She looked at the window with unfocused eyes, at the dim outlines of Malati's porch, recalling her helplessness as every word that Minakshi spoke slid into her like a needle, revenge for her morning's indecision. Anger coursed through her, pure and welcome. She felt her hands ball into fists and a mist cloud her eyes …

The door rattled.

Mankala snapped back to life, just as Malati turned at the sound. 'Is that someone at the door?'

The knock sounded again, sharp upon the wood. They looked at each other. 'Who could it be so late?' Malati said.

The knock came a third time.

'I'll get it,' said Mankala. She walked out of the well-lit study and into the dark hall. She paused at the door, steadied herself, and pulled it open.

Outside stood Tefnakth of the Coterie, his pale eyes gleaming in the darkness.

Mankala took a step back. 'You?'

For a moment Tefnakth's eyes widened, and Mankala remembered the morning by the Wall. But in an instant, he had mastered himself. 'I'm here to speak to the Councillor.'

Mankala pushed past him and stepped out onto the porch. There was nobody there.

'Well,' she said, 'come in, then.'

She led him into the study. 'Councillor Malati,' said Tefnakth, 'may I speak with you alone?'

Malati had turned her chair to face them. 'Mankala-Eleven is my secretary,' she said. 'There are no secrets between us.'

Tefnakth calculated for an instant. 'Very well.'

'You can sit.'

Tefnakth took the chair across from Malati. Mankala remained standing at the edge of the desk. She watched Tefnakth. His hands were clutched tightly together.

'Now, Tefnakth of the Coterie,' Malati said, 'what's this about?'

'They say, Councillor,' said Tefnakth, 'that you are the wisest of the Elders.'

Malati smiled thinly. 'Who's *they*?'

'Those who have no reason to love the Council. I thought that I would come and know that wisdom for myself.'

'Tefnakth,' Malati said, 'I have no love for the Shoortans. That does not mean I will take sides in a factional fight. I have no love for end-of-the-world predictions either. So if you've come for that—'

'I'm not such a fool, Councillor,' Tefnakth interrupted. 'I'm here for something else. You intend to rewrite your Encyclopaedia, don't you?'

'I do, yes.'

'Are you going to put in the Great Fire this time?'

Malati began to tap the desk with one finger. Tefnakth leaned forward. 'Well, Councillor?'

'What's that to you?'

Tefnakth straightened. 'Have you ever thought that we may need to die to live again?'

Malati was still tapping the desk. 'Can't say that I have.' Mankala found her eyes straying to the window.

'The first time you see the leaves fall from the trees,' Tefnakth said softly, 'You think that is death. Until you realise that if Time is truly a Circle, death is necessary.'

'A nice metaphor,' said Malati, 'but symbols are not reality.'

'Why, do you deny the leaf-fall?' said Tefnakth. 'Do you deny the Three Kings? And do you deny the Great Fire?'

Malati's hands went still.

'The end will reflect the beginning,' Tefnakth continued, his voice quiet. 'So the Last Book tells me. And if you want to do something about it, you'll have to do it soon.'

'I see,' said Malati.

Tefnakth rose. 'Consider this all the warning you'll get, Councillor.'

'Is that a threat?'

Tefnakth smiled then, an oddly gentle smile. 'The Circle is turning,' he said. 'Light from light.'

He walked away from the desk, and out of the room. In moments, they heard the door open, and close.

Malati remained sitting, hands on her forehead, her thumbs drawing lines across her temples.

'Councillor?' Mankala said.

She looked up.

'What was he talking about? What Great Fire?'

'The Great Fire.' Malati's voice was flat. 'I uncovered it when we were preparing for the Encyclopaedia. It appears that time out of mind—near the Beginning, if a Beginning there ever was—a fire tore through our City, destroying everything. And it destroyed all evidence of what was there before. There was just one problem: apart from scattered oral sources, we couldn't find evidence that it actually happened. It had destroyed proof of its own existence. So we had to keep it out of the Encyclopaedia.'

'How did Tefnakth find out?'

Malati raised tired eyes. 'I don't know.'

'Right.' Mankala rubbed her nose. 'Is there anything else I should know, Councillor? Leaf-fall? The three kings?'

'The rest of it made no sense.' Malati passed a hand over her brow. 'I'll ask around. But for now—let's finish writing our Bill, hm? We don't have much time before tomorrow.'

'Oh yes, yes of course.'

'Take it down,' said Malati, sounding more assured now. 'The Committee shall have equal representation of farm-owners from the Five and farmers of the Eleventh and Twelfth Mandalas. All decisions about farmland produce, production quotas, and wages, shall be taken by a majority vote. In case of a tie …'

Through the evening, the crown had weighed heavy upon her brow. Minakshi shifted upon her high-backed chair, and looked around the Matriarch's Audience Chamber. 'Is everything clear?'

The ten figures that stood around her, cloaked and cowled, nodded. 'It is,' one said.

'Good,' she said. 'Let me repeat how important this is. Our power is weakest on Carnival Night, you know that—when every transgression's celebrated. And this time it's just hours after the Wall was crossed. I'd heard some rumours that the Council was planning to cancel it because they feared public disorder, but then they backed out, of course. The Carnival will happen. And the Tarafians will try something'—her lip curled—'again.'

'We'll be on our guard,' said Rastogi. 'But if I may ask …' Minakshi raised an eyebrow, 'why did you tell everyone about the breach today, if you knew? Wouldn't it have been safer to wait until after Carnival?'

She favoured him with a smile. 'If your enemy gains a victory, High Priest, you can at least stop them from declaring it, can't you? Would you rather *they* broke the news? Would you risk them doing it at Carnival?'

Rastogi lowered his gaze.

Minakshi looked at him a moment longer. 'Thank you for your time this evening, friends,' she said. 'We will need each other in these coming days.'

She made the sign of the Circle. They reciprocated, and one by one, trooped out of the room. Minakshi waited until they were gone. Then she turned around in her chair, and observed the woodcarving upon its back, intricate little designs, Shoortan circles, scenes from the Creation.

'Nicely carved, ba,' she smiled.

She was still examining the carvings, running her hand along Ananta's keen craftsmanship, when she heard footsteps again. 'Oh what is it now?' she said out loud, without turning.

'Matriarch, a Councillor's asking to speak to you.'

'*Now*?' She groaned. The crown would have to stay on longer. 'Very well. Send them in.'

In a fit of pique, she did not turn even when she heard another set of steps enter the chamber.

'Greetings, Matriarch.'

Now Minakshi did turn.

'What!'

Rama smiled. 'I just thought I'd come and pay respects.'

'Councillor?—*Councillor* Rama.' Minakshi recovered swiftly. She descended. As she approached her, she saw Rama's eyes flit towards her forehead.

'Nice crown, hmm?' Minakshi said, as they faced each other.

'Very fine,' Rama murmured.

'Heavy. A pain. And something I don't need to wear—around you.' Minakshi gestured to her forehead. 'Matriarchs aren't permitted to crown and uncrown themselves. Care to do the honours?'

'Ah—of course.' Rama extended her arms and carefully lifted the Matriarch's crown from her head. It came away in a tangle of hair. She heard Minakshi sigh.

She felt the weight of the crown in her hands: two-tiered, a polished wooden circle atop a black iron band. Inlaid into the iron were three hexagonal surfaces, of a material she had not seen before. They caught and reflected the lamplight in the chamber.

'Replicas of the Heartstone,' said Minakshi, guessing her thoughts. 'Nobody knows what they're made of. The material is no longer in this City.'

Rama passed a finger over the surface. It was cold and smooth. She could see her outline reflected in it, like in the Rasa under sunlight.

'So this is what you won today,' Rama said.

Minakshi met her gaze. 'I won something, yes. And so did you. But it's the loss that you're here for, isn't it?'

Silence hung between them.

'Yes,' said Rama.

Minakshi motioned. 'Spire? This chamber depresses me.'

Rama nodded. Minakshi led her to the exit. Rama stopped to place her crown on the table next to the high chair. They entered a tunnel, which sloped into a spiral stairway.

'Ever thought you'd come up here?' said Minakshi, as they began to climb.

'No. But the Circle turns in strange ways, as we've found.'

'You've replaced your father in the Council?'

'Yes.'

'I'm sorry. But the Council couldn't have chosen better.'

Rama laughed lightly. 'So respectful, Minakshi?'

'Wha—'

'*Doing well for yourself, I see,*' Rama mimicked her voice. 'What you said to your sister the last time we were all together. I didn't know whether to be flattered or not.'

Minakshi almost stumbled on the step, but caught herself. 'I thought you were out of earshot—but that's no excuse. I'm sorry, Rama.'

'Forget it. Everything before this morning now feels like a dream anyway.' Rama was dimly aware that they had slipped into first names.

The stairway twisted and yielded to a circular balcony. The Temple's single spire began here. Rama saw it rise, partitioning the star-dusted sky. The breeze was strong, whipping their hair back.

'Like the view?' Minakshi said, as Rama walked around the balcony.

'Love it.' She came to stand beside Minakshi. They both looked out together, following the Rasa Wallwards, watching little warm firelights blink in and out around the Mandalas of Sumer. 'The last time I saw it,' Rama continued, 'was from the balcony of the Council Tower. With Mithila.'

There it was at last: the name, spoken. She heard Minakshi draw breath.

'You saw her leave, didn't you?' Rama said.

Minakshi made no response.

'*Didn't* you?'

'Yes,' Minakshi whispered. 'Yes. I did.'

'Tell me?'

'She … she flew,' Minakshi spoke slowly. 'Tied to the garudas. It was terrifying. They just carried her in the air, higher and higher. And I was so scared they'd fall, like that old legend of Samati, she'd come tumbling down. I kept picturing her on the ground, limbs shattered, blood—but they took her over the Wall. And she was gone.'

'So reckless, Mith,' Rama murmured, smiling. Little suns were bursting into life in her mind. 'So reckless, and I loved you for it. Tell me more!'

Minakshi stood, rigid.

'*Please?*'

'Tell you *what*, Rama?' Minakshi swung around to face her. Rage crackled in her voice. 'What she said? What she did? What she looked like? You really want to know?'

'I do. I want to know. Everything.'

'She was happy—no, burn that.' Minakshi swallowed. 'She was *joyous*. As if her life was just beginning. No regrets. Not one, dried-up, rotten *rahi* bushel-worth of regret. Not for a father. Not for a sister. Not for … for …'

'A lover,' Rama completed.

'Your words, not mine,' said Minakshi, savagely. 'I thought she wouldn't do it, I thought—'

'But how could you think that?' Rama interrupted. 'Didn't you know her—' She broke off suddenly, when she saw Minakshi flinch. Rama's hand flew to her mouth. 'I'm so sorry—I didn't mean it that way, I just …'

But Minakshi only waved her hand. 'Go on,' she said, tendrils of bitterness running through her voice. 'Say what you think. I *didn't* know her. Six years in the Temple. How could I know her like you? And now I can't. Ever.'

'You wanted to—'

'*Of course* I wanted to!' Minakshi hurled the words into the night, into the Forum, away from Rama. 'I had to tell her why, she needed to see—and all I had to do was become Matriarch, so I could—I could bring her to me, talk to her without looking over my shoulder—she'd have understood me—and then—' Minakshi's voice broke. Her head was lowered, her shoulders shook. But then she stilled herself, and looked up at the sky. 'She's gone,' she said, toneless. 'And the world should be upside-down, but this night is like every other night.'

'I know,' said Rama. 'Like nothing's changed.'

'From the eyes of the Builders, I suppose nothing has.' Minakshi rested her elbows upon the balustrade.

'But we aren't the Builders, Minakshi,' Rama said. 'We hurt. We're allowed to.'

Something in Minakshi snapped like a dry branch. There was a rustle of cloth. And then Rama's arms were full with the unexpected weight of the Matriarch, her head buried Rama's chest. Rama staggered back a step, as Minakshi rocked back and forth in her arms.

'Thank you for coming,' Minakshi said.

Rama stroked her hair gently, awkwardly. 'How could I not? We are the only two, this side of the Wall, who can't mourn her with anyone but each other.'

'I would be mourning with a father,' Minakshi whispered, 'except that nobody knows where he is.'

Rama flinched as the sight of Amrit, lying on the bed, swam in front of her eyes. She drew back. Minakshi felt the movement and straightened.

'I'm sorry,' she said, misunderstanding. 'I've only been talking.'

'Oh no, no.' Rama smiled uncertainly. 'You told me how she was when she left. That's all I needed to know.'

'But why weren't you … your group was there!'

'I don't think they wanted me there.'

Minakshi placed each hand on Rama's shoulders, and looked at her. 'It wasn't them, was it? It was Mithila.'

Rama looked away.

'Didn't we all find out,' Minakshi said, 'that in the end, for Mithila, it was only ever about the Wall?'

Rama closed her eyes and turned her face to the sky. 'I miss her. I miss her so much. All these years we used to talk about how Sumer wasn't room enough—and now I feel like it was all the room I ever needed. And there were so many things I …' she trailed off, shaking her head.

'Do you—do you still—'

'Love her? Builders know! She's gone, and she didn't even let me come say goodbye. What do you do with that feeling? I don't know what to do with it. And I can't even talk to anyone because she made me lose my friends, and today I lost my own father, and now there's nothing left but this City that we can't leave, and she's not in it.'

'Ah. I'm sorry.' Minkashi tried to make her voice comforting, but was so long out of practice that it came out all wrong. Rama found it in her to smile.

Minakshi let her hands fall from Rama's shoulders, and turned back to the balustrade.

'And now what?' said Rama, to no one in particular.

'And now, the rest of our lives,' Minakshi answered the night.

Rama stared into the trackless sky. 'You really think she'll never come back?'

'She can't,' Minakshi said, her voice cracking, then solidifying. 'There's no coming back that way. She's gone.'

Rama hesitated. 'You know, Minakshi, that's also what I came to talk to you about.'

Minakshi turned around at that, as if she had been waiting. Her face was now arranged into a careful expressionlessness. The air between them had turned opaque, intimacies shattered so easily and so finally.

'I know,' said Minakshi. '*Councillor*. Let me tell you. Mithila's gone. But by the bloody Builders, I am not going to let her departure trigger a general insurrection against the Wall. The Tarafians have other ideas, I'm sure, but this will be the first *and last* time.'

'Fair,' said Rama, after a while. 'So let me tell you something as well. I am a Councillor now, no longer of the Tarafians—even if they were to have me back. But I will do everything *I* can to defend the Six Freedoms, and that includes letting people want to go beyond the Wall, to dream about it, to fight for it. That's what the Council stood for this morning. And that's what I'll defend.'

Mithila's presence hung between them.

But then Minakshi laughed. 'Rama, I would hate for us to be enemies. I don't want to fight you, if only for Mithila's sake—no, not even for her sake, she's gone—for the memories we share of her. And you know, I do like you.'

Rama said nothing. A gust of wind blew across them, making her shiver. Minakshi noticed. 'The night draws on,' she said, her voice gentler. 'Should we go down?'

'We should,' Rama said, tired.

They walked down the stairway. 'I'm sorry you came so late,' said Minakshi, as they re-entered the audience chamber. 'I could have shown you around the Temple.'

'I'm sure,' said Rama, following her down the main staircase, 'that there will be other chances.'

'I hope so.' They descended into the hall of the thousand pillars, and Minakshi guided her to the doors of the Temple. The flame lamps glimmered before them, marking the route to the Council Hall—the two towers that faced each other across the width of the Forum.

'If fate does make us enemies, Rama,' Minakshi said, 'I'll always be grateful for tonight.'

Rama turned to face her one last time, silhouetted in the doorway.

'Fate won't make that choice,' she said. 'We will.'

The doors closed between them.

Mankala stepped out of Malati's house, shivering in the cold. She cast a swift look at the porch. It was empty.

She walked out into the street and stood at the gate for a few moments, bracing herself for the long walk back home to the Eleventh.

'Hey!'

Mankala jumped—then laughed. 'So, how long have you been waiting here?'

Elmandar shrugged, his features masked in shadow. 'Not too long, to be honest. I just got here. I know when you get done—'

'Oh no, I meant, how many *days* have you been waiting here?'

'*You* said we were going to—'

'I did. But look, Elmandar—we just won this huge fight in the Council. You may have heard about it. We stood there before the Three Hundred, we won, we beat Amrit himself. So it's just—' she smiled, 'I feel like now you need to raise your game a bit. Remember what you told me? *Good, not great.*'

'You're changing the—'

'I am. Because I can.' Her voice grew light, but it was lightness shod in iron. 'What's the matter, Elmandar? Wasn't it *you* who once said that there was nobody challenging you? I mean, you're interesting enough in your own way, but one can want … more.'

She saw him stare at the ground, and back at her. 'So what exactly do you want me to do?'

'That's for me to know and you to find out.' She waved. 'See you around, Elmandar.'

She turned from him and set off towards the Forum Plaza and the Rasa. She almost looked back—once—but didn't. Behind her, there wasn't a sound.

At the doors of the Council Hall, the President is waiting for her.

'Come, Councillor,' says Hansa. 'Let's walk in together. It's your first time.' Rama nods gratefully.

As they walk, Hansa says: 'By the way—you may soon have a visit from the representatives of the First.'

'What about?'

'From the time of Maliot, it's been tradition that every Mandala has the right to nominate an Elder to represent their interests in Council, when the need might arise. For the First, that was Amrit.'

'Ah. I didn't know.'

'The latter Mandalas don't use it at all,' says Hansa. 'But it's still, you know—one of those conventions.'

'What you're telling me is that I shouldn't refuse.'

'That's right. It's no great burden—just that, sometimes, you'll need to speak for them, when they ask you.'

They arrive at a large door set into the wall. Hansa pushes it open.

Her first time in the Great Hall takes Rama's breath away.

The ascending semi-circles, the high dome, the white bridge midway up that encircles the President's chair. As she enters underneath the statue of Maliot, Hansa directs her to her father's old chair, level with the President's own.

Rama climbs. Around her, the Councillors take their place. When she gets to Amrit's seat, a look below makes her dizzy: the semi-circles plunging beneath, narrowing all the way to the floor a long way below.

After everyone is seated, Hansa says: 'I received an urgent motion of business late last night. I yield to Councillor Malati. But before that, a clarification: I received some representations suggesting we cancel the Carnival, because of how tense the City is, specially after what the Matriarch said at her consecration. My answer: absolutely not. We did not bow to the mob during the trial. And we will not bow now. Go ahead, Councillor Malati.'

'Thank you, President.' Malati stands. A murmur goes around the hall. It sounds hostile.

'My apologies for not circulating this Bill in advance,' Malati says, 'I was only able to finalise it last night. Let me summarise it.

'From the time of Maliot, this Council has always evaded a genuine discussion on the question of just distribution. The structure of farmland ownership has come down to us unchanged from the tyranny of Dichio: the farmers work the land for a wage, which is just enough for them to buy the food that they have produced; and the land is owned by—well, it was Dichio's cronies before the Revolution, and now it is the families of the Upper Circles, who helped Maliot in the Revolution. Maliot, as you know, promised land reform, but it's been two centuries and nothing's happened.

'I say that you can put off these questions no longer. The harvest is declining, the wages have fallen, the farmers are struggling to meet their basic needs—don't mutter at me, I will show you the calculations. The system is broken.'

An outcry at this, a medley of indistinct noises, forcing Hansa to call out sharply: 'Councillors!'

'The Councillor Varsha is outraged,' Malati goes on smoothly. 'But if the Councillor Varsha bothered to pay more attention to her duties as Farmland Administrator, she may find that the situation merits her outrage more than the person who tells her of it.'

Rama steals a quick glance at Varsha. Her face is livid.

'We had proposals,' Malati continues. 'To eliminate the harvesting quota, or to guarantee a third share to the Farmers' Circles. You, Councillors, rejected both. Now I ask for something more modest.

'My Bill proposes a body that will have representatives of the farm-owners and the farmers' circles in an equal *number—there, you're muttering again, anyone would think I was proposing to abolish wage work and put the land back in community ownership, like it was centuries ago. Why does basic fairness scare you so much? This body will decide the questions that I just spoke of, by majority. And in case of a tie, the Farmland Administrator—you, Varsha—will have the casting vote.*

'So, you see, this Bill is not touching anyone's property. Nothing fundamental will change. But the Farmers wish to be heard, Elders, and it's a matter of increasing rage among them that we are refusing to extend

even this much fairness, in such a bad time. With that, I commend this Bill to the Council for its assent.'

She sits.

'We are open for debate,' Hansa says.

Raja stands. 'I oppose this Bill,' he says. 'It seems a backdoor attempt to reopen the question that Sanchika—may he be at rest—and before him, Savarian—had agitated with such tragic results: altering the system of Circles, disrupting the fragile balance, this side of the Wall, that keeps us all alive.

'But that aside, I don't see the point. The Councillor Malati seems to suggest that the declining harvest—and low wages—are a result of some conspiracy by the farm-owners to oppress the farmers. This is nonsense. We have no power over these natural phenomena. And the same goes for the harvesting quota: you know that the soil will die if we don't leave a part of it fallow for a time—and those proportions are given to us by the scientists of the Select. So what will this Committee achieve? We can't fight against the laws of the world.'

'So many assumptions about what is natural,' says Malati dryly. 'Maybe once you actually hear from the farmers, your views will change.'

'And what would they know?' To Rama's right, Councillor Paras stands, impatient. 'Not to disrespect the farmers, but this is what we in Council have spent our whole lives training for.'

After Paras, Elder after Elder stands to oppose the Bill, with variations upon Raja's argument. At first, Malati responds, but there comes a point when she stops. Her face does not change, but Rama notices how her eyes seem to die a little.

'Does anyone else wish to speak?' Hansa asks, after hours have gone by. 'Shall we go to vote?'

Rama stands. Hansa nods to her. 'Councillor Rama.'

'I did not think,' she says, 'that my first speech would be in such a debate. I didn't intend to speak at all, but it seems to me that there's something the Council may want to consider.'

She sees looks of mingled shock and pain around her, as the Councillors hear Amrit's remembered language and phrases in her voice.

'There are moments when Sumer tells us to adapt or die. The Councillor Malati told you two things: the harvest yield is down and wages are down. Let me add something to that. The Wall has been crossed, as the Matriarch told us today.'

There is a stir in the Hall.

'The Councillor Raja said that we cannot fight the laws of the world. That's also what the Select keep saying—that we can't really vote for the Wall to go away. But if the Matriarch is right, then that's no longer the case. And I ask you to think about this: if the farmers know that the Wall can be crossed—that it has *been crossed—how long will they accept the harvest quotas? How long before 'this side of the Wall it must be thus' becomes 'let's try the other side, then'? There are no Elders beyond the Wall—they may understand, at last, that you need them more than they need you.'*

Below her, Raja looks thunderous, and Malati is smiling broadly.

Rama continues: 'We have a choice to compromise now. We can take it. But if we do not, there may soon come a day when the solutions will leave our hands, and will be devised by others—and on that day, we will have no choice.'

She sits to rigid silence. The President waits for more speakers; then she calls for a vote.

The motion falls. Rama is not surprised. But she is surprised at how close it is. 161—138. Just twelve more, and she'd have had them.

When she walks down at the end of the session, she feels the eyes of the Council on her.

Four

The Book of Alora

Through a gap in the clearing, the rising sun called Mithila early. She groaned. Her legs ached, a raking pain that started in her calves and throbbed its way down.

She could hear the river. It reminded her of Sumer, the sound of water never far away. Mithila sat up and looked at the trees, at the leaves that rustled in the morning breeze. Wisps of white-grey clouds floated in the sky.

She closed her eyes, letting herself drift away upon the air, as she so often had in Sumer. This time there was no Wall to stop her. The world was spread out before her, that momentary glimpse, through half-closed eyes, that she had caught from the sky.

She imagined Garuda and Dhara on either side of her, laughing in the morning.

We'll still chase the sun.

Mithila stood on shaky feet. The ascending sun was playing hide-and-seek through the trees, sending little spear-shafts of light through the canopy, turning the leaves into bright, liquid gold.

By slow degrees, the world made itself known to her. The colours of the canopy. The breeze that danced upon her skin and teased her hair. The lush, moist scent that she could almost taste upon her tongue.

She wondered if, in the language that had existed before the Wall, there had been a word for what she was feeling now: for this soft arrival into an unbound world.

She walked down to the river. The world felt dewy, freshly washed. And now, in her second morning, Mithila began to see. It rose above her in layers: the canopy that crowded out the sunlight; shorter trees, waiting for their chance to spring into the sky; a thickness of foliage that surrounded her, branch and leaf that she pushed aside as she walked; an entanglement of grass and tendrils and creeping vines at her feet, through which she picked a path. She turned her head this way and that, until her neck hurt, to see above and around herself: at the curiously tapering, toothed leaves that hung from the canopy, at the longer, slender, darker-green fronds around her, at the serrated, dull-brown barks that spaced out her trail.

All of it new-seen but all of it remembered, passing over the landscape of her mind like the shadow of a garuda upon the ground, as fleeting and as ungraspable.

At the river, sunbeams tossed upon the tumbling water, turning it grey-gold. Mithila was seized by a mad urge to chase them. She slipped off her sandals and waded into the current, stiffening at its coldness, feeling it swirl around her ankles, her knees, her thighs, eddies and whorls that almost took her off her feet. She went no further, but extended her arms and plunged her head into the water, as if to seize the sunbeams. She caught no light, but her eyes and her ears were full of a muddy wetness, and there was a rushing sound that throbbed in her skull. Water entered her nostrils. Mithila surfaced, snorting, feeling it whirl somewhere near the bridge of her nose, its odd taste lodged at the back of her throat.

She clambered back ashore, her clothes soaking. She had barely travelled any distance into the river. Mithila shivered, and walked back to the clearing, where she had abandoned her pack.

Back there, she realized that she was hungry. She rifled through the pack. There was the next portion of *rahi*—and there was something else that she had hurriedly stuffed inside before leaving, and then forgotten. Mithila took out the book with its green cover and ochre lettering.

SUMER LOST, OR THE SONG OF ALORA THE BUILDER

It was always meant to be read in a world without the Wall.

Carina's voice sounded in her ears, just before she'd handed the book back to Mithila, a farewell gift from the Dooma.

Mithila looked around the clearing. Her legs still ached. She lay down and nudged the pack under her head, turning it into a makeshift cushion. Placing the *rahi* within reach of her fingers, she flipped open the book.

The first page, she saw, was written in a fine, calligraphed hand. The black strokes were swift and confident. The words recalled an underground chamber, blue light, another world …

In old Gumfraude, beside Geroun
Come back and wander out with me
To find our way beneath the moon
West of the river, South of the sea

Upon the roads that still recall
Alora's steps; a memory
Of times that were before the fall
West of the river, South of the sea

Come find me by the crystal pool
Beneath the garden of the tree
We will remake Alora's rule
West of the river, South of the sea

Remember what I said to you
Of all that was but could not be
By Mati's shade, my vow renew
West of the river, South of the sea

You asked if we would conquer death
I said there was a galaxy
Bring back my words upon your breath
West of the river, South of the sea

And in those words, the open vein
Will bring you on the road to me
We'll speak the old days back again
West of the river, South of the sea

The City of the Afternoon,
Do you remember? We were free.
In old Gumfraude, beside Gheroun
West of the river, South of the sea.

And if that life you would restore
From Circles of our history
Come walk between the worlds once more
West of the river, South of the sea

'Alora?' she whispered.

She remembered her last night in the City but one, hiding underground in the Dooma, and the dream that had visited her, the dream of the rebel builder, cast down into the depths of Sumer, the dream of Alora.

Slowly, she traced her finger underneath unfamiliar terms. *Crystal pool. Mati.* And then the refrain, ending in the word…

Sea.

There it was once more, a tingling at the back of her brain, a grasping at something insubstantial, a moving shadow upon the ground.

She snapped the book shut, stuffed it into the pack, and pulled herself to her feet.

It was then that she felt, for the first time, that she was not alone.

It lasted an instant. The hairs on her skin rose. Mithila tensed. The clearing remained empty.

A garuda flew across the sky.

Mithila relaxed. Almost laughing at herself, she turned and left the clearing, back to where the river wandered onwards.

Language is incomplete without a word for the flavour of earth after rain.

I remember Sumer. I remember the scent of the woodlands after a shower. But this is something else. It rises from the ground. It fills you up. It dissolves the borders between the world and you.

It runs like the blood in your veins.

The night before our trial, Alvar and I discovered that smara *was not longing. It was memory, memory of a time before the Wall. In that memory there should be a word for this, a word that would spare me this task of describing it for you in the language that we know. But my mind is blank like those maps of Sumer with their white spaces beyond the Wall.*

Sometimes I think I can see—but it's an illusion, like the shadow of a garuda flitting over the ground, which you think you can catch—but the real thing is far beyond your reach.

But we did catch a garuda, didn't we? And maybe we'll have to fill those white spaces up ourselves.

I feel … I feel … I don't know what I feel. My heart could burst. I have cried three times. When the stars came down to me last night. When I heard the rain on the river today afternoon. And just before I stopped to write this. For no reason. I just couldn't stop. In Sumer, I thought my eyes had dried up for good, and I couldn't cry even when I wanted to, like when Garuda died. And now it's so easy.

I don't know why I'm writing this. Maybe because I wish I could show this all to you, but all I have are these words.

Did you know that rain upon a river in the world looks so different from rain upon our Rasa? It creates a curtain over the water, a shimmering—like a mist—a river-mist, I'd call it. Can you see it? Remember our experiments with the lake, remember learning to see the horizon? I'm writing this now because I'm so scared I'll forget—that if I ever come back to you, I'll spend my life trying to make you see without finding the words for it.

I wish there was a better way to know the world than words.

There is taste. Do you know what else I found today, after the rain had stopped? As I walked in the Builders' wood, inhaling that—that flavour into my blood—I saw a low-hanging branch. Blue-black spheres hung from it, in clusters. Again, that shadow across my mind. I plucked them from the branch. I rolled them around my palm. I smelt them. Pungent, sharp, recent.

I bit in.

Bittersweet taste, coolness in my mouth. And I remembered: light and shadow, a low hum, a harper playing Here's to you, Maran and Apar, *two glasses, a gushing dark liquid—and I remembered you, Rama.*

It was something that recalled the taste of the Select's drink.

If I see you again, we will taste our memories.

Mithila closed the diary. The papers were already showing signs of sogginess. She stuffed it into her pack, and stood. The day had worn on, and around her, the world glistened in the aftermath of rain. And as she walked, the occasional drop slid down a leaf-surface, splashed upon her neck, and trickled down her skin, making her shiver.

She kept the river at the edge of her vision as she scrabbled through the undergrowth, branches and leaves brushing against her skin. The scent in the air was growing stronger, as if there was something just beyond, which moved away as she walked.

The world began to change.

The trees grew sparser. Gaps in the canopy began to appear. She caught glimpses of a sky that still bore the promise of rain. Soon, she was walking in an open space—a clearing, but not quite—more like a thinning out, a fading away, the trees around the edges of her sight resembling a boundary.

Mithila stopped. Shading her eyes with her palm, she could see a last row of trees, and beyond that a patch of clear ground.

Beyond that there was *something*. Something that glimmered.

The world turned molten.

Shafts of golden light rent the air. The outlines of the clouds were blinding white, a brightness that almost crackled, before it gave way to rust-red, and then shadow. Streaks of ochre were daubed across the sky, upon a canvas of deeper, darker blue. Somewhere beyond the rim of the world, the sun was going down.

Not Wallset.

*Sun*set.

She tip-toed forward. The line of trees grew closer. The ground began to darken. Like a sigh, the turmoil of colour in the sky was dissolving into a pale, iron-grey monochrome. Around her the wind picked up, a rustling in the trees that matched the rushing of the river. But there was a deeper sound in the distance, deeper even than a roar. A still sound.

She paused at woodland's edge, in a darkling world. She looked behind, at the clearing, at the scattered trees and their shadows, as if she was standing at a threshold, readying to leave a lifetime behind, and walk into the light.

Mithila took one breath to steady herself, and stepped out beyond.

She fell into openness.

Soft earth. Her feet sank into it, almost pitching her forward. Soft earth, until it gave way to water: water that ran up its edges and fled back, leaving behind a curl of whiteness that dissolved into nothingness.

Water that went on forever.

Until yesterday, the Wall.

Today, a boundary of trees.

And now the borders of the world were gone.

West of the river, South of the sea.

Sea.

Mithila tore her eyes out with looking. Her legs carried her towards the sea, but she only had a sense of falling, falling towards it. Beneath her, the ground turned wet. And the water came to her. It chased her feet, spread itself around her ankles, making her gasp with the cold—and retreated, leaving her feet sunk in the ground once more, as if the *world* had moved beneath her feet.

It came back to her, lapped against her sandals. Mithila stood still, tasting tears upon her tongue. Once, long ago, she had lain on her stomach and tried so hard, so very hard, to make the ground beyond the water vanish. Now there was no ground, no Wall—only water and sky. A floating blanket before her, that moved and shifted with the wind, and never ended.

A horizon.

The horizon.

Taraf had known.

Through slits in the clouds, shafts of dying grey light speared the waves. In the far distance, she saw a group of garudas circling above the sea, their cries faint over the air. She followed the light, until she saw the river once more, and the canopy beyond. Mithila turned. To her other side, rising above the trees, away in the distance, saw the Wall.

The wind hit her face. Mithila shivered, feeling the cold in her bones. She stepped back. Something crunched beneath her feet, an unfamiliar sound. She looked down, and saw a multitude of little objects that lay scattered upon the ground.

Ranging from the size of a fingernail to a fist, they were blank and coloured, plain and patterned, smooth, spiked, ridged, corrugated and vertebraed; and all of them were variations upon a spiral, coils and whirls winding around each other in a swirling of structures.

Forgetting the cold, she felt her way among them, picking up the smaller ones—cautiously, and then more boldly, as she realized that they were only *things*—and examining them in her palm. Many of them were caked in the unfamiliar stuff that made up this soft ground, something that slipped through her fingers as she prised it away, like sawdust from her father's workshop but somehow more real, a cleaner smell. The work of her fingers revealed polished surfaces, glimmering in the ascending starlight.

Upon the ground, a peculiar shape caught her eye: dark and striped, it seemed piled in coils around itself, with spirals that widened with every turn. On one end it tapered to a point, and on the other, it opened like a mouth. She picked it up. Unlike some of the other, broken ones, this was whole, a complete, symmetrical design. She brought it up to her face for a closer look. Without quite knowing what she was doing, she cupped it against her right ear.

The boundaries between her body and the world disintegrated. It was as if the world was contained within the spiral, and now it poured into her ears: a rhythmic sound that swelled into a roar.

The sea spilled into her.

Mithila sank to her knees. She felt like her body was holding the world entire, a world without a Wall. The ever-receding horizon was inside her, no, *she* was the horizon. This time she did not hold back the tears.

After a very long time, beneath a pale sky, she looked up again. There was the river to her right. She stood. The sky pressed down on her. Water lapped over her feet, as they dug into the soft ground.

Come find me when you walk ashore
West of the river, South of the sea…

Mithila began to walk.

As her eyes roved across new ground, she saw something standing out of the empty shore. A strange oblong shape, half-buried in the ground, just where the river met the sea, on the edge of the water.

Feet sinking lightly into the ground, she approached it. It was shaped like an arch, covered with patterns, and a smooth black that reminded her of the Wall. As she drew closer, the pattern resolved into the familiar shape of Sumer's alphabet. But it was only when she was standing beside it, with the roar of the river and the beat of the sea sounding in her ears, that Mithila was able to read the words.

Here lies Taraf
The Last

'*No …*' she whispered, her voice taken by a gust of wind from the sea.

The man whose words—like messengers—had found their way to her, six hundred years after his death, to show her a world she was never meant to imagine—here he now lay, in the world she had found. Taraf, whose words had travelled through time and space to her, had made *smara* more bearable, whose songs had vanquished her unspeakable dreams, and whose death—like his life—had been a call and a warning to those who dared see too much. But *here* he was, and he hadn't died in Sumer broken by his Ostracism, no, the Shoortans hadn't defeated him, no, he—like her—had won, had found a way, oh Taraf …

But amidst it all, a sliver of regret crept into her mind. *She wasn't the first after all.*

Around her, the rain began to fall once more. She did not notice. Her eyes were fixed on the black stone—unchipped, unfaded after six hundred years, and the inscription, which could have been carved yesterday.

And Taraf.

She read the words below the inscription.

And if you find my resting place
Traveller, think no more of me
Your steps in mine, so turn your face
West of the river, South of the sea.

Just beneath that, an arrow carved into the stone pointed away from the water.

Rain over the sea. Sheets of rain, billowing over shifting grey water. The dying light. Rain upon the sea. Water upon endless water, moving as one. Behind her, the line of trees shimmered through the curtain of rain.

Between earth and sky, until the horizon, there was only her and the memory of Taraf.

The autumn cold seeped into her again, with all the desolation of an empty world. It seemed as if the circle had turned to its end, and lay broken. Here, a man would have stood, so many years ago, watching the water. And here she stood, an age later, as the rain called time upon autumn and beckoned the winter of the world.

'Taraf'—she smiled a ragged smile, feeling an ache in her heart—'you didn't ever tell us half of it, did you?'

She knelt by the grave, supporting herself on one knee. *Her and no other*. She felt a sudden desire to leap up and run, to run and jump into the sea, and to let the waves carry her away—to end it like it had all begun, in a time out of mind.

It would be so easy ...

The rain around her had begun to fade.

Mithila stood. 'Well, old man,' she said, 'you showed me the world, you brought me here, and you've never been wrong yet.'

She let herself linger no more, but turned in the direction of the arrow. Then, as the darkness began to fall around her, Mithila walked away, away from the grave of Taraf, away from the river, away from the sea.

It was only when she was among the trees again, that the thought crept into her mind.

If Taraf lay there, who wrote that inscription?

In the study, Amrit's presence is everywhere.

He had never been a man for paper. His memory, they said, was unfailing. There are few books, but she sees carven statues from Sumer's history: Maliot, Garlon, other Presidents, even Hansa.

There is paper now, on the desk before her. Rama twirls the pen between her fingers, and looks out of the window. It is raining lightly. She smells the spray in the air, watches little droplets trickle down the petals of the woad flowers in the garden.

A knock on the door. 'Messenger from Councillor Malati.'

'Thank you, Saira. Send them in, please.'

She is turning her chair around when the door opens, and Mankala enters.

Rama stiffens. Mankala inclines her head. 'Sorry, Councillor, did I surprise you? I am *Malati's secretary, you know.'*

'Ah, of course.' Rama motions to a chair. 'Please sit down.' As Mankala does, she continues: 'Does Councillor Malati normally send her personal secretary to deliver messages?'

'If I ask.'

'Ah? So tell me, have you come here as the Councillor's secretary—or as Mankala?'

'Both.'

'The official message first.'

'Councillor Malati thanks you for supporting her Bill in the Council. She requests your company at the Maliot House for a drink tomorrow, and later for dinner at her house, to discuss how you may work together in Council.'

Rama thinks quickly. 'I'm tied up in the early evening—but it would be an honour to join her for dinner.'

Mankala smiles. 'She said you would say exactly this. That is fine.'

Rama feels a surge of anger at being tested for no reason. She suppresses it. Mankala throws up her hands. 'I'm only the messenger!'

'Oh, only *the messenger—you expect me to believe that?' Rama smiles back, in spite of herself. 'And what else, Mankala?'*

'I came to ask you for something, but before that, to ask how you were.'

'As good as I can be, I guess.'

'I want to tell you. I was with Mithila the morning before the trial. And—'

Rama puts up a hand. 'I'd prefer not to know.'

'Oh—yes, yes, of course.' For the first time since she has known her, Rama sees Mankala look uncomfortable. 'I just wanted to tell you how cut up she was about it.'

'Mithila always made her own reality,' Rama says quietly. 'It had space for me. Until it didn't.'

Mankala is staring intently at the ground. 'That's not—'

'I'm not complaining. I chose it.'

Mankala looks up. 'I needed to tell you that—that it wasn't us, and—'

Rama shakes her head, smiling again. 'Do you really think I need a window into Mithila's heart? I don't blame you. I don't even blame her. But right now, in my head, you're all too bound up with her—you, the Young Tarafians—so you'll just have to give me some time.'

Mankala nods, looking like herself again. 'Fair.'

'So why've you come?'

Mankala is silent for a moment. Then she speaks quickly. 'I need to get into the Temple.'

Rama raises an eyebrow.

'Tomorrow,' says Mankala.

Five

The Night of the Carnival

Mankala rapped on the door of the Select's Citadel. After a while, a young man opened it. He was dressed in plain ochre, an Apprentice by his age.

'May I assist you?' he said, looking from Mankala to Alvar.

'Yes,' Mankala replied. 'We're here for Open Day.'

'Wha—oh!' Momentary confusion on the Apprentice's face was swiftly chased away. 'Open Day, of course. Welcome to the Citadel. You can explore any part of the building that is open to visitors, or—'

'That's fine, thanks,' Mankala interrupted. 'We'd like to meet Marwana.'

'Er—yes of course. Follow me.'

They walked through the hall of pillars. In the aisles, small groups of scientists—distinctive in their pale red-ochre cloaks—talked in low voices. From the upper reaches of the Citadel, other noises floated down to them: a regular *thump-thump*; a sound that *felt* like a saw being driven through wood, but not quite; and the occasional call. Alvar's nose twitched. A faint pall of smoke hung in the hall.

As they walked among the pillars—glowing faint blue—Alvar whispered: 'I've never heard of Open Day.'

Mankala shrugged. 'You and everybody else.'

The Apprentice led them up the main stairway and into the heart of the Citadel, through arched hallways and wide, airy corridors. Twice they passed by a pair of scientists in conversation. Alvar heard snatches of talk: '*... the harvest forecast needs to—*', '*new advance on the a. equation by Deva—she's writing it all up—*', '*sure the breakdown actually happens like that?*'

They ascended steadily, until the Apprentice stopped outside a door, and knocked.

'Come in!' Marwana called.

They entered. Marwana was seated at her desk. The soft light of the rain-soaked morning streamed in through the low window behind her. Alvar saw the Forum Plaza spread out far below: the straight line of the Rasa and the white walls of the Academy facing them, through a thin drizzle-curtain.

'Open Day visitors, Chief,' said the Apprentice.

Marwana smiled at them. 'Be welcome.'

Alvar took in the room: shelves on either side, filled with scrolls. The desk was covered with a large map of Sumer.

'Do you want to see the Citadel?' Marwana said.

'Thank you, no' said Mankala, 'We just wanted to talk to you.'

'Of course. Sit, sit.' Mankala gestured at the Apprentice. 'Thanks, Raag.'

Alvar heard the door close behind him. They took their seats opposite Marwana. 'Well, now,' said the scientist. 'Aren't we missing someone?'

'Mithila couldn't make it,' said Mankala.

'Oh my!' Marwana laughed easily. 'I thought you were all joined at the hip—only the Wall could ever separate you!'

Mankala's face didn't change. Alvar fought to keep his still.

'Oh well,' said Marwana, still sounding amused. 'I will not press this. Unless *that's* what you came to talk about?'

'Actually, we came,' said Mankala, 'because we just found out about Open Days. And we wanted to use the chance, as I was expelled from the Academy, and Alvar—' she jerked her thumb at him, 'is finishing this year after his work with the Carers.'

'Go on.'

'So there's one question that's been bothering us,' said Mankala.

'Is this about the Wall?'

'No.'

'Well, that's new.' Was there a hint of boredom underneath the amusement? 'What *is* it about?'

'It concerns architecture.'

'Arch—'

Mankala leaned forward. 'Leader Marwana, why are all the houses beyond the Five made of mud-brick?'

'Why—how else would they be made?'

'Wood? Bamboo?'

'Well, yes—but we need bamboo and wood for other things. For the bridges, for furniture—'

'Marwana,' Mankala cut her short. 'I've done the calculations. If you were to build wooden houses for—say—the Sixth Mandala, and bamboo houses for the Seventh and the Eighth, you would be well within renewal times. We wouldn't run out of either.'

Alvar watched Marwana's eyebrows knit.

'I haven't done any calculations,' the leader of the Select said. 'Let's say you're right. Why does it matter?

'Because that's what's bothering me,' Mankala said. 'Every Mandala is different, every Mandala wants to *show* it's different, with its colours and its banners and its songs. But when it comes to building—the most obvious way—from the Sixth to the Fifteenth, it's all mud-brick, so much sameness. Why?'

Marwana leaned back in her chair, looking into the distance beyond them. Alvar saw a slight smile begin at the edge of her lips.

'Say what you want to say,' said the scientist. 'What's so special about mud-brick?'

'Wood burns, Leader. Bamboo burns. Mud-brick does not.'

'And?'

'And so, there was a time when the City was so terrified of fire that everyone built their house out of mud-brick.'

'Right. And *so*?'

'People aren't that terrified of fire, Leader,' Mankala said quietly. '*Unless they've been burned.*'

Quietness hung between them.

Alvar looked from one to the other. Mankala was still leaning forward, her hands upon the table, her fingers interlocked. Marwana's lips were drawn into a line. Her smile had flickered out.

'Tell me something, Mankala ... Nine,' Marwana said, almost murmuring, 'what was that essay you wrote for which they threw you out of the Academy?'

'I argued that our family structure—the father, the mother, the child—make no economic sense for a world within the Wall,' Mankala said, her voice bored. 'I concluded that this must have been a holdover from the time before the Wall. I proposed studying the family for clues to that past.'

'Ah,' said Marwana. 'I thought I had that story right. It's a hard one to forget.'

'I know.'

'We should have found you younger.' The scientist's voice was so soft that they almost missed it.

'So am I right?' said Mankala impatiently.

Marwana nodded. 'Yes. There is some evidence most of Sumer was destroyed in a fire a very long time ago. The City we live in is not the first Sumer.'

'Sumer is a big place, Leader,' said Mankala, 'with a lot of water. A City-wide fire just ... happened?'

'Probably not,' said Marwana. 'But you see, Mankala-Nine, the thing about fires is that they don't leave a lot of proof behind. Especially after two thousand years.'

The air felt heavy.

'The Forum was untouched?' said Alvar, finding footing for the first time.

'Of course. But, unfortunately, the Select's records don't go that far back. Our Hall of Records is one thousand four hundred and twenty years old—from the time of the Oligarchy, just before the era of

Shoortan rule. But we know from the existence of the older calendar that this City itself is at least two thousand years old. The fire, we think, was near the beginning of … time.'

Alvar cast a sidelong look at Mankala. She was looking down at her fingers. 'So,' he said, 'we don't know why the fire happened, and we don't know what existed before it.'

'Yes.'

'But we do know that someone went to the trouble of setting all Sumer on fire?'

'Probably, yes.'

'And if so, they could do it again?' said Mankala.

Marwana smiled a faint smile.

'But the mud-brick would make it harder, wouldn't it?'

'I know what you're looking for,' Marwana said, her voice gentle. 'The problem is that there are too many gaps in our knowledge, even for someone as good at lateral thinking as you. You put three things together—and then there's this empty space, like a—like a river without a bridge. You know there's something beyond, you can almost see it, but you can't get to it. Our history is just questions.'

Mankala nodded.

'Is there anything else you want to ask me about?' asked Marwana. 'Or do you want to take a look in our Hall of Records? You've done so well on so little that I almost feel you'll spot something we've missed all these years.'

Mankala looked up. 'Ah, thank you, Leader, we'll take you up on that some other time. But that's all for now, I think.'

'Alright,' said Marwana. 'Turn to your right and walk straight on down—you'll get to the main door.' And as they got up and turned to leave, she continued: 'I hope Mithila is safe.'

Mankala paused, but did not turn around. 'We hope so too.'

'And you,' said Marwana, 'stay safe.'

They stood outside the Citadel. The scent of rain lingered in the air. The Forum Plaza looked freshly washed.

'So that's what Tefnakth said,' Mankala finished. 'The Great Fire. Three Kings. The end, like the beginning. All quite mad, you'd think, unless ...' her voice trailed off.

'Now we know about the Great Fire,' Alvar said. 'But the rest—'

'I was hoping we'd get more from Marwana.' Mankala kicked at the grass. 'Apart from just telling me that I was right.'

'You know,' said Alvar, 'She does know something more. But she's not going to give it to us. I feel like it's a test—we have to walk part of the way, for her to take us further.'

'Like we have to prove ourselves,' Mankala muttered. 'You're right.'

They looked at each other, the rain-washed world hazy and glimmering around them.

'Now what?' said Alvar. 'No records. Where do we start?'

Mankala shook her head. 'I don't know. And the Encyclopaedia is burned. Nothing's written down—'

'*Written*!' Alvar exclaimed. 'But of course! Mankala—writing is not the *only way*.'

'Wha—oh!' Mankala drew in a breath. '*Oral* history. The Bards of the Seventh. You think they'll know?'

'I can try!' Alvar's voice rose, excited. 'At least, I can ask. And the Bards have never refused me.'

'Let's do it! When are you going over to the Seventh next?'

'Tonight's Carnival. I'll go tomorrow?'

'Perfect!'

'What should I ask? About the Three Kings?'

'Yes, I think—if any of the old songs talk about three kings? I'm guessing that would need the bards to go *really* far back ... but hey, that reminds me. About the Carnival itself—'

'Oh yes.'

'We can't delay more,' Mankala spoke quickly. 'Minakshi knows. Marwana knows. Tomorrow, the Academy will reopen and Mithila won't be there. They're going to ask questions. And unless we're just going to deny all everything ...'

'That'll just mean all this was for nothing.'

'Yeah.' Mankala took a deep breath, her palms against her eyes. 'So you know that moment, just before midnight, when everyone comes to the Wall, where the Rasa turns—when Carnival ends?'

'Yes.'

'We'll do it then. We'll tell the City. It was us. And that we'd do it again.'

'It's going to be risky,' said Alvar. 'The mood is unpredictable.'

'We have to chance it.'

Alvar glanced beyond the Citadel, to where the stone complex of the First Mandala glistened in the morning. 'Yes.'

Out of the corner of his eye, he saw the doors of the Council Hall open. It was the Watch once again, trooping out of the door. This time there was nobody with them. They marched out in two lines of ten, across the Plaza and towards the Maliot.

They still held swords in their hands.

Rama paddled down the Rasa.

In the early days, she and Mithila had sometimes taken the boat down to the Seventh, before deciding that they liked walking better. After that, she had rarely been on the river.

She docked at the Eleventh and stumbled ashore. There was a milling crowd in the space between the Maliot and the buildings of the Eleventh, gathered around the *rahi* sellers. She overheard snatches of talk about Carnival. Beyond the crowd, the mud-brick façade of the Mandala faced her, concealing its narrow, twisting streets and closely-bunched homes.

As she stepped onto the Maliot, a path cleared for her. She realized with a grimace how visible the blue Elders' stripe was on her tunic. 'Can you please tell me,' she said, 'the way to Konar Hall?'

'Straight down, Elder. On your left, by the tributary. It's the three-storeyed one.'

'Thank you.'

Rama stepped into the Eleventh. Away from the Maliot, she walked in light and shadow, winding around the unevenly-spaced houses. The smell of *rahi* was in the air, mingling with the scent of earth. The streets were empty, but she could hear sounds of movement in the houses, the hum of conversation that told her that preparation for the night was on.

Arriving at the three-storey building, Rama went up to it and knocked on the wooden door.

There was no response. She pushed the door open and stepped inside.

She was in a long hall, with a lofty gable-roof that was held up by wooden rafters. Mild sunlight crept in through arched windows high up on the walls, leaving the hall in swathes of shadow punctuated by dancing motes of light. At the end of the hall was a long, rectangular table. Three men and three women sat behind it, facing her.

Rama strode across the hall, her footsteps echoing. There was a chair waiting for her across from her hosts.

'I received an invitation,' she said as she sat, 'to come to Konar Hall, in the Eleventh, at midday. From the Producers' Organised Union of the Mandalas. I have come. Alone.'

'POUM acknowledges you,' said the man who sat directly across from her. 'We represent a majority of the working farmers from the Eleventh and Twelfth Mandalas. I am Prana-Eleven.'

'I know you,' said Rama. 'You were the one who led those demands for a third share of the harvest. The Charter.'

Prana-Eleven inclined his head. 'I did. But there is a Union now—as there was in the old days before Dichio—and we no longer have leaders.'

'Whom am I speaking to, then?'

'To us all—we represent the POUM. We have heard about yesterday's Council debate on the Farmland Bill.'

'It was all Malati.' Rama shifted in her chair. 'I was only the last speaker—'

'And you supported it.'

'Of course!'

'We are sad to say, Elder Rama,' the woman next to Prana-Eleven said, 'that we have no faith in the Elder Malati. Thirty-four seasons she has been in Council, and her one achievement is—what? Mercy for Savarian's aides twenty-seven years ago? She drafts these Bills, makes all these speeches, and then they fail. She doesn't even consult us before she comes up with these ideas—'

'To be fair,' Rama interrupted, 'POUM never existed all these years. She could hardly have known whom to consult.'

'That's not the point,' Prana said, 'Meghana is right. We work the land. Always have. We know what we want. This is not about her grand ideas. This is about us.'

'Right,' said Rama. 'And where do I come in?'

'Because we have decided,' Prana-Eleven's voice rang in the hall, 'to exercise our ancient right of representation. The Eleventh Mandala resolved this morning to formally ask you, Rama-One, to be our Speaker in Council.'

Rama stiffened. Hansa's words sounded in her ears. '... *one of those unbroken conventions, as old as our Democracy.*'

'Ever since Dichio crushed our Union two centuries ago,' Prana-Eleven continued, 'we have been scattered in the farms of Sumer, working for our separate masters. Nor was there a voice in Council that we could call our own. But no longer.'

'And this—because of my one speech in Council?'

'We know your history, Rama-One,' said Meghana. 'And something of your views. Better, I think, than your own colleagues.' Before Rama could react, she leaned forward. 'Will you deny your own words, the words that you spoke in *The Maliot House* just a few nights ago—that *something of equality is yet to come?*'

Rama's heart lurched. 'How do you ...'

'We know what we need to, this side of the Wall.'

There was no time to think, only to speak. She swallowed.

'I acknowledge your right to a Speaker,' she said, her words tumbling out. 'As you've chosen me, I will do my best to speak for the interests of the Eleventh Mandala in Council … which I *assume* will always be represented by POUM?'

Prana cleared his throat. 'The interests of the farmers of the Eleventh—most of whom belong to POUM, as also the Twelfth.'

'Better hold on to your membership, then—I don't want to decide between competing appeals, each claiming to speak for the Eleventh.'

There was a moment of tension in the room. Then Meghana laughed, snapping it. Chuckles sounded around the table, and even Prana relaxed. 'Then we are decided.'

'Yes.'

'One more thing,' said Meghana. 'When our Charter was rejected by the Council, the reason they gave was that it was impossible, this side of the Wall. That's all they keep saying—that nothing can change because of the Wall, and of course they'd like that, as long as they can sit pretty in their woad blue and chew on their *khire*—no offence to you of course. *But*—' Rama grew alert as she realized what was coming next. 'But now we hear that things have changed. Now, we hear, someone has found a way beyond the Wall. As you were—'

Rama held up a hand. 'We do not go there. It's true that I was once of the Young Tarafians, whose goal was—is—to bring down the Wall. But I belong to the Council now.'

Prana-Eleven leaned back in his chair and steepled his fingers against his lips.

'But what if,' he said, 'we of the Eleventh no longer want the world within the Wall?'

As she stepped out of Malati's house and into the Sumerian evening, Mankala heard the sounds of Carnival. She walked out into the street, and turned towards the Maliot.

In the distance, the Forum Plaza was a whirl of light. Flame lamps bobbed and weaved in the night as people danced around each other. Rhythmic chanting, sharp and quick, carried to her.

The Select—they don't know what they do
The Elders—haven't a fucking clue
We get by—on a prayer and a shout
Builders—when are you letting us out!

Mankala smiled. As she walked she saw two Watchmen in the shadows of the stone houses, hidden but for the curve of their blades glistening in the dim light.

She went past them, feeling the hair on the back of her neck rise. Then she was on the Maliot. The road was filled with people out in their Circle-coloured clothes, holding up lamps. Mankala took a deep breath, and plunged into the crowd.

Two hours later, she was at the Eleventh, bruised and disheveled from navigating drunk revellers who wanted to throw her into the Rasa, and others who had tried to get her to join in the dancing. As she went into the Eleventh, the crowd thinned. By the time she reached her house, the streets were dark and empty.

When Malati had hired her after her expulsion from the Academy, she had been entitled to a house in the Sixth, on equal rank with the Watch. But Mankala had never made the move, shifting instead to this vacant one-roomed home a few streets away from where she'd been born and raised.

She slumped upon her chair. The lamplight showed her the outlines of her bed, the desk upon which some of Malati's papers were stacked neatly, and her one wooden shelf with its few scrolls and books, sometime borrowed from Ananta.

Outside, the night drew on. Soon, the City would head to the Wall. She stood and walked through a short corridor into the bathroom. Her bathing bucket, filled in the morning, waited for her. She kicked off her sandals, slipped out of her clothes, and poured mugs of river-water over herself.

As the water washed away the dirt and weariness of the long walk from the Forum, her mind drifted to what lay in wait: the Wall at midnight, the City assembled, that moment—that *one* moment of stillness when everything was possible—before the day turned and another year of dull resignation began. In that moment, they would have to—

Outside, something struck the floor with a muffled splintering.

Mankala paused, her mug suspended over her head, the water trickling onto her hair.

There was silence.

She shrugged, bent, and lowered the mug into the bucket again. She began to rehearse the words that she would start with, in the moment that she would have by the Wall. *Tonight, the world—*

The air grew burning hot.

Mankala dropped the mug and ran out into the corridor. She stopped at the threshold, just before it widened into the circular room.

The room was on fire.

Flames rose and leapt from the floor, crackling through the wooden shelves, burning up the papers. Before her eyes they consumed her chair and devoured the table.

The air grew burning hot.

Her eyes and throat stung. Mankala retreated through the corridor, back into the bathroom. She looked up. The low, sloping skylight opened into the night sky.

Mankala tossed her clothes through the gap. Measuring the distance with her eye—as she had seen Lamon do so many times—she retreated, crouched, and launched herself forward and into a leap.

Her hands closed around the rim of the skylight. Her arms were almost torn from their sockets. Her face turned to the sky, she breathed cool air even as the heat scorched the bathroom. Mankala clenched her teeth and pulled herself up. She threw out an arm. The sloping roof gave her little purchase, but her head was above the skylight now, as the rest of her body dangled underneath. For a moment, gravity almost dragged her down into the bathroom, where the flames were licking at the threshold. With a final heave, she hauled herself up again, her torso emerging onto the roof. Another pull, and she was out, slipping forwards, her bare knees scraping upon the mud-brick.

At the edge of the roof, she managed to stop sliding. Here, the ground was close—close enough for her to sit on the edge, and let herself go. The soles of her feet stung as she landed, but Mankala didn't care. Shivering in the cold, she picked up her fallen clothes and pulled them back on. She was still wet from her bath, water dripping from her hair. Her scalp felt as if it had been singed, there was a coarse, stabbing pain in her knees, and she had no sandals.

Her house burned.

The ground was cold and hard, an unfamiliar sensation beneath her feet. The window glowed orange. There was no sound.

Mankala shivered again. She backed away—into something solid.

'All alone—on Carnival Night?'

The voice in her ear was rough. She smelt the Select's Drink. Suddenly, her arms were pinioned, and she was immobilized. Mankala twisted her head. Behind her there was a man, tall and bearded. 'Clothes wet—and barefoot,' he continued, his voice slurring. 'Already celebrating Carnival?'

Behind him, another shape.

'My—my house is burning,' she said, stupidly.

'How lucky you're not inside,' a woman said.

'Come with us,' the man spoke again. 'Carnival's no time to be alone, and there's time for another round of drink.'

'I—the Wall—'

'We'll get there.'

Before Mankala knew what was happening, she was being half-pulled, half-dragged down the street, southwards and away from the Maliot. She was trapped: on Carnival Night, this was too familiar a sight. Barefoot and soaking, her cries would be dismissed by anyone they happened to meet.

And then she realized another thing. Though the man's voice had slurred, there was nothing muddled about the way her arms were held: lightly, yet with firmness that killed any thoughts of twisting away.

Mankala relaxed, saving her strength. They were still heading South, into the heart of the last Circles. Every step took her further away from the Rasa, from where she had to be at midnight. They passed a few people, all hurrying North.

'Aren't we going the wrong way?' she said once.

'What way is wrong, when you always end up at the Wall?' the man said. Both of them laughed.

The Circles fell away, the streets narrowed, and the buildings closed in around them. The ground grew rough and uneven, hurting her feet. There was that familiar smell that told her they were in the Dooma: the smell of stagnant water. Then the ladders appeared, hanging from the buildings, joining one roof to another, terrace from terrace.

They approached the bridge that connected the Thirteenth to the Fourteenth. Just beyond that, the buildings came together, and an opening into a black tunnel. Mankala sensed a quickening of pace around her, a shortening of breath.

'You messed up back there didn't you?' she said quietly. 'I wasn't supposed to get out of the house. And now you don't know what to do with me.'

There was no answer. But she felt the grip on her arms tighten. She bit her tongue to stop from gasping in pain.

'Murder is harder than an accident,' she continued. 'What are you thinking of? A drowning? A fall from a high Dooma roof? But you're not from the Dooma. Or—'

'Shut up!' said the man, his nails digging into her skin; but just as he spoke, rattled for a moment, Mankala kicked backwards and up with all the strength that she had.

She felt her heel connect. A scream tore through the night air. In an instant her arms were free. Mankala leapt forward, and onto the bridge. She looked behind her. The man had sunk to the floor, but in the woman's hand, moonlight shone off an iron blade.

Mankala threw herself off the bridge.

The fields by the Wall were a carpet of light.

All through the day, the Fifteenth had trimmed the wick and arrayed the *diyas* upon the barren soil, in preparation for this, the final act of Carnival Night. As Alvar approached the Wall, he had the feeling of walking in a land of fallen stars. The ground glimmered. From one *diya* to the next, curtains of light pierced the dark.

Carnival Night. The one night in the year when the Shoortans retreated, when the 100-metre compact was suspended, when the people of Sumer faced the Wall with nothing in the way. The night of *smara*, they called it. The night Sumer turned upside down.

There were people in the fields already, huddled together in small groups. Alvar walked between the *diyas*, feeling the uneven ground beneath his feet. By the Wall, he turned to face the City.

Sumer was arriving.

Dark shapes moved across the fields. A low hum floated in the air. Motes of light danced upon the ground, making the soil glow orange. The scent of sweat mingled with the smell of the Select's drink, bitter and cloying, so strong that he could almost taste it on his tongue.

The fields began to fill. Waves of people poured in from the Maliot. They all came towards the Wall, outlines of figures that floated a little way above the carpet of light.

There were murmurs in the night, little sounds, words left unshaped. The air tightened, stretched. Alvar felt a curious, cold alertness come over him. A lifetime of *smara* had shattered when Mithila had left. Now it was as if he was hovering high in the air, like a garuda, looking down on it all.

They came on, bodies that passed through light and shadow, walking separately but moving as one, until they were there, massed together, the City by the Wall.

From his garuda's-eye view, Alvar saw them alll: dark heads close together, in and among the *diyas*, beneath the razor-clear moonlight, looking up at the Wall, and the Wall that stared back at them, as it had for two thousand years, unperturbed.

Their faces were masks.

Smara hung in the air like a cold, dank fog, thickening with every breath, cutting off the light.

Until a scream shattered it.

The scream tore through the night, tore through the fields, tore through *smara*, smashed against the Wall. The world broke. Alvar was inside his body again, swaying upon his feet, as the people surged towards the Wall.

The first line hurled itself upon the black stone with boots, fists, nails, teeth, rocks, shovels, knives, sickles, and every other implement that Sumer could yield up to those it bound. The line fell back, and the ones behind elbowed past for their turn. Cries rent the air, cries of an ancient rage, as the people shoved past each other to get to the Wall, to throw themselves upon it. Cries of a different kind, again, as some slipped, fell—and were trod underfoot by the advancing line.

A face pushed past him, contorted, eyes full. On one side of him a man punched the Wall, roaring, until his knuckles split open, blood glistening wetly on the black—and then he punched it again. Next to him a woman, a knife in her hand, stabbed at the Wall, her arm moving faster than he could see, the blade recoiling back in her fist. Before his eyes the man was dragged away and someone else took his place, throwing himself against the Wall with his shoulder.

The air shivered with *smara* like an old man in the last throes of fever. *Smara*, that smelled like blood, tasted like ash, and sounded like the first scream of release from a mouth that had been gagged for a lifetime, a mouth that knew it had time for a single scream before it would be silenced again.

The stars began to fly.

The *diyas* were in the people's hands, flung against the Wall, a thousand tiny pin-pricks of fire. They winked through the air—and winked out of existence when they hit the Wall, and shattered to pieces. A great splintering carried through the air, the splintering of the *diyas*, the splintering of light.

The fields darkened.

Only moonlight remained.

As it drew closer to midnight, as the rage slackened and grief found the end of the body, the people began to retreat, almost by unspoken agreement.

Silence fell.

There was blood in the fields, seeping into the red soil, mingling with it. The black stone stared back, untouched.

Smara receded from the air, like a scent that had been let out from a bottle to explore the world, and would now be stoppered again. It left behind the cold, empty night.

From the darkness, clear and stark, a child's voice rose into the night. It sang the great song of the Wall, a song forgotten on all days but this.

Walking through unbroken darkness
Walking by the silent Wall
In the far and faded Wallset
As the endless evenings fall
We have walked for years unyielding
We have walked this way alone
Walked upon this weary wasteland
By this ring of sightless stone.

The voices of the women and men around him took up the refrain, thousands of voices raised in unison, a chant that could have carried all the way to where Mithila walked upon a barren shore.

Walk with us, our friends, our brethren
Praya *for our nameless crime*
We, the Builders' forlorn captives
We will walk in circling Time

Behind him, the Wall, and the shadows of the remaining lamps upon it. Alvar clenched his fists, waiting. Just a few moments more.

We have often looked above us
With a parched and dreaming eye
Dreamt of when ours sons and daughters
Look upon a boundless sky
When that patch of blue, unbroken
Is a dome above the ground
And instead of dreary Wallrise
Sunrise in a sky unbound ...

He almost shouted out to them, about the horizon, about Taraf, about the truth of all things. He bit back the words upon his tongue.

March with us, our friends, our brethren
By this stone that tells our crime
We have no more strength to wander
Lonely, in this circling Time

Everyone was standing still, facing the Wall. It was only Alvar, who stood with his back to it. *Where was Mankala?* She had not appeared, and the song was moving inexorably towards its climax.

We have dreams, and visions crowding
Dreams of worlds that wait beyond
Dreams of chasing down the Sunrise
In a world without the Wall!
Dreams of never-ending woodlands
Fields that do not stop the eye
And of ranging through the midnight
Till the stars begin to die!

The song rose as the Wall still stood, rose one final time.

Rage with us, our friends, our brethren
Rage against this silent crime

Will you let your dreams lie broken
Silent, walk in circling Time?

Then it was over, just the last notes lingering in the air, unwilling to die. The people grew silent, heads down. Some sunk to the ground, on their knees, in the shadow of the Wall.

That was when Alvar realized that Mankala wasn't coming. He was alone.

It poured into his head, the sight of Mithila, of the garudas taking her away, breaking the Wall and breaking *Smara*, the beginning of the world. He fought to still himself, as silence descended upon the fields. He braced—

And the sky turned red.

It happened exactly like it had happened four moons ago. In an instant, the night was gone. The stars and moon were snuffed out. The world was wrapped in redness: above, a red blanket in place of the sky; the blackness of the Wall appearing through a red mist, and the people before him, as if he was seeing them through a glimmering curtain of red.

Alvar's words died in his throat. Everything was visible—every figure that stood or knelt in the fields, framed in a red halo, transfixed by the change. Nobody moved or spoke. Somewhere at the back of his head, a clock began to tick.

One … two … three…

On *five*, night returned to the world, like it had before.

Alvar opened his mouth and found he had nothing to say.

Out of the corner of his eye, he saw someone shift. He turned his head. It was Minakshi. She too was standing with her back to the Wall, facing the Citizens.

For a moment, their eyes met.

He saw her turn her gaze back to the fields, open her mouth, and begin to speak.

First Interlude

They stand upon the tower, watching Wallrise over Sumer.

'That was close,' says the Mentor.

'It was,' affirms the Young One.

'We human beings are too unpredictable for our own good.' The Mentor shakes their head. 'It makes it … impossible to see all ends. Nonetheless'—a warning finger—'I want no more errors, like what happened with Mithila. We can't afford them. Time's running out.'

The Young One nods. 'Understood.'

The sun comes up over the Wall.

Six

The Lost City

Mithila awoke to a deep, familiar ache in her abdomen and lower back.

'Urgh,' she muttered and sat up. Fumbling in her pack, she took out the first of the cotton pads that Mankala had packed, and staggered down to the river.

Back in the clearing a few minutes later, she stood gingerly. Apart from first day's pain, hours of walking had stiffened her limbs. She reached over her neck and pressed her shoulder-blades, groaning at the ache that flowed down her back. Clenching her teeth, she placed her palms upon her knees, and moved her kneecaps in slow circles.

The sun streamed into the clearing in which she had spent the night, warming her, loosening tendons and ligaments. Her legs chafed. Keeping them apart, she took a look at the furrow she'd drawn the night before, and walked South-West, out of the clearing.

The Builders' woodland returned to fill the space around her. But today, as she walked, Mithila felt an absence around her, an incompleteness, as if something had been torn from the world, leaving a gap wrought in its own shape.

Once, when they were children, she and Dhara had gone wandering Downcircle, traipsing through the Eleventh on a day when the farmers were out in the fields. On the Rasa tributary that circled the Eleventh, they'd come upon a water-wheel, something new. Mithila had stared at the machinery, the flowing water, and the curved blades; but Dhara, who'd never seen a machine without wanting to take it apart, had danced in excitement. She'd turned to Mithila, her face creased into seriousness, and said: '*If you want to know how something works, ask yourself what they were thinking when they made it.*'

She asked herself that question now, as she walked in the Builders' woodland. From time to time, she thought she saw the beginnings of a pattern—a set of trees arrayed in a row or a grove that took the shape of a circle—but before the geometries could settle, there was a rent in the fabric, something out of place. The pattern in her mind disassembled.

It reminded her of the times that she had begun a song but stopped midway, knowing that the opening was all wrong, and let the discordant notes trail in the air. Or the times that Ananta had tossed away a half-done carving, muttering '*the design was wrong from the start.*'

A work little done, and then undone.

What felt most present, but most out of joint, was the quiet. The rustling of leaves was the only sound in the air, yet her senses—*or was it her memories?*—told her that there had been something more, something lost or taken away. It was as if the world beyond the Wall was a larger reflection of Sumer, but just as pared down and bare.

Then the first flagstone interrupted her musings, and changed the world forever.

It was twice the length and breadth of her foot, oblong and white, its borders sharply wrought. She knelt and ran her fingers over it. It was smooth and cold, and felt new.

Mithila's heart raced. She walked on. Before long, she saw the second flagstone, broken and chipped, a crack running through it. A little way ahead, the third one, also broken, grass peeking through the crevice. And then another. Each one more solid, more real than the last. As she walked, the distance between them lessened, until she saw it:

A road through the Builders' Woodland.

The canopy cleared, revealing a ribbon of open sky. She stepped onto the road. Her feet felt light, springy. The flagstones were smooth, like the floors in the Forum's towers. Above her the trees arched, high gateways for her to walk beneath.

Upon the roads that still recall
Alora's steps; a memory…

The road curved.

Suddenly, there was a real gateway.

On either side of the road, two white pillars rose. They met in an arch, which stood at the level of a three-storeyed Sumerian house. They had no light of their own, but reflected the sun: as if giant hands had lifted them from the Forum, stripped them of their glowing hearts, and set them down, lifeless, in the world beyond the Wall. And a little way beyond there was a line of trees, beyond which a brightness shimmered.

She walked beneath the arch. The pillars had cracks running down their sides, fissures in which little shoots and creepers had made their home. The road was now broken in more places, split lengthwise and crosswise, with some stones uprooted and tossed aside. She stepped in and among the gaps, the line drawing closer, the sunlight growing sharper, until at last she was at the border.

Mithila stepped out of the trees. The sky opened and the ground disappeared.

She scrambled back from the edge. She was standing at the cusp of a bowl, which had been chiselled out of the ground. The earth dipped and curved, an outline of perfect symmetry.

Within the bowl, there lay a shattered City.

A lifetime ago, in a little house in the Seventh, Ananta had carved for his children a masterpiece of woodwork: a scale model of Sumer and its fifteen Mandalas, from the Forum to the Dooma. They had assembled it together, on the dusty floor of his workshop, just a City without a Wall. Then without warning, Garuda had run his hand through it, toppling buildings, casting down bridges, upending towers. '*Am I a Builder now?*' He'd laughed.

Ananta had smiled. '*Sometimes, a ruin can be thrilling.*'

Looking upon the broken City, Mithila knew that in this, as in so many other things, Ananta had been wrong.

The towers had been decapitated, leaving mangled throats open to the sky. Between one building and another, an arched bridge began a graceful loop and then ceased to exist, as if someone had hacked it through with an axe. Her eyes rested upon empty plinths, looking as desolate as the Sumerian trees in those brief, fleeting days when they lost their leaves.

Rubble lined the streets.

Mithila looked beneath her. The road turned into a stairway, carved into the side of the bowl. Carefully, she descended. The City was much smaller than Sumer, like a Sumer that ended by the Fifth Mandala.

When she reached the bottom, two more pillars—all that was left standing of a gate—invited her in. Beside them, she saw a statue upon the ground, lying face up. One of its arms was extended, palm outwards, so that when it was still standing, it would have faced the visitor: the eternal signal to halt.

Mithila grinned at that. 'Sorry, not turning back now,' she said out loud, to break the columns of silence around her.

She knelt to look at the face. Her grin died upon her lips.

Short, straight hair that framed high-cut cheekbones, and the beginnings of a smile. A smile that she had seen once and would never forget.

The face of Ghada.

Mithila was back again, in the hall of the Three Kings, where she had fled after the great debate, watching the two of them, Ghada and Samir, listening to them speak strange words, words from another world.

Oh Samir, there was a galaxy.

Her legs swayed. Ghada's statue drew her in, like Ghada's remembered words, like Ghada herself, or the image of her that Mithila had seen in the underground hall.

She forced herself to turn away, and took slow steps into the City.

She picked her way through debris. A stone finger, broken off at the palm, bigger than her foot. A crowned head, upturned, its eyes delicate and alive, as if it had simply decided one day to take leave of its body and rest by the edge of the road. Beyond the plinths, she saw the fronts of buildings, but only the fronts, like masks that somehow lingered even after the faces they covered had been burnt away.

She tried to imagine the fragments that she saw back upon their pedestals, or the white scree remade into the battered buildings by the road. A broken world, put back together.

She tried to imagine it—and failed.

She'd been walking for a while when the principal avenue opened into what had once been the heart of the City: a circular courtyard, ringed by a passage of pillars. The passage was flanked by ravaged towers. Their exteriors had been ripped off to reveal jagged lattices of interior construction, like a human body turned inside out: a crumbling spiral staircase climbing up to nothingness, twisted gaps where doors had once divided space into hallways, windows that no longer separated an inside from an outside.

But Mithila saw none of that. Her gaze was caught by what was in the centre of the courtyard.

It rose from the ground, a rearing of black stone that twined around itself. In a garden of ruin, something made whole. As Mithila approached it, she saw it was human—almost.

It was a man on his knees. His arms extended above his head, in offering or in supplication. His palms cupped a black stone, six-sided, cunningly wrought, almost glowing. Wings sprouted from his back, varicose veins visible and livid against the stone surface, as if they were burning beneath the sun,

But it was his face that caught her. It was turned to the sky, eyes wide open, in a fixed gaze. The mouth twisted in a scream, a scream that had no words but remembered a language lost, a scream that distorted the contours of the face, like a scar.

It was the face of a man who knew, in the moment before death, that he was alone.

Upon his right shoulder stood—or crouched—another man. His knees were bent, his arms spread out, the wings on his back unfolding, ready to catch the air. His face was upturned, so all Mithila could see was the angle of his neck and jawbone, and the very end of his mouth, the lips drawn back in a laugh.

The kneeling man's hands were at her eye level. Tentatively, Mithila extended an arm, remembering how she'd reached out towards the Heartstone in the Temple. She touched the stone, drew her hand back instinctively, then reached out and grasped it. It was black, cold and utterly smooth, just like the surface of the Wall.

Mithila let go.

Remember Samati. Remember me.

Those were the last words that Dhara had said to her. And here, beyond the Wall, in a shattered City, she saw a man holding up a Heartstone to the sky, and burning up, so that another could fly.

She looked away and looked up. In front of her, there rose a high dome, most of it intact. She recognised it at once. It was the face of the Council Hall, seen from the North, walking in from the farmlands of Sumer.

The world blurred. For a moment, she *was* in Sumer again. Around her, the *rahi* stalks waved. The towers gleamed in the summer sun. The Rasa's song was in the air.

Rama's hand was in hers.

The sun-blaze speared the vision away. Mithila sank to her knees. Her palms were on the ground. For the first time in the world, that weight was back in the pit of her chest, forcing her breath into gasps.

Loneliness was still an unfamiliar feeling.

She felt the stone upon her palm, cool and soft. The vice-like grip upon her throat loosened again, let her breathe. She turned her face up to the familiar-unfamiliar dome, the Forum's dome.

Mithila stood, the aftertaste of tears in her mouth. She walked towards the dome, and climbed the chipped steps that fronted the pillared passageway at the end of the courtyard. A doorway opened into dimness.

She entered a large, hexagonal chamber, and passed into the domed hall that she had seen from outside. There was no exit but a spiral stairway, ascending into darkness. Mithila climbed. It yielded her into another empty room, lit by a half-caved in window.

She wandered to the window. It faced the courtyard. She saw the ring of pillars, the black statue, and the City beyond.

She remembered Garuda again, casting down toy-Sumer with a laugh. Had it been so easy for *them* to destroy the City of Ghada, sending her into the arms of an endless sleep, while the ruins above decayed into the Time of the Evening? And would it be even easier to cast down the real Sumer, which did not have even a Ghada to defend it—if that was what they wanted?

Was that what Tefnakth had been warning them about, in those last days before she had left Sumer forever?

Forever?

Sadness washed over her, like summer rain upon the river.

She did not know how long she stood there watching, as the sun climbed overhead, until the dull pangs of hunger returned. Mithila groaned. She straddled the window-sill, her body half in light and half in shadow. High above the City, cool breeze stroked her face. She fumbled around in her pack for today's portion of *rahi*.

Among the broken columns, sunlight shone upon a black cloak.

Mithila stiffened, her hand in her pack.

A flash, a glimpse of black that shifted, caught for a moment in a beam of light—and was gone.

Mithila swung her leg back into the room and tumbled down from the sill. She struggled to her feet and peered out.

In the City, nothing moved.

A man stepped into the courtyard.

From above, she could only make out the top of his bent head. He walked quickly to the black stone statue and stood there, his hands behind his back, staring at the ground.

Mithila leaned out of the window.

The man's head snapped up. Mithila looked into Tefnakth's eyes.

She gasped and threw herself back into the room. For a few moments, she stood in the shadow, heart racing. Then she peeked out of the opening again.

The courtyard was empty.

'*Fuck!*' She scrambled across the chamber, back upon the stairs leading down into the domed hall.

Tefnakth strode into the hall. Mithila halted upon the stairway.

The former Shoortan stopped and peered around.

'Istar?' he called. 'What are you doing up there? Weren't we going to meet by Mati?'

His voice echoed beneath the dome. Tefnakth waited. Then he spoke again, peevish. 'Where are you, Istar? Mentor said midday. It's late.'

Silence answered him. Tefnakth shook his head and came to the stairway.

Mithila forced herself to move. She turned and crept back up and through the chamber. At its far end, she leaned out of the broken window, looking to either side.

Running below the window, across the length of the building, was a thin ledge, the breadth of a human foot. Mithila gulped. She swung one leg over the window and lowered herself upon it, feet perched upon the narrow surface.

Footfall upon the stairs. Mithila did not look back or down. Placing her palms upon the outer wall, her face pressed against the cold white stone, high above the ruined City, she began to inch sideways, step by step. She turned her face to the left once, and almost slipped. Within a short distance, the ledge ran around the corner of the building.

Just as she heard steps in the room, moving towards the window, Mithila turned the corner and passed out of sight. She closed her eyes, breathing hard. Her face throbbed from how hard she had pressed it against the wall. When she opened her eyes again, she saw that a little way away the ledge broadened into a platform, which—long ago—had perhaps been a view-point. From the platform, winding steps climbed around the exterior, all the way up to the dome.

Slowly, she picked her way forward, until she reached the platform. Mithila collapsed against the side of the building and sobbed, feeling the tight knot in her shoulders loosen ever so slowly.

A sound brought her back to life. She stood and hastened up the steps. They took her into a pillared corridor that circled the base of the dome.

Framed by the pillars, she saw the courtyard below her.

Someone stood by the black statue.

It was not Tefnakth. This figure was dressed in blue. A hood covered the face. Their gaze was fixed upon the statue. With a shiver, Mithila realized that she had been climbing, her back to the courtyard, in full view. She moved behind a pillar.

When she peeked out again, she saw Tefnakth striding into the courtyard. The figure in blue advanced to meet him. That walk—surely she knew it, in another world …

They faced each other. A low, indistinct murmur floated up to Mithila. There was a brief conversation. Tefnakth shook his head, violently. The figure in blue spread out their arms, as if to take in the world.

At that, Tefnakth moved to stand by his companion. Both of them faced her, just behind the statue. The figure in blue raised a hand and said something. Before Mithila's eyes, the ground opened up.

One after the other, the two of them stepped in. The ground closed over them once again.

Mithila stiffened, and then hurried along the corridor. Halfway across, she found a doorway that took her into a descending spiral staircase, and opened into the hexagonal chamber. She crossed it at a run and left the domed building for the sunlight.

The courtyard remained empty.

Mithila slowed as she approached the statue. She circled it warily, inspecting the ground. Solid, smooth, featureless. She ran her fingers along face of the kneeling man, looking for a lever, something, anything. Nothing happened.

She let her hands fall to her side. '*Oh, fuck this*,' she muttered to herself. She turned around on the spot, staring at the ground, the statue, the pillars, the sky. She turned a full circle, back to where she started. The world remained the same.

Mithila kicked at the kneeling man, and squealed as it sent a wave of pain shuddering through her right leg. She circled the statue with quick, uneven steps.

'*Tefnakth*,' she spoke into the emptiness, between breaths, her voice escaping through clenched teeth, her body shaking. 'There was a way out. Always has been. You knew it. You. Shoortans. Damn the Builders, you—you—oh, I *hate* you.'

She came to a halt, and forced her mind to still, to think. Tefnakth had not come from underground. Which meant…

Still trembling, Mithila walked to the pillared corridor, and sat down on the steps, with a clear view of the statue. Now to wait.

She ate her portion of *rahi* at last, and took a few careful sips of water. Her aches were back. To distract herself, Mithila pulled out the book of Alora from her bag, flicking its pages open even as she watched the black tree from above the rim of the book.

And if that life you would restore
From Circles of our history
Come walk between the worlds once more
West of the river, South of the sea

She turned the page.

After the poem ended, the words began, thick black strokes, unfaded by time, the lines clear and straight.

In the Time of the Afternoon, we raised a tower to the stars. For our garden, we made a forest. For our chandeliers, we patterned constellations. For our fireworks, we brought down meteor showers.

Tell me, were we wrong to do so?

The shape of the things was not to our liking. So we unspooled the world and wove it anew, nearer to heart's desire. The grammar of being constrained us. So we shattered it and spoke language from nothingness. We brought winged myth to life, to be our chariot in the sky.

Some things were undone. So many more made whole.

Tell me, were we wrong to do so?

We spoke life into existence, we suspended death, we grasped the arrow of time and twisted it into a circle.

Tell me, were we wrong to do so?

Here in Gumfraude, beside the crystal pool, with the Heartstones we made, we drew light from light, burning glass, a bridge to the worlds. So what if that needed sacrifice?

We knew there would be no light without a burning. We accepted it.

Tell me, were we wrong to do so?

This was the world we made.

This is the world you broke.

In the Time of the Evening, in the spindrift of dying seas and the silence of dead forests, you will know that you were wrong to do so.

She read it through, and read it again, her finger pausing at the second line, at the first unfamiliar word.

Forest.

The shadow again, a memory in a word, a vast green carpet she had glimpsed from the sky, smell of leaf and moist earth.

She looked up, beyond the courtyard, towards the invisible edge of the bowl, where the earth rose and met the line of trees.

In the spindrift of dying seas and the silence of dead forests.

Then the story began.

A story filled with unremembered words, words that her eyes paused and tripped over, a language more vast for a world without a Wall—but language nonetheless, grammar and form moulding itself into sense and image, filling her mind.

A story woven out of the scenes that had visited her that night in the Dooma, woven out of all the dreams of Sumerian childhood, the dreams that had faded for others but not for her, that had entwined with *smara*, an unending ache in her heart. Here, by the ruined City, where Ghada's statue lay, a fallen guardian, she read in the Book of Alora those dreams made flesh, and flesh made memory.

The story of Alora, who measured the skies to their last degree, and the story of Ghada, who held time in her fist and altered its form like a piece of wet clay, and the story of Samir, who travelled time and space for the glory of Gumfraude, beside the river Geroun. Here they seized the laws of being and rewrote them by their will, a morning's task to take apart the world and remake it once more. Here was the coruscation that pierced the night, the music that flowed from the stars, and the Heartstones—the three consorts of the sun—because *from light shall break the light.* And for that there came the fall of Gumfraude, the City of the crystal pool, an end of the Afternoon, an eternal sleep beneath the ground, and for the children of Alora, and of Ghada and Samir, a world within a Wall.

And when the story ended, on the last page, she saw the words, all of them familiar.

And you who read this in the Time of the Evening: we have left you our words and our worlds. We know you have the eyes to see. We are waiting for you.

Mithila let slip the book from her hand, and watched it fall to the ground. She rubbed her eyes, wearied to the bone. It was evening. Sunrays slanted into the courtyard.

Hours had passed.

They could not have come back up while she had been reading. She would have seen them. *They* would have seen *her*.

We have left you our words and our worlds.

She picked up the book, which had fallen open to its earliest pages. The words that had brought her here.

In old Gumfraude, beside Geroun
Come back and wander out with me
To find our way beneath the moon
West of the river, South of the sea…

She was here, she had come, she had followed every direction, but *they* were gone, in sleep underneath the Council Hall, never to be woken. But then, as she read on, her eyes paused, and stopped, upon a word.

Remember what I said to you
Of all that was but could not be
By Mati's side, my words renew
West of the river, South of the sea …

Tefnakth's voice came back to her.

'Istar? What are you doing up there? Weren't we going to meet by the Mati?'

Mithila stood. She shouldered her pack. In the declining light, she walked back into the courtyard, and to the black tree.

By Mati's side my words renew …

She closed her eyes.

You asked if we would conquer death
I said there was a galaxy
Bring back my words upon your breath
West of the river, South of the sea …

And in those words, the open vein
Will bring you on the road to me
We'll speak the old days back again
West of the river, South of the sea …

Before a black curtain, the words danced before her, like actors coming onto a stage, words that she had heard a few days ago and a world away, in an underground chamber filled with blue light.

'*Red sprites over the troposphere in Tannor. I wanted to show you the Aurora, dancing in the sky, beyond the Reinmar Gate.*'

We have left you our words.

She opened her eyes.

'*There was a galaxy.*'

She spoke the words that had followed, Ghada's words to Samir, as they stood and watched their sleeping selves.

For a moment in time, nothing happened. Then, with a low rumble, a section of the ground lifted, like a trapdoor.

Below her, there was a ramp. It was aglow with pale white phosphorescence.

Mithila did not hesitate. She stepped inside and onto the ramp.

Above her, the trapdoor closed again. She spun around. *Too late.*

She turned back. The ramp sloped downwards gently. The floor was the smooth white stone of the Council Hall. The walls of the passage were straight. The ceiling was swiftly lost to darkness. The pale glow threw her shadow behind her, and lit up her way.

Mithila walked on.

The passage ended at a ledge that overlooked a vast cavern, stretching as far as she could see.

The ruined towers above the ground had been nothing more than gateways, the broken shadows of a dream.

Before her was the lost City of Gumfraude.

She kneels by her father's bedside, holding his hand.

'Speaker for the Eleventh.' She looks at him, dry-eyed. 'You wouldn't have liked that. But then, I don't think you'd have been surprised.'

Amrit makes no reply. But she has broken the silence, and cannot stop now.

'Remember that time you took me up to the tower balcony, and showed me Sumer? You said that every time, for years, whenever you'd needed clarity, you'd come here. Sumer is always on the move, you said, the Circles turning, things shifting. Sometimes, you said, you need to see it—all the City—to understand.

'But you never prepared me for this. Mithila tore a gap in the world, and now everyone wants to stitch it back together with their own flag. Minakshi thinks she can take things back to the way they were. But that's not going to happen. The Union has returned, the farmers are angry, and this time the same old answers won't work, because they know the world has changed. In Wallshadow, the Dooma stirs. They will see this as their chance to shatter the Circles. They are moving, all of them, and soon, this City will not be able to contain them.

'This will be no second Savarian. This will be much worse, a City riven into so many fragments, broken edges. Sumer cannot hold.

'I would turn to Hansa. But Hansa is worn, like a stone rubbed too smooth, too long, by the Rasa. Did you ever need someone to tell you how to—what to be, what to do?

'Everything is different now, since the morning you left.'

She squeezes his hand with a fierce urgency.

'No, father. You can't leave like this. You promised me. You promised to answer a thousand questions. Now I have just one. Come back so I can ask. Please?'

Does Amrit's breathing quicken? Rama's head jerks up. She puts an ear to his chest, and listens greedily.

She is wrong.

'Give me a sign. Tell me what to do.'

She pulls his elbow around her shoulder and buries her face in the crook of his arm. She stays there until a vague awareness of time begins to burrow into her.

Rama takes a deep breath. She pulls away, and stands. 'I'll do it. I wish you could have known. But you'll be proud.

'And before the end,' she adds in a whisper, 'I will smoke Savarian out of that dead tower. This time, he will die. This I promise you.'

Seven

The Bard's Song

Alvar awoke to a tapping sound. He opened his eyes to see Mankala's face at the window.

He scrambled out of bed and hurried into the hallway. When he opened the door, she shoved past him. Her breathing was ragged, and she smelled of wet clothes and sweat.

'Mankala—what are you—'

'Moving in.'

'*What?*'

'I'm moving in, Alvar,' she turned and almost snapped at him. There were dark circles around her eyes and creases on her forehead. 'Why—are you going to kick me out?'

'No, of course—Mankala, what's going on?'

She shoved past him to his room. Alvar stumbled after her. Inside, she slumped upon on the edge of his bed. '*Fucking* Builders.'

'What happened?'

'Someone, last night ...' Her voice trembled.

Alvar sat beside her. 'Take a breath. You're here. You're safe.'

She took a deep breath and let it out, shuddering.

Alvar waited.

'Someone burned my house down. I don't know how. I got out—and they were waiting for me. Took me to the Dooma. There was a knife—*shit*.' She put her face in her hands. Her shoulders shook.

'Fuck. What. *Who?*'

'I don't know, I've never seen them before!'

She glanced at the window. Alvar wrapped an arm tight against her shoulder. She huddled up against him. 'There's no one outside,' he said gently. 'You're safe.'

She breathed in again.

'What happened?' he said.

'I went for a swim. Not by choice.'

Alvar felt her trembling subside by slow degrees, until she was still, only an odd spasm traveling from her shoulders to his arms.

'You came walking all the way here to the Ninth?' he said. 'Couldn't you have just gone to your parents'—oh *shit*—' He broke off, biting his tongue. 'I'm so sorry, I forgot.'

She grimaced and waved it away. 'Happens.'

Alvar blushed. 'Was it,' he said at last, timidly, 'was it because—'

'The Wall?'

'Yes.'

'Yeah, I guess. They couldn't have me there at midnight.'

'Shoortans.'

'Who else? Must've been Temple acolytes who never come out.'

Alvar sighed. 'Checks.'

She turned to him. 'What happened at the Wall? What did I miss? That red sky …'

'Minakshi came.'

'*Bloody* fucking Builders. Of course she did. And?'

Alvar paused. Darkness lingered before his eyes. Darkness broken by a thousand little pin-pricks of light, and a voice that swirled around him like a cloud of dust, choking him.

And you will die alone.

A voice affirmed by the silence around them, the Carnival's mockery of the Shoortans a distant memory, wiped away by the red sky.

'She's brought back Ostracism.'

Mankala turned to him.

'*What?*'

'Yes.'

'They *let* her?'

'Yes,' he whispered. 'They did. Nobody said a word. As if they wanted it.'

He saw her stare into the distance.

'Well,' she said at last. Her voice was quiet, tired. 'This changes things.'

'Changes?' he said. 'We've lost. She's smashed us. She has the power to make us die alone. They *gave* it to her, so gratefully. They wanted to. And with the sky—'

Mankala turned to him and held his shoulders, her nails digging into his skin.

'Alvar,' she said, '*the Shoortans do not control the bloody sky.* There is some—some—science behind this. We don't know it, *but it's not Minakshi.*'

'How does it matter if that's what it feels like to them?'

They looked at each other. Mankala dropped her hands. 'It was there,' she said softly, looking away. 'We had it in our hands. The time of the Wall was over. We were going to remake the world. And Minakshi's taken it all from us. *Builders,* I hate her.'

She breathed hard. 'Everything we've done is going to be for nothing. Mithila did what she had to do. She brought us all the way here. She flew. All we had to do was take a few more steps. To tell them that we'd broken the circle of Time. But we couldn't. And now we're stuck here. We'll always be stuck here.' Her voice lowered. 'We've failed her.'

Alvar closed his eyes. 'What are we doing this for?' he said.

'What?'

'I feel so lost, Mankala. I thought it was all going to change. She would change everything when she left. But now she's gone and things are worse. Maybe Lamon had the right idea.'

Mankala hugged her knees. 'You really think that?'

'Well, no, but I … I'm not going to do it, but Builders, you can't deny it would be easy. To just walk away. Stop fighting, just become *normal* again. No more Young Tarafians, no more Wall, just doing my thing with the Carers, and you with the Encyclopaedia, the things we love and—would it be the worst life, you think?'

'Normal.' Mankala was silent for a long time, forcing Alvar to open his eyes. He saw her looking past him once more. Just when he thought she wouldn't speak again, she did.

'Remember geometry class, Alvar?' said Mankala.

He was thrown. 'Geo—'

'When they first taught us how to find out the area of a circle, before we learned the formulas?'

'Yeah, we filled the circle with squares,' said Alvar. 'Then we made the squares smaller.'

'And smaller, and smaller,' said Mankala. 'They called it the vanishing point.'

'Yes.'

'And I thought, you know—I thought how true it was. To fit in the Circle, you needed to vanish. If you didn't, your edges would bump against the sides. You'd bruise. And I knew then that bruises would make me.' She looked at him. 'I'm not vanishing, Alvar. I've bruised too much for that, and you have too.'

He knew she was right.

Rama left her father's chamber and came down the stairs. Sunlight poured in through the wide windows of the living room. She walked across the room and entered Amrit's—*her*—study.

Mankala stood. 'Good morning, Speaker for the Eleventh.'

'How,' said Rama, her voice flat, 'did you get in here?'

'Why would your guards stop Councillor Malati's secretary?' Mankala grinned. 'Can you ask them not to brandish their swords so much next time?'

Rama walked to her desk. Her papers were there, and the Bill she'd been drafting last night, half-finished. 'Next time, you will ask before you look at my papers.'

'Oh, is that so? I'm from the Eleventh, remember? You speak for me.'

'No, I *represent* you. According to my best judgment. You don't own me.'

Mankala threw up her arms. 'Builders, Rama! Can't we even make fun of you anymore?'

'Oh.' Rama was still. 'Yes, fine. Idiot,' she said, rolling her eyes. She turned the papers blank side up nonetheless. 'You've come about the Temple, no?'

'Yes.'

'Why, but?'

'I don't yet know. I have a lead—'

'Eesh, but this is not good enough, Mankala,' Rama said. 'You know that I can't just act for myself now? These things have consequences. If I'm going to invent an excuse to land up at the Temple with you, I need to know what I'm inventing for.'

'Can I just—okay, Councillor. The Eleventh asked you to put this Bill into Council today, didn't they? The one proposing a Special Committee to explore options for going beyond the Wall? I read it. Listen to me: don't do it.'

'What? Why?'

'You don't know what happened last night?'

'Carnival? I don't stay up late. What happened?'

'You need to have your own advisors, Rama. While you were sleeping, the sky turned red again, and Minakshi brought Ostracism back to Sumer. Do you want to cross her today?'

Rama tapped her fingers on the desk. 'I see,' she said.

'It takes a lot to rouse the Farmers' Mandalas, Councillor. It takes a lot to overturn a thousand years of—what's that phrase?—*social life*, that's been encrusted in ideology. And once roused—it's so fragile, you know. A gust of air can scatter it to the fields for another thousand years. Pick your moment. You'll get one chance. But you know it's not now.'

Rama nodded. 'Yes. And thanks. You've saved me from a disaster in the Council.'

'Will you trust me now?'

'Ugh, fine,' said Rama, a small smile at the corner of her eyes. 'Come, *secretary*. We have an appointment at the Temple.'

'How much time do you need?' said Rama, as she grabbed the knocker and sent it echoing through the innards of the Temple.

'Fifteen minutes?'

'Yeah, okay. No more, though. Minakshi and I—we're not exactly friends—' she broke off, as the door opened.

'Councillor Rama,' she announced herself to the Acolyte who stood before them. 'I'm here to meet the Matriarch.'

'I—is she expecting you?'

'Yes.' She stared him down. 'Is there a problem?'

'Oh—no no, I wasn't told there were visitors this morning.' He wilted. 'But please come with me.'

Rama walked beside the Acolyte through the hall of pillars. Mankala stepped a little distance behind, a respectful secretary. He took them up and into the Audience Chamber.

Minakshi was on her high chair, crownless.

'Councillor?'

Rama inclined her head. 'Good morning, Matriarch. I came to continue our interrupted conversation.'

'Oh? Of course.'

Minakshi signalled. The priest that she had been talking to quietly left the room. Mankala followed suit, leaving them alone.

Minakshi rose and came to her. They faced each other on the floor of the Audience Chamber. Rama noticed the lines etched into her forehead, the way she held herself erect.

'Long night?' The words she spoke were not the words she intended.

'Aren't they all?' The Matriarch stared into the space beyond Rama's shoulder, her voice spare as withered leaves.

'Did you really have to?'

Minakshi screwed her eyes shut. 'It's done now,' she said.

Rama caught her gaze as she opened them again, and did not let it go.

'Why?' she said. 'What do you think it will bring you? Peace? Unity? Reconciliation? What did Ostracism ever bring Sumer in the old days?'

'I never said I'd use it.'

'A sword that hangs over our necks by a thread, waiting for you to snap it. Is that any better? For you, to hold that power—and for us, to wait?'

'Builders, Rama, I'm not going to use it on *you*—'

'That's not the point. You brought it back into Sumer, after centuries. The memory of our worst days. We just don't do that sort of thing any more, we've—we've *progressed*. And I don't understand why …'

Minakshi raised a hand.

For a while, the Matriarch said nothing. Then she lifted her head and looked at Rama.

'You're Council,' she said. 'You'll understand. Will you hear me out?

'Go on.'

'Circles,' Minakshi let the word drop between them.

'What?'

'Circles,' Minakshi repeated. 'They keep things in place, within the Wall. They allow us to go on. But you know, Rama, nothing really *wants* to move in a circle. Remember when we were children, the slings we used to whirl above our heads, and how they used to fly when we let them go?

'You need force to keep things in a circle, Rama. The tension in the sling. And the Select tell us—Garuda told me—that in the sky, it's gravity that keeps planets in orbit around the sun. Without that, the planets would fly—but the system would collapse. We would collapse.

'In Sumer, I am gravity.'

Her words died upon the silence between them.

You are delusional, Rama almost screamed out, but bit her tongue. 'You need Ostracism to hold Sumer together?'

'I don't know. I might.' Her voice hardened. 'And if I have to—I will use it.'

'And you'll be the one who decides that. Do you think we're going to see this as anything but a power grab?'

'I can't control what you think. Rama …' Minakshi paused. 'Did Mithila ever tell you why I joined the Temple?'

'She never knew. You refused to tell her.'

'I did. The night our father became Savarian.'

'Oh.' For a moment, Rama was winded. She breathed through it. 'I never saw Mithila after that. So, no.'

'If you knew, then you'd also know that power is not what I'm interested in.'

Rama shook her head. 'But why? Just tell me then. Without *her* in between.'

Minakshi dropped her gaze, silent. 'So, what did you come here for?' she said, tired. 'This wasn't our interrupted conversation, was it?'

Rama was suddenly aware of Mankala, somewhere in the Temple, and the slow passage of time. 'No,' she said.

'Then?'

'I came to share a memory.'

'Go on.'

'You know, when we went up to your tower balcony the other night? For what they call the garuda-eye view of Sumer?'

'Yes?'

'For so long, I wanted to show her that. A Sumer she'd never seen, never would. I wanted to give it to her. So I stole the tower key and we—don't look at me like that, you'd do the same—and there we were. Just the two of us, up in the sky, cold moonlight, and Sumer a world beneath us.

'We looked over the City to the Wall, and she talked. And I remember one thing. The wind was whipping her hair around her eyes, and she kept pushing it back to see me. She didn't care, she didn't even notice, because she was talking Taraf and the Wall, but I—it was *distracting*.

'So I waited for her to take a breath and then I said, "*can I fix your hair?*" And she gave me that look, and she said, "*okay, but no pulling.*" And I said, "*yes love, I promise, no pulling.*"' Rama stopped, lost. 'She really was, you know—she could imagine a whole world, but sometimes …'

'I know.'

'So she sat down in front of me and we looked out through the gaps in the parapets. The moon was cut in half. And I remember the feel of her hair—it had been open all day, a tangle! So I just took out the knots and made a weave-braid. And I didn't think she noticed until I was done, but then she leaned back into me and said, "*I told you I never wanted this moment to end.*"

'I remember her look. It's how you look at something that will soon disappear. I should have known then—she, so certain about the Wall, the future—I really should have known that I would—that she—'

Before the silence could take her words entirely, Minakshi spoke.

'I did her hair too. When she was small. Every morning, before we went to the Carers.'

'She would go *ouch* at just a bit of tugging, I felt like I had to do her hair as if I was—'

'Weaving fabric.' Minakshi finished. She smiled faintly.

'Summer of '07,' she said, pronouncing each word separately, like it was a world of its own. 'I, thirteen. She, fifteen. Home. Ananta in his study, Garuda in the Citadel.' Rama found her own eyes closing. The sounds and smells of Ananta's house, and Mithila in it, washed over her.

'She couldn't sleep, because the dreams wouldn't leave her. She should have grown out of it by then, but they never left. She came to my bed in the middle of the night and said, "*I can't stop seeing fires in the sky. And something that shines, in a pit filled with water. And a sun that spins.*" She was too scared to close her eyes. So she climbed into my bed and she put her head into my lap, and she said, "*sing me my song.*"'

Minakshi smiled ironically.

'It was Taraf's song. And I said, *"you sure you want me to sing that one?"* And she said *"yes"*, so I did. *Beyond the Wall, the sunrise swift/ Dispels the iron dawn to lift* ... you know how it goes?'

'Yes. I do.'

'Of course you do. At some point in the night, she fell asleep on my lap and I fell asleep sitting up. I woke up with my legs all pins and needles. Never forgave her for that.' Minakshi laughed once, cleanly.

They were both quiet.

'Thank you,' said Rama at last. 'She would so rarely speak of the ...' She stumbled, hesitated, and then swiftly turned course. 'Of the times before we met.'

Minakshi noticed instantly. 'Can't imagine why,' she said.

'Her little sister had left,' said Rama, trying to make her voice as gentle as she could. 'She tried to forget you, but she couldn't.'

Minakshi's lips twisted in a pale smile. Her hands were in her pockets, making little balls. 'You're very solicitous about my feelings, Councillor,' she said, 'Elders' diplomacy training?'

Rama flushed. 'I'm only trying to be human. Is it always going to be like this, between us?'

'When someone tears themselves out of your life before you're ready,' said Minakshi, 'they leave a jagged edge behind. We're two jagged edges, Rama.' Her eyes glimmered. 'Maybe, in time.'

Rama searched for words, but found nothing.

Minakshi said, 'Want to call your secretary back in?'

Reality came rushing back. Rama swallowed. She looked at Minakshi, silent. The Matriarch favoured her with a brilliant smile. 'What's the matter, Councillor? Isn't she outside?'

'Ye—yes, of course,' Rama stammered. 'Mankala,' she called. 'You can come back in. We're done.'

Five seconds ticked away, unendurable. Then Mankala slipped in and waited by the doorway. Rama breathed.

'Thank you for your time today, Matriarch,' she said.

'Think nothing of it,' said Minakshi, still smiling. 'And here's to peace between us.' She stepped forward. 'May I?'

They hugged each other. Rama let herself relax. She began to pull back, but Minakshi's arm tightened like a vice, holding her in place.

Rama's breath caught in her throat. 'Next time, Councillor,' Minakshi whispered in her ear, 'come up with a better excuse.'

Rama did not say a word. Minakshi let her go and walked away, a sure rhythm in her steps, until she vanished into the passageway towards the balcony.

'So, are you going to tell me why I needed to annoy the most powerful person in Sumer?'

Mankala squirmed and stared sideways, into the Rasa. 'Sorry. I mean, it's just a hunch. I'm not sure.'

'Oh. Well,' said Rama. 'You don't have to. I thought you trusted me, that's all.'

'I do! It was just … the Heartstone.'

'Heartstone?'

The sound of tramping feet carried over the air. The Watch was doing drills in the Forum, swords drawn.

'Yes,' said Minakshi. 'There's a phrase I keep hearing. *Light from light*. I know it's connected to the Heartstone. I wanted to see it for myself, touch it—and because of Mithila's visit here, I knew where it was.'

'And?'

Mankala smiled faintly. 'I felt *something*. A … I don't know, as if I was flint, being wrung for fire. And then it was gone.'

'Well, I hope it was worth it.'

Mankala looked up from the river and at Rama, whose eyes had clouded. She grabbed her wrist. 'Thank you. Really.'

'Oh, don't be silly.' It was Rama's turn to practice a smile. Lightly, she shook Mankala off. 'Be getting back to work, then, Mankala. Come again soon.'

She walked back to the Council Hall, past the marching phalanx of the Watch. The doors of the building closed behind her.

Mankala was alone in the Forum.

There was a tingling in her veins. It moved its way up her body, until it congealed into a cold, clammy hand around her throat.

Mankala choked. Day turned into night. She was underwater once again. There was wetness all around her, and her arms flailing, taking her away from the bridge, away from the woman who stood looking at her, a knife in her hand. Watching from somewhere above, she saw the woman hurl the knife into the river, at her other self, watched it cleave the water and streak towards her back—

The sound of her own breathing tore her back into the world. Mankala knelt on the grass, beside the riverbank. She searched the ground for pebbles, and began to flick them into the Rasa, a calming technique that Lamon had once told her about, in a world gone by.

She leaned back and closed her eyes, letting the sun-warmth play upon her face.

'Mankala-Eleven?'

Mankala started.

Just behind her, there stood a Messenger.

'Yes?'

'To Mankala-Eleven, delivered as spoken.' His voice was quick and flat. 'The end will reflect the beginning. Come to the place of the hidden spears, the labyrinth, and the garden. Come now."

'Who sent this?' she said.

'They said you would know.'

'Oh. Right.' Mankala thought rapidly. 'I have a new job for you.'

The Messenger's eyes sparkled with the good luck. Mankala handed over three iron coins. 'Go to Elmandar-One. Tell him I'm here, if he wants to see me.'

As the Messenger hastened towards the stone-mansion complex of the First Mandala, she turned back to the Rasa, and began to pace. 'If it's a trap,' she muttered at the waters, 'I'm not going in without insurance.'

She didn't have long to wait before she saw Elmandar enter the Forum Plaza from the First Mandala, and hasten towards her. He pushed his hair back as he reached her, breathing hard.

'Hey?' he said.

'That was fast.'

Elmander's face went a curious colour, a mix between pride and furious embarrassment. But then, as he looked at her, his expression changed.

'Are you alright?' he said.

'Yeah. Why?'

'Nothing, I thought … you just looked—I don't know—'

'Oh, I stay alive.' *That was a good one*, a voice inside her snickered. 'Shut up!' she told herself, out loud.

'What?' Elmandar sounded hurt.

'Not you!' She shook her head. 'Ah, listen, Elmandar—we haven't actually seen much of each other since that night at the woad garden, so I was going to ask you'—she smiled at him—'if I could take you out for a walk.'

'*What*?'

'A walk. You. With me.'

He pushed his hair back again and peered at her, looking for a trick. 'Yes?' he said, cautiously.

'Come on, then.'

'Where are we going?'

'On a bit of an adventure.'

'Last time you said this, it was ten thousand booby-traps and a ruined woad garden.'

'Tell me you didn't enjoy it,' she challenged.

'No, no. Of course I did, I—'

'Then come.' She suppressed a sudden shiver that had crept from her blood and into the hairs of her skin, that reminded her of swimming through the river the night before. She swung North, towards the farmlands. As they walked, Elmandar's quick breathing gradually returned to normal.

'And how are your Hedonists doing?' she asked, as they entered the farmlands.

'A little spooked after Carnival, some of them. And that whole business of Ostracism coming back—'

'Mhmm, I can imagine.'

There was an instant of silence.

'You can?' said Elmandar. 'But it was you wasn't it?'

'What?' Her pulse quickened.

'The Wall. You found a way. And now the Matriarch's crazy furious, and—and everything's changed.'

'Why? Are you scared?'

'No, I—'

'Then?'

'I just … I …'

'Just say it!'

He breathed. 'When *you* go, take me with you?'

This time she did stop, and swung around to face him.

Elmandar dropped his gaze.

'What did you just say?'

'It's … it's all I've ever wanted. I think.'

'What, to leave home?'

'Home?' He shook his head. 'I don't know. Sometimes, I look at the Rasa, and I dream. I dream I'm floating on my back, down the river, looking up into the sky. And in my dream, the river doesn't branch at the Wall, because there's no Wall, but it just carries on, it takes me … I don't know where, a place that is not here. Home doesn't force you to stay, does it? It's the place you can *choose* to come back to.'

'You should tell me your dreams more often,' Mankala said.

'I would, if you'd let me.' He grinned at her, uncertain.

She looked back at him. 'Let's go,' she said, before the moment could lengthen too much.

'*The end will reflect the beginning. Come to the place of the hidden spears, the labyrinth, and the garden. Come now.*'

They walked until they reached the edge of the bamboo grove, its cool dark shade welcoming in the late-morning sun.

'Here?' said Elmandar.

'Here.'

'This is the woad garden.'

'Oh thanks.'

'No, I meant … you brought me here just last week.'

'Yeah, with your entire crowd!' She let laughter enter her voice. 'Come on now.' She clasped his hand lightly, palm over palm, and felt him tense. 'Come,' she said again, softer, tugging his hand.

Sunlight trickled in through the tall bamboo trees, ushering them into the grove. As they walked, Mankala darted her eyes above and to the sides, looking out for a sign that someone had been before them. There was nothing.

They reached the line of trees and entered the clearing. Mankala unclenched, letting herself breathe. The hedge-labyrinth was before them, and in the middle of it that familiar stone wall, marking the entrance to the woad garden, outlined in the sunlight.

'Now what?' said Elmandar.

'Now this,' she said, suddenly feeling light-headed. 'We're going inside, so you can pick out the best woad flower in the garden—for me.'

'But—but where's that stick, the one you used to test the ground?'

'Look, here.' She pointed. At the edge of the clearing there lay a stick upon the ground, neatly arranged, as if it had been left for them.

Mankala picked it up. An absolute certainty descended upon her as she tested the ground, and twisted, turned, and changed direction to avoid the spear-filled pits. Elmandar stayed a step behind her, clutching her hand.

Past the booby-trapped ground, at the entrance to the labyrinth, she heard him breathe for the first time. She turned to him, suddenly uncertain. 'Still coming?'

Around them, the sky was bare and the clearing empty, as if nobody had been here or was here.

Elmandar looked at her, his face pale. He nodded, not letting go of her hand.

'Right then.' She threaded her way through the hedges by muscle memory, recalling all the times that Malati had brought her to the woad garden, where they'd discussed the now-burned Encyclopaedia.

They came at last to the final stretch, before the garden wall, where somebody had already let down the white stone slab for them, covering the treacherous ground.

'Someone's here?' said Elmandar.

'Looks like it.'

'Oh.' He seemed like he was going to speak, but then said nothing, only following her to the edge of the garden.

They stopped at the entrance. From inside the garden, there was no sound.

'I've come,' Mankala called out.

Silence answered her.

She lost awareness of Elmandar beside her, as she stood there, balanced on both feet. She let herself take two deep breaths. The knife was at her side, that she'd taken from Alvar's house before leaving.

At a crouch, Mankala entered the woad garden.

She pulled up short.

Since its destruction, there had been an attempt at salvage: the broken plants carried away, new saplings placed in freshly-dug ground. The garden was orderly again, and beautiful as it had once been.

But she saw none of that. Before her Tefnakth lay upon the ground, face down. He was still. He might even have been sleeping, but for the knife in his back, all the way in until the hilt, fresh blood pooling around it.

Mankala's eyes travelled down Tefnakth's body, to his right fist, which clutched a scrap of paper. She knelt and prised open the still-warm fingers to retrieve the paper.

Upon it was a single line of writing, in charred lampblack:

Nobody leaves just yet.

Wallset slanted through the windows of the Tenth Mandala. Outside a hubbub arose, as waves of chattering children pattered into the streets for the last time that day, on their way home. With the quick passing of their feet, it sank into stillness just as suddenly.

'The little ones have gone, Murund,' said Alvar.

There was no reply.

He turned from the window, from the red-gold tint of the empty street beyond. In the darkening room, an elderly man lay upon the bed. His right arm was thrown over his chest. His left ended in a stump above the elbow.

Alvar tiptoed over. The man's eyes were closed. His chest rose and fell. Alvar reached down to the covers, which were tossed around his knees, and gently drew them up to the neck. There was no sound but ragged breathing.

The door creaked open. Kodali entered. There was a young woman beside him. In her arms she cradled a baby, asleep.

'How is he?' Kodali asked.

'Just fallen asleep,' said Alvar. 'I changed a set of bedding earlier, and shaved him. He tends to drift off after that.' He raised an enquiring eyebrow.

'Oh, meet Bhavi-Twelve,' Kodali smiled. 'And Nilan. We gave Nilan away just last week, so he still needs to be brought back here sometimes, to calm down.'

A Third Child, Alvar realized. Adopted, like himself. He grinned at them in fellow-feeling.

Kodali came closer and inspected Murund. 'That's something. Better than many of the others at least.'

'Rough day?'

'You have no idea,' said the head of the Carers' Mandala. 'I've just been telling Bhavi about it. That red sky seems to have uncovered a craphole of repressed feelings among the seniors.'

'He's had to listen to them all day,' Bhavi said. They were all speaking in low voices, to avoid waking Murund and Nilan.

'Yeah,' Kodali said. 'It was bearable while the little ones were here—thank the Builders for the wise soul who first decreed that the Tenth Mandala would care for both the seniors and the little ones together.'

Bhavi grinned. 'Don't I know it?'

'It *always* helps us stay sane in a crisis. But …' Kodali shook his head. 'I'm not looking forward to the night.'

'Ah.' Alvar turned back to look at the sleeping man's face, at his deep-lined forehead, the blotches around the cheeks, and the skin stretched tight around the bone.

'He still calls out for his husband?' Kodali asked.

'Niren? Yes. You know he'd stopped for a while, when he thought I was Niren.' Alvar blushed, as he saw Bhavi staring. Kodali quickly covered his mouth to hide a grin. 'But the last four days—he's gone back to it. *Niren, I can't wait till we win.* Or, *Niren—we haven't made a mistake?* Or, *Niren, where are you—we need to run—the Rasa barricade—Savarian's waiting.* Variants on the last, mostly. It's almost as if he believes the Revolution is coming back.'

For a while, nobody spoke. Bhavi was looking down at her baby, her head bent, holding him to her chest. Then, as the silence began to grow prickly, Kodali said: 'You've brought it here, haven't you?'

The voice was quiet as ever, but it made Alvar swing around. They were both looking at him now. 'What?'

'It was Mithila. Wasn't it?'

'I don't know what you mean.'

Kodali spread out his arms. 'Come on Alvar. You can trust us. Can't you?'

Alvar slumped. He looked away, eyes resting on the cabinet. 'Yes,' he whispered. 'It was.'

'*Builders*, you mad kids. I knew it. The day it happened. I cracked open a bottle of the Select's Drink to celebrate, you know. And I have two. The other one's got your name on it.'

'How did you know? It was Wallrise—'

'Pre-Wallrise feeds, apprentice mine. I was out. Difficult to miss two giant garudas with a girl between them, across our thrice-damned Wall.' He grinned. 'It was glorious though. What a moment.'

Alvar looked at him. 'I've never heard you talk about the Wall before.'

'You never asked.'

Which, as things went, was true. Alvar flushed. Bhavi was looking at him intently. But Kodali was staring at the bed, at Murund's sleeping face, and his gaze was unfocused.

'You know,' Kodali said, and his voice came from very far away, 'if the Circle had a beginning and an end, that's where we of the Tenth live.'

They both turned to him.

'The little ones don't understand that things are permanent. Or that time's a circle. They think the Wall's just another house, and there's an outside waiting for them. They have names for all the places they'll go to. Sometimes I almost believe them.

'But the Seniors. They give them to us, the Carers, in the dying of their days. They can't remember when they stopped imagining the outside, when they *allowed* things to become permanent, until one day, just like that, they realize it's over, they're done, and now they'll never know. How do I comfort them? I can't.

'The young, who refuse to accept the Wall. The old, who wonder when they accepted it. And me, whose fate it is to know how the young will become the old, because I find them at both ends, with the Wall, always the Wall in between, and there's nothing I can do about it.

'That's when I fell in love with Mithila's *horizon*. It was that feeling of brokenness made whole in a word.'

Alvar thought he heard Bhavi sigh.

'Why the past tense, Kodali?' he said. 'Haven't we made it whole?'

Kodali looked at Alvar with something not-unkind in his eyes.

'Mithila left us behind. And you've given us the same world and a red sky at midnight.' He spoke simply, each word measured to its last degree.

'A red sky the Matriarch alone claims to be able to read. A red sky that tells her that now, there must be people who will not come to us to die at ease.'

'The scientific method—' Alvar began, but Kodali cut him short, his voice now low and urgent. 'Mithila's gone. We are here. The Wall's here. I need a reason to believe you. Give me a reason to believe in your horizon, Alvar. Anything will do. But I need *something*. Please.'

Alvar cast around for words. 'Give me some time,' he said. 'A few days. And I'll give you a reason.'

The sun sank beyond the Wall. The world turned pale-grey.

Alvar shifted. Kodali noticed. 'Do you have to go?'

'I—yes. It's my evening with the bards.'

'Go, go.' Kodali gestured at the bed. 'And well done today.'

He remained standing there as Alvar turned and walked away. The last thing he saw was Bhavi, looking out of the window, her face pensive.

Alvar walked North towards the Maliot, and into a commotion.

Just before the Rasa there was a group of people, backs to him. They were holding up flame lamps and chanting. He heard a single sentence.

'Bring back the balance. Bring back the balance. Bring back the balance.'

Facing the people, blocking their path down the Maliot, was the Watch. They stood in tight formation, their faces blank, their swords drawn and extended.

Alvar stopped. Swiftly, he turned and retraced his steps down the tributary, until he came to the first bridge that led into the Ninth. It was guarded at both ends by the Watch. As he passed, they gave him a quick glance, but nothing more.

Above, the sky dulled. At its busiest hour, Sumer was quiet today.

The Ninth was empty. In the narrow paths of the Eighth, where the air should have been dense with the smell of iron, wood-shavings, and musky sweat, as the people trooped back from the swamp furnaces, he only saw little groups of individuals staring up at the sky suspiciously, as though it might change its colour.

Which, Alvar had to allow, was not an unreasonable suspicion.

He exchanged a few desultory greetings with people he knew, but noticed how they kept their distance from him, gazes averted as he went by.

Past another bridge, another set of Watchmen, and he was back there, for the first time, in the Seventh, a Seventh without Mithila.

The light was almost gone by the time the buildings parted, and Alvar entered the large field that covered the Seventh Mandala's sewage chamber. There he saw them, the bards of the Seventh, a loose and merry circle, warmed by a lively fire, a low hum of conversation and laughter swirling around them like a breeze.

'Oho, shadow apprentice!' someone called, as he approached. 'So late!'

Alvar laughed. 'I was delayed!'

Silver-haired Vidusha, the leader of the bards, smiled at him. 'It can get hard, living two lives. Come sit, we're playing *treys.* Malina here just won the last round with *dark as the eyes of the Golden Youth*—inspired, to think of luxury *kajal* when everyone else was thinking of variants on the night.'

Alvar joined the fringes of the circle, as Vidusha turned back to the bards. 'Unexpected as …' She dropped the unfinished sentence into space, leaving it hanging.

'An honest Elder!' someone completed. Vidusha raised an eyebrow. '*Cliché*,' she sniffed.

'Unexpected as a bend in circular Time,' said someone else. Vidusha grinned. 'Better—but trying too hard. A beautiful body is no good if everyone can see its innards.'

'Unexpected as a Matriarch's smile!'

Vidusha snorted and clapped her hands to her mouth. 'Wicked!' she hooted. Laughter filled the circle. Alvar joined in, even as he felt his stomach clench.

'Isn't that going a little too far?' a nervous voice chimed into the pause between laughter.

'Far how, Mir?' said Vidusha.

'Baiting the Matriarch. After last night—'

'Why, what happened last night?'

'You know! The red sky, Ostracism, and today, those crowds, the armed watch. Vidusha, we can't sit weaving words as if Sumer isn't here. You need to take this more seriously.'

Mutters broke out.

'We are the Bards of the Seventh, Mir,' Vidusha said, her smile fixed. 'We are the memory-keepers. You know our song, don't you? Across the ages, steadfast. *Neither you, Builders, nor the Fifteen Circles/ Nor the Elders, nor the Kings/ Nor the Select, nor the Shoortans, nor the Watch, nor the Wall/ Nor circling Time itself/ Understand what language is/Understand what songs there are/ Understand at all.*

'At all.' Vidusha repeated. 'Look at me, Mir. If the Matriarch deserves to be mocked, by the Builders, *we will mock her.*'

'And if we're Ostracized?' Mir came back, 'Whom will we mock in the fields??'

'The fields? The Wall has been breached, man!' Vidusha said, as murmurs of agreement broke out. 'Even the Matriarch's had to face reality. The Circles are dead. We can't see the future any more than we can see past the Wall. What kind of fool would trap herself in a broken cage?'

Instantly, voices shouted over one another.

'Foolish as an Elder with a heart!'

'Foolish as a love that lasts!'

'Foolish as a circle!'

Laughter rocked the circle once more, before a scowling Mir could say anything. Alvar grinned to himself.

'Very funny. Back to *treys!*' Vidusha called.

The bards continued, submitting themselves to Vidusha's judgment on the quality of their similes, sometimes with good grace, and often with grumbling complaints. Alvar took mental notes, as he always did (*'sweet as a First's kiss', 'now that's a good one—a khire-flavoured kiss'*), and settled to wait.

'Old as …' he heard Vidusha say, and his ears perked up.

The standard variations were tried: *the Tenth's love, the Dooma's hate, the taste of khire*—and Vidusha shook them away with a '*Cliché, cliché!*' each time.

Alvar spoke. 'Old as the Three Kings.'

A hush went around the circle. There was no response. Vidusha turned to him, her brow furrowed. 'Is this a reference?'

'N—no, I mean, yes,' he stammered. 'Something I read—'

Vidusha wagged a finger at him. 'What's the rule?' she said. 'If we can't see it, you can't say it!'

'Sorry!' he said, laughing.

He listened as the bards passed from *treys* to composing new endings for old, famous poems, and then to the last part of the night, to the singing of poems. Around the circle they went, each Bard picking their song of the night. To start,the classical scansion of the Age of Tyrants, running into the quicker, uneven tempo of the hidden songs from the time of Dichio. Some scattered love songs ('*… stay, stay, stay awhile/ this side of the Wall…*') wove their way into the lines of City verses speaking of the Rasa and the seasons.

They came at last to Vidusha. 'Any requests?' she asked, as she always did.

Alvar raised his hand. Vidusha laughed. 'I was mean to you earlier this night, no? Come then. What song do you want, Alvar?'

'I don't know,' he said. 'Can you sing us the oldest you know?'

'The *oldest*!' Vidusha said. 'That's a new one. I'll need to think.'

They watched her still. Then, like the rustling of leaves in a breeze, she shook herself to life.

'In the cycle of Time,' she said, 'you cannot sometimes tell the end from the beginning. But here it is, a song so old that it could wear Time strung around its neck. And perhaps, after the breaking of the Wall, it has.'

She closed her eyes and sang, a deep slow note that lingered in the air and descended upon them, soft and heavy, like a raincloud before it burst.

The stars are out.
The Builders will not stay.
But we remain. There was a time, before
And there will be a time to come
Who will remake the broken world?

No more enough, the word.
Where yesterday
We bound into our will the sum of all
Now and today, the bound are we
Who will remake the broken world?

They will not come.
The earth is riven now.
The stones lie scattered. In the coming dusk
Who will put back the shattered three?
Who will remake the broken world?

Hear me.
Upon the dying of the day
Will you renew Samati's sacrifice?
When light from light shall come again
Will you remake the broken world?

And when she was done, nobody spoke. With the rest of the bards, Alvar stood. They dispersed in silence, the sound of their feet quiet against the ground. But Vidusha did not move; and when Alvar turned at the edge of the clearing he saw her sitting unmoving, her head thrown up to the sky.

Alvar left the clearing from the North and caught the tributary, heading back towards the Maliot. The route would take him past Mithila's house. He walked the empty streets until he saw once more that circular mud-brick structure, set apart from the rest.

A light flickered in the window.

Alvar stopped.

Someone had lit a flame lamp in Mithila's house. And the lamp still burned.

Alvar crept to the building. His heart beat with a sudden hope. He placed his hands on the windowsill, stood on tiptoe, and looked through the bars.

Nothing had changed. He saw Ananta's bookshelves, the sculptor's implements scattered around the room, an empty bowl placed upon the floor. There were two chairs in the room, facing each other. And on one of them—

'Why don't you just use the door?' Minakshi said.

He left the window, walked around the house and pushed open the door.

'What are you doing here?' he said, looking around for guards.

'I came home.'

'*Home*? You? This?' He began to laugh.

Minakshi waited for him to stop.

'To remember a father,' she said. 'A brother. And a sister.'

'After they're all gone? You didn't seem to think much of them while they were here.'

'Alvar,' said Minakshi, 'playing nasty is not your thing. Just stop, no?'

Alvar fell silent. Minakshi gestured at the empty chair. 'Come sit? You know,' she continued, as he drew up the chair, 'I had a feeling you'd come by tonight. I did say I'd see you soon.'

'You saw me last night,' Alvar pointed out. 'By the Wall.'

Minakshi shrank in her chair. 'Yes, that. Alvar, I want to explain myself.'

'To *me*?' he almost laughed again. 'Why?'

'Because you're the only one in this City who's never judged me. And I thought that maybe I could ask you for help.'

'Help? I—what is it?' Alvar said, and immediately hated himself for it.

Minakshi leaned forward, fingers entwining, a very Mithila-like gesture of doubt. It disoriented him.

'Do you remember, Alvar, when we were young and used to play in Ananta's workshop? There was a time when Mithila and Garuda were always off together, and it was just the two of us?'

'Yes. Yes, I do.'

'And do you remember when Ananta carved for us that automaton with all those moving gears, and he told us, *think of this like a melody: one note out of place, and everything falls. And then think of Sumer: one thing out of place, and we fall. Every beautiful thing is so easy to break.*'

'I remember,' Alvar whispered.

'Ba was wrong about many things, but he got that right.' Minakshi's fingers were still entwined. 'Sumer is so easy to break. All it needs is one thing to be out of place.'

Alvar looked down at his own hands. For a while, there was silence between them.

'Do you know what I remember about those days?' he said.

'Tell me.'

'We used to draw together. In that same workshop. Cityscapes. We used to try and imitate Synderesis.'

Minakshi smiled. 'Badly.'

'Badly, yes. Do you still draw?'

Minakshi looked away. 'Sometimes.'

'I wanted to show you this.' Alvar reached into his pocket. He took out a square piece of bamboo paper and laid it out upon the table. Minakshi leaned over to look.

Beneath a rising sun, two garudas flew, carrying a girl with them. They flew above a walltop. Beyond the wall, a barren earth extended to meet the sky.

Minakshi's eyes narrowed in concentration. There were worry lines on her forehead.

'There's something different,' she said slowly. 'They're … like at different distances—'

'Look,' said Alvar. '*Look.*'

Minakshi traced the outlines of the figures with her fingers, fascinated. 'Wait!' she said. 'I see what you've done. You've taken a line …' she trailed off. 'You've taken a line. But Alvar, this is not how—'

'Not how Synderesis drew?' he finished. 'Not how anyone draws?'

Minakshi's index finger was on the paper. The fingers of her other hand traced imaginary lines to the figures.

'When I saw Mithila fly,' Alvar said, 'it was like I'd discovered a new way of seeing the world. I can't invent a language but I've been trying, trying to speak what I felt in some way. If I can imagine a horizon,' he gestured at the paper, 'then I can imagine the *horizon line*. Look, here—it's not the Wall at the centre of the world, Minakshi, it's *you*—the world is between you and the horizon line.'

Did he see something glimmer in her eyes?

'Minakshi,' he said, 'Don't you see that that's why we need to go beyond the Wall? It's a world where your one fear is gone forever, because beyond the Wall, *one thing out of place* can't destroy us anymore. Mithila—'

She pushed the piece of paper back to him. Her eyes were quite dry.

'Mithila has gone and nobody can follow her,' said Minakshi, her voice tired. 'But we're still here, we're still easy to break. And I fear her going will bring us to the brink. Alvar, I don't want to make an enemy of the Young Tarafians, but *you* know that we're not crossing the Wall any time soon, so—'

'Oh I see,' Alvar cut in. Minakshi was no longer looking at the drawing. He felt a stab of grief. 'You want my help to staunch the wound,' he said. 'To ensure that it doesn't spread. To tell the City that, if I need to.'

Minakshi winced. 'I'm not asking you to *do* anything. I want to hold this City together, Alvar, and after what's happened … you, Mithila's best friend, who saw her go—what you say and do will turn things. I'm not asking you to let go of your beliefs, Alvar, just to—help keep us together.'

He caught her looking at him, hopefully. Alvar blinked, and yanked his gaze away.

'Minakshi,' he said, 'I'm not making a fool of myself over you a *third* time in three days.' He turned away from her and walked to the threshold of the door. He looked back once. Minakshi was sitting still, her hands steepled beneath her chin, looking at him.

'The drawing's beautiful,' she said. 'Goodbye, Alvar.'

'Uhmm.' Alvar cleared his throat. 'I'd love to see you again, though,' he said, very quickly. 'Away from all *this*.' He was walking away before he finished, before he could hear an answer.

When Alvar stumbled home, his parents were asleep. In his room, Mankala's bundle lay tossed upon the bed, unopened.

Mankala was not there.

'Councillor Malati has called a special session of the Council this evening.' Hansa's voice is taut. 'You may speak, Councillor.'

Malati rises. She looks strained, the skin around her temples tightly drawn.

'Everyone knows what this is about. Last night, the Matriarch proclaimed that she was reviving Ostracism. I have been waiting all day for you—President Hansa—to take action against this reversion to barbarity. You have not, so I am now forced to call this session and move a resolution declaring the Matriarch's so-called revival to be void.'

'I'm not going to dignify this with argument. You know what Ostracism is, you know its place in the darkest times of our history. You know that Sumer is a democracy of laws, not the decrees of the Shoortans. I move.'

'Yes, Councillor Rastogi,' says Hansa, and Rama hears an infinite weariness in her voice. 'You have a response?'

'I do,' says Rastogi, rising. His voice is quiet, almost matter-of-fact. 'Three days ago, the Council voted in favour of the Young Tarafians. I objected strongly, as you all know. But the Council's decision is the Council's decision, and I accepted it. Yet, with all respect, now is the time when the Council needs to season its authority with a dose of humility. The Wall has been crossed, the balance upset, and we have seen the reaction of the Builders. And it is not new. This reaction has been building up for days now. We stand at the edge of peril, Honourable Elders. And in situations where the balance has been upset, the City needs to recalibrate to restore it. This may mean that temporarily, just temporarily, the boundaries of the separate powers that we exercise be redrawn.

He sits.

'Thank you, Councillor Rastogi,' says Hansa. 'There will be no debate. We move to vote.'

A ripple runs around the hall. Malati staggers up, her bristling. 'This is not—'

'In exercise of my authority as President, Councillor.'

'Do I at least get a rejoinder?'

'I cannot deny you that,' says Hansa. 'Make it quick.'

'Just two sentences, then. Three days ago, this Council remembered its traditions, demonstrated what it stood for, and did the right thing—despite all the threats from our Shoortan friends, despite a riot at our gates. If this Council gives in now, all will be undone—and so will we.'

'Alright, thank you,' Hansa almost raps out the words. 'This is not going to be a public vote. I don't want any reprisals later. I am adopting the method of the Three Hundred Pebbles. Black for those who endorse Councillor Malati's resolution. White for those who reject it. You will come up separately, and place your pebble in the appropriate box. Councillor Paras.'

One by one, the Elders leave their seats, ascend and cross the bridge to Hansa's dock. Most of them place their pebbles with their backs to the seats, shielding themselves. Some do not. With all the contempt at her disposal, Malati takes a black pebble, holds it up, and flicks it into the box. Thanu does the same.

'Councillor Rama.'

The last name, the youngest.

She crosses the bridge, amidst the vastness of the hall, the great spaces above and below her. Hansa is sitting there, gaze fixed upon some point in the far distance. Rama turns, hiding her hands from the Council. She takes a black pebble, covers it with her fist, and drops it into the slit.

When she reaches her seat again, Hansa opens the box and mouths numbers to herself.

After many minutes, the President looks up. 'Councillor Malati's motion is rejected,' she announces. 'Two hundred and fourteen votes to eighty-five.'

Malati stands. She looks around the Council as if she is trying to remember something that has disappeared. Without a word, she walks out of the Hall.

Eight

An Unexpected Reunion

Mithila stood on the edge. On either side, the cavern walls curved like a crescent moon. Before her the ground fell away.

From the floor far below, a forest of glowing white stone rose into the vault: sharp curves, clean edges, lattices and traceries woven together, tapering into towers that soared up towards her.

Her eyes measured the distance. It was as if she was perched upon the Wall, looking down, but upon a different City.

Her gaze roamed. Amidst a thicket of needle-like spires, it caught and snagged upon the tallest. She followed its steep, gleaming sides, down into the mist-white nets of stone beneath. Mithila's head swam. She knelt, and holding tight to the ground, leaned over the precipice.

From above, the City looked like a single being. Arched pathways connected the towers, like a network of veins. Streets and avenues of sky-bridges branched and folded back into each other. Her eyes ached. Gumfraude was a stillness that was never at rest.

'*Bloody* Builders,' she breathed.

Long years ago, she and Garuda had stood in the Forum Plaza, and craned their necks to follow the ascent of the four towers into the sky. '*What if,*' Garuda had said, '*we could turn the world around—and look* down *on these, like the Builders from the sky?*' They had closed their eyes and tried, but even Garuda, who had uncovered the horizon for her, could not find that way of seeing.

He'd laughed, as he always did. '*We'll always have the horizon,*' he'd said, '*The sky can wait.*'

Instead, the ground had yielded, to give her the sight that they had not been able to imagine.

'I found our sky, my brother,' she whispered.

The air was still and cool. Mithila stood. In the afterlight of Gumfraude, she saw the dim outlines of the nearby cavern walls, thrown up from the floor like the sides of a vast bowl. The City itself stretched away into the distance, blurring into a white haze. Above, it was as dark as a tunnel in the Dooma at midnight, the roof invisible.

In front of her was the only way forward: an arched bridge, made of the same glowing white stone, just wide enough to walk single file. There was no guardrail.

A little way across the bridge, something lay, as if it had been dropped.

A hunk of roasted *rahi*.

Her mind rushed back up the passage and overground among the ruins, into the shadow of the window where her eyes had met Tefnakth's. Here before her lay a piece of Sumer, a trail, an invitation to step onto the bridge, and into the darkness—or the light—of Gumfraude.

Mithila looked back once.

She put a foot upon the bridge.

Her legs trembled. She stopped. The emptiness of the cavern poured upon her. The City waited beneath.

With infinite slowness, she brought her other foot upon the bridge. The ground was solid, the same phosphorescent material from the Forum. She spread out her arms and inched along the bridge, placing one foot after the other.

She had been walking for a while when she saw the second *rahi* piece upon the ground. She stopped to look down. For the first time on the bridge, her gaze travelled beyond, to the white City. The tower-tops were thickets of spikes, staring at her. Dizziness flooded her. Mithila shut her eyes. And then she remembered doing the same at the first sight of the world beyond the Wall, the world she would never again glimpse from the sky, and all Garuda's regret at seeing forever earthbound.

Mithila forced her eyes open.

Gumfraude shimmered beneath her.

She forced herself to keep looking, until nausea crept along the edges of her throat, and a cold sweat broke out at the back of her neck. Her knees buckled. She knelt quickly upon the bridge.

'*Well that wasn't very smart was it?*'

She would have turned and gone back, and damn the *rahi* trail, but the thought of turning upon the bridge made nausea come rushing back. Mithila laid herself flat upon the bridge, her arms clutching the sides, her cheek to the stone.

The rock walls on either side of her had disappeared, leaving only emptiness.

She felt her breath shorten and shallow, her lungs compress. She gasped for the air that seemed to have been sucked out of the cavernous depths around her. In the cavity of her chest, something screamed.

Mithila realized that she did not want to die.

She closed her eyes, she reached for Sumer, a Sumer that floated before her, daylight upon the Rasa—and heard herself whimper in the darkness.

Her eyes still closed, little dots dancing upon the curtain, she lifted herself to her knees and began to crawl.

Builders, get me out of here, a little voice whispered in her head, *and I promise I'll believe in you.* The world was black around her, the glow of the bridge shut out, a roaring in her ears. From far away, she felt her knees scrape against the stone. Images of home rushed into her mind, each one raking her heart with furrows of regret.

Then her groping hand struck something solid, and there was a vague, *Sumerian* smell in the air. Mithila dared to open her eyes.

Right before her, there was another slice of *rahi*. And just beyond, the bridge ended in a wide platform set into the rock-wall.

She curbed a mad urge to sprint the final few metres to safety. Her legs were tensing, her brain sending signals to her limbs about how close she was. Mithila clenched her fists and forced herself to keep crawling, until her hands—and then the rest of her—were past the bridge and onto safe ground.

She threw herself upon the platform and curled up against the rough cavern wall, her heart pounding.

The platform was a view-point over the City, giving her a garuda's-eye view of Gumfraude. A City of towers, like a thousand Forums packed together, but somewhere in the bones of this world, something felt wrong. She looked again, letting her eyes linger. Then it struck her.

The City was not circular.

She had been searching for a pattern, some symmetry, an *axis* around which the City was organised—like the diameter of a circle—but Gumfraude gave her none. No Wall, no circles, no Rasa to cordon it.

She looked back. The bridge she had crossed stretched across the cavern like a bamboo stalk. The platform extended around her in a semi-circle. Between her and the City below, there was nothing but a sheer drop and the near-perpendicular face of the rock wall.

She stood and walked to the edge of the platform. In a time out of mind, the Samatians had once stood upon an edge, looked on a City far beneath, and trusted the air to break their fall. *Remember Samati,* Dhara's last words rang in her ear again. *Remember me.*

The air felt like a net, waiting to catch her. She inched forwards, until her toes were off the platform. The City was beckoning to her, a softly swirling glimmering of whiteness, not very far away. Perhaps that was where Dhara had gone. And all she had to do was lower herself upon the air, glide down to those white spires, until—

'*No!*'

Mithila scrabbled back from the edge, backing away until she felt the comforting rock wall. *No more looking at Gumfraude.* She let herself slide to the floor and huddled against the wall, her arms around her knees. She took another sight at the bridge. The thought of crawling back upon it set her teeth on edge.

The silence pressed on her, unbearable. 'Remember,' she said out loud, to keep something—she didn't know what—away. 'Remember when we talked about how we'd make new words for what we felt beyond the Wall? Guess what, here's one: the feeling you get when you're looking down from the sky, and everything spins and you want to jump because you—you've forgotten gravity. I get to name it now. I think I'll call it "sky-turn", because that's what it feels like—oh Builders, that's such an ugly word. Come so I can show you. I'll take you out over Gumfraude like you took me out over Sumer, but so much higher, and I'll hold your waist so you don't fall when you look out and forget gravity, and you'll trust me and I won't let go and I—please come? New words, new worlds together, just like it was meant to be.'

She broke off as shards of shame and confusion cut through her. Just for a moment it had been possible to believe that the Council Tower, where Rama had braided her hair as they looked out over Sumer, and the platform from where she now looked out over Gumfraude, belonged to the same world.

But between them was the Wall, keeping out and keeping in.

Mithila looked up into the trackless dark. 'I miss you,' she whispered, 'and I can't even be sorry because I'd do it all over again and if you were there, you'd *make* me do it if you saw me stop. So, what am I going to do with these feelings? Where am I going to keep them in this world beyond the Wall?'

There was no answer.

Mithila sighed, and let her head drop. She drifted by slow degrees into a world of swirling dreams, where Rama and Taraf wandered in the streets of a blood-red Gumfraude, only—but always—a moment in time, or a separation in planes, away from her.

Mithila awoke a few minutes—or few hours—later, still tired. A thought had crept into her mind, interfering with her dreams, and finally pulling her eyes open.

The rahi trail couldn't have led her to a dead end.

She scoured the floor, and soon saw it: inches from the right edge of the platform, just before it met the rock wall, the fourth *rahi* piece.

Cautiously, she approached the edge. Was there a descent into Gumfraude? No. The platform gave way to emptiness, the drop, the same net of air that—

Silently, the lights came on.

It was as if someone was tracing glimmering white lines upon the ground. From the rock wall and from the edge of the platform, they *flowed* towards each other at right angles, separating one patch of ground—upon which Mithila stood—from the rest, a borderline she dared not cross.

Something descended upon her: solid, transparent sheets that met the platform where the lines glimmered, and closed above her head in a curve, as if she was in an upturned bowl. Before she could move, the lines had deepened and the patch she was on *separated* itself from the platform. There was a moment of stillness, and then, noiselessly, the ground shifted and began to take her down the rock wall.

Mithila pressed her hands and face against the sheet—she had no other name for it. It was cold, smooth, hard. *Familiar*. Her skin remembered: a night in the Academy, in an empty room filled with instruments of the same transparent, solid material that she had touched; the night she had come across a secret meeting in a closed room, heard the word *prala* repeated over and over again, and seen—*Tefnakth*.

Tefnakth, there. Tefnakth, here. But Mithila had no time to think. She was moving at a steady pace, noiseless, the platform *sliding* down the rock wall.

She turned to see Gumfraude coming into view beneath, blurred outlines growing sharper and clearer, like a sleeper awakening. Closer drew the sweep of the towers. Her eye measured them to around the height of the Forum. The wreathed mist from which they rose resolved itself into a second level of closely-set buildings, like the denser, lower canopy of the *forest* she had left above ground, connected by that network of sky-bridges.

Closer, the City looked less like a living organism, and more like a corpse: bedecked, preserved, undecayed, lifeless. Its glimmering was no heartbeat, but only the endless, pale death-light of something that had once lived, a memory of radiance. Mithila shivered.

As she descended to the level of the tallest towers, Gumfraude grew unfocused, resisting definition every time she looked too closely. For a while, her eyes rested upon a filigree-thin two-storeyed structure rising from a terrace high above the ground, topped by a set of arches that upheld little domes. A little distance away, two towers, topped by hexagons, rose above a zig-zagging channel that was carrying—water? an illusion of water?—in a steady ascent from the first to the second tower, before it fell back down in a little waterfall, an endless cycle.

Mithila blinked. There was something about the towers that her mind was refusing to accept. It was lodged in her brain like the *rahi* that sometimes stuck in your throat, a feeling coarse and rough-edged.

It was only after she'd descended further and the towers passed out of sight, that she understood. *The water had been flowing both upwards and downwards*, as though for that one small space between the towers, the laws of physics stood suspended.

At last, her transport set her down with the smallest—and quietest—of bumps. The platform immediately *folded* into the cavern floor. The sheets vanished like dew in sunlight. Mithila took a hesitant step forward.

In front of her, a piece of roasted *rahi*.

Around her, the Forum.

The Forum, yes: but a Forum upon a plain of white stone and beneath a black sky; a Forum without the rustling of short grass and the tinkling of the Rasa; a Forum without those little additions the Sumerians had dared make through the centuries—the wooden doors and the wicker gateways with the banners of the Mandalas fluttering in the air; and a Forum without movement or colour; as if this was the original, the archetype, and the one back home a mason's clever copy with a softening around the edges for human eyes.

Four great structures rose before her, in shapes and dimensions that she knew so well. And instead of the river, halfway across the plain, equidistant from each:

Come find me by the crystal pool

A hexagon, whose edges shone with a sharp, cutting light. Mithila looked back once. Her transport seemed to have retreated into the rock wall. She filed away the awareness that someone had likely *sent* it back up for her, and stepped into the plain.

Closer to the hexagon, she saw that it was filled with water so clear, so still, and so transparent, that it might have been a thin sheet of air. She reached the pool, and looked over the rim. On the flat bed, not too deep, there were stones that gleamed, and cast the water in a blue-green sheen.

Do you remember what I said to you ... that evening beside the pool of Gheroun? When the stars were dancing on the water?

Ghada's voice, from another cavern in another world, murmured in her ears. Mithila looked up. There were no stars above, only at the bottom of the water.

You said you would find a way to make this moment last forever.

The pool felt like it had been filled just yesterday, as if the moment *had* lasted forever. Mithila knelt, cupped water in her hands, and brought it to her lips. A taste—*taste?*—unknown filled her mouth, that made her think of cold rock and soft earth. She spat it out, suddenly afraid, and watched it splatter upon the white stone. As she looked up, she saw the *rahi* trail lead from the pool, to the Council Hall.

She followed it to the Hall. At the entrance, she saw the same transparent sheet that had surrounded her upon the platform above.

It fit into the wall without a hinge or joint. She stopped before it and looked up, letting her eyes travel to the top. There was no mistake. It was the Council Hall.

Mithila extended a hand to the sheet and jumped back as it parted of its own accord. At the threshold, a *rahi* piece beckoned to her.

'*Okay, Tefnakth, here I come,*' she muttered, and stepped inside. Behind her, the sheet moved back into place with a soft *click*.

Mithila followed the passage until a *rahi* piece upon a turning brought her into the hall of a thousand pillars. The trail led her through the pillars and ended in another sheet. Beyond it, she knew, was the Elders' conferral room, where she had come with Rama, where they had hidden from Sanchika and Malati, and first heard Tefnakth's name spoken. On a hunch, she puffed out her cheeks and blew at the sheet. Instantly, it parted.

'Responding to motion, eh?' Mithila said. She stepped into the chamber.

Her feet sank into a soft, deep carpet. On the walls, there were shelves of polished, shining wood, filled with books (*so much paper!*). There were four pillars in the centre of the room, and perched on each was a flame lamp. But these lamps were not alight with fire. They had translucent surfaces that glowed from the *inside*, throwing a steady, warm light across the room. At the far end was a desk with more books.

Beside it, there was a bed. It was carefully made, the pillow set plush against the headboard.

There were no *rahi* pieces in the room. Mithila padded to the desk. It was dark-brown, a rich lush colour that she had never seen before. A chair was before it, with angled arms and a thick back. The books were arranged in an orderly stack. In the centre, there was a sheaf of loosely-bound papers—a notebook—with a blue cover, a blue darker than the stripes on the robes of the Elders, as though more woad had been spent to clothe this book than any Sumerian body.

On the cover, she saw the words, in precise block letters, in Sumerian script.

A VOICE IN THE DARK

She picked up the notebook. Her back tingled. She whirled around to face the entrance.

There was nobody.

Mithila sucked in air. Keeping the entrance in her sights, she carefully opened the book.

Have you, unknown reader, ever felt this urge to say something, but nobody to say it to?

The writing was elegant and methodical, strangely familiar—but just out of reach. She read through the first paragraph, and the second:

> *I fear I'm going to ramble some more. In fact, I'm going to play a little game with you. Because it amuses me. I'm not going to tell you who I am. I'll leave you to figure that out. Of course, I'll help you by narrowing things down considerably. You'll know, immediately, that I am one of a small group that used to call itself The Young Tarafians.*

Mithila stopped. She raised her head. Her blood surged. But her eyes were pulled back to the page. The words seemed to twist and writhe upon the page, as if they wanted to escape her.

Who were the Young Tarafians, then? Where did they come from …

It wasn't as if they desired something strange, or radically incomprehensible …

Any fool should have known what he was bargaining for the day Garuda first sang the song about blank spaces …

Take Mithila, for instance. Poor old Mithila, so utterly, so touchingly, so bizarrely convinced of her position. She simply couldn't understand—or perhaps she didn't want to understand—why someone might not, honestly and truthfully desire that the Wall not be breached.

'*The fuck!*' she said out loud, plaintively.

She read faster, turning the pages, turning them with violence, almost tearing the paper out.

You know, I remember playing a game with Mithila once. We were imitating a style of conversation we'd found in the pages of the philosopher Temur, to get at truth.

She closed her eyes. Whom had she played the game with? To whom had she said, '*because it exists*?' Time's circle spun back. Garuda and Dhara sprang back to life, and they were all together once more around the fire, Garuda's laughter, Dhara's quiet force, Alvar's poetry, Lamon's rage, Rama…

She found nothing.

Her memory was a blank. She put her fists to her temples and *pushed*, willing the doors of her memory to open.

Nothing. Resigned, she turned another page:

> *To start with, I knew that the digging was entirely futile. Come now, think about it. Are you seriously going to tell me that the folk who built that Wall, the Forum, the Rasa—folk that powerful would never have never accounted for that primitive an escape? That was exactly what I told Mithila once. And she just gave me her classic Mithila look—you know, the one which says, how-could-you-contemplate-the-possibility-of-the-failure-of-an-enterprise-so-grand-and-noble-as-ours, and delivered a classic Mithila line: "We'll never know until we try, will we?" Huh?*
>
> *But it was something. It let us hope. And even vain hopes are better than despair.*
>
> *And that, I think, is also why I told the Shoortans.*

'*Wha—?!*' Her voice rebounded off the walls. Mithila silenced herself instantly and pricked her ears, her eyes on the door.

Nothing stirred.

Every part of her was trembling: lips and eyes, arms and fingers, knees and feet. She felt her fists clench tightly around the notebook. Once more, a turn of the page.

Oh dear. Oh dear, oh dear, oh dear.
I must confess, I did not foresee this.
This ... changes everything.

And then at last the final entry, written in ink that was fresh and gleaming.

And so, dear reader, it ends. My time in this beloved room, in old Gumfraude. Mentor made it clear that after the last sky-raising, we would have no more use for this dead-undead City, no more secret trips here. There's work to be done back home.

I'm going to miss Gumfraude. Their presence is everywhere, in this carapace of a City. Sometimes, when I stand on the view-point and look down on it all, I can almost make believe I have their power, their timelessness, that if they were to appear before me—Ghada, Samir, Alora—we'd have so much to talk about.

I'd ask them a world. We used their machine like a child uses a rattle without understanding the first thing about sound. How does it really work, this device that blankets the sky in red at the press of a lever? I know the sky isn't really red, I know our eyes are seeing an illusion—but what's the science behind it? Or I'd ask them what really is happening in that chamber underneath Sumer, why we've never been able to open those containers in which the three of them sleep. Or yet again, I'd ask them how rahi *was invented—so little space, such high yield. Or ...*

No more rambling. I was meant to destroy the room before going back this time. But I didn't have the heart. Call it sentiment. I even filled the pool, one final time. It felt right, leaving things as they were meant to be. I will not raise the sky again, no more blood spilt across the firmament.

This was never meant to be mine forever. But what is?

Gumfraude, perhaps. I will leave this notebook here. Gumfraude endures, even we *could not destroy it, and so will my story. And if you, reader from another sky, read my words, be gentle. I was a traitor to the pieces, but not to the whole.*

It's time to go: to dislocation, to confusion, to scatterings. Prala, *not* praya. *All that makes life worth living.*

Goodbye.

There it ended.

'*How could you,*' she whispered. 'Oh, fuck you, fuck you, *fuck you!*'

She threw the notebook on the ground and stamped on it till her feet hurt. There was a red film before her eyes. She turned and swept the books from the table, watching them tumble to the floor. Just beside them was an inkpot, which the author must have used to write those final lines. Mithila hurled it against the wall, heard it shatter, and watched the ink creep along the lush carpet, staining it.

'Fuck you,' she said once more, and sunk to the carpet, on her knees. She screwed her eyes shut. She was in the darkness of the Pit again, stroking the wall of rock and debris before her, imagining Garuda's touch, just before the walls had collapsed on him.

And that, I think, is also why I told the Shoortans...

'Whoever you are,' she said hoarsely, 'I'm going to come back. I'm going to find you. I promise.'

She turned back to the crumpled pages, to unread what she'd read, because it was—it must have been—all a mistake, or there would be an explanation, or—

Then she noticed that the last entry did not end with *goodbye.* A little way down, there was a final, hurried scrawl.

PS. I've had to leave Dhara behind. But I've left her in memory of the garudas, as she'd have wanted. And I've left her light.

Mithila turned ragged eyes to the ceiling. *Left her in memory of the garudas.*

'*Builders!*' She leapt to her feet and ran to the entrance. She almost careened into it before it opened for her. She crossed the hall of a thousand pillars, back out in the corridor, and then she was out of the Council Hall, and sprinting across the plain, to the Citadel. Once more, the doors parted at her approach.

Her breath came in sobs. 'Dhara,' she whispered, 'wait for me.' Her feet echoed as she ran down the main hall of the Citadel, a path remembered from her last evening in Sumer, through the archway, down the sloping passageway, through empty rooms—and suddenly, there was a gleaming light at the end.

And I've left her light.

Mithila burst into the room that—in Sumer—had housed the garudas with whom she had flown beyond the Wall.

The room was not empty.

In the centre of the chamber, floating in mid-air, was a Heartstone: six-sided, throbbing, glowing.

The Heartstone illumined something just beyond it. A container just like the ones in the Chamber of the Three Kings, oblong and suspended in the air, its surface transparent. Inside, resting upon the cushions, eyes closed, face bright under the light of the Heartstone …

'Oh no,' whispered Mithila. 'Oh no, no, no, no, *no!*'

She stood helplessly and stared at the face that would not look back at her.

The face of Dhara.

Ladders hang around her, vanishing into the night. The lamps are unlit, the windows flicker. Murmurs fill the air, the night sound of the Dooma that her father had told her about. Rama stops in the middle of the empty street, before the entrance to a tunnel.

There is a slithering noise behind her. She swings around.

Maji stands there, facing her. Rama raises her hands, palms out.

'A little late to be out in the Dooma.' Maji looks her up and down. 'And what do we have here? Amrit's daughter.' She laughs. 'What an honour for the Dooma.'

There are sounds behind her, shadows that materialize in the corner of her vision. Rama does not turn.

'What are you doing here, Councillor?' Maji asks softly.

'I …' Suddenly, she is tongue-tied. What were you thinking, *a voice in her head screams.*

'Looking for a lost lover?' Maji mocks. 'She was here, yes. Was.'

Rama flinches. 'I've come to talk.'

'The blade comes to talk to the neck?'

Savage chuckles rise around her. Rama sweats. Every line she has prepared, every objection considered, every argument foreseen, is choking in the thick air of reality. And it had been so easy to persuade herself.

'Alright, let's stop playing games,' Maji says. 'We know why you're here. Give us one reason, Councillor, why we should help you.'

She knows it will make no difference. She says it anyway. 'We need to save Sumer.'

*Maji snorts. '*This *Sumer? The Sumer of the Circles? Some things are not worth saving. Not for us.'*

'I know,' said Rama. 'But this time, it's to save Sumer so there can be something—beyond Sumer.'

'We've been hearing this for two thousand years, since the Shoortans took our stories away,' Maji's voice is cold. 'Kings, oligarchs, tyrants, democrats, they come each time with their promises. We die in your quarrels for the sunlight, and you leave us in Wallshadow. What's different this time?'

Rama has her hook. 'You know,' she says, 'you know what's different. And you know who made it so.'

Maji pauses. Around her the shadows shift.

'Does Council know you're here?' Maji says.

'They do not.'

'Audacious. As audacious as her.'

Rama fights to focus. 'I've not come here pretending to be your friend. I won't mock you like that. I'm only here to say that this moment may never come again, and right now it's not us who stand in your way.'

'And why,' says Maji, 'does the burden of fulfilling these moments always fall upon the Dooma?'

'It doesn't,' Rama says. 'Not this time.'

Maji stares at her. 'Speak,' she says. 'And speak quickly.'

Nine

Marwana

Alvar awoke to find Mankala asleep on the edge of the bed.

Relief swept through him. She looked like a small, uncomfortable question mark, curled up into the tiniest possible space to avoid waking him. He got up and walked around the bed to where she was lying.

'*Hey*,' he whispered.

Mankala grunted.

'Move, you big baby.' He lightly nudged her shoulder towards the centre. Mankala grunted again.

'That's it,' said Alvar. He gave her an ungentle shove. Mankala rolled over. He took the pillow and pushed it under her head. Mankala grabbed it and hugged it tightly, her eyes still closed.

'There we go,' said Alvar. He slipped out into the living room. Sekri was sitting at the table, spreading his bread with peanut paste. 'Morning, Da Sekri,' he said, taking the second chair.

Sekri raised an enquiring eyebrow. 'Morning, son. Something you want to tell me?'

Alvar stared.

Sekri gestured at the bedroom and waggled his eyebrows.

'What—da, no! That's Mankala! She's just … she'll be staying with us for a while.'

'Damn, she's my favourite.' Sekri's eyes twinkled. 'I was hoping you were going to break some good news.'

'Priorities straight as ever, I see. Just because *you've* always been in the sacred union.'

'No need to get jealous now, son, nobody's perfect.' Sekri held up a hand, grinning. 'She's welcome here, of course. What happened, but?'

'Oh, I—there was an accident in her house,' Alvar stammered, 'and she can't—uhm—go back to her parents now.'

Sekri nodded, good-humoured. 'No questions asked, I get it.'

Alvar steered away from the subject. 'And why are *you* up so early, da?' Mild sunlight streamed in through the arched window.

'Big new order today,' Sekri said. 'Long day of work.'

'From whom? I thought demand was dead because of the harvest.'

'Right. Downcircles, yeah, I don't think anyone's buying clothes this season. But when have these things ever hurt the Forum?'

'Elders?'

'No, actually.' Sekri gave him a side-eye. 'Shoortans.'

'*Shoortans*? New clothes? What for?'

'Not clothes. Flags. Banners, rather.'

'Banners?'

'Don't ask. Seems a waste. But they bring the linen, they pay us, so can't complain, eh?'

'Fair. Da Suneer left early then, I guess?'

Sekri swallowed the last crumbs of bread and pushed his plate away. 'Yes, he kissed me goodbye at Wallrise. He's already in the workshop, with everyone else.'

'Prasanna?'

'Ha! Refused outright. Said that after Ostracism he'd never work for the Shoortans again.'

'He'd better be careful now, they may just Ostracize *him* for it.'

They burst out laughing together, and then stopped together, as darkness crept around the edge of mirth.

'Well,' said Sekri, just before the silence grew uncomfortable. 'I'll be off then. It's going to be a long day.'

'I can imagine,' Alvar grinned. 'Show me one of those banners before you hand them over to the Temple, no?'

'If you bother coming home from the Bards at a sensible hour some day!' Sekri stood and gave him a good-natured little jab in the ribs. 'Be seeing you.'

'Work hard!'

'Shut up. Love you, son.'

The door closed behind Sekri. Alvar leaned back in his chair, stretching his arms behind his head. There was no sound from his bedroom. He began to turn over Vidusha's song in his head. *Who will remake the broken world?* The refrain drew him, the beginning from a high note that lowered swiftly and crested again at the end. He ran over the other lines. Nothing there, apart from those recurring three words: *light from light.*

Alvar stood, and wandered to the bathroom. He was hit by a sudden, sharp memory of Mithila. It washed over him and he let it, an ache at the back of his head.

He dragged the water bucket to the corner of the bathroom, slathered himself with oil, and emptied the river water upon himself, gasping at the coldness.

When he walked back into the living room, his hair still wet, he found Mankala sitting on Sekri's chair. Her face was slightly pale.

'I'm trying to figure out,' he said, 'if I'm expected to worry about you or not.'

Mankala only held up a piece of paper. 'What's this, Alvar?'

It was his sketch, that he'd left lying on the table where he'd been working last night.

'Oh,' he said. 'I've been drawing.'

Mankala looked at the sketch, and then back at him. 'How did you do this? The distances—depth—it's like *I'm* seeing the world, instead of the Wall looking over me, like in all the other paintings.'

Alvar shifted and grinned embarrassed. 'You know when you talked about vanishing points yesterday? I was already thinking of Mithila, I was trying to imagine the world from her eyes—if you could see a horizon, if you could see that vanishing point where the earth and sky meet—and if you could draw it—'

'Alvar. Have you just been *hiding* this talent from us all these years while playing at being a poet and a carer?'

'Shut up, it's a bad drawing!'

'It's literally something nobody has ever seen before. There's—there's—*depth*!'

He walked over to her and tried to grab at the paper. Mankala held it away, laughing.

'Let me work on it, okay! I just started.'

She handed it back to him, still laughing. 'Just be careful, alright? Pretty sure this is an Ostracizable offence in Minakshi's New Sumer.'

'Oh.' *Shit.* Alvar shook his head. *No, Minakshi wouldn't …*

'Is that why you didn't come back last night? Shoortan trouble?'

'Oh—no. Sorry, Alvar, for getting you worried. There's blockades all over the upper Circles. I just couldn't be damned to get through them last night.'

'Blockades?'

'Elders seem to be *very* jittery last night. Watch with swords at every check-point. I think they're expecting violence.'

'Malati put you up?'

'Elmandar.'

'Ooo. I *see*.'

'I'm sure you do,' said Mankala primly. 'Did you get anything from the Seventh?'

'Nothing about the three kings. Something random about three stones.' He sang the song for her.

Mankala pursed her lips. 'Yeah, that doesn't tell us much.'

'Why don't you ask you-know-who?' Alvar snorted.

'Builders, Alvar, nothing is happening. Stop prodding.'

'All the more reason to ask, before the prodding starts.'

'*This* is what they're teaching you in the Seventh? Terrible puns?'

'It was a good one! But seriously, why not? The Upper Circles get access to all kinds of historical documents that we'll never see. Ask Elmandar.'

'Thoo. No. And, besides I may have asked too much of him yesterday.' Mankala's voice grew quiet. 'Actually, I'll tell you on the way. Give me a bit to bathe. Do I need to drag a bucket from the river?'

'I left enough for you … but on the way where? I have to go to work.'

'Take today off, Alvar. It's the endgame.'

'I—what game?'

'The kids will get by without you for one day. As for the elders, they can argue with Kodali for a change.'

Alvar held up his hands. 'I do a lot more than that.'

'*Fine*. Just come. I'll explain. I promise.'

'Well …' he hesitated. 'Kodali won't mind this once, I guess. But you owe me.'

'Good. Wait for me.'

She slipped back into the bedroom, reappeared with the clothes that he'd left for her, and disappeared into the bathroom. Alvar heard water sloshing around on the floor. He stayed seated, wondering.

Mankala came back into the room, no longer smelling of sweat. Alvar wrinkled his nose. 'Phew, the air's fit to breathe again.'

'Idiot!' She sprinkled him with water droplets as she ran her hands violently through her hair. 'Need to get this cut short,' she muttered.

'Where are we going?' he asked.

'Back to the Citadel.'

This time, Mankala simply pushed the doors open. Across the hall and up the stairs they went, through the corridors, until they stopped before Marwana's door. Nobody interrupted them.

Mankala took a deep breath, and knocked.

'Come in,' Marwana's voice said.

'Here we go,' said Mankala. They walked in.

Marwana was waiting for them, sitting upright, her elbows resting upon the desk, her fingers steepled in front of her lips. Streams of sunlight from the large window at her back—with the Academy silhouetted in the distance—cast her face in shadow.

There were two chairs, facing her. They sat.

'I thought you'd be back,' Marwana said. 'Tell me.'

'Marwana,' said Mankala, without preliminaries. 'We believe that the Builders are still in Sumer. We believe that there exists a secret organization dedicated to fighting them. And we believe you lead it.'

Marwana smiled, and raised an eyebrow.

'The story of Malan,' Mankala said, 'is a lie. He never crossed any line. Probably he never existed. There was no covenant and no punishment. But there was a battle. And when it was over, the victors imprisoned the vanquished within the Wall. But they still feared them. So they—the Builders—left some of themselves behind, in secret, to ensure we'd stay down. That we'd never get out. Soon after, to erase our memories, they destroyed Sumer in a great fire. And they will do it again, if they must. We don't even know how many times they've already done it.

'But they didn't just have it all their way. There were those among the defeated who resisted. Who resist. Two thousand years is a long time to endure, but they did it. They formed a secret group. They trained in isolation. And they chose their own successors, each generation.

'Or, should I say, *selected*.'

Mankala subsided, breathless, her eyes shining.

'Um,' Alvar said.

Marwana was still smiling.

'Am I right?' Mankala said.

'I'm sure you'll tell me,' Marwana said quietly. 'So, finish.'

'We should have known,' there was a slight tremble in Mankala's voice. 'You were there at the Pit, you saved them after Garuda died. That night when the sky turned red for the first time—when Mithila could've been lynched in the *maidan*—you were there, you saved her. That speech you gave at our trial, that turned the tide. You got us the time we needed to do what we had to. Always, Leader Marwana. Right time, right place. All too perfect. Scientific neutrality? *You were never what you seemed.*'

Marwana only gazed into the distance beyond them.

'I wish I'd saved Garuda,' the leader of the scientists said, unexpectedly. 'One of our best hopes. Such an analytical mind, but he knew how to dream. And he dreamed too much.' She shook her head. 'I thought I'd get to the Pit in the morning, to make it look like we'd just found out, to avoid the Shoortans suspecting us—but it was too late. I've regretted that every day of my life.'

Alvar saw something glimmering at the corner of her eye, but Marwana blinked rapidly, and it was gone.

'Sorry,' said Mankala, 'I didn't … didn't mean to remind you of—'

Marwana waved a hand. 'Who can change it now? Not even the Builders—'

The word unlocked Alvar's mouth. 'So wait,' he said. 'Then you actually *are* a secret society that wants to fight these people? And you've been helping us—'

'Go beyond the Wall,' Mankala finished for him. 'Destroy the hold they have over Sumer. Discover the horizon.'

'So far, so fascinating.' Marwana was looking at Mankala with an intense, almost hungry look. 'And will you now explain to me why we live in secret?'

'Because that's your only hope.' Mankala's words ran into Marwana's. 'The myth of Malan, the legend of the Builders—two thousand years they've been around, you can't just fight them outright. You'd be smashed, like they smashed Taraf. So you've built, and all through time, when you can, you've given history a little *push*—here or there, to send this City down a path that will better resist the Builders.'

Something struck Alvar, and he joined his words to hers, finishing her thoughts: 'And Taraf was one of yours, wasn't he?'

Marwana's sudden start was all the answer they needed.

'Tell us, Leader,' Mankala whispered. 'One of us is dead. Another, vanished. A third beyond the Wall. We've given our blood in this, your war. There's just the two of us left now, and they're coming for us. Who are we fighting? What are we fighting for? We've earned the right to know, haven't we?'

Marwana started again. 'Coming for you? What do you—'

'They burned my house,' said Mankala steadily. 'And they came for me with a knife.'

'You should've told me!' Marwana's voice rose. 'There's no way we're losing you. I'm going to arrange security for you now, I—'

'Yes, okay,' Mankala said. 'I appreciate that, but if my luck runs out, I'd at least like to know what my life meant.'

Marwana stopped, as though stung. She put her arms on the desk, her fingers entwining. Silence lingered between them, stretching into a minute. At last, she leaned forward.

'If you've deduced things this far,' she said, 'then you'll understand why I couldn't just tell you, the last time you came.'

'Last time? You should've told us after the Pit, after Garuda. Then Dhara might still be here with us today,' Mankala burst out. 'Perhaps we'd have known what we were fighting, what to be careful of. Perhaps things would've turned out differently.'

'That can't be,' said Marwana heavily. 'Once you set the rules, you can't say you're going to break them when you want to. If we did that, everything would be lost.'

'What rules?' said Alvar.

Marwana turned to him.

'The rules of non-intervention, of course. You heard her. Every time we—the Select—intervene, we risk ruin. So we've decided to bind our own hands. And so that we're not tempted to backslide, we've bound ourselves to that publicly, openly, before Sumer. We can't start making exceptions—'

'You are the scientists,' Mankala interrupted. 'It's your job to deduce the rule and the exception.'

'We are the scientists, yes,' said Marwana. 'And that's why we know to trust ourselves even less than we trust others. You'll have to admit,' she added, as Mankala opened her mouth, 'that it's worked so far. Sumer respects us. Sumer believes us. If the day comes when we need to step in, it's our two thousand years of silence that will let us speak and be heard.'

'And that will be if ...?' Mankala prompted.

'Oh Builders, persistent, aren't you?'

'Sorry,' Mankala said simply, 'but we're not leaving here without an answer. What are you worried of, we'll sell you out? Mithila's already changed the world, Leader, we—her friends—are more marked than you'll ever be. So stop trying to save us, and just tell us what we need to know so we can save ourselves—and maybe even help you, if you'll have us.'

'I ... alright.' Marwana put up a hand. 'You didn't have to say all this. I knew you'd figure it out. I was waiting for you. I don't even have much more to tell.'

She took a breath.

'Yes, there was a battle. Yes, our ancestors lost. Yes, the victors put the defeated within the Wall. But the point was not just punishment, as far as we can tell. It was, is, an experiment. A social experiment. Put so many human beings in a confined space, set conditions that allow them to stay alive. Then watch what they do, and what they do to each other.'

Alvar felt his gorge rise. Mankala was looking at Marwana, revolted.

'The Builders have patience,' Marwana continued, 'they could watch for a thousand years. Two thousand. Longer. But, of course, you'd have to ensure that the conditions of the experiment were not altered: nobody could cross the Wall. So yes, you're right. The Builders left their own in Sumer, this side of the Wall, to ensure that.'

'The Shoortans!' Alvar burst out.

'Wrong,' said Marwana, matter-of-factly. '*Not* the Shoortans, Alvar. You know a social experiment can't work if everyone can see the conditions under which it has been set up. Don't hate me for saying this, but the Shoortans are actually of Sumer.' She allowed them a moment. 'I know this is hard—but they are us, and we are them.

'No, they're not going to stick out like that. They are all over Sumer—in the Council, among the Shoortans, in the Mandalas, upper and lower—and here in the Citadel, we know. We call them the *Overseers,* these Builders-born. Always watching, always maintaining the control conditions of the experiment. Sometimes we think we've identified one, but you can never be sure.'

'And you—'

'Yes, us. We are, as you've guessed, not *just* scientists. We live to fight the Overseers. But the stakes are a little more … life or death.'

She looked at them, waiting for them to work it out.

'No experiment,' Alvar said slowly, 'lasts forever.'

Marwana nodded. 'Correct. And what happens when an experiment has served its purpose?'

'You … dismantle it?' said Alvar. 'Throw it away?'

'Yes again,' said Marwana. 'And what other purpose does a circular Wall serve?'

'Control,' Alvar breathed. 'If you want to end the experiment you can erase it completely. Nobody can get out.'

'Exactly. That's what Mithila hit upon at the trial, when she spoke about the Rasa drying up. We don't know where it comes from, but *they* do. What if they decided to just stop it one day? What if they tore it all down because they could?'

'But you don't even know,' said Alvar, 'who they are. The Overseers.'

'And that's why we're building back.'

Marwana's voice was the smelting of iron in a furnace, a cold blade in the moonlight, the wingbeat of a Garuda, and the weight of the Forum.

'It's not just about scientific neutrality as a cover. Never was. It *had* to be the scientists, because in this closed system, to prevent a single disruption from killing us, someone needs to invent alternatives to everything that the experiment provides.' She smiled. 'Water—theirs. *Rahi*—theirs. But the air we breathe is ours, and the earth beneath our feet, and *we are building.* Beneath the quarries, an underground City, room for us all. We've invented a variant of *rahi* that does not need natural sunlight to grow. And for years, we've been drawing water from the Rasa into the soil, creating aquifers that will last a generation. I don't know if it will be enough—but *fuck the Builders*, and fuck their Overseers. We're going to put up a fight.' Her voice turned inwards, softer, sharper. 'I hope our ancestors did. I hope they were put here screaming and scratching, that they didn't just walk in meekly to become the great Experiment within the Wall.'

'Marwana, that's not enough!' Mankala said. 'It'll only buy us some time, but not a forever. That can't be all we have.'

'No,' said Marwana. 'Unless …'

'Unless there's a way beyond,' Mankala finished. 'And we find it.'

'Right again,' said Marwana. 'There is. We know they use it.'

'Wait. How?' said Alvar.

'Little things, little signs across the years that generations of us have put together, bound by threads of memory.'

'What?'

'Tell me something, Alvar. Do you know of someone in this City, someone who just disappeared?'

'Dhara?'

Marwana shook her head. 'Another mystery, that. But, no. Someone who was hunted, from the Forum to the Wall, quarry to the lake. Someone who was never found. Someone that the City thought was dead, until—'

'Oh no,' whispered Mankala.

'Oh yes,' said Marwana. 'Do you think he hid out for years in Sumer with every damned Watchman looking for him—and one day, walked into the Seventh and began his life over again? Where would you start searching for that lost time? Let me tell you: not this side of the Wall.'

'No, no, no, this makes no sense,' said Alvar. 'He fought against the Elders—'

This time, Marwana's smile was weary. 'Oh, you think so? Have you ever *really* thought about what happened twenty-seven years ago? We had a City, peaceful. A City at rest for two hundred years. Out of nowhere, a man rose up and appointed himself leader of a revolution. Blood in the streets, blood in the river. He conquered all. The Watch, the Shoortans, the Elders—just shadows in his light. The people were with him. Every Circle on his side. He was at the Forum, on the verge of abolishing the Circles.

'And then Savarian lost. Just like that.'

'But we know now,' Mankala said. 'Mithila read it in the Encyclopaedia, it was because of—'

'Dhanurashi,' Marwana snorted. 'Now isn't *that* a story we all love. All hope has faded but then, at the first light of Wallrise, the hero appears—and defeat turns into victory. That's not how real life works, Mankala. Not unless it's scripted. There was only one thing more impossible than Savarian's rise, and that was his fall.'

'You're telling us the Blue Revolution was a put-up job? For what?'

'To ensure that no force in Sumer could be allowed to grow too powerful. The Elders were at the peak of their power, they were even talking about abolishing voting in the *maidan*—and then the barricades came up, and even after they tore them down, the City's never been the same. Savarian was an Overseer, Mankala. And he sacrificed himself for his—whatever twisted *cause* that his ilk have.'

Alvar had been shifting in his seat throughout Marwana's words. Now, in the silence that she left, he spoke.

'But if there's a way out these Overseers know, then—then they can find Mithila.'

'Find her?' Marwana said. 'They probably already have. What Mithila did—what you all did—was the most serious breach of the experiment's conditions in all our history. They're going to hunt her down beyond.'

'Oh, Builders! Will they—?'

'She's good at staying alive, that one,' Marwana said gently. 'Bit like her father, that way.'

A breath passed between them. Mankala shifted in her chair.

'You need to get out, don't you?' she said. '*We* need to get out.'

'We've been looking for the Road for centuries,' said Marwana. 'But how can we find it, unless we find *them*?'

'You can't,' said Mankala, 'unless they reveal themselves.'

Alvar saw a look pass between Marwana and Mankala, a look of sudden understanding.

Mankala nodded slightly.

'I come from the Eleventh, Leader,' she said. 'From the Farmers' Mandala. We have a story there, for the fields: of Garuda, who flew too close to the sun, and of Samati, who lost his wings to protect him.'

'We remember,' Marwana said, 'much too well. There was a time when that story was too popular. Too many people thought they could fly.'

'They're hunting me, Leader,' said Mankala. 'And I can be Garuda. Not to chase the sun, but to draw her out. Fly close, but not close enough.'

'Wait—fuck, no,' Alvar interrupted. 'You're not sacrificing yourself, Mankala.'

She turned to him and gave his arm a quick squeeze. 'Of course not, Alvar. I like being alive too much to sacrifice myself. I'm just bait. Flint for fire.'

'I would not ask this of anyone,' said Marwana. 'That parable does not end well.'

'You don't have to,' said Mankala. 'Look around you, Leader. The sky turns red. The Matriarch's brought back Ostracism. The Watch is arming. In the Farmers' Circle, the Union rises again. In what's going to come, they could end the experiment if they wanted, kill us all. If there was a time to take a chance, it's now. You know that if they've come after me before, they'll come again—and that's when you catch them.'

'I'm going to give you security anyway,' said Marwana. 'You won't know they're there, but they will be. We have long practice in making ourselves invisible when we wish. But you, Mankala—don't be rash. Don't go *looking* for them, please.'

Mankala shrugged. 'And oh, Leader, speaking of which: I thought you should know. Tefnakth is dead.'

Marwana didn't flinch. 'That took longer than we expected,' she said.

'Wait, so he—wasn't one of yours?' Mankala stammered. 'A double-agent? We thought he was betraying the Shoortans for your side.'

'What, Tefnakth?' Marwana scoffed. 'Of course not. We think that he was one of the Overseers, but became a renegade.'

'Oh!' said Mankala. She paused. 'Leader, last question. Who are the Three Kings?'

Marwana smiled. 'Come, let me show you.'

Once more Rama stepped into Konar Hall, with its high roof, and lambent dust rising underneath her feet to dance in thin, sun-pierced clouds. Once more the Union members were waiting for her behind the table, faces carved into silence.

'Well?' asked Prana, before she could sit.

'The time was not right,' Rama said.

'We gave you instructions, *speaker*.'

'You asked me,' said Rama, 'to be the Speaker for the Eleventh. I do not take orders from you, I *represent* you.'

'We asked for a Bill—'

'That I drafted.' She withdrew the sheaf of paper from her pocket and placed it on the table. 'Then I went into a Council that voted to uphold Ostracism by a huge majority, because they were terrified. What do you think they would have done to your Bill, Prana-Eleven?' She looked around her, at the faces that were creasing into uncertainty. 'You know it. They would have thrown it out, marked you enemies—enemies of the Shoortans, of the Elders, of the *Circles*. Your Union would have been smashed before it could begin. Is that what you want?'

'Do you think,' said Prana, 'that we are afraid of the Shoortans?'

'No,' said Rama, 'but I think that you underestimate their power. Tell me, Prana-Eleven: how many of you will dare face Ostracism?' She heard little indrawings of breath across the table. 'How many will dare to care for those who are?' she continued. 'What will you do if the sky goes red again? Tell me that your Farmers' Union will hold, Prana-

Eleven. Promise me that the Eleventh and the Twelfth will stand as one, and I will go back to the Forum now and call a special session this night for your Bill. But if not, then let me do my job.'

'*How* dare—' Prana spluttered out, but Meghana cut in. 'She's right.'

'Dead on, in fact,' she continued, before Prana could speak. 'The Shoortans have been around for centuries. We were born last week. What are we going to offer people, the memory of the Union from three hundred years ago?'

'The harvest—'

'Not enough, man. Look, for this to work, our people need to see how the Wall *is* the reason for what's happening to us. We thought this Bill would be the first step—to break all this bloody reverence around the Wall. Then we could start talking—about everything: the farming quota, the shit wages. But how do we begin when Ostracism hangs over us?'

'So what are we going to do then,' Prana grumbled. 'The Matriarch and the Shoortans can stretch this out forever, this *balance-balance* thing. We're stuck. And if we don't have anything to show to our people, why will they trust the Union?'

'You can't go it alone anymore,' said Rama.

'Right,' said Prana. 'And which Circle will come stand with us?'

Rama smiled. 'Pull up another chair, will you?' She turned to the door, and called out: 'You can come in now.'

The door was thrown open, and Maji stood silhouetted against the light.

Prana's eyes widened. Nobody spoke.

Unhurried, Maji approached them. The occasional beam of sunlight glanced off her silver hair.

'The chair?' Rama repeated.

Prana almost jumped to attention, and dragged a chair from the corner of the hall, just as Maji reached the table.

'Greetings to the Producers' Organised Union of the Mandalas—or should I say, the POUM,' Maji said. She placed her right fist against her forehead, then extended it in a sixty-degree angle from her elbow.

Prana started. 'That's the old Union salute!'

'Well caught.'

'Greetings to—I'm sorry, who are you?' asked Meghana.

'My name is Maji,' she sat. 'Maji-Fifteen.'

The air between them hardened.

'Dooma?' someone asked.

'Dooma,' Maji replied.

'And what does the Dooma want here?' said Prana.

'*Alora*,' said Maji, her voice ringing out. '*We will carry the memory of your name like a hot iron beneath the tongue*. We remember, Eleven. We remember more than any of the Mandalas. The creation of the Circles, the myth of Malan, and the fall of Alora. We remember what the Shoortans did to us. And now that the Wall is breached, we will break their power: this side or *that*.'

'That's all well and good,' said Meghana, 'but what are you doing here?'

'I'm told you could use some help.'

'Why, what do you have to offer?' said Prana.

'Power,' said Maji. 'You cannot get what you want as long as the Shoortans have control, as long as Ostracism looms over anyone who dares question the Wall. Until today, you thought you could use the Council. But now you know, Council and Shoortan, they're just two branches of the Rasa that flow away and towards, an eternal circle. You have one option: confront them, power against power, upon the street. We know how this works. We've seen before. We can help.'

Prana fidgeted with his hands upon the table. 'You want violence, like Savarian did,' he said dully. 'What if it's not worth it? What if we don't want to choose with our lives—'

'Then they will choose for you,' Maji said. 'They always have. Now that you have shown your hand—*POUM*—once they're done shadow-fighting each other, they will join and come after you. This window that opened when the Wall was crossed—it will close forever, because you'll have had your chance, you'll have let it go, and they will have no fear of you, because they know you can't do anything. They will crush you. Forget the Wall. Tighter farmland quotas. Wages at their whim. Your Union a sad joke. Did you really think it would be so easy?'

Prana's eyes flashed. 'Of course not. But violence—'

'Can't always help it.'

'Spoken like someone who has nothing to lose,' muttered a man from the corner of the table. Rama stiffened. Meghana brought her hand down on the table. 'That is *not* how we speak to guests here. I'm sorry, Maji-Fifteen, that was—'

'Twenty-seven years ago, we lost a Revolution,' Maji said.

Gasps ran across the table.

'*You*,' said Prana slowly, 'are the Unforgiven. Savarian's guard.'

'We are who we are,' said Maji.

Meghana was the first to recover. 'No offence, Maji-Fifteen,' she said, 'and no judgment either, but if this is going to be a fight against the Shoortans, no Mandala will stand with us if we ally with the Unforgiven.'

'Let me answer you,' said Maji. 'Twenty-seven years ago, a man from the Eleventh told me a story: the story of Garuda and Samati.'

A hush descended upon the hall.

'He asked me what I thought it meant. I said to him: if you want to fly, someone must sacrifice themselves for you. And so he did.

'His name was Rahul-*Eleven*.'

A sharp movement. Meghana was looking at Maji as though she was seeing her for the first time.

'And just before he died in a rain of Council arrows—arrows that were meant for me—he said to me: *remember Samati. Remember me.* I have never forgotten. I remember the day a man of the Eleventh gave his life so that a woman of the Fifteenth could have a chance to live, and it did not matter, Dooma or Unforgiven, because it was a revolution. And I say to you: in the day the Wall lies broken, it will not matter if there *is* a revolution. Come and make it with us.'

Meghana stood. Her hands gripped the edges of the table.

'Rahul-Eleven was my father,' she whispered, her voice trembling. 'We never got his body. You must tell me everything. *Please*?'

'I will. In time,' Maji said gently. 'There is so much to tell.'

Bodies shifted around the table. 'Alright,' said Prana, 'We obviously can't take any decision here, the six of us. We'll need time.'

Outside the hall, a commotion broke out. It crawled through the windows and into their ears: footsteps, thumps, the calls of people.

'We have no more time,' said Rama.

A knock upon Rama's office door.

Sweat—noise—blood—in her mind.

'Come in,' she calls.

It is a Messenger. She looks at him, heavy-eyed. 'Yes?'

'Special session of the Council. Now.'

Rama stands. A thought strikes her. 'Have you been around to Councillor Malati's yet?'

'No, but she's on my beat.'

'When you get there, I'd like you to deliver a separate message to her secretary.'

Rama walks up to the Messenger and whispers a few words into his ear. An eyebrow flickers, but he is too professional to ask her what she means. She drops the money into his pocket.

Once he is gone, Rama walks back to the desk. She pulls open the only drawer.

It is there, the gleaming dagger that has been passed down in their family, Elder to Elder, for a time of crisis; and a roll of thread next to it.

She withdraws it from the sheath. The blade shines. She runs her fingers lightly down the edge. It is as sharp as the last time Amrit had made her practice. She sheathes it and slips it up her sleeve, strapping it with the thread like he'd taught her.

She calls a quick farewell to her mother, who is up in the chamber, and steps out. One of the members of the Watch is standing at the gate. The other—

'Where's Chana?' she asks.

The Watchman looks uneasy. 'He left an hour ago—didn't tell me where he was going. Haven't seen him since.'

'Can't wait for him. Come on, let's go.'

She strides out into the street. In minutes, she's at the Forum, part of a long queue of Elders. There is an entire cohort of the Watch standing guard, swords drawn.

They enter, hurry down the passageway, and into the Great Hall.

In moments, everybody is seated. Hansa rises.

'The Councillor Raja has called this special session. Councillor, you may speak.'

Her voice is weary, so weary.

Raja stands. For the first time, he is subdued.

'I regret to inform this Council,' he says, 'of an unfortunate event that occurred earlier today on the Maliot, near the Eleventh. There was a posting of the Watch on the bridge, by my orders. They were doing standard checks. And there was a congregation of Shoortans who—I am told—objected. Things escalated. Unfortunately, one of the Watch drew …'

'Bloody Builders, Raja!' Hansa does not address him as "Councillor". 'Did we not agree that only the flats would be used?'

'I'm aware,' says Raja stiffly. 'I take full responsibility. But what is done is done. I regret to inform the Council that one of the Shoortan High Priests is dead.'

A chill silence descends upon the hall. At her seat, Hansa's head is in her hands, as if she no longer cares about acting the part. Rama shuts her eyes.

Hansa raises her gaze to the hall. Her face is pale.

'This is,' she says, 'a complication.' Rama could laugh.

'I will speak to the Temple, on behalf of the Council,' Hansa continues. 'But first, I must offer our apologies to Councillor Rastogi, the Temple's representative-in-Council. Councillor Rastogi, I—' She stops, looking around.

'Where,' she says, 'is the Councillor Rastogi?'

Ten

The Maidan

There was a bamboo stick.

It was pushed into the ground. Its thin shadow extended upon the furrowed field, matching its length. At one point on the shadowline, a twig marked the spot.

'What are you doing?' Mithila said.

Bent over, tracing a line from the twig along the shadow, Dhara did not reply. The summer sun blazed down upon them, making Mithila squint. The Wall was a pen-sketch in the background.

Dhara dropped another twig a foot from the shadow-tip. She straightened. Mithila saw her place her left foot on the first twig, and her right foot on the second.

Dhara turned to her, still standing like that.

'North,' she said.

Her eyes were shining.

'What?'

'My body turns to the North.'

'Um, yes?' said Mithila. She cast a look around once, to make sure that this wasn't some bizarre test. The Towers of Rebirth were to her right—the map of Sumer was in her head—and yes, that meant Dhara had her back to the Rasa.

'North!' Dhara repeated, looking at her intently, as if she expected a reaction.

'I know! So?'

Dhara pushed a strand of hair out of her eyes, a familiar gesture. 'Don't you see?'

'I see a bamboo stick, I see you standing here, I hear you saying 'North, North', like you've invented directions! What, Dhara?'

'Uff.' Dhara huffed. 'Mithila. Wallrise is from the East. Or rather, East is what we call where Wallrise happens.'

'Yes?'

'So as the sun travels from Wall to Wall, East to West, shadows will travel the other way. And if we want to know where North is, we follow the path of the shadow.'

Mithila's eyes began to glaze. 'Dhara, we *know* what North is!'

'We do? Go on, tell me what North is.'

'North is—' she began mechanically, 'North is what you face when the quarries are to your right, like now. North is when you stand at right angles to the Rasa's flow, when your back is to the Mandalas and the farms are before you. North is—'

'Full marks, well done. Now tell me North without naming anything of Sumer.'

'What?' It was as if her mind was pushing up against something opaque. 'That makes no sense—we understand—'

'Don't you see what I've done?' Dhara said softly. She gestured at the stick, the shadow, and the twigs. 'This is North—everywhere. This is North not—not in the terms of Sumer. You see? When there is no Rasa, no Forum, no *Wall*—this will still be North. Always.'

Mithila struggled with the concept. 'North everywhere, always,' she said slowly, running her tongue around the unfamiliar combination of words. They made her dizzy, as if behind them there was something too large to contain. 'And we need this …'

Dhara smiled.

'When we go chase the sun.'

We'll still chase the sun.

Mithila sat upon the floor, hugging her knees, her face buried in her chest. She raised her head. Dhara's container hovered above her.

'Why didn't you wait for me, you idiot?' Mithila whispered.

A year had not changed Dhara. It could have been the morning after they had last met. There was her wiry dark hair framing her cheekbones, her pursed lips half-curious, half-mocking, her fingers locked together. But it was her eyes that Mithila remembered most, the eyes that were never at rest—and those eyes were closed.

Mithila's heart ached.

'You could've waited,' she repeated. 'We'd have done this together. Out in that forest, you would have measured shadowlines and taken me North to find the sea. And you'd have been writing it all down, discovering the design of this world, altering it with every new thing we found—*find*—Dhara, *we still can.*'

She struggled to her feet, and pressed her nose against the cold, hard surface.

She noticed for the first time that Dhara was dressed in a plain cotton smock that reached to her knees. Her feet were bare. There was the faintest hint of bluish light around her body.

'Who took your sandals away?' The thought sent little tendrils of anger creeping through her. 'Did they drag you here? Did you fight them, Dhara? I bet you did. I bet you hurt them. Tell me you hurt them.'

She ran her hands along the sides of the container, this time more carefully, looking for a gap, a crack, a lever, a handle—but found only a surface barren in its smoothness.

Shards of memories came rushing back into her, as she looked at Dhara's face: evening in the Forum, the light of Wallset gleaming upon the towers, and Dhara saying, '*just tell me what it will be like. The moment … the moment when we see true at last.*'

The knot in her throat loosened into tears. Mithila felt herself smile. 'Dhara, won't you laugh if you knew,' she said, 'that when the moment came, I closed my eyes and saw nothing? You'd laugh, and I'd be embarrassed, and—please laugh at me now, Dhara—*please.*'

She felt her cheeks wet again.

'No,' she said. 'This is not going to be the end. I'm going to find the person who did this to you, and drag them back here to undo it.'

And with that, the diary from the Council Hall floated into her mind.

I've had to leave Dhara behind.

There's work to be done back home.

'Home,' Mithila whispered, 'They left you here and went back *there*.'

She swallowed. There was a weight in her chest, as if *smara* had just invited itself in again. The Wall floated before her, and the image of Sumer in circles that she had seen with Rama from the Council Tower, and Mithila suddenly felt like somebody was choking her.

'There was a world to discover,' she said to Dhara, suddenly angry all over again. 'I had just started to see. Find new words. Create a language. And now?'

There was no answer.

'Wait for me,' she said through clenched teeth. 'Don't you go anywhere.' One last time, she flung her arms around the sarcophagus, willing herself to feel Dhara through it, to believe that she stirred.

Then she stepped back. 'Sorry,' she said, 'but I'm going to have to take your light, Dhara. I need it.'

Mithila plucked the Heartstone out of the air. There was a moment when it sent a tingling through her arms, making her hair stand on end. Holding it in front of her, she let its light shine into the corners of the room, and spotted the passageway where she knew it would be. Mithila walked over to it, leaving the container—and the room behind her—in steadily growing darkness.

She took one last look behind her, at the container floating in the air, and the sleeping figure inside it. 'Wait for me,' she repeated.

Then Mithila began to walk down the ramp, Heartstone held in front of her, lighting up her way into the depths of Gumfraude.

'... stubborn, block-headed conservatism,' Malati was saying. Rama had never seen her so angry. 'And the Council refusing to see past its own nose. Had you not given in to the blackmail that was Ostracism—like I *begged* you—we wouldn't today be in this—'

'Do you have a point?' Hansa cut in, tired. 'Any solution, other than I-told-you-so?'

'I'm only stating facts,' Malati replied, cold. 'If you actually thought the Citizens would protect us, *this* Council, after we murdered Sanchika in coldly blood, then—'

The door crashed open, and one of the Watch dashed in.

Malati's words died on her lips.

'President Hansa, Councillors,' a half-gasp, half-shout from the floor, that carried up to all of them. 'The Shoortans—marching on the Forum—huge crowd. They just crossed into the First.'

'How many?' snapped Hansa. It seemed that she was relieved at having something to do at last.

'A few hundred—mainly the Middle Circles. Just like the last mob.'

Hansa jerked into action. 'Get your men into defensive formation around the Hall. Make a wall. Swords out, but you *will not* use them unless attacked. We need some time to decide.'

The Watchman did not reply.

'What is it?' Hansa said. 'Was I unclear?'

The Watchman swallowed.

'Speak, man!'

'President Hansa—I'm sorry, but—half the guards from the Forum have joined the Shoortans, and a lot of the others just ... left. There are fewer than fifty of us in the Plaza right now.'

'And how many marching on us?'

'At least six hundred.'

Rama saw Hansa grip the bars of the dock, as if for support.

'Thank you,' she said, her voice like ash. 'I will go out and meet them.'

Raja jumped up. 'President—no! Remember the mob at the trial?'

Hansa gave him a look. 'You've done enough damage for today, haven't you, Councillor?'

Raja sat, face purple. Hansa swept the Hall with her gaze. 'I will go out,' she said, calmer.

As the silence stretched like a string on the point of snapping, Marwana rose to break it. 'I will come with you, President. This is a crisis. And if the Select can help now, we will.'

Hansa nodded. She came down from the dock, and met Marwana at the floor of the Great Hall. They walked out together.

The first sound of marching footsteps came, piercing through the thick walls of the Council Hall.

A stiff breeze whipped their hair and cloaks back, and sent ripples along the Rasa. 'Give way,' said Hansa, to the few members of the Watch who had stayed. They parted, and Hansa saw the mob rise.

They were entering the Plaza in waves from the First Mandala, holding up great red banners painted with the Shoortan Circle, the first time Hansa had ever seen such a thing. At the front, four men held a bier upon their shoulders. Behind them, people came in with hard faces, carrying tapering bamboo blades, sticks or staffs, and some even had—Hansa drew breath—swords, glinting in the sun.

The line was disciplined, walking in step, almost a formation. *Not a mob,* a part of her registered. *They are led.*

At the head marched Minakshi and Rastogi.

Ten metres from her, they halted. The marchers stopped behind them, without breaking formation. *Almost,* Hansa thought, *almost as if they'd been drilled.*

Minakshi broke the silence. 'President Hansa,' she said, her voice harsh. 'We come for reparations.'

'The Council acknowledges and regrets what happened,' Hansa said. 'We will determine the facts, and in accordance with our laws—'

'No,' Minakshi said, 'that will not do.'

A dense silence hung between them. Behind Hansa, the Watch was standing together, a thin line.

'If you have specific demands, Matriarch,' said Hansa, 'then within the framework of our laws, we can meet and—'

'No, President Hansa,' Minakshi said coolly, interrupting her a second time. 'I don't think you understand what's happening here.'

Hansa shot a quick glance behind Minakshi. The faces that looked back at her were still.

'Sumer has changed forever,' Minakshi said. 'The balance is shattered. The first time when the Wall was breached. The second time today, when your Watch murdered a High Priest of the Wall.'

'You had Baku killed!' came a shout from the crowd.

'Yes, they did,' Minakshi agreed. 'And you, President, are responsible. Your Council was asked to ban the group that set itself against the Wall. You did not. Instead, you set up checkpoints with armed Watchmen around the City, to harass us—and finally killed a Shoortan. *You* have broken the balance, President Hansa. You and your Council.'

'We kept the laws,' Hansa said.

'You *made* those laws. There are others. Do you remember the Compact? Do you remember Taraf?'

Hansa drew herself up to her full height. 'Are you threatening the Council?'

'It's not a threat anymore, President.'

Hansa turned from Minakshi. She cast a gaze across the front line of the people, letting it pass from face to face, before coming to linger upon one of them.

She locked gazes with him, but addressed them all. 'So quiet, Citizens?' Out of the corner of her eye she saw Minakshi fold her arms and regard her with a lazy half-smile. 'Are you for this blackmail, this bullying of your lawgivers?' Hansa continued. 'Does the Matriarch speak for all of you? You, Rudeer-Eight. Look at me. I know you. You're an honest man of the Eighth. You do an honest day's work, making our boats. You've come all this way, surely you came with something to say?'

Rudeer did not flinch. 'We stand with the Matriarch,' he said shortly. 'And I don't make the boats. I keep them afloat.'

A rattle of agreement shook through the mob. Hansa betrayed no change in expression. 'That answers exactly half a question. I asked you many more.'

'Let *me* answer,' said someone two voices to Rudeer's left. Hansa found her gaze travelling, before coming to rest upon a younger woman, who had streaks of grey in her hair. She was dressed in brown. The brown of the Watch.

Hansa's fists clenched. She kept her voice even. 'Go on then, Niri-Six. You who swore an oath to serve. I'm listening.'

Niri looked unperturbed. 'You stand there, President, you look so surprised. You think you know all ends, you know what's best, that your judgment will never go wrong. You forget that we watch you, we see your mistakes, we see your refusal to accept when you were wrong. You were wrong about the Builders, about the Wall, and every time you've been wrong, they've sent us warnings, they've changed the colour of the sky—and you've only grown more stubborn—and finally today, you fell to violence. You think *you* are the Builders, President, that you'll decide what you want and we'll follow. We don't want leaders like that.'

'You—*what?*' Momentarily, Hansa lost her grip. She took two steps forward, towards the line of people.

A spear came sailing through the air.

Hansa leapt back, stumbled, and fell over, her legs waving in the air. The spear struck the ground a foot from her and buried itself in the grass, its handle quivering.

Raucous laughter rose from the crowd.

Her elbows stung painfully. Hansa struggled to her feet, feeling tears of rage and shame prick the ends of her eyelids. Beside her, Marwana had not moved.

Minakshi, who had decorously looked away while Hansa found her bearings, now walked forward and plucked the spear from the ground.

'The time for blustering' she said, her voice ringing in the Plaza, 'is over. President, look around you. You have set yourself against the

Builders, against the Heartstone. You insult the faith of the people, and you killed one of us, one of theirs. We gave your people care when you gave them laws. Sumer has responded. Can you feel their anger, President? Do you know what it can do?'

Silence fell again.

Hansa stared down at the grass, Niri's words swirling in her head.

It was Marwana who spoke.

'Tell us what you want, Matriarch.'

'Not very much,' said Minakhi. 'We don't want to rule Sumer. We only ask that the balance be restored, that was shattered once—twice—by your hand. That hand will need to be held, if only for a moment. To see, and for it to be seen, that if one swings too far, another holds it back.'

'When you say *held*, Matriarch,' Marwana said quietly, 'do you mean *tied*?'

'We can talk about that. We're confident that the Council has learnt, and will no more insult the Builders.' Minakshi's voice gentled.

Hansa looked up. 'We can talk—'

Before she could speak another word, Minakshi cut in, voice hardening again. 'But let one thing be clear: we will not treat with those who voted for the Young Tarafians and encouraged them to challenge the Wall. We will not treat with those who put swords on every street and took a Shoortan life. We will not treat with those who have blood on their hands.'

Silence fell between them.

'You want a coup,' Hansa said heavily.

'This is where I stand,' said Minakshi, 'and I have spoken for those who stand with me. I—'

A restless stirring had been passing through the crowd all this while, and now suddenly, it broke.

'Shoortan killers, down, down!'

'Shoortan killers, down, down!'

The chant passed from mouth to mouth, cohering into an indistinct roar, until all Hansa could hear was the word *down*, spoken in a hundred voices, to a hundred different rhythms, rending the air, entering her ears, shuddering within her.

For the first time in twenty-seven years, Hansa felt afraid.

With her back still to the crowd, Minakshi raised both arms. Silence came back slowly, like an ashamed child creeping home.

Minakshi looked at Hansa. 'How long,' she said conversationally, 'do you think I can hold them back?'

Hansa searched for the remnants of dignity.

'What do you want me to say?' she said, and heard her voice crack as she spoke. 'You give us no choices.'

'Is that really true, President?' Marwana asked softly. Hansa turned to her. 'There is one answer,' her voice was so quiet now that even Minakshi couldn't overhear.

For a moment, Hansa's brow furrowed. 'Ah.' She paused. '*That's* an answer?'

'It is one,' Marwana murmured. 'Whether it is the answer you want to give—'

Hansa nodded. She straightened. 'I will consult with the Council,' she said to Minakshi. 'I cannot'—she took a deep breath to still herself, to pacify something that was tearing at her throat—'I cannot answer you here. '

Minakshi smiled graciously. 'By all means,' she said. 'Take your time.'

As they turned from her, Hansa heard her voice one final time.

'But try not to take forever.'

Hansa stood at her place, high up in the centre of the Great Hall. She looked into the eyes of each of the Three Hundred. They looked back at her, waiting—waiting for something.

'Elders,' Hansa said, 'we have spoken with the Matriarch. This knot will not be untied. We have to slash it. I have come to a decision. I only ask that you let me finish what I have to say.'

Rama shivered.

'I have been President,' said Hansa, 'for twenty-seven years. You have always trusted me from the beginning. You called upon me when Anguli stumbled. A new President, in a time of conflict, of mutiny. I was young then, and untested. You could have made my task impossible. But you united behind me. We won, we smashed Savarian. So far we have always won.

'But now we are in peril, Elders. It is a peril of our own making. We have made mistakes. We must own them. *I* have made mistakes. I must atone. And you know our Democratic traditions offer a President only one path to atonement.'

Rama realized she was listening to a resignation speech. She cast a look around. The faces of the Council were schooled into careful silence.

'The President is First in the Council,' Hansa continued, 'because someone must be. But nothing more. Once we step into Council, all are deemed equally ready to take up the mantle.

'And that is why I will remind you of one thing more. In Council, we vote on everything—*but succession*. When a President chooses to lay down their burden, they select their successor, for stability, for continuity. The Council has never refused to ratify a President's choice.

'I hope this will not be the first time.'

The first stir, a great rustling of cloth, as people shifted in their seats.

'Here are my two decisions,' said Hansa, tonelessly. 'First, I resign as President.'

There was no reaction. She had given them time to prepare.

'Second,' said Hansa. 'My successor will be Rama-One.'

Rama reeled in her seat.

Hansa turned to her, catching her with her iron gaze. Every eye in the Council was upon her.

'Does anyone,' said Hansa, 'have any questions?'

After a moment, the Councillor Varsha, Farmland Administrator and effective second in command, rose. Rama held her breath.

'My President,' Varsha said. 'On behalf of the Council, I must ask: is this your final position?'

'It is.'

'On both counts?'

'Yes.'

'There is no chance of you reconsidering—or delaying—at least until this crisis passes?'

'None.'

'I am satisfied, then.' Varsha sat.

Things were moving too quickly. Rama's legs were iron, and her stomach sloshed like water in a bath-bucket.

'Why are you doing this, President Hansa?' Raja said from across the Hall.

The President looked at Raja, strangely.

'Because,' she said, pronouncing every syllable, 'we need to survive.'

Fuck, Rama's heart raced. *Minakshi.* Behind the masks of inscrutability, she sensed the Elders calculating.

The Councillor Paras of the Second Mandala stood. 'May I ask,' he said, 'if the Leader of the Select was party to this decision?'

Marwana rose. 'No,' she said, 'The President's decision is her own. But the Select will work to the best of its ability, and its goodwill, with—President Rama—to solve this crisis, if such be the decision of the Council.'

President Rama.

Marwana looked around the Hall. 'The Select do not intervene in the politics of the City,' she went on, 'and sometimes that lets us see clear. Permit me to make an observation. Three days ago, you voted down Councillor Malati's farmland Bill. May I suggest that you would not have been in this desperate pass had you accepted one, just one, of the compromises that it offered? One compromise that would have ensured that when this moment came, you would not stand alone?'

At her seat, Malati had her eyes closed.

'On that day, Councillor Rama spoke for the Bill, in just these pragmatic terms. With respect, Council, it is not always about long years of experience. Sometimes, it is a rare blessing to come at a problem with fresh eyes, unburdened by habit.'

Nobody spoke.

'A second thing,' said Marwana. 'This City is cleverer than you think, Elders. They know what you say. They know what you think. And they judge you.

'The Councillor Rama has not told you this yet: but after that vote, on her first day, the Eleventh asked her to be their Speaker. You know what that means—what it *could* mean for you, at a time when you need every bit of support you can find. Consider well, Elders, where power lies. You're good at that. I have spoken.'

In the silence that rushed in to fill Marwana's words, Rama realized that she had been offered a way out. To graciously decline, because she had committed to the Eleventh, a commitment that Maliot's democracy did not allow her to renege on. And the Eleventh was relying on her, their only voice …

'Any more questions?' said Hansa.

There were none.

'Very well then. I formally propose my successor to the Council: Rama-One will be the next President. If anyone objects, we shall go to vote. Are there any objections? Speak now.'

There was nothing. Hansa waited. Then she asked again, 'for the second time: does anyone object? Speak now.'

Again, silence. Out of the corner of her eye, Rama saw some of the Elders lean back in their seats.

'One final time, I ask you,' Hansa said. 'Does anyone object? Speak now.'

I'm twenty-one, she almost screamed out. *How can you do this to us? To me?*

'It is done,' said Hansa. She turned to Rama. 'Rama-One,' she said, her voice gentle. 'You may refuse. Many have, in the past. None will judge you for it. But if you accept, it must be of your free will and with full knowledge of all that it will bring you. No rest, no peace, little power, all responsibility. Will you lead?'

She waited.

'Will you lead?'

Rama stood on unsteady feet, as though a whiff of air would dislodge her, send her floating over the hall and out into Sumer.

'I will lead.'

'*I'm sorry,*' Hansa whispered, as they stepped out into the Plaza together.

Which was not, Rama reflected as she saw the mob for the first time, a particularly promising start.

As they got within earshot of Minakshi and her followers, Hansa wasted no words.

'It is done,' she said. 'We have chosen a new leader for these times, for harmony and for balance. Rama-One joined our Council two days ago. She is untainted by our two mistakes. We have given you what you asked for. And now we ask you to show an equal grace. Let this end here.'

There was a moment of quiet. Then Minakshi inclined her head. 'We will talk.'

'I yield to the President-Elect,' Hansa said. She stepped back, motioning to Rama.

Her own legs took her forward, unbidden. Rama tried not to stumble. Minakshi walked to her, calm and assured. They met in the centre, alone.

Minakshi smiled. 'President in just three days, huh?'

'Three days in which you won absolute power in Sumer,' Rama replied. 'Was it so easy?'

'Some parts.' Minakshi leaned forward and whispered, 'Like making you President.'

Rama was suddenly aware of the knife beneath her sleeve.

It would take a moment …

'I'd rather you didn't,' said Minakshi.

Rama looked at her.

'Unless you think that the President killing the Matriarch will give you what you want,' Minakshi said lightly. 'In that case, go on.'

'What do I want?' said Rama. Her right hand lingered around her elbow.

'You want to remake the broken world.'

Rama's hand went limp.

'I don't want your power, Rama,' Minakshi continued, her voice soft. '*Something of equality is yet to come* ... I don't want to stand in your path.'

'Then what do you want?'

'Just my own shot at remaking this broken world. Like you.'

Rama gritted her teeth. 'Yes, but what do you want from *me*? From the Council?'

'Not here, not now,' said Minakshi. 'We'll meet in the Temple tonight. Congratulations on the new job, Rama—my President.'

She turned to leave.

'One thing,' said Rama.

Minakshi paused.

'You didn't know. At Carnival. That the sky would turn red.'

Minakshi's face was carved out of rock. 'Yes, well,' she murmured. 'Right place. Right time. Sometimes that's all it takes.' Then she was gone.

'Well done, President-Elect,' a low voice came. She turned. Marwana was standing beside her.

'I haven't done anything.'

'You took the job. Not many would, with all this.'

'Not at all,' Rama quipped. 'Always wanted to be President one day.'

They started walking back.

'The Council did not look too happy about it,' Rama continued.

'The Council has been doing this for years,' said Marwana. 'They understand power, Rama. They'll do what you tell them. For now.'

'What do I do?'

'I don't know, you're the President,' Marwana said. 'I can only tell you what I've seen. Hansa—she needed to break Savarian for them to trust her, to follow her. It won her three decades of peace.' She saluted Rama smartly. 'If you need anything from the Select, ask. You know our constraints, but'—her voice lowered, 'I will do what I can. You know that too.'

Rama nodded. 'Thank you, Leader Marwana.' She paused. 'Tell me something. If I ought to ask you one question, what would it be?'

Marwana's eyes gleamed. 'I would ask about the Select's Protocol.'

Rama nodded. She glanced back. The Shoortans had not yet moved. She reached the doors of the Council Hall where Hansa stood, waiting for her, away from Marwana.

'Well?'

'She wants to negotiate tonight. At the Temple.'

'They'll cage us here till then. A show of power.'

'Yes,' said Rama, 'but also so that *she* can tell the City that you've been stepped down.'

Something like respect appeared in Hansa's eyes. 'Yes,' said the former President. 'That too.'

'Will you help me?' Rama said.

'All that I can do,' Hansa said. Her fingers were tightly entwined. 'This wasn't how I wanted it to be. But I suppose Anguli didn't either, until the Mutiny. And then it was.' She looked into the distance. 'Sometimes the lamp is taken from you before you can pass it on. I can advise you how to hold the light in the wind, but you'll have to carry it yourself, Rama.'

Rama turned back to the Council Hall. 'Come then,' she said, 'Councillor.'

Hansa flinched.

From the beginning, Mithila had known that Sumer's Forum was built in the reflection of Gumfraude. And that meant that Dhara's room would yield to the underground passage that connected its towers.

She walked that passage now, the Heartstone lighting her way. The light she had taken, to leave Dhara in the dark.

A year ago, on a cold autumn evening in the Forum, she had listened to Dhara speak the story of Garuda and Samati: one who gave up his wings so that the other could chase the sun.

Remember Samati, Dhara had said.

She remembered. How could she not, when those lineaments of loss limned her own life in much the same way? In darkness underground, Garuda had given himself up, searching for the light, and the horizon, *their* horizon, more Samati than his own namesake. In the sweat and heat and brittle noise of the Forum, Ananta had given himself up for Sumer, a Samati burning his wings to shield the idea of a revolution.

Sometimes it had been for her.

In a dim room of the Academy, Rama had read a curt note addressed to her, and walked quietly into the night. On the Maliot Road, Lamon had thrown himself into the river—and thrown away a future—to clear her path to the Wall. Each time she had asked, and each time it had been given to her, uncomplainingly. And now, without asking, she had left Dhara alone in the dark to light up her own way back.

She was Garuda, her wings unsinged, while Samatis around her burnt up and fell to earth.

Perhaps the lesson is that some of us know how to burn.

Ahead of her, the passage forked. On a prayer she took the broader road.

Deep in her pocket, she knew there were those scraps of paper that had told her to fly, no matter what she was leaving behind, the words that would now tell her not to mourn for those who had burned. Savarian's missives.

The Rebel lives for no one, least of all for themselves. The Revolution will have your heart—all of it—or it will have none of you.

But here again, she knew now, her father had been wrong.

She turned her mind back to the parable. Why did it end? Why did it suggest that it was Garuda's fate to forever circle the sky over a Wall-bound world, looking down upon a memory of ash, a gift of wings weighed down by unending remorse? Was there no better use for such a gift, asked and freely given?

And some of us to make sure that they burned for something.

'I'm coming back,' she said, hearing her voice rebound off the walls. 'I'm coming back to earn my wings.'

The passage opened into an empty chamber, shorn of blue light, floating containers, or the voices of Samir and Ghada. Gumfraude's pale shadow in Sumer housed its masters, and here there was emptiness. Mithila cursed, and retraced her steps.

She clutched the Heartstone tighter as she walked. Its throbbing light reminded her of its companion in the Temple, that she had reached out to touch just before there had been a hand on her shoulder, turning her away. There was Minakshi, who had taken, would take more, who would erect a tower of ash and say that she had rebuilt the broken world. And Minakshi would be there.

She came back to the fork. Mithila took the second path, the final path. She walked.

Mankala sat in her usual chair in Malati's study, leaning back. Alvar sat across from her, swivelling around in the Councillor's seat, chomping on a plate of *khire*.

'Oh, stop it,' Mankala said. 'You know you're not supposed to be sitting there anyway.'

The Elder had welcomed them in without even a raised eyebrow at Alvar, but had left for the Council Hall, telling them to make themselves at home. Alvar had immediately called for *khire*—and they'd brought it for him too.

'What are you, Rastogi? *That's not allowed!*' he mimicked the High Priest. 'Let me, for once in my life, enjoy this, no?' He rocked in the chair. 'Oh, is that oil they've put in the joint, to let it swivel? Imagine that, Mankala: to be able to afford oil for *chairs*.'

'You'll break that if you're not careful,' said Mankala.

'Pfft,' said Alvar rudely, but subsided.

'Okay, now that I have your attention,' Mankala said, 'help me think through this. What do we know so far, Alvar? We know that we are an experiment. We know that the Overseers—the descendants of the Builders—are here in this City, to keep the experiment going. We know that they've burned down Sumer to wipe away memory, and can do it again. We know the Select are fighting them. And we know that one day the experiment will end. What we don't know: who they are, when they'll end it, and how.'

'Which are some rather basic things not to know. And we also don't know what *light from light* means,' Alvar added helpfully.

'All of which comes down to finding the Overseers first. Well, we know they're nervous. Nervous enough to murder Tefnakth. Nervous because Mithila's flight was not part of the plan, and now they're going after me. So what we need to do—'

A soft knock interrupted her. 'I'll get it,' Mankala said.

'I'll come with you,' Alvar rose.

When they opened the door, they found a Messenger outside. 'I bring word to you from Rama-One,' he said.

Mankala's brow furrowed. 'Go on.'

'She says: "*Dear Mankala, could you take my Bill back home? I'm afraid that the hosts of our last journey together have proven uncharitable.*"'

'Bill? Bill—*ah!*' said Mankala. 'Thank you very much.' She closed the door.

Alvar turned to her, confused. 'What did that mean?'

Mankala swung around to him. 'It means we have to leave, Alvar. Now. And run.'

'Where to?'

'Home. Eleventh Mandala.'

'I come from the Speaker,' Mankala panted.

At the long table, in Konar Hall, three people turned to them. Each of them was a face Alvar knew. In the centre was Maji. On the right, Carina. And on the left, Prana-Eleven.

The last of them spoke now. 'And?' Prana said.

'The Shoortans have surrounded the Council,' Mankala said.

A hubbub rose around the table.

Maji stood. 'I warned you,' she said tightly. 'While we negotiate, the Shoortans have already moved. Now, all of you, decide. If the Shoortans are unopposed before the day is done, if the Elders fall, tomorrow they will rule this City. And you won't be able to do anything about it. So, I say to you again: *decide*. Maybe you want no part of this. Maybe you want to back out. So be it—we'll all go home. But if you hold off now, if you sit here and argue with me about the Unforgiven, about Savarian, about alliances—they will come for you, and they will smash you. So what's it going to be?'

A tense silence filled the air.

Meghana spoke. 'We know we have to move, Maji. We've already called a Union muster after our morning's meeting. They should be coming together any time now, and we'll try to have this ratified at once.'

A snort of impatience escaped Maji, but she did not say anything.

'In the meantime,' Meghana said, 'what do you suggest?'

'It's too late to break the siege,' said Maji. 'Here is what we can do. The Matriarch has made a move. It needs legitimacy. She will have to convince the City. Tonight.'

'The Maidan!' Prana said.

'Yes,' said Maji. 'After the Elders bend, she will come to the Maidan. She will fill it with her own, but not everyone will be hers. We surprise the Shoortans there, we can break them in a street fight. She is projecting strength right now, but she doesn't have it yet.' She leaned towards the Union members, her fists on the table. 'My people can move now. They've been waiting twenty-seven years. They are ready, so ready. Will yours join?'

Prana nodded. 'We see it. We'll be with you, Dooma—as soon as we get this ratified.'

'You don't sit around for a damn vote with the Shoortans out on the streets!' Maji snapped.

'Oh, but we do,' Prana snapped back. 'And we damn well will. This is how POUM will work, Maji—every decision democratically taken. And if you don't like that—'

'Builders take you all, just be quick about it!'

'We will.' Prana was now looking at them directly. 'Thank you for this message,' he said. 'Tell the President that we have heard. Watch for us in the Maidan.'

The last crumb of *rahi* had been swallowed, the last sip of water squeezed from the bottle and into her throat. Her legs were chafed raw, making her wince with each step. Her arms, held out before her for hours, ached even with the weightlessness of the Heartstone. The darkness of the passage and the throbbing light in her hands blurred into each other, a canvas of shifting black and white. Mithila felt her eyes close. Walking blind was easier when the circular world had unravelled into a single straight line.

Through the dim veils that blanketed her vision, she concentrated until the dancing black dots resolved themselves into the outlines of Garuda and Dhara as she last remembered them in moments of gladness, the last evening by the fireside, before the Pit. They beckoned her onwards, retreating as she advanced, her steps in theirs.

Every other moment, little feelers of worry crept through the hallways of her mind, expecting the path to be blocked by that impassable black stone that they had once hurled their shovels against, on the other side, in another world. But arrow-straight, the road went on.

'Look, you were wrong,' she muttered to the outline before her, just out of her reach. 'North everywhere, but what's North when there's no sunlight or shadow—and can't be? I'm going to come back for you just so I can see you solve this problem.'

Then she heard the dull, roaring sound against the walls of the passage.

Instantly familiar, instantly known. And with it, a sudden urgency speared her mind. Gritting her teeth, squeezing back tears with each chafing step, Mithila ran.

At dusk, Alvar walked into the Maidan. There was nobody there.

Cautiously, he fingered the red-ochre cloth in his pocket. '*Keep a look-out in the Maidan*,' Maji had said, just as they were leaving. '*If something goes wrong—wave it. And when* you *see someone wave this from Maliot's statue—that's when things will get hot, so just get out of the way.*'

He passed beneath the statues of Maliot and Garlon. The Fifth surrounded him, blocking out the sun. Wallset was almost here.

He leaned against one of the plinths, keeping an eye on the empty stage, feeling exposed. Time dragged. There was deathly silence in the air, as if all Sumer had gone home, waiting for something.

As Wallset passed into twilight, he began to hear people.

They called to each other, a few streets beyond. The tread of footsteps, hurrying back and forth. *Thumps* upon the ground, the sound of things dragged along the streets. A rustling in the air that came from the Forum.

From the North, two men entered the Maidan. They were dressed in the uniform of the Eighth. They held sticks in their hands, tapered into sharp points. They advanced towards the Rostrum. One of them saw him, and quickly hid his stick behind his back.

'Who's there?' he challenged.

Alvar left the shadow of the statue. He made the sign of the Circle. 'Here for the Matriarch's speech.'

'You're early. She only left the Forum half an hour ago. At least another half hour to get here.'

Alvar spread out his arms. 'Best seats in the house.'

They laughed with him. Then they got busy with something near the Rostrum, and Alvar gratefully slipped back into the shadow.

A slow trickle of people began to enter the Maidan from all sides. Alvar waited a few moments longer. Once there were enough people for him to blend in, he slipped out and made his way towards the Rostrum. Behind him, the Maidan began to fill. Alvar looked around, trying to identify faces. The gathering darkness cloaked them: but again and again, he saw spears, and on occasion, moonlight glinting off a blade.

Bodies moved close together. The smell of sweat rose in the sky. Murmurs began to rise. Flame lamps bobbed above the heads of the people.

There was no red flag on Maliot's statue. Yet.

He heard a rhythmic noise approach, the beat of footsteps upon the ground, steps marching in time.

From the North, Minakshi entered the Maidan.

For an instant, the voices in the Maidan rose, and then dropped into a murmur. Rastogi walked behind Minakshi, and two priests alongside him. They were flanked by men whose faces were veiled in Shoortan flags (had his fathers stitched them last night?).

'Anytime now, Maji,' Alvar muttered.

Minakshi ascended the Rostrum. Rastogi did not follow her.

Looking down upon them all, she extended her arms, palms out. With her left hand, she made the sign of the Circle. The Maidan hushed.

'Greetings once more, Citizens,' she said. 'Three nights ago, we met by the Wall. And we talked.'

'*You did*,' Alvar muttered under his breath.

'I told you the balance was disturbed because the Wall had been breached.' *Yeah right.* 'I told you what the Heartstone said. And the sky answered me true.' *It did not.* 'Since then, we the Shoortans tried to restore that balance. But the Council … disagreed.'

Alvar held his breath. This was the moment. And there was no response from the Maidan, no objection, no questions.

Minakshi went on smoothly. 'But this morning, they went too far. The balance was torn when they murdered High Priest Baku.'

'*Elders' Council, down, down!*' someone shouted quickly, too quickly, seamlessly taking up Minakshi's lowering tone and raising it to a crescendo. Immediately, two others—conveniently positioned at different ends of the Maidan—joined in.

'*Elders' Council, down, down!*'

Minakshi raised a hand. 'I hear you now, and I heard you this morning. So we marched to the Council Hall. And then, a miracle happened: some of the Watch joined us. In the heart of every Citizen, there is—for ever lit—the flame of justice; and no law in this City can snuff that out.'

Little rivulets of conversation broke out across the Maidan. Minakshi didn't wait.

'President Hansa accepted the error of her ways. She has resigned.'

The rivulets swelled into gasps of shock, exclamations, expletives—and, from strategic places in the Maidan—cheers.

Nobody protested.

Nobody spoke for the Elders or for Hansa.

The second test that night. She passed it.

Minakshi went on, authority hardening around her.

'And now, listen to me. There is one other thing I must do, before this night is done. So we can heal, and renew.'

'Now what?' Alvar muttered, but Minakshi was speaking again.

'Three nights ago, by the Wall, we brought back Ostracism. We did so against our will. Punishment wounds us too, as it wounds the City. But these are extraordinary times.

'Any Ostracism must be proclaimed publicly to the City, so that none may deny knowledge of it. And so, I tell you: tonight is the first Ostracism in four hundred years.'

Her voice rose and deepened, as if it was pitched from the sky.

'For the tear that she made, which must be repaired; for the wound that she opened, which must be staunched; for the healing that needs a fever to burn the sickness away; for the City, that is emptier with her than without; I Ostracize the first to break the balance.'

'I Ostracize Mithila-Seven.'

Alvar choked.

'If Mithila-Seven comes back, she has no home among us. If you see her on the road, turn away. If she speaks to you, harden your ears, and if she weeps, lock your hearts. If her clothes are torn, she must wear the wind. If she hungers'—the pitch broke, for a moment so swift that Alvar might have imagined it, and then it was back—'she must live on air.'

A heavy instant, before she went on.

'And to anyone who shelters her: you will join her in the cold. So it must be, and so I have spoken.

'I Ostracize Mithila-Seven.'

His heart raced. Alvar craned his neck. The exits stayed empty, and Maliot's statue was bare.

All his life, Alvar thought, he had waited for someone who would never come.

Upon the Rostrum, Minakshi's hands were clasped together, and she was staring at her feet. When she raised her face again, in the glancing moonlight, he saw that her cheeks were wet.

'The Heartstone tells me,' she said, 'that the Builders will exact their own vengeance upon her, beyond the Wall. But when the balance is broken, we cannot stay silent.' Her voice softened, but still carried. 'I say to you, no longer as Matriarch, but one of you: she is my flesh, my blood, all that is left to me in this world. But I cannot leave this City broken to keep myself whole. I cannot have this wound open, just to spare myself the cut. She has left me with no choice. I do what I must.'

In the gathering silence, Alvar felt his heart lurch, as every moment of the Night of the Carnival repeated itself, as though time was a Circle because the Shoortans said so.

Not this time.

He laughed into the stillness.

Faces turned, eyes fixed him. Light-headed, Alvar strode up to the stage and leapt upon it.

'Lies,' he shouted. 'All lies, Minakshi.'

Minakshi turned to him in astonishment—and then her eyes grew cold. 'You—challenge your Matriarch?'

'First of all,' said Alvar, 'you're younger than me. And you've been jealous of Mithila since you were babies.'

Minakshi drew back as if she'd been slapped.

'Mithila,' Alvar called out above the heads of the crowd, 'crossed the Wall to show us that it could be done.'

Where are you, Maji? What am I even doing?

Minakshi's face was telling him: '*Don't make me do this to you.*' He ignored her.

'She's found the horizon.' (Did some heads snap up at that word?) 'And she's going to bring us back a world. What do you bring, Matriarch?' He laughed again.

There was a stir, but Minakshi was back.

'I don't bring,' she said, turning to the crowd. 'I keep. Dreams will not keep Sumer alive. But they can kill us. Here is another Tarafian. They have fought the Wall too long now. For the balance, this ends here.'

'*What* balance?' Alvar shot back. 'The one in your own head? That's not real, Minakshi.' *Maji's on her way.* 'But do you know what's real?' he went on. 'Our Six Freedoms. You forget that in Sumer, it is no crime to speak. So I say: we did right. She did right.'

'Is that what you believe, Tarafian?' Minakshi's voice was grey like leaf-fall. 'You have nothing to show for it. Because she left.'

'She did not—'

'Oh, but she did. She left all of you.' Minakshi spread out her arms to the crowd. 'She chose to leave. But Sumer is for those who stay. We fight for those who stay. We are not an idea in the waiting-room of Time—we are here, we are real. But *where is she*?

Alvar opened his mouth, found no words, and stumbled. Minakshi's eyes gleamed in triumph and in sorrow, and she opened her mouth to say the words, and—

'*Here!*'

Every head in the Maidan turned towards the North Exit, where the voice had come from.

Mithila was there. In one hand she held a green book. In the other, raised high above her head, there was the Heartstone, a light from another world.

PART THREE

MIDDLEGAME

Second Interlude

'Do you know,' the Mentor says, 'what the word *apoptosis* means?'

Next to them, the Three Kings slumber.

The Young One shakes their head.

'The leaves must fall for the trees to begin afresh. Sometimes, you must die to live again.'

Ghada and Samir walk into the chamber. By now, the Young One is accustomed to their presence.

'The thing about apoptosis,' the Mentor continues, 'is that once it starts, it cannot stop. So, every step towards death must be overseen with great care. In the bodies of plants, of trees, and in the cells of our own bodies there are designated overseers to usher in death, the way it should be done.'

Why have you brought me here? Samir asks Ghada.

'But unlike bodies,' the Young One says, 'human beings—like you said—are unpredictable. And so, nobody can see all ends.'

The Mentor smiles. 'That is the challenge, isn't it?'

Eleven

The Council Hall

Raja entered the room, two Watchmen at his heels.

'Mithila-Seven,' he said.

Mithila, sprawled on the chair, looked at him. 'Can we assume you've threatened me already, and get straight to the interrogation?'

Raja's hands curled into fists.

'You think this is a joke?'

'The fuck am I doing here, Raja? I didn't break any laws.'

'Did you go beyond the Wall?'

'Tsk tsk, Raja, didn't your father teach you how to ask nicely? Speaking of which, caught *my* father yet? No? Didn't think so.'

Raja drew closer. She felt his hot dry breath, saw a vein bulge. She made a face, scrunched her eyes, and looked away.

'What's beyond the Wall?'

'Oh, *now* you want to know?' She laughed. 'Can't show you from here, can I?'

'You fool of a *child*!' Raja snapped. 'You're in protective custody. For your own safety.'

'Take your protection where someone wants it. Let me out, Raja.'

Raja almost choked. He puffed out his cheeks, breathing hard. 'I'm done. The President can deal with this.'

'Sure,' said Mithila. 'Low bar, but I'm sure President Hansa will be more interesting than this.'

Raja smirked. 'Hansa isn't President anymore.'

'What?'

'Oh, *now* you want to know?' Raja spat out an ugly laugh. He turned on his heel and left the room.

Mithila sat up. The room she was in was somewhere high up in the Council Hall. It was sparse and unfurnished, other than her single chair, a desk at one end, and a shuttered window. She had a vague feeling of familiarity.

She closed her eyes. She was back in the Maidan. The world stopped, and Time was hers to command. Once again she walked to the Rostrum, faces parting before her. She climbed onto the platform, the two figures on the stage turned towards her, captured in mid-motion like dancing sculptures. She walked up to her sister and held up the Heartstone.

'I'm back. I brought the horizon.'

Chaos unleashed. Shouts rang out in the Maidan, running feet, the crunch of wood striking flesh, and out of nowhere, there was a red flag waving from Maliot's statue. She saw Minakshi's eyes widen at something behind her, her mouth open to scream—but before Mithila could turn, something crashed into her, and everything went black.

She had woken, head aching, in the arms of a Watchman, being carried up the stairs of the Council Hall.

Now, Mithila gingerly felt her temple. She winced. There had been no time to think.

Footsteps sounded, light.

No time to think now, either.

She put her hands in her pockets and stretched out her feet, a portrait of insolence.

The door opened.

'No,' Mithila whispered. 'No. I'm not awake. I'm dreaming.'

Rama walked into the room, moving in the light.

'Welcome back,' she said, '*Mithila-Seven*.'

Mithila gawped.

'Home so soon?' said Rama. 'Did you miss us?'

Mithila struggled to her feet. Her eyes shifted from Rama's face, to the blue stripe down her robe.

'President. Rama.' she croaked.

'Well caught,' said Rama.

She halted a few steps from Mithila. The air between them shimmered. Lamplight dallied on Rama's cheekbones, dancing in her hair, playing with shadow. And something darker—*she's put kajal around her eyes*, Mithila thought stupidly. Her throat felt dry.

The space between them slowly filled up a world.

From far away, she heard Rama speak. 'Well?'

And in that voice, whose measure she knew better than any other, Mithila felt she caught the slightest quiver. Her feet found solid ground. She looked Rama in the eye.

'My President,' she said. 'Should I kneel?'

Rama walked up to her.

'Rama, I—'

The slap stung her across the face. Mithila staggered back in shock. She raised a hand to her throbbing cheek.

In front of her, Rama was furiously wiping her eyes with the heel of her palm.

'Alright,' said Mithila softly, not moving her face from where it had turned. 'I deserved that.'

'Yes,' Rama said, her voice unsteady. 'You did.'

Mithila looked back at her. Rama shoved a piece of paper onto her chest.

'Explain.'

She caught it in her hands as it slipped from her chest. The paper was crumpled but legible.

R

I feel that it would be best if you did not join us tomorrow for the trial.

Please, Rama, don't take this in any other way, this hurts to write. Right now, this is the only thing that I can do.

Blue, I dream you, blue, always.

M

'Er—ah.' Mithila looked up and cleared her throat.

'Brave enough to defy the Elders. Brave enough to mock the Shoortans. Brave enough to cross the Wall. But not'—Rama's voice lanced her—'brave enough to look me in the eye when you decided you wanted no more of me.'

Mithila cast her eyes down. Her ears burned.

'Do you remember,' Rama said, dry-eyed now, 'when you asked me: *you think I'll ever leave without you knowing?*'

'Rama—'

'I did know. Because I woke up and Sumer was empty. But I didn't know it from you. So what did it matter?'

'I thought—' Mithila stammered, 'you'd ignore it—you'd still come…'

'After *this*? After you told me to stay away?' A glint appeared in Rama's eyes. 'Were you testing me? Is that what you do to those who love you, Mithila? Loyalty tests? And if they fail—no longer worthy of the world beyond the Wall, no longer good enough for you?'

'No, that's not—*ugh*,' Mithila buried her face in her hands.

'Not what?'

'I—I don't know what to say—'

'Easy, just imagine you're talking about the Wall, and you'll find the words.'

Mithila flinched. 'Okay.' She took a deep breath. 'I—I wasn't thinking. It was—that night was—Ba became Savarian and there was the trial, and—oh, Builders, Rama!' She looked up. 'The world is so different now. It feels like a lifetime ago. There's nothing I can say to make it right. But I will say this: it was the stupidest thing I've ever done. I shouldn't have—I'm sorry.'

'Yes,' said Rama again.

Mithila looked at her. 'Yes?'

'It *was* the stupidest thing you've ever done.'

Once, that familiar wryness would have made Mithila laugh. Now, she did not dare.

'Does it matter now?' she asked.

'We'll see.'

Mithila exhaled. 'I thought about you so much. I want to tell you so much. The horizon, out there—'

Rama threw up a hand. 'Wait, wait. Some things have changed—in here.'

'What? I've just been gone four days.'

'Yes, well. First, Minakshi has become the Matriarch. Second, she has revived Ostracism. Third, she has Ostacized—you.'

Mithila blinked. 'Say—what?'

'Your sister has cast you out. In Sumer's eyes, you no longer exist.'

Mithila felt her knees buckle, felt herself slump into the chair.

'My sister?'

Rama looked at her, eyes softer. 'She didn't think you would, *could*, come back.'

Mithila laughed, a hollow sound. 'Not very comforting, that.'

'I know.'

For a moment, Mithila thought that Rama was going to move closer to her, but she didn't.

'That's why you're with us,' she continued. 'Protective custody.'

Mithila nodded. Her chest constricted. 'Shoortans won't be pleased.'

Rama smiled, grim. 'Lucky for you I *am* President.'

Mithila returned it feebly. 'Feeling very protected right now.' She touched her cheek.

There was a moment of silence, which stretched endlessly.

Then Rama burst out laughing.

'*Bloody* Builders,' she said, 'but you are impossible.'

Mithila grinned back, and stood. 'Anyone told you,' she said, 'how good you look in that robe? Always did dream you blue.'

'I'm still mad at you, you know.'

'I do. But it's true!'

'Fine,' said Rama. 'Now tell me. Did you find the horizon?'

'Yes,' said Mithila. 'Yes, yes, yes. I did. The sky came down to meet the earth, and it was called the sea. And the sea was—bigger than anything we know. Bigger than the Wall. It was water, water forever, but somehow … more. It didn't end.'

Rama listened. 'Are the Builders truly a lie then?' she asked.

'Yes. No. As in, I don't know. There was a City. It was theirs. A song of white stone that dazzled. The doors opened and there was nobody there. Rama, there is a world. And now everyone can see it.'

Rama cocked her head. 'Everyone?'

'What?'

'We have,' said Rama, 'a bit of a Shoortan problem on our hands.'

Mithila stared at her. 'But it's done,' she said. 'The Wall's been crossed. Everyone knows they're lying. We have the world. What do *they* have?'

'No,' said Rama. 'Only you have it. The Wall is still here. All we have are your words.'

'I have new ones now. I've found them.'

'I hope so. Because Minakshi will have hers.' Rama nodded at her. 'I will hear the whole story from you. But I have to go now. This night's madness needs handling.'

'Wait!' said Mithila. 'When are you letting me go?'

'I don't know,' Rama smiled faintly. 'The Council will decide, keeping in mind what's best for the City. Anything else?'

'Oh, but—alright. By the way …'

'Yes?'

'Thank you for leaving my Heartstone with me.'

Rama flushed. 'I'm not a thief.'

'Debatable,' Mithila murmured.

Rama looked at her. 'You—oh, *Builders*, Mithila!' she said, helplessly.

'Sorry, sorry,' Mithila said, suddenly uncertain, looking away. 'I'll stop. You're President now, you have to—'

Her words died in her throat, as Rama took a step towards her—and then another—until she was standing in front of her, a breath away. Suddenly, her throat was dry all over again.

Rama took her by the shoulders, hard enough so that Mithila gasped. Slipping one hand underneath her chin, Rama tilted her face up until Mithila was looking into her eyes.

'How is it,' Rama whispered, 'that you can see past the Wall, but—'

'Wha—'

Rama drew her close and kissed her. Mithila gasped out loud. Rama halted in alarm, and began to pull away. 'No—*yes* …' Mithila murmured, and wrapped her arms around Rama's neck and drew her back. For a moment, she forgot how to breathe.

Then Rama did pull back. She leaned her forehead against Mithila's, eyes closed. Mithila felt tears on her face. She did not know to whom they belonged.

Rama stepped back, out of Mithila's arms. Mithila looked at her, dazed.

'This doesn't mean I'm not mad any more.'

Mithila nodded wordlessly.

'*Do you have any idea how scared I've been for you these last four days?*'

Mithila nodded again.

'I'll see you when this is done,' Rama said. She turned and walked away quickly, without looking back.

Rama strode down the stairs, fists clenched, heartbeat loud. She crossed through the Hall of a Thousand Pillars and stopped outside the conferral room, closing her eyes and leaning against the door. She let herself breathe.

She opened the door and walked in.

'Good evening, Elders,' she said.

The Councillors Hansa, Raja, Paras, Varsha, and Thanu, standing together by the pillars, stopped talking. They turned to face her.

'Could be better,' Raja muttered.

Rama smiled. 'Why, yes. And that's why I've called this meeting.'

He stared at her.

'For those who haven't heard,' Rama said, 'the Shoortans' coup ran into some trouble tonight.'

'We've all heard,' said Hansa, a little wearily.

'They came because I sent for them.'

Hansa stilled. 'You raised a militia?'

'Not quite,' said Rama. 'I just found some people who hate the Shoortans more than they hate us. And I introduced them to each other.'

She saw them shift, and exchange glances.

'We've got some space now,' she went on. 'But we're still in big trouble. We've lost half the Watch. The people are not on our side. Who can blame them? We've hardly been on theirs. The Matriarch knows this. She is going to ask for what we cannot give, and when the people see us refuse, again, they will fight for her. Again.'

'We know,' said Hansa. 'We know how serious things are.'

'I know you do. And you also know that we can't meet this moment in the normal manner. This is now about whether we'll last this night—and the next. So I ask you: will you give me Special Emergency Powers?'

'Emergency Powers? You don't need the Council for that,' said Hansa. 'A President may at any time proclaim a State of Emergency, which can last for fifteen days until we vote to renew or end it.'

'Yes,' said Rama. 'But I'm asking for *Special* Emergency Powers.'

'*Special*—oh.' Hansa's voice died away. The glances that the Elders exchanged were longer. Rama let the silence settle, waiting for one of them to speak.

It was Varsha who did.

'But that will let you change all that's sacred. The property laws, that Maliot preserved so carefully in the Constitution.' she said. 'You'd be able to override the rule of two-thirds majority, acting all on your own. We've never allowed this before—because this is—'

'Fundamental. I know. I'm not asking lightly.'

Varsha went on, her voice hardening. 'This would make you a dictator for fifteen days. You'd have more power than even Maliot had, you'd have the power of a tyrant, a Dichio. Anything you choose to do—if you get it wrong, the scars will last a generation.'

'I *know*,' said Rama. 'I know what it means Councillor, what I'm asking. I ask because there is no other way.'

'So you're telling us,' said Thanu, his eyebrows raised, 'that you have to destroy democracy to save it.'

'Suspend it. For a while. I know this sounds unseemly in one so young, and that's why I called upon you first. The Council trusts all of you, and—'

'But what do you intend to do with this power?' Varsha interrupted. 'We can't trust you blind, Rama—President.'

'I don't know yet,' said Rama, 'because I don't know what the Matriarch will ask of me tonight when I go over to the Temple. But I need to know that I can react, that I have the power of the Council behind me to act in the moment. Trust me, I will do what it takes to beat the Shoortans. I *need* you to trust me on that, on just that, if nothing else.'

The Councilors were silent. She saw Hansa with her fingers steepled, and Varsha staring at the ground. *Not enough*, a voice in her mind warned.

'You're right to pause,' she said. 'This is not easy. So will it help you to decide if I say this? Any changes will be subject to Council's renewal in fifteen days. If, by then, we have not won, I will resign, and the next President can put things back where they were that very day.

This time she heard the sound of drawn breath.

'You think we can win this in fifteen days?' Thanu said, disbelieving.

'If we don't,' said Rama, 'we've already lost.'

Some of them nodded.

'Alright,' said Hansa, 'but we'll still need a blueprint. I've given you my seat, President Rama, but I'm not going to sign away the Council to you even if the Matriarch is battering down our doors, without some idea of what you're doing.'

'I understand,' said Rama. 'Listen, then.'

In the room upstairs, Mithila paced.

As soon as Rama left, she had gone to the door and opened it. Two Watchmen stood outside, facing her. She'd glared at them and closed the door again.

Now she measured the length and breadth of the room with her feet, feeling her muscles clench. From time to time she heard sounds from somewhere in the Council Hall,

President Rama. *Matriarch* Minakshi.

Outside, a world.

'Bloody Builders, let me out Rama!' she called. 'I need to be out there. Now.'

There was no reply.

Mithila approached the door. 'Watchmen, I know you're there,' she said softly. 'I know you can hear me. Listen. I have been beyond the Wall. There is a horizon. You walk and you walk and the sky retreats, and you're chasing the sun, until you see—not Wallset. *Sunset.* I just want to show it to you.'

Silence answered her.

'Come on, you're not the President's slaves, you can think.' She drew closer to the door. 'You heard what she said—I'm here for protective custody. But I don't need protection, I've been beyond the Wall and I have returned, and I have—I have seen the Builders.'

A thought struck her. She hurried back to her chair, reached into her pack, and brought out the spiral that she had picked up by the sea.

'I've even brought something back for all of you. It's a slice of the world, and it shelters the world. Let me show you?'

When there was still dead silence, she went over to the door. Outside, nothing moved. She tried it.

It was locked.

Mithila kicked the door, and squealed as a stinging pain traveled up her foot.

'Rama, you fucking locked me in!'

She turned away from the door. Every time that big square window caught her eye, something began niggling away at the back of her mind, a feeling of things repeating, as if Time really was wheeling back in a circle. She tried to recall those hazy moments after recovering consciousness, in the arms of the Watchman. He'd carried her into a domed hall, up a winding stairway, and into—

'*Builders!*' Mithila breathed. She was looking at it.

She strode forward and pushed upon the shutter. The window swung open. Mithila leaned out. Just below her, a foot-wide ledge ran around the outside of the Council Hall, and disappeared into the dark.

And she knew exactly where that ledge went, here in this reflection of a ruined City.

Mithila turned back. There was no sound from outside. Once more, she pulled her pack over her shoulder, and just like she had done the day before, swung her legs over the windowsill and onto the ledge.

Below her, as the wall fell away, there was nothing but trackless dark—a darkness that grew as she moved away from the window and the light. She felt her legs tremble, and a strange drowsiness take her, a temptation to let go and float backwards, into the Sumerian night ...

She turned her head. Just beyond the corner of the wall, there was the huge Temple spire, outlined in the dark.

'*Fuck you, Minakshi*,' Mithila muttered. Life flooded back. She dragged herself around the corner, and onto the high platform. It gave her a garuda-eye's view of the Forum, spread out far below her, the lamps flickering in their symmetrical lines between the towers. She sensed a stirring in the Forum Plaza, the presence of many bodies close together.

Something moved at the edge of her vision. Mithila turned to the Shoortan Temple. Upon the wall, there was a shadow. It was moving up, scaling the sheer wall-face. Mithila watched, fascinated. The shadow reached a lit window, she saw a rustle of black, and then it was gone, so quickly that it might have been a dream.

Mithila returned to reality. The ascent circled around the outside of the dome, just as it had in the ruined City. Mithila retraced her recent journey to the top, around the pillared passage, and to the stairway set into the inner wall.

She descended. The stairway was dim, but there were lamps on the wall, at just the right distance to prevent complete darkness. A little way down, she passed a door. She began to wonder who had lit the lamps …

'Who is it up there?

Mithila stopped dead. She looked back up. Nowhere to climb to but a dead-end passageway. But that voice, surely she knew it.

'Are you hearing things again?'

That voice. Yes. Mithila remembered. She squeezed herself against the wall.

'I heard something.'

'You're going soft, Two. Every time we're told to go down into the crystal hall, you're like this after.'

She heard the footsteps and saw them come up around the bend in the stairs, the two sightless men who had led her to the Three Kings, the day of the trial. Mithila held her breath as they went past. She let their steps fade away before hurrying down again.

So *that* was who was behind the door.

She began to see exits from the stairway, arches that yielded into well-lit corridors. She stopped at one and looked out, into a narrow, carpeted passage, where portraits of Elders dominated the walls. A sudden sound made her withdraw her head. Two Councillors hurried past, talking to each other, flanked by the Watch.

Mithila climbed down. She didn't look out again, until the stairway ended, and she saw a throbbing, white light in the distance.

Cautiously, she peeked out.

She was back at ground level, looking out into the Hall of a Thousand Pillars, two doors away from freedom.

In the President's Office, Rama rose from her chair. She had put on the President's blue cloak. On her hands, she wore the President's blue gloves, last used during Savarian's Mutiny.

'*We wear this when we go to battle*,' Hansa had told her that evening, when she'd given her those gloves. '*You will have blood on your hands. Best not to let it show*.'

Her hair was smoothed down, and her dagger hidden more carefully than last time.

'I'm ready,' she said to nobody.

Voices sounded outside. The door opened.

Raja stood at the threshold. 'You sent for me, President Rama?'

'Yes, thank you. Do we still have the Watch patrolling the Towers of Rebirth?'

'Yes.'

'Recall them.'

'What?' said Raja. 'But Savarian—'

'I know. But what can he do? Start another Mutiny? Let him run to the Dooma—he'll only create more confusion there, but we can't have ten men stuck at the other end of Sumer right now.'

'Alright,' said Raja, doubtfully.

Rama held his gaze. 'Savarian took my father,' she said softly. 'Before this is done, we will deal with him. And the third time will be the last.'

'Yes, President. I—'

The sound of running footsteps interrupted him. The door burst open, and a young Watchman rushed into the room.

'She's gone!'

Rama raised an eyebrow.

'Mithila-Seven! She escaped, President. As you'd instructed us, we didn't stop her.'

'Took her long enough.' Rama smiled. 'And so it begins.' She flexed the fingers of her right hand, watching them move beneath her blue glove. She turned to Raja.

'Now for the other sister.'

Mithila staggered into the Forum Plaza. Climbing out of that window had made her bones hurt. She was astonished that she had made it this far. *Just get to the Dooma*, a voice buzzed in her head. *They'll keep you.*

The Shoortan Temple stood a little way from her. Its sight sent her heart racing. In the night, she saw flickering lights and figures moving back and forth in the Plaza, and voices carried to her. She crept along the edges, making herself small. *To the Rasa and the boats ...*

A pair of arms cut through her thoughts, one hand on her mouth and the other at her throat. Instinctively, she struggled—and opened her mouth.

The hand pressed down on her throat, cutting off her scream. Mithila saw the world dim, and then her body went slack.

Twelve

The Banner

Mankala rapped on the door. Somebody shuffled inside.

'Come in, Mankala.'

She walked in. 'How did you know it was me?'

Marwana raised her head. Her eyes were tired. 'No hidden science. I was looking out of the window and saw you coming.'

'Where is everyone?' said Mankala. 'The Citadel's empty.'

Marwana smiled. 'I'd like to say that the Select takes a very long lunch-break, but I suspect it has more to do with that.' She gestured at the window. Mithila walked over to it and looked down upon the Forum Plaza. She saw lamps in the night, gathered together in little groups, tense and waiting.

'So, what new ideas have you brought me?' said Marwana.

'I need you to know something,' said Mankala. 'I think we're in some danger. But I can't see it clear.'

Marwana, still looking tired, leaned forward. 'What is this about?'

'It's about the Three Kings.'

'Go on.'

'Ever since you took me down there, I haven't been able to get it out of my head. It's like—it's like a story that begins in the middle and ends at the beginning and has pieces bitten off on all sides. But there's one thing, Leader, it's just been playing in my mind. Samir says to Ghada, "*it's so hot.*" But it was *cold* down there. We were shivering.'

'We think the cold has something to do with how they've preserved themselves. But we don't know—'

'But where's that heat coming from? He says, *it's so hot*. She says, *any surprise, given what's happening above?*'

Marwana was silent for a moment. 'You think they're referring to the Great Fire.'

'Yes. I think … don't know—'

'We've considered that. But the Great Fire never touched the Forum,' said Marwana. 'It didn't melt the stone. How could they have felt it so far down?'

'Except that the same people who made the Forum made the fire, Leader. The Builders,' Mankala said, 'or the Overseers. Maybe the Forum's bones were made as strong as the fire would be. Our quarries never held stone so smooth and white, which glowed so. Maybe we've never had fire like that either. *This* fire would be incandescent. Would it not, for it to wipe out Sumer so completely that nothing remained but an echo of a memory?'

'And you're basing this on three words that Samir says?'

Mankala smiled faintly. 'Something a little more direct, Leader. A few days ago, they tossed something through my window and my house burnt down in moments. I suspect that's the smallest part of what they can do with fire.'

'What!'

'Just like that, Leader. No trimming of the wick, no slow travelling of flame, just a burst of fire. And then, I think of that cold chamber, Samir saying *it's so hot* …'

Marwana steepled her fingers and looked at the desk.

'Because they can do it again.' Mankala placed her own palms on the desk and leaned towards Marwana. 'And Leader—I think it's sooner than we imagine.'

Marwana stiffened. 'What?'

'That night Tefnakth came to see Malati, he said *that the end will reflect the beginning*. To begin in fire and to end in it? Then they murdered him. And now—' she pointed at the window. 'You see what's happening? We're on the brink of something much worse than Savarian. If ever there was a time for them to act, that time is now, as Sumer starts to tear itself apart. And if that fire comes again,what chance does mud-brick have? Or the refuge you are building underground?'

Marwana nodded. 'I—thanks for telling me this, about Tefnakth. We couldn't have known.' The tiredness had gone from her voice. 'You're right, Sumer's on edge, and we don't even know if it's *them* who've brought it to the edge this time. We're going to have to secure the City.'

'The Select? How?' said Mankala. 'You've sworn an oath not to intervene.'

Mankala smiled suddenly. 'The Select do not intervene *of our own will*. But if we need to, we'll find a way.' She sobered. 'Have there been more attacks on you, Mankala?'

'None.'

'Don't drop your guard. We have our people shadowing you. And we're keeping an eye on our suspects. At least this civil war we're slipping into has brought them all out.'

Brought them all out.

Her voice echoed in the room. Mankala looked at the lamp on the wall, at the slow-burning flame, and in her mind's eye it grew, enveloping the room with a crackle and a roar, and in that fire a face appeared before her, floating in the air …

'All?' she whispered.

'Yes.' Marwana stared at her. 'What do you mean?'

Mankala rose, kicking the chair out behind her. 'I have to go. I'll come see you tomorrow.'

Marwana stared after her as she hurried from the room.

Mankala hastened back through a restless Forum Plaza, giving the murmured voices and twinkling lights a wide berth. When she reached

Malati's house in the First, she found Alvar and the Councillor already there.

'Are you joining the office, Alvar?' she said.

'Where else was I going to find you?' Alvar grinned.

'I think the more immediate question,'—Malati raised an eyebrow—'is whether I still have a secretary?'

'Sorry!' Mankala stammered. 'A lot's been happening!'

Malati waved a hand. 'Don't worry about it. I'm told we're voting to give Special Emergency Powers to the President tomorrow morning, so there's not going to be much work for me soon. But that means we have the time to get the Encyclopaedia started again, Mankala.'

'Councillor, you're going to sit this one out?' Alvar said.

Malati raised her hands. 'Some of us fight. And some of us shelter.' Her eyes clouded, as if remembering something. 'They have no need of me now. Maybe after, to pick up the pieces. Maybe.'

'I'll come tomorrow,' Mankala promised. 'But before that, Councillor, a question: where in Sumer is Savarian? Surely the Council has some intelligence?'

'More than Savarian?' Malati laughed. 'If he could disappear for twenty-seven years, what hope do they have now?'

'Let me rephrase,' said Mankala. 'Where do you think he is?'

Malati's brow wrinkled. 'On the night of the Carnival, Amrit had sent an urgent message that Savarian had been seen leaving the Dooma. But Amrit's not going to be speaking again.'

'Leaving for where?'

Malati shrugged. 'Wrong person to ask. If something happened after that, the inner circle—Hansa, Raja, perhaps Paras and Varsha—would know. They wouldn't tell me, the voice of mercy.'

Mankala shook her head, frustrated. 'I *need* to find him.'

Out of the silence, Alvar spoke: 'I think I know where he's gone.'

'*... utter nonsense ...*'

Mithila's eyes opened to dim light and angry voices.

She was lying on a rough pallet. Above her was a gabled roof. To her left, there was a long table, crowded with people.

'If you had waited, Maji—' from across the table, Prana-Eleven began.

'Waited. *Waited.* Is that all you do, Prana, all your Union can do? You'd stand by the Rasa and just *wait* for a boat to arrive, and wonder why it never came.' Maji's voice grew dangerously soft. 'You wanted to wait for the Shoortans to rule the City? For the President to be in jail? Or did you want to wait till you could slink back to your homes and tell your Mandalas you lost before you began?'

'Unlike you, Maji, we care about the consent of the many rather than the dreams of a few,' Prana said, his voice tight.

Maji looked down upon him. 'You arrogant little man.' Contempt simmered in her voice. 'What leader worth a bushel does not know the pulse of his people? If you didn't know what they wanted, what makes you think *you* could ever give it to them?'

'Spoken like a true successor of Savarian,' Prana sneered. 'And that's why nobody remembers your Revolution. That's why they all know it as the Mutiny of the Unforgiven. Don't glare at me—you have a problem, argue with history.'

'I've a *problem* with the fact that you promised women and men on the ground, and failed.' Maji lashed at him. 'This could have ended tonight. Instead, all we did was inflict a flesh wound and reveal ourselves before time.'

'We *told* you, if we got the signatures—'

'Builders, Prana, you don't have the choice to go around collecting signatures!' Maji said. 'You never did. You can fight, or your Mandalas can be ground into the dust in some unholy Shoortan-Council power transfer. Do you think Rastogi will be a better master than the Elders? Do you think *you*—POUM—will be allowed to exist?'

She paused, her fists clenched on the table. 'The Shoortans will sit down with the Council, and then—after what we did tonight—both will come after us, with all the Circles behind them. If the Farmers'

Mandalas sit this one out, the Dooma will not—*cannot*—withstand them. Do you understand me, POUM? If *we* fall now, you will never rise.'

'And do *you* understand that all the Circles would prefer to march with the Shoortans rather than stand with the Unforgiven?' Prana began to shout.

'Are you two *quite* done?' a third voice came, to instant silence. Mithila pricked her ears at the familiar tone.

Maji and Prana turned to look at Carina.

'There's an obvious solution,' said Carina, 'But nobody wants to be the first to say it.'

'Do tell,' said Meghana.

'You know what I'm going to say. Your Banner can't be any of you. Not the Dooma, nor the farmers. Your Banner must unburdened by the weight of history, but weightier than the desires of any one Circle.'

There was a hush.

'After Savarian,' said Maji slowly, 'we swore we would never fight under another. If defeat was to be our unending future, it would be *our* defeat.'

'That's just a bit too bad, isn't it?' Prana said. 'Because here you are, here *we* are, and—as someone's so fond of saying—we're out of choices.'

Maji did not speak. The silence lengthened.

'I'm going to cut this short,' Carina said at last. 'Because, to quote from a failed revolution, *we have no time.* Mithila-Seven, you can stop pretending to be asleep.'

The table turned to stare at her. Mithila scrabbled clumsily to her feet, almost tripping herself up. She looked back at them, at their doubtful faces.

'Welcome back.' Carina grinned. 'Care to lead a revolution?'

'Absolutely not,' said Mithila.

Halfway through their dash across the farmlands, they saw lights coming at them. Mankala seized Alvar's shoulder and forced him to the ground. As the *rahi* stalks scratched against his skin, Alvar heard running footsteps. Shadows rushed by them, swiftly swallowed by the dark.

'That was the Watch,' said Mankala, as Alvar got to his feet.

'Coming from the North?' he said, confused. 'There's nothing there but—*oh!*'

'Shit!' Mankala swore. 'We may be too late. *Run*, Alvar.'

They sprinted once more, through the *rahi* stalks and over the bridges, until at last they saw them in the night.

The Towers of Rebirth.

They rose like a group of conspirators, dark-cloaked and bunched up close together, looming above the barren ground. Behind them, the Wall was like an ink-spill of lampblack, daubed upon a canvas of shadow.

Mankala stared at the towers, jutting into the sky.

Alvar bent over, his hands on his knees. 'You do know we have boats, right?' he panted. 'To get across the City.'

'Too obvious,' she said absently. 'Which one, Alvar?'

'The Third, that's where the Gatekeeper who was a former revolutionary—wait, let me.' He led her to the towers. 'Here.'

'*Helloo!*' Mankala cried out to the night. 'Open the door please! We come in peace.'

'That's not going to work,' Alvar said. 'Here, I'll try.' He rapped on the wooden door. 'Gatekeeper, please will you open? It's me, Alvar-Nine. You gave me sanctuary.'

There was silence.

He knocked again, harder. 'We're friends of Mithila. Mithila Maloran. We mean Savarian no harm.'

The wild *rahi* at the foot of the tower swayed gently in the breeze.

Mankala looked around. There was nobody in sight.

'Wait,' she said, as Alvar lifted his hand again. She pushed at the door.

It swung open.

'What!' Alvar whispered. 'That's *always* supposed to be locked, it's sanctuary.'

A lamp marked the beginning of the ascending ramp.

'Well,' said Mankala, 'here we are.' She stepped in. Alvar followed.

'Careful now,' Mankala said, 'watch the rear.'

He walked behind her, as they climbed into the darkness. The passage twisted around itself. At each curve, they saw the looming bays and the woven basket-lids that covered them. That smell was there, the mixture of wood shavings and decaying death.

Alvar edged closer, and lifted one of the lids.

'Don't!' Mankala hissed.

'As if you've never wondered.'

'When I was *ten*, yes. But I'm not interested in sniffing corpses anymore, and we're in a hurry—what—'

She broke off as Alvar jumped back. The lid snapped shut.

'Will you be *quiet*!' she whispered.

'I thought … there was a hand—'

'Of course there is a hand. What do you think they do with the hands?'

Alvar shook his head. 'Let's just go,' he muttered.

'Thank you.'

The passageway brought them out to the top of the tower, and into the circular corridor that ringed the open shaft. Moonlight streamed in from the window. The roof, inches above their heads, pressed down on them. Alvar walked to the edge of the balcony, and looked down into the shaft. He saw the bays disappear into the dark, all the way to the waiting, moist earth.

He shuddered and turned back to Mankala, who was staring at the empty corridor.

'There's nobody here,' said Mankala. 'Savarian's gone.'

Three floors beneath them, a door creaked open.

'For the last time,' said Mithila, 'I *will not* be used like … like a Shoortan priestess, selling shine while telling them, "I bring you light."'

'Nobody's selling anything,' said Maji. 'What you have is real.'

'Then let them come and see it for themselves. You're not listening to me, Maji. I don't care about who rules Sumer. I'm leaving, and anyone who wants can come back with me.'

'Oh Mithila,' Carina smiled, 'do you really believe you can walk out of here and just—*leave*?'

Mithila turned to her. 'What?'

'You have a choice,' said Carina. 'Be Mithila Worldfarer. Or be Mithila *the Ostracized*.'

The word ran through her mind, turning it bloody.

'Or I could run away,' she whispered. 'Not be anything.'

'Where will you run to?' said Carina. 'The Maliot is crawling with Shoortans. The moment you leave this hall—'

Then the woman next to Prana, the one they called Meghana, spoke quietly.

'Mithila Worldfarer. Take power, when it is given to you.'

'I will not be anyone's Banner,' said Mithila.

'Mithila-Seven,' said Prana, 'I don't think you understand. In the hours since you returned to Sumer, the whisper has run through the Mandalas: *the Worldfarer is back*. You have ceased to be Mithila, Mithila-Seven. Now you are *Worldfarer*, Wall-conqueror. Mithila the Unpunished, because you crossed the *raika*, looked the Builders in the eye, and came back.'

'Can you go easy on the fucking titles?' said Mithila.

Chuckles rose around the table. Prana flushed.

Meghana took up his words. 'That's why you will be leading us as the Worldfarer,' she said. 'You have the authority we need. And we—we have power to give, for you to wield when they come to crush you.'

'And why should I—'

'Because if you want to go back into the world you will have to go through the Shoortans and the Council. If they win, Worldfarer, the Circles will remain, something of equality will never come, they will smash our Union—and you will never get out of Sumer, as long as you live. So we march together, Worldfarer—or we fall. What's it going to be?'

Dhara, I will find out who did this to you, and make them undo it.

'Will the people join the banner of an Ostracized?' she said.

Meghana smiled thinly. 'It's for you to give them reasons why.'

'The Shoortans will attack the moment that banner is raised,' Maji said. This is not something they can let pass. We aren't enough here. We'll need barricades. And we'll need the Mandalas with us. Every second house, at least.'

'We know, Maji,' said Carina. 'We weren't idling while you raided the Maidan. We've called for a vote. Eleventh to the Fifteenth. The people will decide.'

Maji started. 'What? That is so risky. What if they say no? We couldn't fight at all, then.'

'Isn't that what democracy is?' Carina said, laughing. 'The democracy that Savarian, and you, wanted?'

'Fine,' said Maji slowly. 'I can't argue with that. Where are the people?'

'Outside. Waiting for the Worldfarer.'

'Wait—*what*?' Mithila felt her world spin.

'Come,' said Carina. 'Come out and meet them.'

'N—no,' Mithila stammered. 'I'm not ready. I've just seen a bunch of things beyond the Wall that I don't have the words for—and I don't even know what I saw or why—'

Maji grasped her shoulder. 'Then find those words now,' she said. 'Or make your own.'

Mithila stepped out of Konar Hall. She shielded her eyes from the sudden light. Flame lamps had been placed across the front wall, and more were hanging by the houses across the street. In front of her, a few steps away, the road that led up to the Hall was thronged. Mithila looked up, to the row of buildings beyond the road. There were lights in the windows. More flickered on the rooftops, where people were standing and watching.

Prana gestured to her right. Mithila saw a rough platform, wood crates stacked together with planks laid across. At the centre, balanced upon a thick log, there was an iron bowl, from which a crackling fire leapt into the sky.

'We gave you a stage,' Prana whispered. 'Better than the Maidan. Make it count.'

'The easier to pull me down from?' she whispered back.

'This is no time for jokes, *Worldfarer*.'

Mithila turned to him. 'What's the point of a revolution that can't make you laugh?'

Before he could reply, she lightly leaped up the uneven log-steps and onto the platform.

The eyes that looked at her were curious and watchful.

Mithila placed her right fist against her forehead, and extended it out to them. 'I have been beyond the Wall,' she said, 'and I have come back.'

Silence fell.

'The Builders are dead. *Smara* is not longing. It is memory. *Praya* is not penance. It is hate. And the time of the Circles is over.'

Their faces gave away nothing. Mithila picked out one, at an even distance from her: a man, middle-aged, a shock of dark hair falling across his temple. She held his gaze as she spoke.

'There is a City that I saw. Its doors opened for me. Imagine our Forum. Imagine a thousand Forums, stone upon stone, shining with their own light. These Builders knew no walls, no bounds, no circles. Theirs was a world without endings, a world with a horizon.

'It was called Gumfraude.'

'Who told you?' a voice came from the crowd.

Mithila did not take her eyes away. 'Taraf,' she said. 'In a faraway place he lies alone. But in death he showed me the way, a map to Gumfraude on his headstone.

'And there, in the light of that City, in the footsteps of Taraf, I walked and I saw, and I have come back to tell you of it. These Builders shaped the world in their image, they unspooled Time, they spoke life into stone. But that was not enough. They wanted to go on forever, and if they could not, to be the last who would live in a boundless world. So they turned their deaths into an endless sleep, and for us, who came after, they raised the Wall to keep us in forever.

'They built this Wall, they built this City, and they poured the last scraps of Time into it, forever a circle. Perhaps they meant to be kind. They did give us food, and water, and the warmth of bamboo soup. And perhaps they thought that if we had a reason, it would be easier to stay. So they gave us the myth of Malan, and an eternity of repentance—*but for a crime we never committed.*'

She took a long breath. 'And *these* are the Builders whose forgiveness you must ask, through all the days and nights of *praya*. But if anyone should be asking for forgiveness …' she let her voice fall.

'And why should we believe this story over what the Matriarch says?'a man shouted into the silence.

Now she did turn, towards the voice. 'Because the Council Hall is up the road, and there you will find your Builders.'

'*What!*' a wave of unrest passed through the people.

'Deep underground, beyond a vast hall of pillars, there is a chamber. In that chamber, the Builders lie dreaming. You can see them. You don't even have to cross the Wall.'

'*You* are Ostracized,' someone said it at last.

'I was. I am.' She inclined her head. 'And now you know why. Was I wrong?'

'You set yourself against the Shoortans.'

'They set themselves against me,' she said. 'With their weapon of despair. They offer you Ostracism. I offer you the world. What will it be?'

'So you want us to rise against the Council, fight the Shoortans, bleed and die for you before this is over—all for a story?'

'For the world they don't want you to have.'

'But they're here with us,' someone said. 'They have what we have.'

'And what do *you* have?' Mithila said softly, 'this side of the Wall? You work on land that isn't yours, to grow crop that you don't own, at a time that is given to you, and just so much that the Wall allows. You, of the Eleventh Mandala, and the Twelfth—yes, it is to you I speak. Not a week ago you took your troubles to the President, the *old* President, and she told you, "*if you have a problem with the conditions of our existence, you can try changing them.*" Yes, your faces tell me that you remember. You remember how the Council jeered you, when the President said with such sympathy, *oh, but what can we do for you this side of the Wall, but farming quotas.* That's all you get—*what can we do this side of the Wall*—because they've never let you ask, "*but what about that side?*"'

'You're dodging,' someone hissed. 'You were telling us a story about the Builders. And you still haven't told us—*how do you know?* How do you know if the Builders lie sleeping here in Sumer, and there are none beyond to tell you?'

And underneath the question, Mithila heard: *did you even go beyond the Wall, Worldfarer? Were you just hiding here? Is this another con?* She touched the Heartstone absently. *Not now. Not yet.*

'Because I have seen things,' she said, 'you wouldn't believe. Did you know that when the sun sets—*sunset,* not Wallset—the sky is on fire at the rim of the world? I walked over a bridge that rose above the City of Stone, and its spires were at my feet. For two thousand years Gumfraude has waited for you. That is what you lose if you stay.'

Little debates had sprung up in various parts of the crowd, but the majority was still focused upon her. Then a voice cracked through the night, stilling all other sounds for a moment.

'All we have is your word for it.'

'And now you will have yours.' She turned to the man whose gaze she had held all this while, and gestured to him. 'Will you join me here?' As he hesitated, she beckoned. 'Only for a moment.'

He pushed his way to her. She reached into her pack, pulled out the spiral that she had found on the edge of the sea, and cupped it in her fist. He clambered up on the stage.

'What do they call you?' she said.

'Ronin-Thirteen.'

'Ronin-Thirteen, you will be the first. Don't be surprised at anything I do, I promise that you will come to no harm.' Gently, she turned him by the shoulder, until he was facing the crowd.

Mithila reached into the darkest recess of her memory, and pulled out Garuda's voice.

'Listen to me,' she said to the crowd. 'Close your eyes. Think of Lake Sumer. Fix it in your mind. Is it there? Stay.

'Imagine the Wall. Let it move away. Let it shrink. And let the water grow. Slowly. Slowly. Are you with me? Now, listen. I want you to do something you've never done before. I want you to believe. At the count of three, I will give you a word, and you will see the Wall vanish. One … two ….'

At *three*, she spoke the word that Garuda could not have known, and as she did, in one movement, she raised the spiral to the ear of Ronin-Thirteen.

'The *sea*.'

Eyes flew open. Faces altered. Bodies shifted.

It was here. The first word from beyond the Wall.

Ronin fell to his knees. His face was buried in his hands. His shoulders shook.

'I saw the sea,' Mithila said. 'It moves like its alive. It tastes like tears. And it goes on forever.' She placed a hand on Ronin's shoulder. 'Tell them.'

Still on his knees, Ronin looked up at her, his eyes glistening.

She looked back at him. 'Tell them.'

'I—' His voice cracked. He stared into the night sky and took a long breath. 'I heard—it was the sound of the world. It was—it was—' He turned back to her. 'I want to hear it again.'

'As many times as you want.' Mithila held her hand out so they could all see the spiral, resting in her palm. 'Put it to your ears, and you will hear what you've longed to hear every Carnival Night, when you've gone to bloody yourselves upon the Wall. The call of the world.' She caught the eye of one of the people closest to the platform. She knelt and extended the spiral to him. 'Go on. Try. And then pass it on.'

As she straightened, she saw him put it to his ear, heard him gasp, saw his eyes widen in confusion, in exhilaration, saw him turn to his neighbour. The chatter from various sections of the crowd was growing louder. It felt as if some of them were already deciding how to vote. She looked from face to face, lingering on those still unconvinced.

'Is this little thing all you brought from beyond?' someone called, as the people at the back muttered, restless, waiting for it to reach.

Mithila smiled again. 'I was waiting for you to ask.'

In a swift movement, she drew out the Heartstone and held it out, over the crowd. Its throbbing white light mingled with the lamps and cast her face in a halo. The chattering died.

'It is a Heartstone,' she said, her voice flowing around and over them. 'Here I hold it, and there are no Builders to stop me. This is the Heartstone I found in Gumfraude, the Lost City. You of the Fifteenth, you know the words—*light from light.* It has broken. And we have a world to discover. Will you come?'

A storm broke out in the street, an argument that would not be contained. Mithila stood still, holding out the Heartstone, letting them all see it, as undeniable as the sea.

Then she turned and descended the platform. It was over. They would decide.

The doors of the community hall opened, and Maji and Prana fell in beside her as she entered.

'*So* much drama,' Maji drawled.

'What did you want, a lecture?'

'No no, I was just reminded of …' Maji left the last bit unsaid. She looked at Mithila. 'Was that whole story about the Builders a lie?'

'Why?' Mithila murmured. 'Were you not persuaded?'

'As long as *they* were,' Prana grunted. 'In two hours, the Matriarch will know exactly what happened. By Wallrise, they'll be here.'

'How did it go?' asked Carina, as they approached the long table.

'Alright. I guess,' Prana said. 'We'll know. Soon enough.'

Mithila sat. An oppressive silence settled around the table. Prana tapped his fingers on the wood, until Meghana told him to stop. Maji stared at the ceiling with a fixed gaze, not looking at any of them.

Then Carina—who was sitting next to Mithila—began to hum one of old Taraf's songs under her breath, just the tune, leaving Mithila to fill in the words in her mind.

Beyond the Wall, the sunrise swift
Dispels the iron dawn to lift …

The lights faded. The ceiling receded. The air shimmered. The world entered her, diffident, like a curious child. It ran through her with a child's un-heavy feet. It danced in her blood like they danced with the lights on Carnival Night. And it came to settle in the cavity of her chest, where once *smara* had been.

She was, once more, at Taraf's grave by the sea. The rain fell in ropes. The sky arched above her, unwalled and free. She wondered if other eyes had seen that sky, before Taraf had walked that shore, or after, unseen footprints lost like a breath on water. Had Gumfraude called to them, like it had called to her, and cast them down in an endless sleep, their names the shadow of a whisper, like Dhara's would soon become?

And she wondered if she would be the last person to see the unrimmed world, for another six hundred years, until another Mithila rose and crossed the Wall, ahead of another unwilling Sumer.

She closed her eyes and let herself breathe. She felt dewy ground beneath her feet, the smell of the rain-washed forest, and the motes of fire that had danced around her in the night. Weariness was inside her. She tried to keep her eyes open, but she could feel herself drifting, as though she was floating in a weightless world …

'*Wake up!*'

Mithila came to life with a jerk. Carina was shaking her. 'They're here!' she whispered in her ear.

Mithila struggled to her feet. She turned. There were five who had entered the hall, three men and two women. She knew them by their Circle colours, by the signs embroidered into their shirts, moving from right to left, from the Fifteenth to the Eleventh: the candlewick, the sandals, the broom, the bamboo stalk, and the bushel of *rahi*.

Mithila rubbed her eyes. 'How long was I asleep?'

'Three hours.'

Her head hurt like someone had carefully driven an iron nail into it. Mithila put her palm upon the table, and pushed herself erect.

The group stopped a metre away, facing her. Her eyes passed from one to the other. They looked back at her, motionless. Moments slipped away.

'Yes?' she said uncertainly.

From the right, a man advanced, until he was standing inches from her. He pointed to the lampwick emblazoned upon his shirt. 'Under the banner of the Worldfarer,' he said, 'the Fifteenth will march. Until the Worldfarer gives us a world without Circles. We march for that world and nothing more.'

He raised his right fist to his forehead, and extended it to her. Without knowing what she was doing, Mithila cupped his fist in her palms, and drew it to her.

'I won't fail you,' she said.

She dropped her hands. The man of the Fifteenth retreated.

His neighbour walked forward. 'The Fourteenth will march,' he said. 'Under the Worldfarer, on the same terms.' Mithila performed the ritual again, smoother this time, her voice stronger. He too moved back into line when she was done, and the man in the middle advanced. 'The Thirteenth will march,' he said, his words tumbling into one another. 'With the Worldfarer. On these terms.'

Mithila heard Maji exhale. That was the last three Circles, Maji's people, the memory of Savarian. That left the two women to her left.

Eleventh and Twelfth. She stole a look to her side. Prana was sweating, and Meghana was staring firmly at the floor.

The first of the women stepped forward. She looked directly at Mithila. 'Worldfarer,' she said. 'You asked us not to believe. But following you demands belief. No more circles, yes, but how do we square this one?'

Before Mithila could answer, the woman raised her right fist to her forehead, and extended it. 'The Twelfth will believe—and the Twelfth will march.' Mithila sighed in relief. Smiling, she reached out once more—to find a knife-point at her palm, its edge pricking her skin.

Mithila stilled. She kept her hand steady, in place.

'Until you betray,' said the woman of the Twelfth, very softly.

The knife retreated from her palm. Mithila dropped her hand. The woman of the Twelfth nodded, once.

The last representative stepped forward. Her voice was mild and unhurried. 'Under Worldfarer *and no other*,' she said, 'the Eleventh will march. Until the world.'

Behind her, a great loosening of limbs.

'It begins,' said Maji, and her voice shone.

She strode past Mithila and grasped the representative of the Fifteenth by the shoulder. 'Gather the company, Ranat. We need the barricade up on the Maliot before Wallrise. This is a *revolution*.'

Ranat turned to Mithila. Maji took a step back, pale.

'Field command is with Maji of the Fifteenth,' Mithila said, 'until I say otherwise.'

Maji mastered herself. Turning quickly to Carina, she said, 'I'll leave the Charter to you.' She strode towards the door, almost dragging Ranat along with her. Halfway across the hall, she turned around once.

'Thankfully,' she said, 'one of us remembers the last time.' And then she was gone.

Mithila turned back to the table, where the Union members and Carina were looking at her in silence.

'By the way,' she said, 'where is my banner?'

Thirteen

The Barricade

Rama stood on the balcony of the Council Tower. She watched the sun spill up from behind the Wall, striking the white stone of the Forum with its first light.

The City took shape before her eyes.

Beneath her, the Forum stirred.

Rama looked down. Next to the Temple, the Shoortan forces had begun to move. They left the Forum in lines of five, and took the Maliot, Wallwards.

Rama watched them out of sight.

'At this rate,' Carina said, 'The Matriarch will come down upon us, and we'll still be arguing.'

'If you would stop objecting—' Prana began, but Carina cut him short.

'Why, am I delaying you, Prana?' she said, sweetly. 'Should we have another *Committee*?'

Prana brought his hand down on the table. 'We had an agreement. Until you, Dooma, decided to obstruct—yet again.'

'Yet again?' Carina's voice grew dangerous. 'Want to explain that?'

Meghana put a warning hand on Prana's shoulder, but he shook her off. 'Everyone knows this. Clever Dooma, you had Savarian's ear in the

Blue Revolution. You refused to let him compromise, because for you, *nothing* less than the total destruction of the Circles would do. You goaded him to defeat—and now again—'

'So it's back to sly old Dooma bringing everyone else down, is it?'

'You're always in it for yourselves, you—'

'Oh, *shut up*, Prana,' Meghana interrupted. 'Do I need to remind you what my father died for?'

Little mutterings broke out among the other members of the Union. Prana turned to Meghana. 'You don't see. Our mothers and fathers, those who joined Savarian, lost everything because the Dooma didn't know when to stop. And now again—'

'Alright, that *really* is enough.' Mithila stood. She walked over to Carina, and looked over her shoulder, at the roll of paper spread out on the table.

CHARTER FOR A NEW SUMER

Article 1: Every Citizen of Sumer has absolute freedom to venture beyond the Wall, temporarily or for all time, alone or in company. This freedom shall not be infringed under any circumstance.

Article 2: The farmland belongs to those who work it.
All questions about production and distribution, including harvest quotas, shares in produce, etc. shall be decided democratically, in a manner to be determined.

After that, there were illegible words, crossed out or smudged.

'What's the problem?' said Mithila.

'Carina wants a third article calling for an immediate tearing down of the Mandalas and rebuilding the City without Circles.'

'Yes, what's the matter?' said Carina, 'afraid you'll find the Dooma in your kitchen?'

'Why do you Dooma always have to speak so *harshly*?' Prana protested. 'We've signed up to going beyond the Wall, we've put a Shoortan target on the backs of our Mandalas. We've signed up to take back the farms—and that means take the food right off the Elders' plates.'

'What a lovely sacrifice,' Carina said. 'Now let me rephrase this. The Worldfarer gets what she wants. You get what you want. And what do we get? Don't say "our eternal thanks."'

Prana turned to Mithila, his eyes appealing. 'I've been trying to explain this all night. Look. Imagine—imagine we're winning, alright? The Council sees it. They come and say, "let's make terms." Are you going to tell them, "no terms till we've thrown you out of your houses and moved in?" You're making compromise impossible.'

'Oh, because taking the food from their plates is a grand compromise, isn't it? What are you trying to be, a half-revolutionary?'

'Why don't we get into power first, and then—'

'And then you'll throw us some scraps, after you get your land back? That's how every betrayal has begun: with a man saying "stand with me, let me get into power, and then …" And then he stabs us in the front and sends us back into the shadow of the Wall to lick our wounds.'

Prana blanched. Carina took a breath and calmed herself. 'Here is our chance,' she said, her voice quieter, 'to start the world over again. This Charter is our dream, made words. And you, POUM, want to dream by halves? When it comes to the farmlands, your lands, you will have a revolution, and then you will stop? Can't you see that that won't work? It's all bound together—you leave any part of this City standing, then one day *it* will come back and break *you*.'

Meghana spoke. 'Carina, we understand this. *I* understand this. But you know this too: twenty-seven years ago there was a revolution. We were too young, but our parents were there, and the Dooma and at least a small part of the Farmer's Mandalas fought together. The Revolution failed, and you know why: Savarian Refused to compromise. All or nothing—and he got nothing. Now we have another chance. At least this time …'

The shadow of a smile flitted across Carina's face. 'As always, you want us to fight for you, but you will not fight for us. We are invisible even in your dreams. I will say no more. Let the Worldfarer decide. She is our Banner after all.'

Mithila felt the eyes of the room on her. A part of her had known it would come down to this. She cleared her throat. 'Alright, Carina. Please write.'

Carina took up the pen once more, and looked up at Mithila inquiringly.

'*Article 3. The Marriage License Law stands abolished.*'

Silence fell, broken only by the scratching of Carina's pen. She finished writing. 'Alright. And?'

'That's it. That's the Article.'

'Oh.'

Silence lingered in the air. Everyone around the table was staring at her.

'What the bloody Builders is this?' said Carina at last.

'It's weaker than even Thanu's Social Law,' Prana said.

'But strong enough to destroy the Circles,' said Mithila.

'What do you mean?'

'Just this,' said Mithila. 'The Circles rest upon three things. The first is the Wall. This, we will destroy. The second is control over land, which locks them in place. This, we will transform. And the third is the Marriage License Law, which holds people to their Circles. This, we will abolish. I promise you, Carina, that once we strip these powers from those who sit in the Forum, the Circles themselves will wither away. And you will be free.'

'Wither away in a thousand years?' Carina said heavily.

'Not so long.'

'Many generations, at least. And until then the Dooma—waits?'

Mithila said nothing. Carina's face slipped into a mask.

'We promised to follow you,' she said. 'And so it will be.'

'Would it help if I told you that Savarian considered the abolition of the Marriage License Law fundamental to his Revolution?' Mithila said. '*I* would know.'

She sensed a stir in the hall, as people remembered afresh who her father had been—no, *was*. Mithila shrugged to herself. It would take some getting used to.

'It will also make it easier for the Middle Circles to join in,' she said. '*Everyone* outside the Five wants the marriage license laws abolished. And this doesn't threaten them.'

'Ah, that reminds me,' said Carina. 'Article 4. *Any Mandala wishing to join the Banner does so on the above terms, and is at liberty to propose any further terms, to be ratified by a majority of existing Mandalas. In case of a tie, the Banner will have the casting vote.*'

Prana nodded. 'Logical.'

Carina's pen moved swiftly. 'Done,' she said.

An exhalation went around the table. Mithila looked up. A grey light was trickling in from the high windows. Wallrise approached.

'The Worldfarer first,' Carina said.

Mithila leaned across the table. She took the pen, turned the paper towards herself, and signed her name below the last article.

One by one, they signed for their Circles.

'We are bound now,' said Prana, 'to each other, and to the Banner.'

'And now that we are …' said Carina. She clapped her hands.

The door to the hall scraped open. A man entered, a bundle in his hand. 'As you asked,' he said. He walked up to them and unrolled it on the floor.

It was thick cloth, swiftly made, rough and blood-red. Upon it was stitched a black wall, cracked through the middle. Through the crack in the wall, in a mesh of finely-woven threads, Mithila saw the sun peering through.

The first light of Wallrise streamed through the windows and stuck the sun on the banner, making it blaze gold.

In the conferral room, the senior Councillors were waiting.

'She finally talked last night,' Rama said. 'The Matriarch demands complete power over any matter concerning the Wall. She also demands that she alone will decide what matters concern the Wall.'

'What nonsense,' Varsha snapped. 'Everything this side of the Wall has *something* to do with the Wall. She wants control through Ostracism.'

'She denied that,' Rama said mildly. 'She was only insistent about a free hand in dealing with the Young Tarafians, and matters like those. Oh also, by the way, she was very angry about something. It turns out someone broke into the Temple last night, ambushed two of the priests, knocked them on the head, tied them up, and painted a big crossed circle on their faces. In lampblack.'

Raja snorted into his arm. Even Varsha smiled.

'She did accuse me in the beginning,' said Rama, 'until I told her if we had someone capable of such a thing, we'd have gone straight for her instead of wasting time with priests.'

Chortles again. Then Hansa brought them all back to earth.

'What did you say to her demands?'

'I asked her for some time.' Rama gave them a demure smile. 'After all, the Council hasn't granted me Emergency Powers yet. She gave me a day.'

'This is bad,' Varsha said gloomily. 'She has the mob. What can we even do?'

'A lot, as it turns out,' Rama said. 'Councillor Raja—could you report, please?'

Raja cleared his throat. 'Uhm—so, late last night there was a meeting of the Mandalas Eleventh to the Fifteenth. They have come together under the banner of Mithila-Seven, whom they now call the *Worldfarer*. They've made a barricade on the Maliot Road, and blocked off the routes beyond the Tenth.'

Rama laughed out loud. '*Never doubted you, Mith,*' she murmured under her breath. The Elders looked at her strangely.

'The Shoortans have just left the Plaza,' Raja continued. 'They're marching Wallwards.'

'And there you have it,' Rama said. 'Respite. The foot is off our necks. For a while.'

Hansa flashed her a sudden, appreciative grin. But Varsha was frowning. 'How did you know this would happen?'

'I devised it,' said Rama, her voice flat. 'Why, were you thinking I would allow such a threat to this City to escape—because of my feelings?'

Varsha coloured. 'No—no—of course not. But this is risky, this creation of a third force.'

'The President's right.' Councillor Paras—who hadn't spoken yet, in either of the gatherings—now did. 'We needed to gamble.'

'Ha!' Hansa said, rubbing her hands. 'Gamble? Rama, this was genius. Don't worry, Varsha—this so-called Five Mandala Alliance will collapse very soon. Farmers and the Dooma—what unites them? History? Shared interests? Nothing. Even Savarian couldn't stop them from bickering all the time. We only need to find out what divides them now—and then a little push.'

'Exactly,' said Rama, 'which is why—'

The door to the Audience Chamber opened, and Malati walked in.

Rama looked up. 'Councillor Malati, can we speak in a bit? This is a bit of an emergency—'

'I know,' said Malati, 'this is too.'

Rama saw annoyance flash on the faces of the other Councillors. Quickly, she asked: 'how can I help?'

'I understand that the Council will be fighting again. The last time we fought, there was a weapon that was decisive in our victory. It could shoot missiles very far, very fast, and—'

'We know that,' Hansa interrupted. 'Except that that knowledge is lost. The Dhanurashi will not make us a trebuchet again. Builders, he won't make us a chair!'

'Oh, I wonder why,' Malati said sarcastically. 'And I wonder who warned you not to destroy every single person you thought *might* be a threat to you after the Mutiny.'

'Is there a point?' said Hansa.

'Yes, if you let me finish. I came to tell you Councillor Amrit wrote out the workings of the trebuchet in the Encyclopaedia of Sumer.'

Rama started. 'Which was burned, wasn't it?'

'All of it,' said Malati, and her voice cracked for just an instant, 'except this.'

She reached into her pocket and extracted a sheaf of paper from it. Raja looked at it and jumped to his feet.

'Saved from the fire,' said Malati. 'By quite a stroke of luck, no? It is, I believe'—she smiled drily at them—'*particularly* useful against barricades.' She moved around the chairs, and handed the sheets to Rama. 'Here you are—President.'

'Where did you get this?' Raja said.

Malati ignored him, and looked at Rama.

Rama was staring down at the writing and the diagrams. 'Iron and wood,' she said. 'And stone?'

'We have it,' Hansa said. 'We have all of it. There are stocks in the Council Hall, for desperate times. I do believe this qualifies. But we need people from the Eighth to actually make it.'

'Ah,' said Rama. She thought for a moment. 'I'll handle that.' She turned to Malati. 'Thank you for this, Councillor.'

'Just doing my duty,' said Malati. 'Just one more request, President.'

'Go on.'

'I'm done.'

Rama started. 'What?'

'I resign.'

'Yes, but why?'

'I find fighting distasteful.' Malati's voice was toneless, prepared. 'And I find this conflict—and whatever will emerge from it—distasteful. At the time of Savarian, I was still young. I am no longer young, and I will not have the time to find my place in the new order that you're going to build. I would prefer to retire, so I can use that time to remake the Encyclopaedia.' Malati smiled. 'You're not going to miss me.'

There was, Rama thought, some relief floating upon the faces of the Councillors, but their masks were on.

'I can't—won't—stop you, of course,' she said. 'I wish you would reconsider, but if you've thought about it—'

'I have.'

'Well then,' said Rama. 'The Council is so thankful for all your years of service, Councilor Malati. We will give you a worthy farewell once we've sorted this trouble out.'

Malati nodded smartly.

She turned to the Councillors. 'I do remember,' she said, 'that all these years, in Council, some of these people sitting here questioned my allegiance. They accused me of giving shelter and comfort to rebels. Sometimes they hinted that secretly, I would have been pleased if Savarian had won. I wanted this to be my last act here—so that when you remember me, you remember what loyalty means.'

Before anyone could say anything, Malati turned and strode out of the room.

'Thank Builders,' said Raja, the moment she was gone. 'No stupid mercy petitions this time, no "*but what about their rights.*"'

'Forget that,' Hansa said. 'This has changed everything. We don't have to play defence anymore.'

Rama felt rising excitement in the room. 'No time to lose then,' she said, holding up the sheets. 'By the way—Special Emergency Powers? The Council meets in half an hour.'

The Councillors exchanged glances. Finally, Varsha said: 'We will support it.'

Rama fought to keep her voice steady. 'I am glad.'

'We don't like it,' Varsha said.

'I don't either.'

'But we recognize that it is necessary.'

'Indeed.'

'Subject to what you said—this will be reviewed in fifteen days.'

Rama smiled. 'I hope to finish this much before that.'

They nodded to her and walked out of the room, faces set. Hansa lingered.

'Your father would be very proud if he could see you now,' she said, once just the two of them were left in the room.

Rama stared at the floor. 'I hope so.'

'I know he would. How strangely the Circle turns ...' Hansa tailed off, shaking her head. 'You know,' she continued, 'I still remember how, for most of the Mutiny, Savarian was destroying us. His forces had reached the Fifth. We were on our knees. He was on the barricade, laughing at us. Then he asked us for a debate, like—like he wanted to play with us before he cut us down. I wasn't going to accept, I wasn't going to allow another humiliation, but there was one among us who insisted.

'Amrit.'

Rama's throat was dry. 'And then?' she whispered.

'He went. To the foot of the barricade. There, before the eyes of Sumer, they spoke. Savarian wove his dreams of deceit, as he always did. But Amrit'—Hansa smiled fondly—'I never knew it, but *Builders*, he could speak. I still remember the moment, when he said, '*and when the Circles are gone, what then? What will take their place? In this City within the Wall, what do you have to promise us that there will always be enough, so that we do not exhaust and perish? And if you're wrong, what will we lose? What would we have lost, but Sumer?*' I remember because Savarian had no answer, he'd never really thought this through, all he could say was, "*the people will decide*"—and when the people heard that, they realized they did not know either.'

'And then?'

'Nothing changed just then,' Hansa said. 'But I knew we were going to win. And we did. I'll always know it turned that day. After it was all over'—she smiled again—'we called it the duel on the barricade.'

'That's why Savarian hated my father so much?'

'Yes. After we smashed them, he sent a message over the barricades, just for Amrit: *one day I will drag you down with me.*' Hansa's voice broke. 'And Time circled.'

Rama locked her fingers together. 'I see. The duel on the barricade.'

'We're going to win again,' said Hansa. 'And I will know the moment that we do, my President.'

She nodded and walked away from the Rama. As she opened the door to leave, a young man slipped through the gap.

'President.'

'Ah, there you are, Sanap,' Rama said to the secretary, hearing her voice tremble. 'I need you to get to the Eighth Mandala. Be careful, Shoortans on the prowl. Once you're in the Eighth, ask for a man called Lamon. He's an ironworker.'

'I'll find him.'

'When you do,' said Rama, 'give him this message.' She turned to her desk, and began to write.

Light crept across the sky, as the barricade rose above the river.

Water barrels rolled out of their houses, filled with earth. Chairs, dragged from their tables, smashed to their bones, lashed together with bamboo. Flagstones, worried and uprooted like teeth from the Maliot Road. Somewhere in the Dooma, there was a gaping hole in the wall where a window-shutter had once filtered Wallrise. In the Twelfth, earth breathed again inside a home with no more floorboards.

The barricade rose three storeys high, stretching from the river to the houses of the Eleventh. On the outside, facing the faraway Forum, sharpened bamboo stakes protruded into the air, level with a man's throat. By the river, little fortifications stood, security against bowshot from the other bank.

Inside the barricade, people swarmed up and down the structure, shouting orders. The banner of the Worldfarer was planted atop, waving in the grey sky.

'You built this in the small hours of the night?' Mithila gaped.

Maji smiled. 'A banked fire needs only moments to come alive, Worldfarer. The challenge was to not let it die for twenty-seven years.'

For the first time it struck Mithila, how long Maji had waited. She looked at her with new-found respect—and then her gaze was caught by the banner, and from there to the woman standing next to it, looking out over the Maliot, with a sling at her back.

'Why is there a baby at the barricade, Maji?'

Maji shrugged. 'You think the Revolution won't have mothers? Bhavi-Twelve was among the first to sign up. And she specifically asked for guard duty.'

'But the carers—'

'Are the Tenth Circle. You know. On the other side.'

'I can't allow—'

'You do not *allow*, Worldfarer,' Maji growled. 'We aren't here because you allowed us. Do you intend to volunteer for babysitting duties while we fight on the barricade? No? Then I suggest you stop pretending you know better than the mothers, and do your job—you know, as the Banner we're marching under. And if you really care about the babies'—she gestured beyond the barricade at the Tenth, looking Mithila in the eye—'*persuade* them to join us. Then we can have Carers again.'

Mithila dropped her gaze. 'Right,' she said. 'No pressure, then.'

She looked around her. On their side of the barricade, little camps had been thrown up on the Maliot. Women and men together in small groups. In their hands, they held bamboo staves, sharpened into points. At the edge of the Maliot, she saw people: people of all ages—and a *lot* of children—watching them. Some held on to their parents' hands by the finger, while others chased each other round in a circle, raising a clatter of noise.

'What is this, a holiday picnic?' she muttered to Maji.

'I think we roused a whole lot of them when we were requisitioning for the barricade,' Maji said wryly. 'But I know how this goes. They'll only watch for now. If we start winning, they'll join.'

'You're really going to be insufferable with all your *twenty-seven years ago, it was like this* no?'

Maji narrowed her eyes at Mithila for a moment, but then she laughed. 'Your father always said—'

But what it was her father always said Mithila never found out, because Maji was interrupted by a shout. They turned. Prana was hurrying towards them, from the Eleventh.

'Is it done?' Maji said.

Prana nodded. 'We've secured about half the Circle. East Quarter. Barricades on three bridges.'

'Good,' said Maji. 'And how many will join us?'

Prana looked down at the ground. 'From the Eleventh and the Twelfth? Not—ah—not as many as we'd hoped.'

'Oh well,' said Maji. 'It always begins like that. Will they at least give us quiet support? Shelter, if we need it? Provisions and supplies? And if it comes to the streets—doors opened to us, and closed to them?'

Prana looked outraged. 'Of course! They're with us, it's just that—'

'They're not quite ready to die yet.' Maji nodded. 'That's fair.'

In the distance, Mithila heard a faint, rhythmic noise.

It was the sound of marching feet.

'They're here,' she said quietly. 'What are we doing?'

'Twenty-seven years ago—' Maji began, but bit her tongue, as she saw Mithila's expression. 'Sorry! I'll keep this brief. Watch.'

The marching feet grew louder, until there was a sudden shout from the top. 'They're here!'

'Here we go,' said Maji. She turned back to the buildings of the Eleventh, looming above them, and made a quick signal. Mithila followed her gaze—and it was then that she saw the plumes of smoke rising from the direction of the Wall, somewhere along the Rasa.

'What the—'

Maji saw her look, and smiled calmly. 'Don't worry—just to stop them from circling around us.'

'*You* did that?'

'Just burnt our bridges, Worldfarer.' Maji spread out her hands. 'We've left one to cross over.'

'White flag!' Bhavi shouted from the top of the barricade. 'They want to talk.'

'That means you,' Maji said, with an iron smile.

Mithila walked up to the barricade, trying to still the frantic beating of her heart. There was an easy path, almost a stairway leading up on their side. She climbed gingerly, searching for support. Near the top, Bhavi caught her arm and dragged her to the rim of the barricade.

'All good, Worldfarer?'

'Yes, thanks.' Mithila looked down. Before her lay the Maliot, glimmering in the morning sun, running with the Rasa, studded with bridges. One bridge was directly beneath her, vaulting the tributary that separated the Tenth and the Eleventh. Marching towards it were the Shoortans, in well-disciplined rows, a phalanx that stretched halfway back into the Tenth Mandala.

Flags waved in the breeze, black flags with the white patch of the Heartstone etched in the centre. There was no sound from the marchers, just the steady *dhoom-dhoom* of their tramping feet upon the flagstones.

At their head walked Rastogi.

Mithila turned to the windows and the terraces of the Tenth, at the level of her eyes and below. They were lined with people. On a rooftop, she saw Kodali.

The Shoortans halted before the bridge. Rastogi walked towards the barricade alone, carrying the white flag. He stopped beneath her.

'Who is the leader?' he cried out.

'Oh hello there, Rastogi,' Mithila said.

Rastogi looked at the Worldfarer's banner waving by her side. His nostrils flared. 'Mithila-Seven,' he said, his voice as harsh as ever, 'I cannot speak with you.'

'Is that so?' said Mithila. 'Send my little sister out to play, then. You're following her orders anyway.'

Rastogi glared at her. 'Was it one of your cowards who attacked our priests in the Temple last night? And *painted their faces*?'

'What!' Mithila said. Out of the corner of her eye, she saw Bhavi suddenly cover her mouth with her elbow, as if she was trying not to laugh. 'I didn't do it, but there's nothing wrong with a Shoortan face that a little paint wouldn't improve.'

Chuckles rose below the barricade.

'Stop this mutiny,' Rastogi snapped. 'I know you're desperate, but setting yourself up at the head of a bunch of farmers with sticks—you're not seriously thinking of fighting us! The Matriarch says that if you surrender now she will reconsider your Ostracism. No one will be hurt. On Shoortan honour.'

His words fell like pebbles on the ground.

'How kind,' Mithila said. 'But I'll pass.'

She drew herself up. 'And go back and tell her this: I am the Worldfarer. I have been beyond the Wall. I have seen the sea and the lost City of Gumfraude, and I have come back. Do you think your lies have any power over us now?'

Behind her, a cheer went up. She raised her arm, holding Rastogi's gaze.

'The Circles have come together, under the banner of the Worldfarer. From the Eleventh to the Fifteenth, we say that *we are done with you*, Shoortans. You've had two thousand years. Now get out of our way.'

Rastogi looked past her. He pitched his voice beyond the barricade, to those he could not see.

'Citizens. Your Worldfarer is Ostracized. Those who stand with her stand against the Wall. Leave her now, and the Matriarch will still be merci—'

'That's enough,' Mithila cut in. 'If you're not out of here on the count of ten—'

'Oh?' Rastogi sneered. 'What will you do?'

Two well-aimed arrows, fired from the rooftops of the Eleventh, sheared the air, whistled past Mithila's ears, and bounced off the flagstones on either side of Rastogi.

He fell backwards squealing, a high-pitched sound none of them had ever heard from him.

Laughter rose from the barricade. Rastogi looked up—and at that moment the third arrow struck the ground, just in front of him.

The High Priest scrabbled to his feet and ran, his black cloak flapping around his legs. The laughter followed him back to the Shoortan phalanx.

Mithila leapt down from the barricade.

Maji, grinning, cracked out: '*Archers!*'

Three women and three men hurried forward to the barricade and positioned themselves before small, strategically created gaps in the structure. There were bamboo bows in their hands, and quivers at their back.

Mithila went up to the barricade, and peered through one of the cracks. Across the bridge, the Shoortan phalanx was still.

She turned around. Maji's fighters had left their camps and were positioned upon the Maliot, weapons out. The crowd on the edge of the road had melted away into the morning, but its presence lingered.

Mithila looked through the crack again. Her eyes traced the lengths of the bamboo stakes leaning out of the barricade, to their sharp points.

'They're going to try and wear us out,' Maji said.

She was wrong.

Before Mithila knew what was happening, the Shoortans moved. The first row sprinted towards the barricade, shields up, swords drawn.

'*Matriarch!*' they cried, '*For the Wall!*'

'Fire,' said Maji.

The arrows flew from the cracks in the barricade. From the rooftops of the Eleventh more came, arcing downwards onto the Maliot. Mithila saw men stumble and fall, replaced by the ones immediately behind them.

'Barricade!' Maji called.

Women and men rushed past Mithila to the barricade, and as they ran, she could hear them sing, sharp and joyous:

Alora, arise, your children call
Alora, the day is here again

Her mind had just enough time to register *Alora*, to think of Gumfraude and of Ghada, before the fighters of the Dooma leapt onto the barricade, and she thought of nothing else. Remnants of flagstones in their hands, they took aim and hurled them on the Shoortans, finding shields, helmets, eyes, fingers, necks. From the bottom, more flagstones were passed.

The Shoortan line halted—and then came on again.

Through the crack, Mithila watched. Amidst a rain of stones, the front line was hacking away at the bamboo stakes. The first of them began to climb, and then there were bodies falling back upon the Maliot, hitting the ground with a crunch, or falling upon their companions, who slashed at them, trying to get away. Screams pierced the air, as the frontline retreated from the stones, but was swept against the barricade by those behind them, in a mad rush from the arrows that came from above.

The smell of sweat and blood rose into the sky.

Was the barricade shaking?

Mithila instinctively reached for her side—and found nothing. Maji had not given her a weapon. She cursed.

'Arrows!' Bhavi's shout cut through the chaos.

Mithila's eyes snapped up. At the top of the barricade, she saw Bhavi duck, pulling the sling to her front and curling her body over her baby.

'Clear the Maliot!'

Arrows came flying over the barricade, launched on a hope and a prayer, passed over all of them, and struck the empty road harmlessly.

Maji laughed. 'Shoortan, meet barricade.'

'They're retreating!' Bhavi called.

Maji raised her arm. 'Hold fire.'

Through the crack, Mithila saw the Shoortan phalanx running down the Maliot, in panic. Behind her, the archers had stopped. On the road she saw bodies, face down in the street, impossible to recognise. Something began to build in her chest. Turning away, she hurried to the Rasa and let herself into the river, wading across the barricade. She stumbled and looked down, and saw threads of red running through the water. Blood, channeled between the flagstones, was flowing into the river.

There was a hand on her shoulder, and a voice in her ear.

'What the *fuck* do you think you're doing?'

Mithila gestured at the pile of bodies next to the barricade. 'We can save some—'

Maji seized her collar, and with a strength that surprised Mithila, dragged her back to their side of the barricade, splashing water as she went. Hands reached for them, grabbing Mithila under her arms and lifting her up onto the Maliot. Behind her, Maji hauled herself up, droplets of water spilling from her clothes.

The fighters on the barricade surrounded her. From the streets of the Eleventh, the others began to emerge.

'Nobody,' said Maji quietly, 'crosses the barricade without my word.' She looked at Mithila. '*Especially* not the Banner. The first time they see us doing this, there'll be an ambush waiting. Let the Shoortans come and get their own.'

'Fourteen dead,' said Mithila numbly. But before she could say anything, one of the Dooma—a young man—was on his knees, and throwing up his breakfast upon the Maliot.

Maji walked back to the river, and knelt by the shore. When she straightened again, they saw that she had soaked a cloth in the water. She walked back to them and helped the man to his feet.

'It is hard, the first time,' said Maji, to the circle. She gave him the wet cloth, and put an arm around him.

'I wish I could tell you it becomes easier,' said Maji. 'But if I did, I'd be lying.'

The Carers came out onto the Maliot. Working silently, they lifted the Shoortan bodies, and under Kodali's direction, carried them to makeshift biers, destined for the Towers of Rebirth. This was their job, after all.

They came back once, to run water over the Maliot, to wash away the blood.

But this had never been the Carers' job.

They left, and a dark-red bloom remained upon the flagstones of the Maliot.

On the other side of the barricade, Mithila sat against the foot of the barricade, looking up at the sky. Upon the Maliot, the Revolution ate: Leaf plates on their knees, fresh bread and peanut paste, dipped into little cups of bamboo soup.

Mithila leaned back against the barricade.

She heard a slithering noise above. Bhavi leaped lightly to the ground. The barricade guard came and sat beside her.

'Hey, Worldfarer.'

Mithila turned to her. The baby was awake now, and regarding her with utmost seriousness. Bhavi grinned. 'Say hi to Nilan.'

'Ah—hello, Nilan,' Mithila said throatily. She had very little memory of babies. She raised an index finger and passed it back and forth over his eyes. Nilan followed it with his gaze and made a sudden grab for it. Mithila let herself be caught. Bhavi laughed, a clear sound.

'Why don't you hold him?' she said. And before Mithila could protest, she found her arms full of baby, surprisingly heavy. For a moment she was terrified that she would drop him, or he would cry, but Nilan only looked at her curiously. She cradled him in her arms, and clumsily rocked him back and forth.

'Oh well done!' said Bhavi. 'Almost as if you've been practicing.'

'You sure it's safe up there, Bhavi?'

'Safest place in the Revolution, Worldfarer. The top of the barricade is the last to fall. And when it's truly dangerous I leave him behind with Aashna.' Her eyes twinkled. 'Like last night at the Temple.'

Mithila gaped. 'That was you?'

'May have been,' Bhavi smiled, guileless. 'I had some fun with the priests, won't lie. And it got them mad enough to hurl themselves at us, didn't it?'

Mithila sighed. '*You* should be leading this thing.'

Bhavi shot her a quick look. 'You okay, Worldfarer?'

The weight of Nilan in her arms, his eyes upon her, gave her the complicity she needed.

'No,' said Mithila. 'I'm not.'

Bhavi raised an eyebrow.

'Blood was fine in theory,' Mithila said. 'In practice? I don't know. I'm not Maji. I'm not my father. Maybe I'll get used to it? I don't know.'

'You don't have to get used to it,' said Bhavi.

'But if I don't, I need to know what it's worth,' said Mithila. 'I need to know you're all here for *something*, not just because your Mandala voted to follow the Banner. Why are you here, Bhavi, upon this barricade?'

Bhavi was quiet, looking at Nilan, who'd gone to sleep in Mithila's arms.

'You know,' she said, 'a few years ago, we used to hear about a girl whose dreams were not leaving her with the years.'

'I see,' said Mithila. 'I was that famous, huh?'

'Not you by name,' Bhavi said. 'Just the stories. This was when I had turned eighteen, that time when the last of the dreams leave forever, and *smara* is all that remains. You know most people can't wait to be rid of the dreams, because they're frightening, but I—I wanted them to stay. Fires in the sky. Stars upon the ground. Shifting water. I wanted them all to stay. But they wouldn't. And I had to make my peace with it, like we all do.

'Then you did what you did, Worldfarer. And I knew that though my dreams were gone, *he*'—she pointed at Nilan—'could grow up in a world where dreams never had to leave, a world without the Wall. So I came.' She took in the Maliot with a sweep of the arm. 'The Mandala vote doesn't say we *have* to fight, Worldfarer. It says we can *choose* to fight. They're here because they choose to be. And they will leave if they so choose.'

She held out her arms. Mithila carefully deposited Nilan back in them. He did not wake.

'Sorry, Worldfarer.' Bhavi smiled at her, a full, rich smile. 'But you're stuck leading, I'm afraid. Until the world.'

'Then I better start acting like that I guess,' Mithila muttered. She stood, brushing dust off her clothes. 'I'll see you soon,' she said to Bhavi. She walked down the Maliot, where Maji's people had just finished eating, and Maji herself was standing in the middle.

Mithila walked up to Maji, and cleared her throat.

'Yes, Worldfarer?'

'I need a weapon,' said Mithila.

Maji turned, an eyebrow raised. 'You?'

'No, Rastogi. Yes, *me*.'

'You are the Banner,' Maji said slowly. 'Not a fighter.'

'Maji, I'm not going to stand on the barricade like I'm some Golden Youth, while people fight and die around me, for me. Now, for the last time: *give me a weapon.*'

Maji's lip curled. 'Temper, Worldfarer.'

Mithila stared at her.

'You'd be a liability in a fight. I'd have to waste two of ours just to keep you safe. We can't afford to lose you, *Banner*.'

Mithila smiled sweetly. 'You sound like you wish you could.'

'Don't provoke me, Worldfarer. Not now. I'm not wasting a weapon on you.'

'In that case,' said Mithila, 'I'll fight you for yours.'

Maji's eyes widened. 'What?'

'You're important too, Maji. My field commander. What would we do without you? Seems fair to keep you safe—'

'Don't be bloody stu—'

'With *respect*, Maji,' Mithila made her voice iron. 'Shouldn't my field commander trust her Banner?'

Mithila saw a flash behind Maji's eyes, for the girl who had come out of nowhere and taken over a revolution that Maji had dreamed of for twenty-seven years. It was what she'd been counting on.

She bared her teeth in a grin. 'Well?'

Maji turned around. 'Swords!' she snapped out. 'No, you idiot—not the *real* ones. We aren't killing each other yet.'

A ripple ran down the Maliot, as people quickly realized that something was happening. Two practice swords, tips blunted, were brought over to them. Maji tossed one to Mithila, who caught it clumsily, nearly dropping it. Maji's eyes lit up in amusement.

Mithila balanced upon the balls of her feet. The sword was light. She gripped it in her right hand, holding it slightly bent, protecting her right side.

Around them, a circle was forming, breathless excitement in the air.

Maji faced her.

'You're still our Banner,' she said quietly, so only the two of them could hear. 'I have no desire to humiliate you here before everyone.'

Mithila yawned.

Maji lunged.

She was quick for her years, but her lunge was half-hearted. She was holding back, still unwilling to shame her Banner. Mithila stepped out of distance and mockingly beat away Maji's blade, even as the older woman withdrew.

'What's the matter?' she taunted. 'Forgotten how to fight after *twenty-seven years?*'

Maji's eyes narrowed. Warily, they circled each other. Mithila was dimly aware of the crowd around them, of bets being placed, of children watching wide-eyed. She blocked them out.

Maji came on more slowly this time, feinting to Mithila's neck and then to her stomach, watching for her reaction, waiting to see how she would parry. Mithila danced out of range, offering nothing. Out of the corner of her eye, she kept a watch on Maji's feet, waiting for movement.

Maji attacked again, and this time it was not a feint.

Mithila was ready. She saw the blade coming at her chest, teased a parry across her body, and—as Maji tried to go around it—stepped back and flicked her blade away. For a moment, Maji's side was unprotected, but Mithila's own blade had turned in her hand, and by the time she had it under control, Maji had jumped back, out of distance.

There was applause from the circle, but Mithila cursed.

Maji would not be taking her lightly forever. Mithila pressed forward, trying to catch Maji's blade at close quarters; she felt her retreat. Mithila advanced, looking for Maji's blade, to turn it away or to trap it, and it was Maji who was avoiding engagement, clumsily parrying her inches away from her body, stumbling back towards the circle that surrounded them. Mithila saw uncertainty glimmer in the Field Commander's eyes; she felt the sun on her neck, exultant, young and immortal—

Rashly, she stepped into Maji's range, her blade extended, an invitation.

Maji exploded into her, beating her blade away with a blow that made her shoulder sting, and the next moment Mithila's chest had split apart in a blaze of pure pain.

She collapsed on her knees, wheezing. Somehow, she'd kept hold of her blade, but her lungs were on fire, and her stomach felt like every last bit of air had been pumped out of it. She doubled over, breathing hard.

A hand around her shoulder, pulling her up, not ungently. She sucked in air.

Maji murmured: 'How many years did he teach you—banking fire?'

'Since I was four,' Mithila gasped, 'all three of us. Every day, an hour. Never knew why … a sculptor was so into—duelling.'

'It shows,' said Maji.

Mithila straightened, still breathless. 'Do I get my weapon now?'

'No.'

'*What?*'

'You lost, Worldfarer. '

'But—'

'Come now,' said Maji, her voice lowering again for just the two of them. 'You've impressed them all. The stories of your skill with the blade are already going down the Mandalas. They will respect you. But

I cannot—I *will not* have my Banner throw her life away playing the hero, when everything depends on her.'

'But—'

'If you argue with me anymore,' said Maji, 'I *will* tie you to a post made specially for you before battle. I am your Field Commander, Worldfarer. It's my barricade.'

Mithila opened her mouth again, saw Maji's eyes flash, but before she could speak—or not—another voice chopped the air.

'Worldfarer! Council!'

Bhavi stood at the edge of the circle.

'What?' said Maji.

'Council's at the barricade.'

'*Council?*' Maji began to laugh. 'What in Sumer—'

But a nameless dread had begun to creep up Mithila's throat.

'I know what this is,' she said.

She climbed up the barricade, still feeling heady, with Maji and her fighters at her back. At the top, she peered out over the rim. The road was clear, but stained with blood.

She looked up, further, and then she saw her.

Upon the bridge, a single figure stood, looking up at them.

'Greetings, Worldfarer,' Rama said.

Fourteen

The President's Proposal

Above the Wall, a garuda flew in the sky.

The world stopped to catch its breath.

The brilliant sun, the shadow of the barricade, the red stain upon the road, the needle-line of the river, and the two figures who faced each other, one upon the road and one upon the barricade. It could have been a painting by Synderesis.

Aeons passed them by.

'The President is welcome,' said Mithila at last.

'You know, Mith,' Rama said, 'They liked me better before you showed up. No barricade then.'

'Occupational hazard,' said Mithila, trying to keep her voice airy.

'Could've avoided it if you'd just let me know before leaving, *again. Off to start a revolution, Rama, won't be back for dinner, but anyway, blue I dream you blue*. It would've been polite.'

'Avoided?' Mithila repeated. '*Avoided?*'

'A world ago,' said Rama, with that half-smile that Mithila knew so well, 'I heard these words: *something of equality is yet to come*.'

The memory that pierced her was so sharp that Mithila's knees trembled. She grabbed at the barricade to keep her balance. The air before her shimmered. She was in the Maliot House again, her hand in Rama's, aware of her only good tunic, worn for the occasion, laughter in the room. And she heard once more the harper's music, weaving the air into song.

The world split into two, blood upon the Maliot, the sweetness of *khire*, the barricade beneath her, Rama's fingers in her hair, her own breath caught in her throat, *tell me something, talk to me, what will you do when you're in the Council*, Rama's voice, *I know you'll be telling me it's not enough, that something of equality is yet to come,* and Rama knew, Mithila thought savagely, she *knew* that one day it would come to this, but not so soon, not when she was so unprepared ...

Mithila blinked that world away.

'That,' she said, 'was a long time ago.'

Behind her, in the windows and along the rooftops, she sensed the people listening.

Rama looked at her with clear eyes. 'What do you dream of now, Worldfarer?'

We'll betray our dreams of each other, but I won't have it any other way.

Her own eyes blurred. The world was out of place.

Just, don't wake me up too soon, and I'll live.

'I'm sorry,' she said, 'but I woke up.'

Rama went rigid. A fist closed around Mithila's heart, and squeezed.

'I read your Charter,' Rama said, 'for a New Sumer. Do you know so little of me to think I would disagree?'

Mithila's head *hurt*. She looked to her left, to the windows, to her Revolution, watching.

'Rama would not,' she said. 'But I do not know the President.'

'Then hear your President,' Rama said. Her voice changed into something deeper, carrying across the barricade. 'I stand here in the Council's stead. I speak in the Council's voice.'

Mithila kept her eyes up. 'Go on.'

'This is to you, Mithila Worldfarer, and to those who follow you. I speak to you, the women and men of the Eleventh, the Twelfth, the Thirteenth, the Fourteenth and the Fifteenth.

'We are sorry.'

Whispers broke out, like gravel thrown into the lake, little ripples crossing into one another.

'In the past, you asked us for what was rightly yours.' Rama's gaze travelled beyond Mithila, to the rooftops and balconies. 'In our greed, we said no. For that I say to you, the Council says to you, we were wrong. We are sorry.

'We know that you've taken up arms against us only because you had no choice. For that, the blame is ours. We broke the ties that bind. For that I say to you, the Council says to you: we are sorry.

'But I also say: what is broken can be repaired.'

Rama knelt upon the road, heedless of the blood. On one knee, she looked up at them.

'And here, now, I ask you to give me a chance to repair it.'

Below Mithila, Prana growled: '*here we go again.*'

The whispers had grown into mutterings, sharp and heated.

Rama went on: 'As your President, I say: do not trust me. We have squandered any right to your trust. A Council that murdered Sanchika in cold blood—you should not trust. A Council that dismissed the meagre pleas in Malati's Bill—you should not trust. My hands are empty of platitudes and promises. But I come with amends.'

She paused. And then again: 'Will you hear me?'

'We're listening,' said Mithila, her answer lost in the scatter of voices from above and below.

'This morning, the Constitution of Sumer was changed,' said Rama. 'The old order is dead.'

'We call it the New Settlement. These are our three changes. First,' she said, raising her hand with a finger up, 'we have abolished the Marriage License laws in this City. Forever.'

Somewhere in Sumer, Mithila thought, Lamon was smiling.

Rama raised her second finger.

'Second: we accept Malati's original Bill. Farmers will decide, with us, what becomes of farmland. But more importantly: the Eleventh and the Twelfth will receive a third share of all the income from the farmland produce, to do with as they see fit.'

A third share, a third share! The voices of the farmers echoed in Mithila's mind, on the night she had seen them march to the Council

Hall, when crossing the Wall had been no more than a dream. Mithila shot a glance below. Prana's face was blank.

'And third,' said Rama, 'the people of Sumer are no longer bound to live in the Circles defined by their work. From this day, you are free—free to love and to live, across the City.'

And the voices rose again, higher than before, cries of excitement, of jubilation.

'This is not a promise. It is *already* done.' Rama's words ascended above the noise. She stood. 'It is done, no matter what. Something of equality is yet to come—but *something* of it is here.'

Mithila looked at Rama, standing there alone upon the Maliot, in front of the barricade. She was gazing past her, as if following her words as they wound their way into the latter Circles.

'Aren't you forgetting something, my President?' Mithila called out.

Rama went still.

'The Wall,' said Mithila.

Rama shifted. 'I'm sorry, but the Wall is not part of the New Settlement. This—all of this, this blood beneath my feet—this is not about the Wall. It's about us, our lives here, in Sumer.'

'But not those who want to leave it.' Mithila heard her voice shake. 'You are taking the world away from us, and offering us a few bushels of *rahi* in its place. Is that the price you've put on the horizon? A house, a lover, a third of your money?'

I know you'll be telling me, telling me always that it's not enough, and sometimes you'll make me angry because you'll accuse me of compromising, and I'll make you sad because I will really be compromising.

'Your people cannot eat the horizon,' said Rama, her voice trembling.

'But they have tasted the world. You have the power to do this now. And you *won't*—'

'I *can't*.' The words stretched taut, a rope between them. 'Don't you see? I can't. Not yet.'

'Not yet? Or not ever?'

Rama flinched. 'Did we not once promise that we would always be honest with each other?'

'In another world, a long time ago,' Mithila said. 'But I no longer ask for honesty. Just tell me a lie that I can forgive.'

There was silence.

'You called me *Worldfarer*,' Mithila said, after a while. 'Do you understand what that means?'

'Yes—no—*Worldfarer*,' said Rama. 'The Wall has been there, two thousand years. It has waited. It can wait a little longer. Let there be peace first.'

'There cannot be peace within the Wall.'

'Mithila—listen to me. Please.' Rama's voice grew urgent. 'A week ago, when we dreamed of the future in the *Maliot House*, this was unthinkable. Today it's already here. And you cannot lose what you never had. It is only you who will know the loss of a world that only you have seen. But your people—their dreams are here. Will you trample on them for the sake of yours?'

We'll betray our dreams of each other.

Mithila looked at her, aching. 'They have heard the sound of the world,' she said. 'We are not going back to what we were, Rama. The lies that kept us chained for two thousand years—they're broken. And *that* is something you'll never repair.'

Rama smiled at her, a slow sad smile. It broke her heart.

Numbly, Mithila knelt and picked up the banner, from where it was folded up beside her, and unfurled it. It whipped over the side of the barricade, twisting in the wind.

'Look, Rama,' she said, and Rama looked.

'This is the banner under which we've come together. Under this banner, and with a blade held to my palm, I have made my promise. It is the Wall—or it is nothing.'

There was a long silence.

The world shifted.

I'm sorry, Mithila said with her eyes. *I'm so sorry*. Rama was looking away from her, at the ground.

'I will take your answer,' Rama said finally. 'If you change your mind, come and find me. These laws will stand for fifteen days. If we have not resolved this by then, they will be gone—and so will I. Think about that, Mith.'

'I—alright,' said Mithila.

'Farewell,' said Rama. She turned and walked away, over the bridge.

And I thought, when you left at last, in that morning, how unfinished words became themselves in you, how effortless you made everything seem, how the world was suddenly so much more.

The world grew smaller, and greyer.

Beyond the bridge, Rama turned back once. Mithila bit down on her tongue, and watched her in silence.

Rama nodded. And then she was gone on the Maliot, towards the Forum.

'Well done,' Bhavi whispered. Nilan was looking at Mithila, wide-eyed, as if he'd understood the entire conversation.

Mithila nodded, not trusting herself to speak. She climbed down from the barricade, feeling sick.

'You heard that,' Maji said behind her, loud enough for her voice to carry to the terraces. 'Council's scared. Council's weak. Council thinks they can buy us.' She laughed harshly. 'As soon as we lay down our arms, they'll take it all back. We've seen this game before, haven't we?'

There were a few murmurs around her, which sounded like agreement. Mithila walked past her, into the Eleventh.

'She lies as well as the last President,' Prana muttered behind her.

'Is there any chance,' Mithila said, 'that it might work?'

'Not a chance,' Prana replied. 'You have the POUM, and you have the votes of the Eleventh and the Twelfth. We will not be swayed. We know better.'

When they reached Konar Hall again, Mithila found that it had been converted into Maji's control room. Tables and chairs had been dragged in, scale maps of various parts of Sumer spread out, and the hall was full of little groups of people, many of them bearing weapons, who stood close together and talked in low voices.

She threw herself into a chair, put her face in her hands, and took a long breath.

'Hey,' Maji said, 'there's no need for that. You did *well.* They always do this. First the bribes. Then the violence. Always. Also, Worldfarer ...' She paused. 'There's someone here to see you.'

'Please,' Mithila said, her hands pressed to her eyes. 'Can it wait?'

Unexpectedly, Maji knelt and put an arm around her shoulder. 'I know. But trust me, this might make you feel better.'

Mithila gave her a wan smile, and got to her feet. 'Well then. Where?'

Maji pointed to the wall. Mithila noticed for the first time, the outlines of a doorway. 'Go on.'

Mithila walked to the door, and pushed it open.

She entered a circular chamber with a low roof, and sunlight streaming in through large, rectangular windows. A bench ran around the circumference of the room. In the centre, two chairs faced each other across a table. One of them was occupied.

He smiled. His eyes came to life.

'My love,' her father said.

Once again, time graciously slowed down the world for her.

Sunlight fell in gentle veils, bathing Ananta's face in a glow that brought back the taste of hot bamboo soup, the scent of wood shavings, and the measure of the night to the rhythm of song in an old house in the Seventh.

She did not know when she stumbled across the distance between them, when she fell into his open arms, and when she let herself sob into his sleeve. Ananta said nothing, only held her, his touch as soft as she had always known, until the tears dried themselves.

She pulled back and looked at him.

He wore a tattered smock that hung loose from his body. His face had sunk in upon itself. The cheekbones stood out, the eyes deep-set, the mouth drawn.

'Sorry I've been away for a bit, Ila,' he murmured.

The name slid into her, the nickname she had not heard from him after she'd turned six and insisted that he only call her *Mithila*.

She lifted her head, sniffed hard, and dragged the back of her hand across her eyes. Since the day in the Maidan, when Ananta had become Savarian, she had covered up the hole in her heart with layers of forgetfulness, as though it was a wound that could be bandaged away. And now those bandages had been ripped off, but there was no scab, only an open wound. 'The Rebel didn't have a daughter either, Ba?' she said, half laugh, half hiccup.

For a moment, he looked at her. Then, with a strength she did not recall, he pulled her back into a tight, familiar hug. 'Forget that *rebel* nonsense,' he said, his voice strangled. 'If I could burn up those words I wrote, I would. I will always have a daughter. Won't I?'

This time she didn't cry, but let her head rest upon his shoulder, and allowed her eyes to close. He did not smell of fresh wood, sawdust, paper. He smelled tired.

'So,' said Ananta softly. '*Worldfarer*, I hear. You did take the moment.'

Mithila stepped back. She felt herself tremble. Carefully, she pulled up a chair and sat down. Ananta followed suit. For a moment, it felt faintly ridiculous, the two of them across each other. Mithila stood up and dragged her chair around, until she was next to Ananta, and they were both sitting together, facing the windows.

She dropped her head sideways, onto his shoulder, winding her arm through his to hold it to her.

'Almost didn't,' she said. 'Just as I was about to leave, Minakshi came and told me you'd been seen in the Dooma, that Rastogi would have you killed unless I stayed back. I didn't know what to do, I—'

'What? She said I'd been seen—when?'

'The night of the Race.'

'But I never left the underground until I fled to the Towers of Rebirth. Your sister lied to you.'

'Ah.' Mithila stared intently at the table. 'That little shit.'

'Don't use that language about your sister, Mithila,' Ananta said automatically. But then he caught himself, and his face split into a mischievous, familiar grin. 'Though I will say: as someone who failed at revolution, you've done—you've been perfect. Mithila Maloran. Worldfarer. And I have never been prouder.'

She grinned and looked away, suddenly shy. 'It just … took me up.'

Ananta laughed freely. 'No no, I didn't mean crossing over. You do that once, and it's done. I mean this, all this. The barricade, the Banner. You have to do it once, and then all over again, and again—and each time could be your last, but never *the* last. Oh, Builders!'

'You'd know.' Mithila groaned, as she felt the day's weariness finally seep into her. 'But I … I don't know how barricades work. I don't know how *anything* works. I didn't make this Revolution, Ba. The Revolution made me, and I know it will unmake me. The Union, the Dooma—they have their own desires. I'm their vessel. I am the Banner, only the Banner. They know it. I know it.'

'You didn't think you could beat the Wall. But you did.'

'Oh, the Wall!' she let out a quick laugh. 'At least the Wall's just there. I always knew where *I* was, with the Wall.'

'And I always told you, didn't I, that people are harder?' Ananta grinned. 'So annoying, no?'

'I only need,' Mithila whispered, 'to get back into the world. To take them with me. I just need to—hold this together till then.'

'Feels like holding water, doesn't it?' Ananta said gently.

Mithila lowered her head. 'Yeah. If only there was someone …'

Someone who knew barricades.

Someone who had led a revolution.

Someone who had wanted a world, and fought for it.

She looked up, and the words came unbidden.

'Will you help me?'

A slow deep smile spread across Ananta's face.

'I thought you'd never ask,' he said.

For a moment, she felt a great, painful relief. He would know what to do. He *was* the Revolution, the unfinished Revolution, the Blue Revolution, and this time there would be no Salva and no trebuchets and no Council. This time he *would* finish it, and she—she would be Worldfarer, but only that, Mithila-beyond-the-Wall, no more the Banner.

Just her and the world, like it was always meant to be.

'I can't wait to see Council's faces when Savarian appears over the barricade.' Ananta laughed.

Savarian.

And at that name, the world came crashing back in, sweeping away the dreams she had woven in the moments before, like the waves of the sea that only she had seen.

In his absence, there had been a revolution in search of a Banner, it had found her, it had become hers, but not hers to give away.

'No,' she whispered.

Ananta stilled. 'What?'

'It can't be you, Ba,' she said miserably. 'It can't be Savarian—anymore. Don't you see?'

Her father looked stricken. *That's two in a morning*, Mithila thought, numb. *How many will I have to give up before the end*?'

'Tell me why?' Ananta said quietly.

She forced the words out, one by one, each hurting her throat more than the one before. 'You're not going to be commanding some irrelevant barricade deep in the Twelfth. If Savarian is in a revolution, then it is *Savarian's* Revolution. And the moment it becomes Savarian's Revolution, this coalition will shatter.' Suddenly, she found herself repeating. 'This is the banner under which we've come together. Under this banner, and with a blade held to my palm, I have made my promise. And it's the banner of the broken Wall, not the Blue Revolution. It is not mine to give up to you.'

'Ah,' said Ananta. An eternity of silence fell between them.

When her father smiled again, it was a rueful smile, and it broke her heart once more.

'What was I thinking?' Ananta said. 'I was a revolutionary. We don't get second chances.'

'Oh, Ba,' she whispered.

Ananta spread out his arms. 'Is there nothing I can help you with?'

Mithila made herself say it.

'Don't be seen until we win.'

Ananta *almost* winced at that. But when he looked at her, she saw in his face a curious mixture of pain and pride.

'Builders, so ruthless,' he said. 'I wonder where you got *that* quality from.'

Mithila stood, not trusting the sharp, painful ball in her throat to stay in its place. 'I'll see you after we've won,' she said.

She walked to the door. Ananta remained seated, staring at the window.

At the threshold, she paused and turned around. Her father had his back to her, but he seemed to know.

'Mithila?'

'Yes, Ba?'

'There are three things I need to tell you.'

'I'm listening.'

'On the night I fled to the Towers, the Council followed. Just outside the sanctuary, Amrit caught up with me. We fought. I believe I killed him.'

Rama's father. Mithila breathed in. 'Ah,' she said. 'And the next?'

'For twenty-seven years, I've thought about what I could have done differently. What I would do. If I had the chance.'

'And that is?'

'I would bend. So that I wouldn't break.'

'Ah,' said Mithila again. Her mind, it seemed, had shut itself down. 'I'll remember. And the last thing?'

'There was a song for the Blue Revolution. Our song. After they destroyed us, they turned it into a love song. But if there comes a day when you need help, a day that you need to come find us, any of us—remember it.'

'What is it?' Mithila whispered.

And Ananta sang once more the song Mithila had heard, the night before her father had become Savarian.

Before I gave you my heart,
Oh revolution,
I dipped my brush in the sky
To paint it blue
Blue I dream you
Blue.

I ask from the sky its colour,
Oh revolution
To dress you in blue
I ask from the river its wellspring
To bathe you in blue
Blue I dream you
Blue …

Ananta stopped. Mithila's hands were crushed into her pockets, her nails digging into her skin.

'Anything else, Ba?'

'That's it.'

'Alright.' She smiled a ghastly smile at Ananta's back. 'See you very soon.'

Mithila walked out of the Konar Hall. There was a small crowd gathered around the entrance. They immediately parted for her. Belatedly, she raised her arm to give them the union salute. It felt heavy, as though someone had attached weights to her muscles. She turned away from them, suffocated.

She plunged into the heart of the Eleventh, into the twisting streets, the closed doors that lined them, and the shuttered windows. Here and there she saw a hole in the wall, or the remnants of a door, wood and iron given up willingly, or unwillingly, to the scaffolding of a revolution.

Lines hung from window to window. The drying clothes fluttered in the breeze, dappling her path.

She walked further in.

The sharp winter sun daubed the mud-brick houses with patches of light so brilliant that they were almost white. She shaded her eyes as she walked. On another day, these streets would have brimmed at this hour: footsteps, laughter, the smell of fresh *rahi* cooking outdoors. Today it was barren. After the Shoortan attack, Maji had sent word to the Mandalas to stay home. Nobody seemed to have disobeyed.

Like the desolation of Gumfraude—no, she quashed the thought as soon as it came. The stillness of the Eleventh was not the stillness of abandonment, but of waiting, waiting for the Revolution to be born.

She walked faster. The path curved. Above her, someone shut their window with a crack. She heard a wail. A door opened and a harried-looking man hurried out, snatching at a piece of white cloth from a pile on a slab. He did not look at her as the door closed again.

She turned and slipped into another lane. More doors. Someone had planted bamboo in pots outdoors, and the stalks waved at her. Ahead of her, a patch of water, freshly thrown, shimmered in the glancing light. She kept walking, turning back, losing herself, turning wrong at every familiar corner, her feet aching.

Around a bend, she came upon the charred remains of what had once been a house. A shapeless, roofless husk of blackened mud-brick stared at her. Mithila stopped in alarm. *Surely the Shoortans had not …* no, all around her, the quietness still lingered. And every other house in the neighbourhood was untouched.

She left the burned house behind, wandering onwards. Inevitably, she wound her way at last back to the Maliot, where all roads led. Her walk had carried her to Wallset. Beyond the river, the *rahi* stalks danced in the unworked fields. They shone red-gold under the declining sun. To her South, the mud-brick houses were bathed in liquid light. The evening breeze kissed cool the sweat at her nape.

Sumer felt too beautiful for words.

She turned and walked along the Maliot until the barricade was visible again. One of the men was keeping a watch up top, while the others relaxed beneath. A plume of smoke rose in the air. And they were singing, low and sweet.

She dragged her feet back to the Konar Hall.

Outside, the crowd had grown.

She heard talking as she approached. As she came into view, they fell suddenly quiet. Mithila saw Prana in the crowd.

She saluted. 'All good?'

Prana saluted back, and a few others did as well. 'All good, Worldfarer.'

Mithila nodded, and entered the Hall. She closed the door shut and leaned against the wood, putting her ear to the crack.

'… without my idiot son getting his brains splattered out onto the street!' someone was saying.

'Sindu, listen to yourself!' Prana's voice was strained. 'The Council murdered Sanchika literally one week ago. They stabbed him one by one and nobody lifted a finger. You will trust them over someone fighting by your side?'

'*Our* side?' another voice came. 'Did I miss her working the fields with us, Prana? You all dropped her on us as Banner—and she's from the Seventh, all they do is sing and dance for the Council, they might as well *be* Council. What's the damn difference?'

'Seriously?' Prana said. 'She's no longer of the Seventh, Nayam. She's been Ostracized. She's risking more here than all of us put together.'

'Prana,' the first voice came back, calmer. 'We're not doubting the Worldfarer, but remember *you* asked to have the President as Speaker for the Eleventh. *You* told us she was an ally.'

'And I was wrong! Because she abandoned us the moment they dangled the Presidency before her.'

'But even the Worldfarer trusts her—'

'Builders, Sindu, are you still in school? They have a history, don't you—'

Mithila jerked away from the door, her ears burning.

She walked slowly, back to the long table.

'Ah there you are,' said Maji. 'There's someone waiting for you.'

Mithila gave her an ugly look. 'Not again.'

'No no—this is nothing like that,' Maji said quickly. She pointed at the two strangers around the table. They were looking at her in silence. Two men, dressed in their circle colours: green, with the hammer-and-chair upon the shirt; and ochre yellow, with the scale-and-needle.

Mithila's heart quickened.

'Welcome,' she said.

'I am Naman-Eight,' the first of them said.

'Zohar-Nine,' the second one nodded.

'Please speak freely,' said Mithila.

'Thank you, Worldfarer,' Naman replied. 'We are charged by the Eighth and the Ninth to tell you this: we have heard of how the Worldfarer crossed the Wall, the Heartstone she has brought back from the world, and of the lost City of Gumfraude. We have heard of what was spoken here last night, and we have read the Charter that was pasted on our walls this morning.' Mithila shot a quick glance at Maji, who looked away demurely.

'We would like the honour,' Zohar said, 'of the Worldfarer speaking to us directly. We ask this for the Eighth and the Ninth together.'

'The honour,' said Mithila carefully, 'is mine. However. You understand that I am Ostracized?'

'Yes,' Naman said. 'We take full responsibility for your safety, Worldfarer. From the time you leave this Hall to the time you are back, nobody shall harm you. This, on the word of our Circles.'

'Can you give me a moment?' Mithila said. When they nodded, she gestured to Maji, and they walked away from the table.

'Well?' said Mithila.

'Do it,' said Maji.

'You think so?'

'Yes, Worldfarer. We won today because the Shoortans underestimated us. They thought we were a bunch of goons with sticks. They're not going to run at a barricade again. Neither will Council. But they *can* wait us out. And we—we can't win this without the Middle Circles.'

Mithila steepled her fingers. 'I don't even know what to say to them. The Dooma wants dignity. The farmers want land. I don't know what the Eighth and Ninth want from me, or what I can give them.'

'That's why you lead us, Worldfarer,' Maji said. 'You have what nobody else does: your words from beyond the Wall.' She paused. 'You know what we call them in the Dooma? *The Comfortable Ones*: the blacksmiths, the carpenters, the architects, the weavers. Comfortable above us, comfortable in their work, comfortable in their wage, comfortable enough to hate risk. Savarian couldn't persuade enough of them. You will have to.'

'Easy enough,' Mithila whispered. 'Just win the Revolution that my father lost.'

Maji shifted. 'I will say this. If the Eighth and the Ninth join us tomorrow, the Tenth will follow. We can have half the City by noon.'

'Right.' Mithila let herself smile at Maji. 'Let's do it, then.'

Together they walked back to the table.

'I will come,' said Mithila. 'Name your time and place.'

'Tomorrow, at Wallrise. In the open ground of the Ninth. It's big enough. We'll all be there.'

'Done.'

To her surprise, Naman and Zohar gave her the union salute. Mithila saluted back, fist against her forehead. 'Be well, Worldfarer,' said Naman, before he and Zohar turned and walked the long passage to the end of the hall.

'Now to do it all over again,' Mithila said. Exhaustion flooded into her with the words. She stumbled.

Maji noticed. 'There's a room above that's yours.' She looked at Mithila critically. 'Get some sleep, Worldfarer. You need to pace yourself. The days will only get longer.'

Mithila stood. Just as she was about to retire, she stopped.

'One thing,' she said. 'During the Blue Revolution, did you have deserters?'

Maji suddenly got busy staring at the piece of cloth wrapped around her wrist. Nobody else spoke.

'Well?' said Mithila.

'Sometimes we did.'

'What did you do to them?'

Maji's smile was tight. 'They were executed. People's Court. No questions.'

'What?'

'Your father's orders.' Maji looked her in the eye. 'Being soft doesn't win a revolution.'

Mithila held her gaze. 'But you didn't win.'

Maji said nothing.

Mithila looked around the table. 'I am not my father. And this is not the Blue Revolution. If anyone wants to leave—they leave. We don't stop them. And we *absolutely* do not execute them.'

'You'll give the Shoortans all our plans,' Maji's voice rose. 'You'll give them every barricade, every password. They'll have the names of all those who're with us, the ones they'll kill for sport after they win, because of what *you* give them.' She stood. 'No, I will not allow this. As Field Commander—'

'You really think you're going to force people to be free?' Mithila said. 'How did that work out last time, Maji?'

'What do you want to do?' Maji laughed scornfully. 'Send them away with our love and a packet of *rahi*? We did not lose the Blue Revolution because of this, *Banner*, and I'd thank you to remember—'

'That the blade is at my neck?' Mithila said coldly. 'I remember, Maji. And I am still *your* Banner. Do you want to find another one?'

Their eyes locked again. Maji was the first to look away.

'Are my instructions clear?' Mithila said.

Maji's face was made carefully blank. 'They are clear, Worldfarer.'

'Good,' said Mithila. 'You can tell Prana when he comes back in. And you,' she turned to the others in the room, 'can tell everyone else. Nobody is forced to stay.'

Mithila turned and walked up the stairs without a look back. She found the chamber they had made up for her. The bed was two soft mattresses piled up on the floor. She bent to sit, and with her knees by her face, undid her sandals. *I should have a bath*, she thought, *they've got the water up for me.*

Like a stone in river, she fell asleep.

'*Red sprites over the troposphere in Tannor. I wanted to show you the Aurora, dancing in the sky, beyond the Reinmar Gate. There was a galaxy, Samir. And now all those dreams will pass, frozen in a suspended future, like so many little beetles in amber … like us.*'

In the cold blue light of the Crystal Hall, Mankala wrote furiously, every word that Samir and Ghada spoke to each other. The new words had already begun to sound familiar: as though they were not unknown, but only lost. The images that they summoned glimmered in the distance, *just* out of reach.

'*I love you. Farewell.*' She heard their footsteps fade away into the darkness.

Moments later, the blue light flickered twice, so briefly that she wondered if she'd imagined it. Mankala blinked.

'*It's so hot*, hmm?' she muttered. She walked to the containers and inspected the three figures. She took in the older king's crown, and the Heartstone in Ghada's hand. She tapped on the transparent surfaces, and went around to the back for a closer look.

The side of Ghada's container was slightly different from the other two. Protruding from the dark, opaque surface was something that looked like a circle, with spokes—something that, it seemed, could be grasped and turned …

Mankala knelt down and held it—but no. Her hands slipped around and over the circle, but it was somehow beyond her touch, as if it was not all there. She straightened, frowning. She checked the other two containers, ran her hands against their smooth sides. Nothing.

'Ugh!' she said.

'Found anything?' The voice was at her back.

'No, Leader,' Mankala said. 'Nothing new. I feel like I could sit here for years and it would just be the same thing, in a circle—forever.'

'And you wouldn't be the first,' said Marwana gently. 'Come on, let's go.'

They went back through the passage, and up into the Citadel. Mankala rubbed her eyes. 'What's been going on out there?'

At the doors of the Citadel, Marwana turned to her. 'Nothing good. Blood on the streets. By tomorrow, the City will be divided three ways. The roads will be be closed. Some bridges are already burned. You won't be moving around anywhere.'

'Wha—' Mankala breathed. 'What happened while I was down there all day?'

'Your friend Mithila is at the head of an alliance of the latter Circles. They've already beaten the Shoortans in one battle. People have died. More will die.'

'There's a *revolution* on?'

Marwana smiled. 'Like father, like daughter.'

'Father—oh,' said Mankala. '*Oh*.'

Marwana stared at her. 'What?'

'The Elders had Savarian trapped in the Towers of Rebirth, Leader. But he's gone—vanished.'

'So that's where you went when you left here so suddenly?'

'I had a hunch. But I was too late. We met the Doorkeeper of the Third Tower. He told us that the guard had suddenly withdrawn—and the moment that happened, Savarian left.'

'Almost as if it's scripted, isn't it?' Marwana murmured. Her eyes flickered. 'Savarian running loose in the middle of a revolution—all we needed now.'

Mankala looked at the Rasa, vanishing Wallwards into the distance. 'Where's Mithila, Leader?'

'Eleventh.'

'Oh.'

'Isn't that your Circle?'

'Not anymore. My house was burned, remember? I don't really have anywhere to go.'

'Your parents—'

'There is no home for me there,' Mankala pushed a shock of hair out of her eyes, blinking suddenly. 'Remember the time when you said you wish you'd found me earlier?'

'Yes. I so wish we had.'

'I didn't tell you back then, but so do I, Leader. I'd have been with you, and I'd still have had a home.'

'Ah,' Marwana paused. 'Was it your expulsion?'

Mankala nodded. She paused—and then spoke in a rush, words that had long been buried, now finding their way to light.

'The Academy gave me a month to recant. Of course, they didn't *call* it "recant"—that would've made the Shoortan pressure too obvious. "*Reconsider,*" they said, "*and acknowledge the errors in this essay*". I remember the day I came home and told my father, and he looked at me, relief in his eyes, and said, "*so they let you off*", and I laughed and said to him, "*let who off?*" and I watched his eyes change. And later that evening, my mother came back from the fields, and—things got worse.'

'They didn't understand?'

'They made it clear that no one in the family had ever been expelled from the Academy, and their child wasn't going to be the first. I told them that they were only proving the point I made in the essay about the illogicality of our family structures this side of the Wall. That did not go down well. After our third fight, they said that if I didn't take the Academy's offer, they would—I was—I would no longer be ...'

Mankala choked, and tailed off. 'So on the thirtieth day,' she continued again, 'I took my things and walked out.'

'Oh, Builders!' said Marwana.

'Yes.'

'Did you ever wonder why people reacted like this to an essay?'

Mankala shrugged. 'Isn't Shoortanism two thousand years of overreaction?'

'Unless it wasn't the Shoortans,' Marwana said softly. 'And the reason why you terrified someone so much was because if you proved that there was a time when the world was not like this, it would become possible to imagine a time when the world *would* not be like this.'

They looked at each other. The moment lingered.

'Well, I'd better go,' said Mankala. She turned.

'Wait!' said Marwana.

Mankala stopped.

'I read your essay,' said Marwana, 'You argued that this side of the Wall, families chosen were a more logical way of structuring our society than families given.'

'I did, yes.'

'And I know we found you late,' said Marwana, 'but it's never *too* late, Mankala. Do you want to stay here with us until this is over? You won't be able to come back to the Forum once you leave it, now. You can stay—and you can start to see our work, and …' she left the unsaid, unsaid.

For a long moment, Mankala stood there, her back to Marwana.

Finally, she shook her head. 'If only I could,' she whispered. 'But not now, Leader. I can't. I have to go to Mithila.'

Marwana smiled again, with a hint of sadness. 'I thought you'd say that. Perhaps another day. Go well, Mankala. And be safe. Life becomes cheap in a revolution, for greater things.'

Mankala nodded. 'I'll be back—we *will* solve this.'

She began to walk away.

'Tell me something,' said Marwana.

'Yes?'

'Why didn't you just agree to reconsider?'

'Because,' said Mankala, without turning, 'I was right.'

Marwana watched her until she was out of sight.

Mankala threw the door open, and marched into Malati's office.

Alvar stood, crumbs of *khire* falling off his clothes. 'Where were you all day—'

'Alvar! We need to get to the Eleventh before they block off the roads.'

'The Eleventh? Why—'

'Mithila's there, leading a revolution.

'*What!*'

'Come on! Also, where's Malati?'

'Locked up in her room for hours. Won't answer the door.'

Mankala stood still for a moment, then muttered: 'Oh, there's no time—I'll see her later. Come on, Alvar.'

They rushed out of Malati's house, and into the street. 'By Maliot?' said Alvar. Mankala laughed. 'Why, aching for some Shoortan company? No, we're going inside.' She cut South-East.

The wide, paved roads of the First were empty. They went past the mansions of the Elders—strangely dark and quiet—and past the sewage chamber of the First. At the bridge over the tributary dividing the Second and the First Mandalas, they saw the Watch.

'Halt!' said one of the Watchmen, as they were spotted. 'Roads closed tonight.'

Mankala held up her hands. 'I'm authorized. Elders' business.'

'Which Elder?'

'I'm Councillor Malati's secretary—you know this.'

The Watchman's face did not change. 'The roads are closed.'

'What!' Mankala burst out. 'Malati has—'

'Mankala-Eleven,' the Watchman's companion, older than him, spoke gently. 'Didn't you know? Malati resigned today.'

'Oh,' Mankala's face went blank.

'We can't let you through tonight. Orders.'

'But I have to get home!'

'Erm … honestly, you're safer here, Mankala-Eleven. Nasty business afoot tonight in the end Circles. Just spend the night with Malati.'

'I see,' said Mankala. Alvar waited for her to do something, but she only said: 'Guess you saved us some trouble. Let's go, Alvar.'

He caught up to her as she walked quickly back into the First. 'We're going back? Just like that?'

'Not so loud. They were never letting us through. Time for the backup.'

'Backup?'

'You'll see.'

In the dying light, she led him North, towards the Forum. At the cusp of the Circle, they stopped at the largest stone mansion in the First Mandala.

The house of the former President.

Alvar tilted his head up, taking in the lights at the windows. But the house was silent, and there were no watchmen at the gate. Mankala quietly lifted the bar and moved it inwards, trying not to let it creak. They walked up to the door. It opened before they could knock.

'I've always told you,' said Elmandar, 'that it won't whine if you do it quickly.'

'We can talk about your gate, Elmandar,' Mankala said, 'or you could take me home.'

Elmandar stepped back. 'What?'

Alvar coughed delicately.

'Roads blocked,' said Mankala, rolling her eyes. 'I need to get home, but they won't let me.'

'Oh. Didn't you know?' Elmandar said. 'Council's left the Forum. They've all moved to *The Maliot House*.'

'Why the *Maliot House*?' said Alvar.

'I don't know, mother doesn't tell me anything,' said Elmandar plaintively. 'I figure it's because there's going to be fighting tomorrow. You can't really direct stuff from the Forum.'

'Alright, but then the Maliot should be clear,' said Mankala. 'And they'd let *you* through, surely. Former President's son and all.'

Elmandar's eyes glinted with a sudden light. 'A trip Downcircle on the night before a battle, huh?'

Mankala shrugged. 'I mean, it *is* where I live, but whatever makes you happy.'

Elmandar stepped out of the house, and past them. 'I'll be right back,' he said, disappearing into the darkness of the street.

Mankala turned and sat on the steps, leaning back on her elbows, closing her eyes.

'Please tell me,' Alvar said, sitting next to her, 'how this relationship works.'

'Smoothly.'

They did not speak again after that. Mankala leaned all the way back, her hands behind her head, until she was lying on the porch and staring up at the sky. The silence around them was stifling. Alvar jumped up and walked into the garden.

After a few minutes, he heard running footsteps, and a rattling sound. Alvar hurried back to the gate. Mankala came out and stood beside him, grinning. The rattling grew louder.

They burst out from around a street corner, seven figures riding the night. They had one foot upon their vehicles' base—a plank supported by four wheels—while they used their other foot to push upon the ground. Their hands were upon the handlebars, which branched out from the wooden frame of the mount. The wheels were of iron. *Scarce, but never scarce enough*, Alvar thought.

They sped down the road at a frightening pace, straight at them. Alvar's heart leapt as they approached, but then Elmandar, who was leading, raised a hand and the group split into a semi-circle, coming to a stop. Alvar saw that they had lashed sharpened sticks to their belts.

'The Hedonists are here,' Elmandar flashed them a grin. 'An armed escort.'

Mankala sniffed. 'I suppose it'll do.'

'We got chariots for you as well,' said Elmandar. 'Made two of us ride one-handed.' At a gesture from him, two were wheeled out for them. Mankala's eyes widened. Alvar caught one just before it fell to the ground.

'Ready?' said Elmandar.

'No,' she said. 'How do these things work?'

'You'll understand better with your feet than your head,' Elmandar laughed. Without waiting for an answer, he kicked off.

And so began the strangest journey Alvar had ever taken in Sumer.

Both hands on the handle, one foot on the *thing* with wheels, Alvar tamped down his trembling. As they moved, he stumbled, and gripped the handlebars tightly. His mind was giving orders that his body did not know how to follow, and it felt like they were far more than a few centimeters above the ground. He turned, and saw that Mankala was struggling too, her jaw set, her knuckles white around the handlebars.

The Hedonists fanned out, giving them cover, as they reached the Maliot. Alvar sensed his body settling into the chariot's rhythm, his foot shifting imperceptibly to give him balance. Around him, there was darkness: nobody had lit the lamps by the river tonight.

On the road, they picked up the pace. The night wind was on his face, whipping his hair back, cold gusts lashing his cheeks, drawing tears from his eyes. The boards rattled beneath his feet, and he grinned into the night. He had never gone so fast before.

'*Out of the way!*' Elmandar's shout ripped the air, and suddenly everyone sped up. Alvar had moments to see the two Watchmen who stood guard upon the bridge to the Second, see their eyes widen, and see them tumble out of the way as they passed through. Cries followed them from behind, but they were past.

Wallwards, they met nobody else upon an abandoned Maliot. Just beyond the Fifth, Elmandar raised a hand. Alvar stopped with the rest, his heart racing.

'Let's cut in from here,' Elmandar said. 'There'll be no watch beyond the Fifth.'

They entered the Sixth, at a steadier pace, and turned South-East, towards the heart of Sumer. The houses of the Watchmen were dark and quiet. Here too, like in the rest of the City, the lamps were unlit.

Beyond the Seventh's Bridge, into what had once been Mithila's Circle, the roads narrowed, forcing them into a walk. The night closed in, until they were almost groping their way forward. The Seventh was deserted.

Alvar shivered. 'Where is everyone?' he whispered to Mankala.

'I don't know,' she whispered back. 'I thought—'

'*Who goes there?*'

Alvar stopped dead. Elmandar and two Hedonists had just stepped around the corner and into the next street, temporarily out of sight.

'It's a street in Sumer, what do you mean who goes there, *I* go there,' Elmandar drawled. 'Who's asking stupid questions?'

The remaining Hedonists slipped past Alvar and Mankala, and joined Elmandar around the corner.

The first voice came back, cold. 'You had better control that tongue, Elmandar-One, unless you want it pulled out by the root.'

'Oh, your father would weep for—'

'*Enough!*' the first voice snapped. 'I haven't the patience for your brand of foolery tonight, Golden Boy. Have you seen those companions of Mithila the Ostracized?

Alvar clapped a hand to his mouth.

'I don't know, Shoortan, *have I*?' Elmandar said. 'Maybe I have. Maybe I haven't. Maybe they're in my *pocket*.'

'You were seen a while ago with them in the First Mandala,' another voice spoke, in clipped tones. 'We don't have time for this. Your party will be searched now.'

'Come on love, search away, if you want to get your head smashed in like a pot,' Elmandar said cheerfully.

There was a sudden hush, broken by the sound of muttering.

'Elmandar-One,' the second voice spoke calmly. 'The Matriarch only wants to speak to them. There's no need for violence. Would your mother like to know you've been making a scene?'

'Some of us don't have to ask for mummy's approval before doing anything. Isn't that lucky?'

'Our fight is not with you, Elmandar,' again the second voice, still calm. 'Don't force our hand.'

'Oh, just let your hands own their urges,' Elmandar hooted gleefully. 'Why would I force anybody to do what they already want?'

'*Bloody* Builders, let me choke them out of him, I beg you,' the first voice was a low, furious snarl.

'Is that a threat or a promise?'

There was a moment of deathly silence. Then Mankala and Alvar heard a sickening crunch, and pandemonium broke out. The night air resounded with cries, insults, the sound of wood meeting wood, and roars of pain.

Mankala nudged him. 'Alvar. Time to leave.'

They crept away, and started running as soon as they were out of earshot.

'You know,' Alvar panted as they ran, 'I see why you like him.'

Music woke Mithila.

Her eyes flickered open. The full moon came in through the window. It touched the edges of the room.

The music floated up to her. A flute, sweet and clear, its lilt entering her ears, becoming a song she knew.

Blue, I dream you, blue …

Mithila rose and went to the window.

Beneath her, on the street, people were walking.

They held flame lamps, glimmering in the night. They walked down the road in single file, some holding their children by the hand, still in their nightclothes, stumbling. She followed them with her eyes, and saw them cross over one by one into the Tenth Mandala, heading towards the Forum. She could not see how many there were.

And the music continued.

Blue, I dream you, blue …

Mithila straightened, and took a deep breath. From her window, she watched the procession until the last of them had vanished into the darkness of the Tenth.

Fifteen

The Select's Protocol

There was urgent rapping at the door.

Mithila awoke. Her legs felt desperately stiff. For a moment, she lay in bed, staring at the iron sky outside the window. There was a scent of rain in the air.

The rapping came again.

Mithila rolled out of the bed and staggered to the door, opening it.

'Worldfarer, you need to be down in five minutes.' The man handed her a fresh pair of clothes. 'Hurry.'

Mithila nodded and closed the door. She walked to the bathroom and washed the sleep out of her eyes, swiftly running water behind her neck and under her arms, regretting last night's decision to skip a bath. As she changed, she noticed that the linen shirt they had brought her had the design of the broken wall with the sun peering through, emblazoned upon the front.

She hastened down. Maji was the only person in the hall.

'Barricade,' she said without looking up. 'Now.'

'Where are the rest?'

'There.'

Mithila followed her out. They stepped out into the cold half-light. Wallrise was still an hour or so away.

'Tell me, Maji,' she said, as they walked towards the Maliot. 'How many deserted last night?'

Maji looked back at her, something like pity in her eyes. 'What did you expect?'

'Just answer the question.'

'Quite a few from the Eleventh and the Twelfth. We'll know better later.'

As they approached the Maliot, Maji turned them away from the barricade. She took Mithila into one of the houses on the edge of the Mandala. They went up the staircase, and onto the roof, where a group of people had gathered.

Maji strode to the edge of the roof. She pointed beyond the barricade.

Mithila saw them: massed ranks of the Watch, in familiar brown, facing the barricade.

'The Council,' said Maji.

'*What!* Didn't you tell me the Watch had abandoned them?'

'Enough seemed to have stayed. Or some went back,' said Maji. 'Whatever it is, they're here now.'

'They must have marched half the night,' said Mithila. She looked down at the barricade, and saw her own forces in position. 'This makes no sense,' she continued, her voice low. 'They saw what happened to the Shoortans. This is suicide.'

Maji tapped upon the bars of the balcony, 'Or they were told you'd be speaking at the Ninth this morning. And they figured they couldn't afford that.'

'Maji, we'll lose the best chance we have.'

'Of course, you have to speak. And the Eighth and the Ninth *have* guaranteed your safety,' Maji calculated. 'Okay, but we're going to give you an escort. I think …'

Mithila leaned upon the balcony, as Maji's voice washed over her. *No, this isn't it*, she thought. *Something's off here.* She knew she was forgetting something vital. The Watch was just standing there. As if they were toys, only for show.

Out from a street in the Tenth it came. Memory hit her like cold water.

It was just when the Watch halted upon the Maliot, that Nilan began crying.

'Not now!' Bhavi cursed. She stole a quick glance over the barricade. The Watch was well out of bowshot range, and seemed in no hurry to move, to attack, or to do anything at all. Below her, on their side, Maji's forces were armed.

She had time. Bhavi sat upon a protruding chair-leg, making sure her head was below the top of the barricade, and gently rocked her baby in her arms.

'*"Dream of fields and flowers blue,"*' she sang softly, '*"Dream of Wallrise bright and new/ Dreams today will shelter you."*'

She kept her head turned sideways, a corner of her eye upon the ranks of the Watch. Nothing moved.

Nilan's crying began to subside. Bhavi smiled tiredly. There had been long arguments at home about who would go to fight and who would stay, but she'd known all along that Aashna's heart moved to the rhythm of the *rahi* harvest cycle, and not to the ebb and flow upon a barricade.

'Stay, love,' Bhavi had said at last. 'I'll come back with the stories, and you'll tell them better than I ever can.'

Aashna had conceded at last. 'I'll get things ready for our move to the stone mansions when we win,' she'd said, kissing Bhavi goodbye. 'Imagine, a garden for Nilan to play in.'

Bhavi smiled again at the memory. It *had* meant sleepless nights on the barricade, as she'd been the one breastfeeding.

Nilan had now gone back to sleep in her arms, and there was no noise or movement behind the barricade, so—

Her thoughts were interrupted by sudden movement on her side, just above her eye level. Bhavi looked up. On one of the rooftops of the Eleventh, someone was gesturing frantically, gesturing at … *her*?

She began to rise to her feet.

'*Bhavi!*' Maji's voice rent the silence. 'Get—'

A rush of air at her back. A whistling noise. Instinctively, Bhavi threw out her arms to protect Nilan.

Her eardrums exploded with a sound that filled the iron sky, and Bhavi's world went dark.

'*NO!*' Mithila screamed.

The first stone from the trebuchet smashed into the top of the barricade, where Bhavi had been standing. A creaking, groaning shriek tore through the air, and pieces of the barricade flew in all directions. They saw Bhavi's body tumble halfway down the barricade, where it snagged upon an outlying piece, and hung there, suspended.

Maji's head was tilted towards the balustrade, resting on her fists. She raised a ragged gaze to the barricade.

'*How?*' Her voice came out strangled. 'They destroyed those—*things* after the battle of the Rasa. Cast away Salva, so that nobody could ever do this again. Who did this?'

And Mithila remembered the two torn pages of the Encyclopaedia that she had carefully carried to Malati on the night before the flight, her last gesture of sentiment before leaving Sumer.

What have I done?

Before she could say a word, the trebuchet fired again.

Like a dream, they watched the stone arc across the sky. It travelled slowly, as though it was floating in the air, gliding upon open wings; as if they had an eternity to trace its parabolic path, measure it to the last centimeter—

It smashed into the barricade, making it shiver like an old man in the last throes of fever.

What have I done?

Maji jerked to life. 'Noor, Rami!' she cracked out. 'Pass the word down the signalmen—I want all posts retreating to the Twelfth, right now.' As the two of them darted down the staircase, she turned to another. 'Pania, take the Worldfarer to the Twelfth. We'll cover you.'

'But—' began Mithila.

Maji threw up a hand. 'No debate. You go or you die here. Those are your options.'

'But I have to—'

'No, *you do not,*' Maji snapped. 'Your orders. Nobody is to be killed.'

Mithila felt a hand on her shoulder. She let herself be pulled away. Pania hurried her down the stairs. They broke out running, running down the Maliot, Wallwards. Behind them, Maji and her people also entered the Maliot, and ran towards the barricade.

Mithila turned back once, just in time to see the barricade come crashing down in a cloud of dust and debris with the impact of the third stone. She stood there as the dust cleared, and Maji's forces arrayed themselves into formation.

The barricade was gone.

Across the levelled ground, the Watch began to march towards them, sunlight glinting upon their blades.

As afternoon came, Mithila stared out of the window, onto an empty street.

The room Pania had left her in was similar to the one she had been in last night, a Circle up. Only, these walls were empty of sconces, there was a single, ragged mattress on the floor, and her water jug was chipped.

The silence below her, in the Hall of the Twelfth, was unnerving.

Inexorably, her mind slid away from the objects around her, like hands sliding off a slippery stone, back into the maw of memory. *I have to do this one thing*, she had told Alvar, so smugly, and then she'd gone to Malati, given her those two torn sheets of the Encyclopaedia, watched her weep, and felt—

I didn't know!

She had given the Council the weapon they needed to destroy the Revolution, which they had used once already to destroy a Revolution.

Would you have let this happen, Ba?

She walked to the rough-hewn chair, and began to worry the grain with her thumbnail.

She didn't know how long she'd been doing that when a door slammed below, and a medley of noises came through to her. *Finally, something to do.* Mithila turned and hurried down, into the Hall.

Maji stood in the middle, covered with dirt and blood. Others crowded behind her.

'There you are,' said Maji.

'How many?' Mithila asked.

'Bhavi, lost. Two on the barricade, broken bones. Five wounded when we were covering your retreat.'

Mithila took a shuddering breath, her shoulders unclenching after hours.

'Bhavi—and Nilan, no?' she whispered.

'Amazingly, the baby lives.' Maji almost smiled. 'She managed to shield him as she fell. Builders' luck. But it would have been worse had they given chase after the first skirmish. More would have died.'

'Why didn't they?'

This time Maji did smile, mirthlessly. 'Twenty-seven years ago, they tore down a barricade, and drove forward to finish us off. Ten barricades came up behind them. They died trapped and screaming. Raja remembers. The memory of Savarian saved our lives today.'

'Just not enough for Bhavi,' Mithila said bitterly.

'It's a revolution, Worldfarer.'

Would you have let this happen, Ba?

Guilt roiled over Mithila in waves. 'So, what's the Council doing?' she said.

'They will secure the Eleventh. Make sure there's no threat from behind. Then they'll come for us.'

'How long do we have?'

'A few hours.'

Standing next to Maji, Pania spoke. 'Let's get out of here. Back to the Dooma, I say. Our streets. That machine won't fit—'

'No,' said Mithila.

They looked at her.

'The Revolution can't be the Dooma. That's what they want—to break us this way. Yesterday, some of the farmers left us because of the President's promises. Today we lost the Eleventh. Are we going to abandon the Twelfth now? Are we going to let them *see* us abandoning them, at the first fall of a barricade, the first death of one of theirs? Would the Union stick with us a moment longer? Would we have any right to ask them to?'

'She's right.' Maji nodded. 'We don't retreat. We can't.'

'But we can't fight them on the Maliot!' Pania protested. 'Our sticks and sickles against their swords? It'll be a massacre. We had the barricade and now we have the inner streets. There's nothing else.'

'Can't we get around the back and take out the trebuchet? Set it on fire, destroy it—something?' said Mithila.

'Shoortans in the way,' Maji said. 'Last night they occupied the Middle Circles. They're working together.'

Rama and Minakshi. Mithila could have screamed.

'Then what do we do!' Prana burst out. 'I can't ransack my farmers' homes for a barricade that will get smashed—'

Maji turned to him. 'We'll have to make our stand here. And their stone won't last forever, we'll—'

'But …'

Their voices washed over her. Mithila turned her head away, feeling sick. *Saved by Savarian's memory.* Maji's words lashed at her. She gazed out of the windows with unfocused eyes.

The windows of the Hall were set low, and Mithila found herself looking out at the tributary of the Twelfth.

Right there was that familiar farmers' water-wheel, a memory from childhood, spinning as it always had, as if the world was unchanged, as though the water didn't remember blood.

From the depths of memory, Dhara's voice came back to her, on that summer's day when they had wandered together by the Eleventh.

'And do you know how this works? Can you imagine water hitting a flat surface at this speed? Now think... '

The world jerked backed into focus. Ananta's last words rang in her head.

I would bend. So that I would not break.

'... fucking lives on this barricade, not that you care!' Prana's voice was the first she heard again.

'Stop,' said Mithila.

There was silence in an instant. They all looked at her.

'Not this barricade,' she said. 'We need another one.'

'Are you paying *attention*!' Prana exploded at her. 'The last one's dust.'

'I noticed,' she said mildly. 'And I say we have to build a barricade.'

'Build it yourself, then.'

Maji's eyes flashed, but before she could speak, Mithila said: 'You know what? I think I will.'

She walked out of the Hall, to where a crowd was waiting them. There was a stir when they saw her.

'I need a barricade' Mithila called out, 'and on my word as the Banner, *this* one they will not be laughing at. I know I've asked too much of you—but one last time—we need iron and wood. Will you help?'

One of them gestured towards a side street. 'Houses begin here.'

She heard them troop behind her as she turned the corner, into the beginning of the street. She marched up to the first house, and knocked.

There was silence inside. Mithila knocked again.

After a very long time she heard footsteps slowly come up to the door. At the threshold, they stopped.

Just as Mithila raised her hand to knock for the third time, the door opened.

She stepped back, her hand hanging limp in the air. Before her there stood a woman. Her face wore lines of exhaustion. Her eyes were lightless. And in her arms—

'Nilan?' whispered Mithila.

'Get his name out of your mouth,' the woman said. Her voice was quiet, very quiet.

'Aashna,' Mithila said, stupidly.

'Clever. And where was that cleverness when you sacrificed Bhavi to the barricade?'

'*I* didn't—' Mithila began instinctively, but stopped herself. Around her, she sensed the crowd, pressing in.

'I heard you out there,' Aashna continued in the same toneless voice. 'You've come for iron and wood. For a barricade. A *barricade*. How dare you.'

'I—'

'Oh no you don't. We ripped our house apart for your Revolution. And I don't mean the chairs and the floorboards we gave to your Commander when she came around begging. And now you won't even leave me alone—you come back *and you want more*. I will give you nothing, Worldfarer, nor will anybody in this Circle.'

Her words had woken Nilan. He was looking at Mithila fearlessly, at the face he knew.

'Bhavi said—'

'And now you say *her* name.' Aashna stepped out of the house. At close quarters, she towered over Mithila. Mithila fought the instinctive urge to back away, still feeling the gaze of the crowd at her back.

Aashna's eyes bored into hers. 'She believed. She believed so much. In your Revolution. I couldn't stop her from going to you. She couldn't stop herself. *A leader should do better, Worldfarer.*'

'I should have. Yes. I'm sorry. And I know how she believed,' said Mithila.

'*Liar*. When did you even speak to her? We know you leaders, you push us to the front to die for you, to die for your ideas, and we die, and the ideas die, but *you* always stay alive—'

'Except that's not how it happened,' Mithila said desperately. 'We were there together. We talked. And she didn't just tell me she believed, she told me why.'

Aashna's lip curled. 'And why did she believe?'

'Dreams,' Mithila swallowed.

'What did you do with those dreams?'

'They're still there. They weren't just for herself. They were for everyone. They were for—for *him*.' She didn't speak Nilan's name. 'And I'm saying nothing you don't already know. But you know I'm speaking true.'

Aashna turned away. Mithila looked down at the floor. Her cheeks flamed in shame and guilt.

'I'm—I'm sorry,' she stammered. 'I shouldn't have come. I have no right here. I'll—'

She turned away, choking. The people in the street had watched in silence. Slowly, ever so slowly, Mithila began to walk away.

'Wait.'

The voice, at her back, halted her. Mithila turned.

Rock-still, Aashna jerked one thumb back towards her house. 'Take the bed. Builders know this home doesn't need one anymore.'

'I—'

'*Just take it, Worldfarer*. Before I change my mind.'

The voice was raw. Mithila nodded. She signalled. From the crowd, two others detached themselves to follow her in.

As she passed the threshold, Aashna caught her arm, forcing her to turn, until they were looking directly at each other. Her grip was vice-like.

'*Dreams*, you said.' Aashna spoke very softly. 'You're carrying hers now, Worldfarer. I'll be watching to see what you do with them.'

'We're ready,' said Raja.

'Is the Eleventh secured?' Rama asked.

'Yes. As you said: nobody harmed, but we've told them if they fight, they will be considered rebels, and dealt with accordingly.'

'Good.' She looked at the Rasa, glistening under the bright afternoon sun, a spear-shaft of light upon the water. 'Let's finish this.'

Raja gave the order. The Watch—thronged with new recruits from the night before—began to march down the Maliot. Rama looked up at the buildings of the Eleventh. Watchmen were stationed on the terraces, and the houses were quiet. It was a risk, she knew. One arrow from one window was all that it would take.

Behind them, the trebuchet followed, rolling down the Maliot.

'Tell me,' said Rama, 'how much longer can we use this?'

'We're almost out of stone,' said Raja, 'and this time, forever. Those were the emergency reserves. We'll also need fresh wood, which will take—I don't know …'

'Then we'd *better* finish this,' said Rama.

They marched Wallwards, the Eleventh falling away to their South.

'Look, President Rama,' Raja said.

Beyond the bridge to the Twelfth, there was a barricade.

They halted.

'So,' said Rama, 'they're going to fight it out.'

Raja looked at her. 'Should we clear it?'

Rama almost nodded, but stopped herself. 'Wait. Let me give this one chance. Pass me that white flag?'

He handed it to her. 'Get the machine in range anyway,' she said, 'I doubt this will work.'

Rama held up the white flag and walked down the Maliot, towards the barricade. But as she approached, she saw a completely different structure.

She was looking at the point of a triangle. The barricade extended back from that point on both sides, meeting the houses on one edge, and the Rasa on the other. Together, they formed a V-shape, whose tip stretched out and towards her. It seemed to be bound together with iron bands. Rama frowned.

Beyond the barricade, there was silence. The houses of the Twelfth stared down at her, as narrowly set as their companions in the Eleventh.

'I come in peace,' Rama said. 'Is anyone here?'

For a few moments, nothing happened.

Mithila's head appeared over the barricade.

'Yes, Rama?'

Rama's heart leapt. She felt her fists clench, and stuck them behind her back. She looked up at the barricade.

'Are these our mornings now, Mith?'

'If you like.'

'Why are you doing this?' Rama said quietly. 'You know you can't win.'

'If that's what you think, why are you here?'

'Because I have a duty to this City,' Rama said. 'Nobody else wants what you want. Nobody else wants to die for an idea. Don't throw lives away.'

Mithila's face did not change. 'Tell me something,' she said. 'You would have negotiated with the Shoortans for safe passage here today. What was the price they asked? Your proposal already leaves out the Wall. Are you going to sell me out to them when this is done?'

Rama blanched. 'There was no selling out.'

Mithila was silent.

Rama looked up at her. 'Will you force me to do this?'

'Nobody forces anyone to do anything, Rama. We choose.'

'I don't *have* a choice.'

Mithila straightened, looking ahead of her. 'Do what you have to do,' she said. 'Because I will.' She ducked from the barricade, and there was silence again.

Rama felt the beginning of tears prick the edges of her eyelids. She blinked them away, turned, and strode back to the company. 'Let's get this over with,' she said.

'With joy, my President,' Raja grinned. He turned back and called to where the trebuchet stood. 'Load.'

Once more, Rama watched in fascination.

A chain of people passed up smaller rocks to make up the counterweight. A single Watchman oiled the shaft. Then a large rock, which reached their knees, was rolled up and put into the throwing arm.

'Launch!' Raja shouted. A man slashed the rope holding the arm down. It swung the rock into the air. She saw it fly, graceful parabolic motion, effortlessly making for the centre of the barricade, and—

—just as she braced herself, something went wrong.

The stone crashed into the barricade, but the barricade did not shatter. Instead, it *bent* backwards, almost as if it was absorbing the force of the blow.

The barricade sprang back, without damage.

The stone rolled harmlessly along the road—and into the river.

'What ...?' murmured Rama.

Beside her Raja shouted: 'Fire.'

The reload. The second stone. The second hit. And once again, the impression that the barrier bent, bent more than last time, but again, after impact, was left standing.

'Fire!' Raja called a third time. She spun to stop him, but watched helplessly as the last of their stones sailed into oblivion. The barricade still stood after the hit, although sunk in upon itself.

'We're out of stone,' said Raja.

'I was *telling* you to wait,' Rama said, annoyed. 'They've discovered some new design. But we were making a dent, it'll just take more time. Find something else. Maybe melt down some iron, so we—'

'Look out!' a voice from the side. Rama turned, just in time to see three flaming arrows hit the trebuchet.

The dry wood caught fire. A crackling noise came to her ears. Heat rose into the air.

Around her, there were cries. 'Stay back!' she shouted, as Watchmen rushed to the trebuchet—and stood, helpless.

The fire rushed through the wood, devouring it whole. Flames danced in the sunlight. The smoke brought tears to her eyes. A Watchman ran from the river, water in a helmet—and then threw up his arms to shield himself from the blaze. The helmet fell to earth. Water spilt uselessly upon the Maliot.

'Back to me,' Raja roared, as Rama saw more flaming arrows fly into the trebuchet. 'Leave it, by the Builders—'

'How did this happen,' she swung to him. 'Did you know they—'

'It's not coming from the barricade,' Raja said. 'They don't have the reach on us, we're too far—President, the arrows are coming from the Eleventh. *From behind us.*'

For a split second, they looked at each other, and together, they turned to the watching houses behind them, through the choking haze of fire and smoke.

'The other fucking sister,' Rama whispered.

In the fading daylight, the rough-hewn wooden container wore a pale sheen.

Mithila had watched as they'd gently lowered Bhavi into it, as Aashna—her face a mask—had knelt one final time to kiss the side of the container. Now Kodali and two of the Carers stood before it, ready.

They will expect something from you, Maji had said.

What can I say, she had asked. *I've never done this before.*

And Maji had looked at the cloth around her wrist, the cloth she had tied every morning for twenty-seven years, and she had only said: *nor had I, until I had to say farewell to Upar. You won't know. Until you do.*

They were looking at her now—Kodali, the Carers, Aashna even Nilan—and on the Maliot, a ring of people. Looking to her, before Bhavi made her last journey to the Towers of Rebirth.

Mithila stepped forward.

'Out there in the world,' she said, speaking the words softly, as they came to her, 'by the shore of the sea that never ends, there is a memory-stone. It keeps the memory of Taraf, through sun and wind and rain, through the turning of the years.

'Bhavi dreamed of being in that world, a world where dreams themselves have no ending. We can't give that world to her anymore. But she—like Taraf—will live as long as the last of us remember. And we will not forget. She will be with us when we find the sea, when we find Taraf, when we live in their dreams. There we will build for her—and for everyone that we have lost, will lose—a memory stone to last forever. So that we remember, and they never become just a name.'

She paused. Aashna had turned her face away. From the mists of memory, Mithila remembered a night in the Seventh, the taste of bamboo soup, Ananta sitting across from her, and the memory of Garuda in the air.

'And I know,' she said, 'I know that it is the hardest thing in the world to trust someone else with your dream.' She looked down at the container. 'But I ask that you trust us with yours.'

Mithila knelt, and draped the container in the Banner, which had hung that morning from the barricade. She rose and stepped back. Kodali and the carers came forward. Smoothly, they lifted it upon their shoulders. Nobody moved or spoke.

Bhavi was soon lost to the oncoming Wallset.

'Prana,' said Maji, her voice hoarse, 'can you report, please?'

Back in Konar Hall again, Prana cleared his throat. He looked down at the map of Sumer that was spread back on the table. 'We're back where we were. Morning positions. All we've lost is a day and a barricade, and even that, they didn't bother taking the wood.' He traced the line of the Eleventh, from the Rasa to the end of the eastern Quarter. 'We have the new ones built at each crossing point.'

'Why did we stop? We could have taken the Tenth,' Carina said. 'With them so busy fighting each other …'

'Heh,' said Mithila. 'I don't know about you, but I just wanted to watch.'

'I can't believe it,' Maji said wonderingly. 'Shoortans, stabbing Council in the back. Now if *that* had happened twenty-seven years ago …'

'Do we know,' asked Mithila, 'what's happening out there? The Maliot was very quiet when we let go of Bhavi.'

'There's no more fighting,' Prana said, 'and the Shoortans are licking their wounds in the Seventh.'

'Bet my sister's taken our house,' Mithila muttered.

'Council still holds the Upper Circles. The Maliot's clear.'

'That's screwed up our plans of speaking in the Ninth, then,' Mithila said.

There was a long silence.

'This is going to be a longer fight than we thought,' said Maji, tiredly. 'We need to think about food.'

'There is all of North Sumer,' said Carina.

'Who's going to waste forces there?'

'Whoever wants to starve out the others,' Carina said lightly.

Maji frowned. But before she could say anything, the door at the end of the Hall scraped open.

The man who walked in was dressed in the simple robes of a scientist; a sudden, almost absurd memory of Sumer as it once had been. Nobody spoke as he approached them.

'Greetings,' he said, as he came up to the table. 'I come from Marwana and the Select, with a message.'

'Be welcome,' said Mithila. 'We're listening.'

'The Select offers to mediate this dispute, in keeping with its historical role as neutral arbiter in this City. Leader Marwana proposes a meeting between the three—the President, the Matriarch and you, Worldfarer, under her auspices.'

'I see,' said Mithila. 'Where and when?'

'Tomorrow, at Wallrise, in the Maidan. If you agree, you commit to no further violence until the Mediation is over.'

Mithila narrowed her eyes. 'The other two?'

'They have agreed—subject to your like agreement.'

'A minute, please,' said Mithila.

Someone showed the scientist to the Audience Chamber. The rest of them gathered closely around the table.

'Sanchika was killed with less planning,' Mithila said. 'It would be easier to end it now by ending me.'

'Not necessarily,' said Meghana. 'First, we would go on fighting, Worldfarer, no offence meant.'

'None taken,' murmured Mithila.

'But last time,' said Maji, 'Marwana took a lot of heat for not stepping in during the Blue Revolution. People said the blood was on their hands.'

'What do I do?' Mithila asked.

'I think you'll have to go,' Carina said. 'If the other two have agreed … it's not going to look good if we're the only ones resisting a solution.'

Mithila grimaced. 'They're just going to try and change the Charter—*again*.'

Prana smiled at her. It had the slightest hint of irony. 'You have absolute freedom to negotiate, of course.'

Mithila looked back at him. 'Your Mandala,' she said, 'saluted me with a knife before signing the Charter. I am not fool enough to forget that when I go into the Maidan.'

There was a long silence. Then Maji spoke, decisively. 'You'll go. We got back the Eleventh, but our position is delicate. The weapons situation is bad, and there's only so long we can manage with the food we have. I'd give it two weeks before we run out.' She looked to Mithila. 'But they don't know this. It's a negotiation.' A pause. 'We trust you.'

Mithila nodded. 'Understood.'

'I thank you,' said Marwana, 'for coming.'

A gentle Wallrise bathed the Maidan, casting pink edges along the buildings. There was a nip in the air, the slightest hint of winter's cold, and the beginnings of a breeze. Clouds were gathering in the skies above them.

Mithila had never been in the Maidan like this: empty and silent, with a round table set in the middle, around which the four of them sat, surrounded by the Fifth Mandala. She stared at the table, pointedly ignoring Minakshi.

'Now,' said Marwana, 'we have one chance to sort this out. Nothing discussed here will go beyond the walls of the Maidan. You can all speak freely. I know that none of you is *absolutely* free. But if we know what binds us, we can discover what doesn't.'

Minakshi spoke first.

'We will withdraw the Ostracism,' she said. She looked directly at Mithila, so that Mithila was forced to meet her gaze. 'I haven't had the chance to talk to you as my sister. I just—I can admit, here, where it's just us, that I made a mistake. I didn't think you would come back, so the Ostracism—it wasn't real.' She smiled narrowly. 'And if it can help us—frankly, even if it doesn't—I'm sorry.'

'Rescind the Worldfarer's Ostracism,' Marwana repeated. 'Is there anything else, Matriarch?'

'I would like to hear what the *Worldfarer* has to say.'

'I'm thrilled that the idea of my slow and painful death doesn't appeal to you, Minakshi,' Mithila said, 'but we all need to get one thing clear. The Council and its President seem to have taken a … ah … *neutral* stand on the Wall.' She curled her lip. 'They have no views about it one way or another, it appears. That leaves us and the Shoortans. And nothing's going to be solved unless the question of the Wall is decided. So, let's get straight to that. Are the Shoortans prepared to change their minds about the Wall?'

'Of course not,' said Minakshi.

'Then—' Mithila began, before Marwana cut her short.

'Wait just a minute. Let's hear the President.'

Now Rama spoke. 'The Council has come in good faith, willing to overlook everything so far—including what happened yesterday.' She looked straight ahead as she spoke, not turning to Minakshi. 'Yesterday, I made a proposal. The Shoortans do not object to it, but the Worldfarer does. I can compromise on that. But that said,' she said, turning to face Mithila. 'I believe your Revolution cares for democracy, for the good of the people. Have you not realized how an uncontrolled outflux of people from Sumer beyond the Wall will cripple those of us in here—'

'Why, you might have to wash your own floors or something?' Mithila cut in.

'Be that as it may,' Rama said after a pause, sliding her eyes to Marwana, and keeping them there. 'An unforeseen number of people leaving us will mean that this City will collapse. We will *all* be left with just one choice: leave or die, which is no choice at all. I imagine the Worldfarer is better than that—'

'Value of human life seems to have risen overnight,' Mithila murmured.

Rama turned to her and spoke, coldly: 'What's that supposed to mean? Spit it out now, so that we can have a conversation without you interrupting.'

'Sorry about my bad manners,' Mithila said. 'It's almost as bad as you trying to kill me yesterday.'

Rama stiffened.

Mithila locked eyes with her. 'I was on the barricade when you sent in your stones,' she said. 'You knew that. You talked to me moments before.'

Rama did not look away. 'I gave you enough time to leave. And you're here now.'

'You wanted me to choose between death or submission,' Mithila said. 'I'm here despite you, not by your mercy.'

Rama gave her a long look. 'As you like,' she said, and with her face carefully blank, turned to Marwana.

'As the Worldfarer pointed out, while we clearly can't wait to see each other dead,' she said, her voice almost cracking but not quite, 'none of us wants to kill the people of Sumer. We're not Dichio, are we? I propose we set up a committee—with representation from all three of us—to decide if, when, and in what manner the citizens of Sumer can go beyond the Wall. It is not too much to ask. We acknowledge that there is a way beyond the Wall, and you, Worldfarer, accept a democratic decision on whether we go.'

Silence fell between them.

Then Minakshi said, her lips pursed. 'We are willing to consider this.'

Marwana turned to Mithila. 'Worldfarer?'

'Democracy, like it was?' Mithila felt anger. *The stitch up.*

'Pass,' she said. 'You really believe we'll trust you on these Committees, after all these years? You'll make us disarm, blood mopped up, and then you'll mention that the Committee will operate by majority, and we'll find, funnily enough, that Veto has formed an alliance.'

She heard her voice rise, and calmed it with effort. 'I don't think you understand. You no longer have the right to stop us from going beyond the Wall. I said this in the Council Hall, I said this to all the Elders: we're not forcing anyone to come with us. We're not Shoortans here—'

'I can't believe we have to go through this all over again,' Minakshi interrupted. 'The old Matriarch told you this. I told you this. Rama is telling you this. That is *exactly* what you are doing. Sumer will change permanently, unacceptably, with this—'

'That you believe the present is acceptable, is your whole problem,' Mithila snapped.

'It is acceptable because we're alive.'

'And some of us want to *live*.'

'Children, children.' Marwana's cool voice stilled them both. 'That's enough please. You've come here as leaders. Now then: the Committee idea is not acceptable to the Worldfarer. But the President has a point, as does the Matriarch, when they say that such a decision should not be taken without asking our democracy. How about this: you, Worldfarer, and you, Matriarch—put your cases to the City. You can have a debate in the Maidan, if you so wish. Go to each Mandala. Speak. Persuade. If the Council has a view, they can too. After you've had enough time, we conduct a vote across the City, where we count every Citizen's vote separately. And if there is a majority for going beyond the Wall, we work out the ways—'

'No!' all three of them spoke together. Mithila almost laughed at that.

Marwana did laugh. 'So you do have something in common.'

'Let me suggest something,' said Mithila. 'I can accept the President's idea of a Committee, but *after* a delegation of Citizens has gone beyond the Wall, unconditionally, to give you a full report of the beyond. We can't talk about this in the dark.'

Rama's eyebrows rose. 'Interesting. I'm not averse to this.'

'The Shoortans absolutely are,' Minakshi said. 'This is what you told Soma too—one of us will have to give up everything. If even one goes beyond the Wall, our faith is laid waste, over two thousand years of it. You want us to give up everything.'

'You eavesdropped on your own dying Matriarch?'

Minakshi's nostrils flared, but Marwana cut in before she could speak. 'None of you,' she said, 'is actually willing to give up anything.'

Quiet poured back into the Maidan.

'If you insist,' said Marwana, 'on sorting this out through battle, then the Select cannot, *will* not, stop you. Sumer has had bloodletting before. I suppose it will have it again.'

Rama turned to her. 'Leader Marwana,' she said, 'I would like to know about the Select's Protocol.'

Marwana smiled slightly. 'I am glad,' she said, 'that someone asked. You know that a conflict between the Mandalas can destroy everyone. It can poison our water supply, like in the days of Dichio, and bring a great plague upon us. A race to control the woodlands or the iron furnaces for weapons can deplete them faster than they regenerate. If the fighting spills over into the farms, we may starve.

'The Select's Protocol comes into force when, in our judgment, conflicting parties in Sumer are so equally balanced in strength that a long-drawn conflict—where all this may happen—is a real possibility. In that situation, if—*if*, I remind you—the conflicting parties agree, the Select takes over absolute management of North Sumer, of the Rasa and of the sewage chambers. We ensure that until the conflict comes to a resolution, our resources are not destroyed.'

'What exactly,' said Mithila, 'does the Protocol entail?'

'No fighting North of the Rasa,' said Marwana. Her voice was sharp and clear. 'None may cross the river except with prior permission of the

Select. Sewage chambers in the Mandalas will be off-limits. And the Select will ensure that production from the farms, the woodlands, and the furnaces will continue at a minimum level. For this, we may direct Citizens to continue work in North Sumer. Finally, to maintain strict neutrality, our Citadel shuts its doors. To *everyone*.'

'Basically,' said Mithila, 'fight it out in the Mandalas until one of us wins.'

'If you refuse to find a solution here, Worldfarer,' said Marwana, 'then, yes, that is what we are saying. The Select is not an insurance against your collective folly.'

Rama leaned back in her chair. 'The Council has made all the compromises it could. If this does not satisfy you, we have no further choice but to fight. I agree with the terms of the Protocol. I'd rather not have the City burn in our war.'

'I think we're done here,' said Minakshi. 'I was open to the President's proposal, but the Shoortans too have gone far beyond what our faith allows. We will abide by the Protocol.'

'Why do I feel,' said Mithila, 'that you two agreed about this beforehand?'

Rama's lips tightened. 'The Matriarch attacked us in the back yesterday.'

Minakshi smiled. 'Just restoring some … balance, President. There's no need to take it so personally.'

Marwana sighed. 'This is pointless. There's one thing left. Worldfarer, do you agree to the Protocol?'

'I cannot believe we are having this discussion,' Mithila said, 'just to stop some people from *leaving* this Builders-damned City. But I guess that's why we have to fight for it. Yes. We will abide by the Protocol.'

'I am glad that none of you is entirely self-destructive … yet,' Marwana said. Protocol kicks in from Wallset. I hope you sort this out amongst yourselves. Fast.'

There was something in the way she said *fast* that filled Mithila with unease.

As if it were a plea or a warning. Or both.

PART FOUR

ENDGAME

Sixteen

The Ambush

Mithila stepped back into Konar Hall.

'Truce till Wallset,' she announced.

'And then?' said Prana.

'What do you think? More of the bloody same.'

'That's it?' said Meghana. 'No compromises?'

'No compromises,' Mithila said, as she reached the long table. 'They'll give us the Circles, but they'll keep the Wall. They'll give us the fields, but they'll keep the Wall. They'll let us *think* about it—but, Builders, they will keep the Wall. Oh yes, my little sister did apologise for trying to starve me to death.'

Prana coughed. 'So we get ready, then.'

'Yes,' said Mithila. Just then, tiredness hit her. 'But not now. I—we can't keep going all the time.'

Maji took a look at her, and stood. 'Alright everyone, it's been a long two days. Afternoon's off. Rest yourselves.'

Around the table, people rose. 'That means you too, Worldfarer,' Maji said. 'When was the last time you properly slept?'

Mithila looked at her, blank.

'Can't have our Banner losing her mind,' Maji said briskly. 'Go upstairs. Feel better.'

Mithila walked up the stairs, to her door. She stood outside it and took a shuddering breath. Here, last night, *blue I dream you blue*, hope turned into abandonment. She pushed the door open.

Alvar stood, grinning, Mankala with him. Mithila gaped.

'Missed us too much to stay away, huh?'

Laughing, she fell into their arms.

'And as I told you at the start,' Mithila finished, 'I found only questions. Spirals that sing the sea in your ear. Stars that dance in the night. And a place where water flows up and geometry stops making sense.'

'Geometry? More like they broke the laws of reality.' Mankala punched her thigh. 'And I can't *believe* people have been going in and out, as if the Wall was a damned fence. Yes, Marwana said the same thing but I didn't really believe her.' She paused. 'Do you think she—Dhara—went? Herself?'

'I don't know,' said Mithila. 'But she didn't stay because she wanted to.'

'We can save her, right?' said Alvar.

'We can't,' said Mithila. 'Not yet. But we can find the people who did this to her, and make them put her back. Once we get out. That's why I accepted this Banner.'

'We're going to have to make them do a lot,' said Mankala slowly.

'What do you mean?'

'We learned things, too, Mithila, while you were gone. It turns out that the Builders, the ones who put us here, left their descendants behind to keep us here. I'll bet it's the same people who did that to Dhara.'

'The Shoortans?' said Mithila, automatically.

'That's what we thought,' Alvar said. 'But Marwana says it's not. It's about a battle our ancestors lost. She thinks that they were put in here as a punishment or an experiment.'

'And they must have lived out there in Gumfraude, our ancestors,' Mankala jumped in. 'Ghada, Samir—and Alora—the king in the middle, the one between the two of them. Until this battle happened, and some of them, the ones who escaped, went into these Eternity

Containers beneath the Council Hall, hoping that one day one of us, their children, would bring them back. That's what Ghada says to Samir in the chamber, remember? And it all makes sense now—Ghada's statue that you saw overground, the story you said you read in *The Book of Alora*—and this.'

'*Tefnakth*!' Mithila exclaimed. 'We have to find him. He must be one of them, the—'

'Overseers,' Mankala finished. 'That's what Marwana calls them. And no. He's dead.'

'W—what!' Mithila stammered. 'I saw him out there, he was alive three—no five—days ago. He can't just *die*.'

'Killed,' said Mankala. 'Stabbed in the Woad Garden.'

'Oh,' said Mithila. She was quiet for a few moments. Then she shook her head. 'This doesn't make sense. Why wouldn't *they* just kill the ancestors—Builders, whatever—outright? They'd just need to go down, get into that chamber—'

'I'm sure they've tried,' said Mankala. 'I don't think anyone knows how to break into those containers they're in. Ghada even boasts about it.'

'But these Overseers,' said Mithila, 'who are they?'

'Brilliant question,' said Mankala. 'I wish we knew. But you will soon, I expect,' she added.

Over Mithila's head, Alvar's eyes asked Mankala the question. Mankala shook her head ever so slightly. *Let's not burden her with what Marwana said about her father just yet.*

'What do you mean?' Mithila said to Mankala.

'What's the one thing the Overseers cannot allow? What's the one thing that literally destroys their experiment? It's you, Mith. You've already destroyed the idea of the Wall. And if you take Sumer with you beyond the Wall—their experiment's over. They have to stop you.'

'They're going to come after me, aren't they?' Mithila said.

Mankala grinned. 'You get used to it after the first time. Trust me.'

Alvar sent her a quelling look. 'It hasn't come to that yet. They'll only make a move if you're winning, Mith. If it looks like the Time of the Wall is coming to an end.'

'Or they'll end the experiment,' Mankala spoke the unspoken.

Mithila laughed. 'So you're saying I have to lose to save myself from these Overseers?'

'No,' said Alvar. 'You're going to win, and we're going to beat the Overseers.'

'No pressure at all,' said Mithila. 'Win the Revolution. Make the Overseers show themselves. Stop them from destroying Sumer. Leave.'

She sat down on the mattress, hugging her knees. Alvar sat down beside her.

'This is too big, Alvar,' she whispered. 'I only wanted one thing. To go beyond the Wall. And then to return, tell them what I did, and take them back with me, if they wanted. And to save Dhara, if I could. But now there's a revolution, and Sumer could end, and …' She buried her face in her knees.

Alvar bumped her knee with hers. 'It could be worse, no?' he said, very seriously. 'At least your girlfriend isn't trying to kill you.'

Mithila stared at him. Suddenly, she giggled. 'I know, right? What if she'd taken really drastic measures instead?'

'What if it was catching?' Alvar said. 'What if your sister had tried to kill you first?'

'Thank the Builders, she would *never* do that.'

'Could have been worse,' Mankala joined in. 'At least your father didn't turn into Sumer's most wanted rebel overnight.'

Mithila burst out laughing. 'Could have been *even* worse,' she gasped out between breaths. 'At least he didn't kill my girlfriend's father.'

'Wait—*what*?' Alvar's hand flew to his mouth. 'I'm so sorry, I thought—I thought you two would figure it out … in the end.'

Mithila chuckled helplessly.

'Life happens, Alvar, what to do? I should look for other people—I'm a Banner now, they'd better be lining up.' She laughed again, softer this time, a little choked. 'Or not. In the end, I push them all away.'

Alvar gently put an arm around her, as Mankala plopped down on her other side.

'What do you think, Alvar, is she any good at pushing people away?' she said, leaning into Mithila so hard, that she almost fell upon Alvar.

'I don't know,' Alvar said, pushing back. 'She's so far away, isn't she?'

'You're squashing me!' Mithila protested

'Oh, what a shame,' Mankala said. 'We'll just have to tell Maji that we wrung out her banner.'

Mithila laughed, a small watery laugh.

Alvar squeezed her shoulder. 'Now let's get to the important things. What have you brought me from beyond the Wall?'

Mithila was quiet for a few moments. Then she straightened. 'Actually—I *did* get you something. I got you a forgotten song. You'll be the envy of the bards when you go next.'

Alvar looked at her, his eyes dancing. 'A song from beyond the Wall? From Gumfraude?'

'Well, I'm cheating a bit,' she admitted. 'It's from the Dooma. The same book—*The Book of Alora*—that Maji gave me. But I read it in the ruined City, and it opened the passage to Gumfraude.'

'Tell, tell.'

Mithila reached into her bag—lying in her lap—and took out the book. She leaned back again, settling into the gentleness of Alvar's arm, and Mankala's knee falling on her thigh. She flipped open the book and began to read to them.

In old Gumfraude, beside Geroun
Come back and wander out with me
To find our way beneath the moon
West of the river, South of the sea

Upon the roads that still recall
Alora's steps; a memory
Of times that were before the fall
West of the river, South of the sea

Come find me by the crystal pool
Beneath the garden of the tree
We will remake Alora's rule
West of the river, South of the sea

Remember what I said to you
Of all that was but could not be
By Mati's shade, my vow renew
West of the river, South of the sea

You asked if we would conquer death
I said there was a galaxy
Bring back my words upon your breath
West of the river, South of the sea

And in those words, the open vein
Will bring you on the road to me
We'll speak the old days back again
West of the river, South of the sea

The City of the Afternoon,
Do you remember? We were free.
In old Gumfraude, beside Gheroun
West of the river, South of the sea.

And if that life you would restore
From circles of our history
Come walk between the worlds once more
West of—

She was cut off by Mankala turning violently. Suddenly she was facing Mithila, her hands on her shoulders.

'What did you say?'

'What?'

Mankala gestured at the book, frantically. 'The last lines. *What were they?*'

'Oh!' Mithila repeated, glancing down. '*And if that life you would restore/ from circles of our history/ Come walk between the worlds once more —*'

'*Circles!*' Mankala's fists were clenched against her eyes, and her neck was turned to the ceiling. Alvar and Mithila looked at each other, bewildered.

'Between the worlds. *It's so hot.* Oh, I am such an *idiot*!' Mankala whispered.

'What are you talking about—'

'Mithila.' Mankala opened her eyes. 'Tell me what you saw in Gumfraude—those pillars.'

'What?'

'I mean the water, the water flowing up—isn't that what you said?'

'Oh, yes.'

'Describe it to me.' Mankala squeezed her eyes shut again. 'Exactly.'

'Oh, I … ' Mithila thought back. 'So there was a channel of water. It was flowing in a … a Z shape?'

'A zig-zag,' Mankala prompted.

'Yes, yes—kind of. And there were these two pillars …' Mithila looked up at the ceiling, bringing the dead, white City back into her mind. 'They were facing each other, the channel was passing through them at each point of the zig-zag, and then it just—fell down to start over.'

'Can you show me?' said Mankala. She jumped up and fetched the paper and pen from the table. 'Draw it.'

Mithila looked at her. 'Go on!' Mankala said.

Mithila bent her head over the paper. She drew one pillar, and then the other. At the base of the second, she sketched the falling water, and started with the zig-zag channel. The pen scratched on the paper, one turn, then another, slowing down as it went, and—

Mithila stopped.

'What happened?' said Mankala.

She let the pen fall. 'I can't do it.'

'Why?'

'I don't know how to. It's like—it's like pieces of—'

'Two different worlds,' Mankala said.

'Brought together,' Mithila finished.

'Yes!' Mankala stood. She was smiling.

'Come on, you two,' she said. 'There's work to do. We have to wake the Three Kings.'

The late afternoon sun came in through the high windows of the hall.

'What is this about?' said Maji. '*You* were meant to be resting, Worldfarer.'

They had all gathered by the table, at Mithila's call. Mithila now pointed to Mankala, at the end of the table. 'This is something you need to hear. And it can't wait.'

Heads and eyes turned as Mankala stood.

'I know your situation,' she said. 'I have an idea. The way you break a stalemate is by doing something you haven't already tried in the last Revolution.'

Maji looked at Mithila, her expression saying: *you made us give up our sleep for this?* 'What do you mean?' she said. 'Also, who are you?'

'I trust her,' said Mithila. 'Tell them, Mankala.'

'We're going to bring back Alora and Ghada,' said Mankala, quickly.

A stir passed around the table. Maji stared. 'What did you just say?'

'Beneath the Council Hall, there is a Chamber. There lie Alora and Ghada and Samir—and so many others—waiting for us.'

Maji swung around to Mithila. 'That night you spoke of Builders underneath the Council Hall. *Alora*?'

Mithila nodded. 'The three of them lie together—Alora in the middle, Samir and Ghada at his side.'

'We'd always heard the rumours.' Maji took a deep breath. 'But—but you said they sleep the sleep of the dead.'

'That's because she didn't know we can wake them up,' said Mankala.

Maji's chair clattered to the floor, as she leapt to her feet. 'Explain. *Now.*'

'In that chamber, they preserved a slice of time,' said Mankala. 'Time that circles back upon itself, an infinite circle. There are two realities, two worlds: ours and theirs. Their spun time lies upon ours. It is more real than reality. We cannot touch it. But there is a moment—one moment—before the circle begins anew, when their world stops. In that chamber, in that moment, there is only one world—ours. That is when we can wake them. They left us that moment, and they left us signs, in the hope that one day—one day—someone would understand, and now …' She let herself smile. 'And *now* we do.'

'What in the Builders—*two* realities?' Prana said, disbelieving. 'You think Time works like a blanket?' He turned to Mithila. 'Worldfarer, you can't stake this Revolution on a metaphor.'

'She's found a way to open Ghada's container, Prana,' Mithila said. 'And Ghada will know how to wake the rest. We'll have our truth from the source.'

'How are you so sure about this?' Meghana frowned.

'I stayed in that chamber for six hours,' said Mankala, 'I heard them speak. I had nothing but confusion. But then the Worldfarer told me of what she saw in Gumfraude. And I understood.'

'Alora.' Maji's voice echoed in the hall. 'We will carry the memory of your name like hot iron beneath the tongue.'

There was sudden silence. Mithila shivered.

Maji looked straight at Mankala. 'Your story, and ours, they come together. You have seen with your own eyes what we have known all these years: that somewhere underneath this City, Alora lies sleeping, with Ghada and Samir beside him. We have kept his memory alive. *All will be remembered.* Through the pathless years, in secret we speak his name to each other, hot iron beneath the tongue: Alora, cast down into darkness because he, a Builder, rebelled, for *us*. And for all these years we had the book of Alora but never knew what it was telling us.'

'How could you have known,' said Mankala, 'when the sign they left for us was in Gumfraude, where nobody ever went—till now?'

'If this is true—' Maji began, but Meghana cut her short.

'But these are—these still are the *Builders*, aren't they?' she said. 'How do we know they're going to be on our side?'

'Because we are Alora's children.'

It was not Mankala who answered, but Carina. She too was on her feet, and her eyes were shining.

'Yes, it was the Builders who put us within this Wall of Sumer. In that the Shoortans speak true. But they do not give you the whole truth. Since the beginning of Time, there were those who resisted—Alora, and Ghada, and Samir—and this side of the Wall, it was us—the Unforgiven—who remembered how to fight. Yes, we remembered freedom, and we remembered loss—we remembered Alora—and for that, we were condemned to eternity in the shadow of the Wall, the last of the Circles. We lived in hatred and contempt, because the Shoortans taught you to believe the myth of Malan, turned *smara* into guilt and repentance, and taught you to believe that we were nothing more than carriers of madness. But we—*we* remembered. And now, at last, the time has come. The words of our Book made real, Alora, Ghada and Samir to return, to take back the world they made, a world without Walls or Circles.'

Mithila remembered the words she had read among the ruins.

We know you have the eyes to see. We are waiting for you.

Prana looked at Carina strangely. 'They will fight with us, then?'

'Fight with us?' Maji's voice rang out. 'They will fight the Wall, and they will destroy it—*for* us. If they return to this world, the Wall will crumble and fall.'

'A—ah.' Prana swallowed.

'Let's be seeing what trebuchets do against the Builders, huh?' Mithila chuckled.

Maji laughed. 'Like the wind that sweeps the leaves from the ground, they will sweep all of *them*—Council and Shoortan and the Circles—away.'

'Yes, okay, and how are we sweeping to the Council Hall to get to them?' Meghana interrupted. 'Maliot's blocked remember?'

Mithila turned to Maji.

'Field Commander, I need you to clear the Maliot for us.'

A long silence fell upon the table. Maji was looking down at her hands.

'But we can't attack,' she said at last, heavily. 'Not now.'

Mithila raised an eyebrow.

'Defending,' said Maji, 'is collective. The entire Mandala comes together. The enemy fears every street corner, every open window, every quiet roof. We can defend against better weapons, greater numbers. But attacking, the Mandala will be against us, and they know their own streets better. In the Blue Revolution, we only attacked when we knew the people were already with us. That's not the case this time.'

'Is it impossible?' said Mithila.

For a while, Maji was quiet.

'No,' she said, finally. 'It is possible. But we will need two things. One: bait, to draw the Shoortans away from the Maliot. And two: every last body we have. If we do this, Worldfarer, and we fail, or if you fail to wake Alora, then it ends. The Revolution dies tonight.'

'Right,' said Mithila. She swallowed.

'I …' Maji paused. 'I am of the Dooma, and to see Alora rise, it is … even in our dreams we could not desire it.' Her voice grew toneless. 'But as your Field Commander, I must say—we don't *have* to do this, Worldfarer. It's not our only strategy. But it is your decision. We will follow.'

'I know,' said Mithila. She turned to Mankala, who was still standing.

'Tell me,' she said, 'are you sure this will work?'

Mankala raised her chin and held her gaze.

'As sure as I've been of anything in my life.'

Mithila nodded. 'We do it. Tonight.'

There was a long exhalation around the table. 'I can plan the attack, Worldfarer,' Maji said, her voice soft. 'But how do we draw them out?'

With her mind clear, like the Rasa on a blazing afternoon, Mithila caught Alvar's eye. Alvar, who had been sitting quietly through the meeting, saying nothing; and as her heart swelled with love, the beginnings of a plan began to form in her head.

Alvar stepped across the bridge and into the Tenth Mandala.

The Circle he had come to know so well was a husk of emptiness. His ears strained for familiar sounds: the calls of children at the end of a long day, and the pattering of their feet; the low murmurs, as the older ones took their evening air, leaning upon their carers' arms; and the roll of the wagon, back and forth, upon the streets.

All of it gone tonight, the Mandala wrapped in silence. The only sound was the stone he kicked ahead of him, as he walked.

An hour to Wallset. An hour to the end of the Select's Truce, the moment that would cleave day from night, peace from fray, like the snapping of a dry branch.

From a neighbouring street, he heard the hurried sound of footsteps.

Alvar stopped.

Tap-tap, tap-tap; the steps grew louder, passed him—and faded away.

Alvar moved again, heading West, towards the Maidan and the Forum. He crossed an empty Ninth, and entered the Eighth. In the sky, the light began to fade.

'Alvar-Nine.'

A line of men and women blocked the road.

In the middle stood Rastogi.

Alvar stopped dead. He threw up his hands. 'Truce!'

Rastogi threw him an amused laugh. 'Nobody's hurting you.'

'Let me pass, then.'

'The Truce doesn't say we have to lay out a carpet for you,' said Rastogi. 'Alvar-Nine. Where are you taking the Heartstone? To the Maidan? Giving it to that—the President?'

'I have no Heartstone.'

'You lie. We know when someone dares put their hands around the Builder's stone.'

'You didn't even know another Heartstone existed beyond the Wall until the Worldfarer brought it back,' Alvar said mildly.

'There is no *Worldfarer*,' Rastogi snapped. 'There is the Ostracized.'

Alvar grew aware of the ever-dimming sky, and the silent, watchful houses around him. His eyes darted to either side, to the little openings that led further into the Eighth.

'This is a Truce,' he said once again. 'You have no right—'

'We have no right to *harm* you,' Rastogi interrupted. He too looked up the sky. 'For another fifteen minutes?'

Alvar spun around and darted back into the lane he had come from.

Behind him, Rastogi shouted: 'Follow him. Wait till Wallset. *And then get the Heartstone*.'

Before Alvar could take a step into the lane, two Shoortans appeared at the end of it, blocking the exit. He cursed, pulled himself out, and turned the other direction, away from Rastogi. He turned the corner. The way North, to the Maliot, was blocked again.

It was almost dark.

Alvar stopped.

He was out of time.

He calculated, turning and turning over the map of the Eighth Mandala in his head. Then he set his face southwards, and sprinted.

The evening wind whipped his hair back, and whistled in his ears. Sounds carried to his ear—running feet behind him, shouted commands—and his own breath, ragged and torn, louder than anything else.

Under a lowering sky, he turned the corner. There it was: the Eighth Mandala's sewage chamber, a large circular field open to the sky, separated from the row of mud-brick houses by a wide street.

The sewage chamber: inviolate ground under the Protocol, under the protection of the Select. Alvar flew down the street, past the two bemused scientists who stood at the edge, and dived into the space just as the Shoortans entered the street from either end.

Wallset fell.

He ran till he reached the centre, and fell on his knees, panting. On the edge of the sewage chamber, the Shoortans quietly fanned out and formed a large ring, surrounding him from all sides.

From behind the line, he heard Rastogi's voice.

'He has to eat. We'll wait.'

Mithila looked up at the darkening sky. 'It's time,' she said.

'If only your friend keeps up his end of the bargain,' said Maji.

'He's never let me down,' Mithila said. *Don't let this be the first time, Alvar.*

'That's reassuring,' Maji said. 'Otherwise we're all dead.'

They stood on the bridge over the tributary, the Tenth Mandala silent behind them. Maji turned now, away from Mithila, and faced the massed ranks gathered upon the street, extending either side of the Community Hall.

'Companions,' she said, and her voice carried upon the air.

'Two days and two nights old is our Revolution. Two days ago, the Shoortans came down on us. We beat them. Yesterday, the Council came down on us. We beat them too.'

Cheers rose into the sky. Maji smiled, her teeth bared.

'Now they have both retreated into their Upper Mandalas. And tonight, we march upon *them*.

'But this is no ordinary fight.'

She paused.

'For two thousand years, we have laboured and lived in Sumer, the Sumer given to us. But ever since the Worldfarer came among us, we have known that our dreams are no longer bound by a bounded City, measured by a *Wall*rise and *Wall*set. Forget the Circles, forget the

Farmlands and their quotas, forget the Wall—when we march with the Worldfarer, we can start the *world* over again.

'And we will start that tonight.'

Silence hung upon her words.

'Tonight, we awaken the Builders, who have lain sleeping since the Wall came to be. No, these are not the Builders of the myth of Malan—the *lie* of Malan—but the Builders who once reigned in the world beyond, Builders who knew no Walls, Builders who have been waiting to be woken so that they can tear down this one. These Builders are our ancestors. And now, thanks to the Worldfarer, they will soon be by our side.'

A stir.

Maji spoke before it settled. 'But for that, we need to fight. Tonight, we march on the Eighth. There we shall find the Shoortans—and we shall defeat them, so that the Worldfarer may go to the Council Hall, and bring back our Builders to us.

'I won't hide from you the peril of what is to come. Twenty-seven years ago, there were some of us who marched—and lost. You know that story. There is not a house—from the Fifteenth to the Eleventh—that does not know someone who died in the Blue Revolution. Some died for their dreams. And a man of the Eleventh died to save the life of a girl of the Fifteenth, telling her the story of Samati, that *if you want to fly, someone must sacrifice themselves for you.* He died so that the dream would live, banked fire, until the day came when it could burn again.

'Tonight that death unites us, Fifteenth to the Eleventh, because our dreams have returned, and this time they burn too strong to be killed, by Shoortan or Councillor. We march for the world that we'll make, but also for the memory of those, like Bhavi, who will never see it. We remember the fierce and the gentle. We remember the disappeared, the ones whose bodies they did not leave for us mourn. And we remember Maran and Upar.'

She raised her right hand, clenched in a fist. Around her wrist, they all saw the worn and faded cloth whose story they knew, the cloth that had once belonged to Savarian, and had witnessed the first—and last—Marriage of Truth in Sumer. The cloth that bound together a revolution past and a revolution present, the dreams that were dead and those that refused to die, Maji and Upar, Mithila and her father.

And Maji began to sing, a song that Mithila remembered, a song whose strains she had heard thrice before.

Here's to you, Maran and Upar
In our hearts and never afar
Your eyes are closed, but we won't forget
The fire you left, that still remains …

A great rustling in the crowd. There were some who sang the words with her, slipping into the refrain as easily and as naturally as if they sang it every day; and others who joined in humming, their voices like of the waves of the sea.

'We march,' said Maji. 'Garuda formation.'

Mithila stepped off the bridge and stood aside. One by one, in silence, the people crossed the bridge after Maji, and fanned out on the street beyond, before vanishing into the Tenth. In moments, the space outside Konar Hall was empty.

Mankala stood by the door, watching Mithila across the vacant space. Beside her were the two chariots she had brought that afternoon.

'Shall we?' Mankala said.

Mithila felt the hilt of the sword at her waist, which Maji had finally given to her.

'Let's go.'

'*Just stay in the Circle,*' Maji had said to him. '*When we attack, they'll think it's to save you, to save the Heartstone—and they'll draw the rest of their forces away from the Maliot to stop us from getting you out. No matter what, just stay there.*'

'*So basically, first I'm bait, and then you're bait?*'

'Basically.'

In the beginning, it had all gone to plan.

Night had fallen. The Shoortans surrounding the sewage chamber had become outlines. He'd stood in the centre of that wide-open space, shivering a little. He'd started to sing—to infuriate Rastogi—that old, pre-Oligarchy song of lovers beyond the Wall: *Oh father, tell your children/Not to look where we have gone/For we have gone to live, this day/In the world of the rising Sun …'*

At *sun*, the Eighth exploded around him.

A ball of flame arced through the air and hit the ground with a muffled *whump*. There was fire on the road, tongues of flame leaping into the night. Alvar ducked, shielding his eyes. When he looked again, arrows were whistling through the air.

The night filled with cries of *Dooma! Worldfarer!*

Alvar rushed to the edge of the sewage chamber, staying back from its boundary line, as Maji had ordered him. The fire on the road painted the buildings of the Eighth in a lurid light. Just beyond the flames he saw the Shoortans rushing to-and-fro, shouting commands.

From the South, the Dooma advanced. Alvar saw Maji at the head. She had a blade in each hand, and she was running—they were all running. The gap narrowed in seconds. The two forces met with a *crack* and a shower of yells. Alvar's eyes followed Maji. Her blades were a blur, he could almost *feel* them singing, singeing the air, and *she* was a blur, catching a blow on her thigh—Alvar winced—that seemed not to slow her down a whit, while around her the two forces heaved and struggled—and then Maji was lost in a crush of bodies.

The fight on the road turned into a melee. The narrow space only allowed combat at close quarters between the frontlines, with the forces behind them almost pushing their way into advancing, like a battering ram. But Alvar saw the centre of the fight begin to shift North, the Shoortans being pushed back, on their heels, up the road—

'Matriarch!'

The shout came from the North.

Alvar turned.

Flame lamps weaved and bobbed and moved towards the fight, carried by black cloaks. Alvar danced from foot to foot, unable to move beyond the circle, feeling the weight of the Heartstone beneath his shirt, the weight that kept him tied to where he was, and—

Something's wrong, his mind whispered to him. *It's POUM that's supposed to be coming in from the North, driving a wedge through the enemy—not the Shoortans.*

They poured in, lines of black cloaks from the dim distance, visible first only as pin-pricks of light, then as things made flesh and blade. Alvar's heart began to sink. He looked for Maji again in the fight. There she was, moving just a *little* slower, and she'd been pushed just a *little* back, and—

A building by the road went up in flames.

The fire came from somewhere inside, flames emerging from the windows as the mud-brick itself refused to burn. Alvar danced around at the edge of the sewage chamber. He was close enough to smell the heat, the smoke, the sweat, and the blood, and it seemed that there was nobody in the burning house, nobody that he could see, at least.

But in the new light, there were things that he *could* see, and they were the Shoortan banners, that now outnumbered the banners of the broken Wall. He shaded his eyes and searched: yes, there was Maji—and she had lost one of her blades, she was now fighting with a sword in one hand and a bamboo staff in the other, he could see her hair matted with sweat, a line of black cloaks pressing upon her—

An arrow came flying through the air and buried itself in the ground inches from his feet.

Alvar leapt backwards. Suddenly he realized he was unarmed, standing right at the edge of the battle.

He hurried back into the shadows and the shelter of the sewage chamber, trying not to lose sight of Maji, who—

'Alvar!'

The sudden, sharp voice made him jerk. Alvar swung around.

On the other edge of the sewage chamber, away from the fighting, stood Lamon, a flame lamp in his hand.

Alvar stared at him dumbly.

'Come here!' Lamon called.

'Lamon, wha—'

'You need to come with me, this is a disaster—Dooma's losing and POUM got ambushed on the way, they're not getting here in time—'

'How do you—'

'No *time*, Alvar!' Lamon cut in again. 'We need to get you out. The Eighth is mine. They won't find us.'

No matter what, just stay there.

Alvar hesitated. He turned—and saw a blade come whistling down upon Maji's bamboo staff, slicing it in half. Maji spun and hurled her half-staff at an advancing black cloak. But then she was retreating, and the Dooma was retreating South, pressed by the Shoortans, the line holding—just about.

He felt the Heartstone against his skin again. Mithila's, from beyond the Wall.

The Dooma's line broke, and the first of them began to turn and run.

'*Matriarch!*' came the shouts.

Alvar felt sick, as if a rock had settled in the base of his stomach. He hurried to the edge of the sewage chamber, where Lamon waited, past the single Select member who stood guard, seemingly unconcerned by the battle that raged a little distance away, or by anything they did.

'Come,' Lamon beckoned.

They hastened South-West, deeper into the Eighth. Behind them, the noise of the fight grew fainter. The paths were empty and dark, the buildings quiet.

'The next bridge,' said Lamon, 'takes you to the Ninth, and it's unguarded. From there—'

Before Lamon finished his sentence, there was a rustle behind them. The next moment, there was a gag around Alvar's mouth, a sack descended on his head, and the world was plunged into blackness.

They waited at the edge of the barricade, gripping their two chariots, as the Rasa wound its way towards the Wall.

'I cannot believe that at the end of all things,' said Mithila ruefully, 'we're going to ask the Builders—the *Builders*—to save us.'

'Rebels, Mithila,' Mankala said. There was an unfamiliar lightness in her voice. 'Rebels, just like us. Is that so hard?'

'A little.' Then, because they were alone, she went on: 'are you *actually* sure about this?'

'Mith. Worldfarer. The bravest fool I know.' Mankala turned to her and grinned in the darkness, her teeth gleaming. 'When have we been sure about anything? You bound your waist to the garudas and threw yourself into the sky.'

'That was just my own life, no-one else's.'

'What is it that Ghada says to Samir? *All my life I've only known doubt.* You think we deserve more certainty than they had?'

'I suppose,' said Mithila, 'we'll find out together.'

A flaming arrow arched across the sky and plunged into the Rasa. The signal.

'Time to meet the Builders,' said Mankala softly. 'We give them their lives. They give us the world. You ready, Worldfarer?'

'Let's go,' breathed Mithila.

They sped down the Maliot.

Someone removed the sack from his head, and undid the gag.

Alvar gulped air. Piece by piece, the blurry world began to come into focus: a small round room, open windows, flickering lamplight.

Rama stood in front of him.

Alvar started and then winced as the ropes cut into his arms. They had bound him to a chair.

He turned his eyes up again, and met hers.

'Hello, Alvar,' Rama said. 'It's been a while.'

'Why the fuck have you tied me up?' Alvar spat.

'Easy. It's just a precaution. You won't be harmed.'

Alvar looked around. His chair was the only piece of furniture in the room, resting unevenly upon an earthen floor. The walls were chipped and cracked.

'That was cleverly done, I'll give you that,' Rama's voice washed over him. 'The Worldfarer's soul-friend, walking into enemy territory with the Heartstone. Anyone else, and they'd have smelled a trap—but you—you were believable. I don't suppose you'll tell me why?

He stared straight ahead. 'Where am I?'

'Safe.'

'From whom? All those dangerous rebels?' When there was no answer, it struck him. 'Rama, you're not seriously going to keep me as a hostage!'

Rama looked at him. 'What do you think she'd give me, to have you back?'

Alvar stiffened. 'She's smarter than that.'

'Smarter? Is that what we're calling it now?' she said quietly.

There was something unbearable in her eyes. Alvar wrenched his gaze away. A grey Wallrise loomed before him, Minakshi running up to them, the garudas—and Mithila, who put her father's life in the balance and then left anyway.

'Welcome,' said Rama, 'to the Know Your Mithila class. I've spent a few days here already. The lessons are not always pleasant.'

Alvar exhaled, staring at a point on the wall before him.

'And yet,' he said, 'only one of us is tied to a chair. Seems like the Know Your Rama classes aren't a picnic either.'

Rama's smile was tight.

'How did I get here, *my* President?' Alvar said.

'Don't you remember?'

He thought back. Lamon had called him from the South, and he'd followed him away from the fight, into the Eighth Mandala, turning into darkness, and then—

A horrible suspicion took root in Alvar's mind.

Rama saw his face change. 'He didn't do it to hurt you,' she said quickly. 'I promised him you wouldn't be harmed.'

He could have screamed. But Alvar only clenched his teeth. 'Oh. I see.'

Rama walked to the window, and stared out into the night.

'Don't blame Lamon,' she said after a while, still looking out of the window. 'I gave him—well, I'm sure Mithila didn't mean to make him sacrifice his chance at a life with the person he loved, just so she could go beyond the Wall?' She laughed softly. 'Who'd do *such* a thing?'

'But he—he—' Alvar began, and found he had nothing to say.

'He saw his future bound up with ours,' Rama finished, 'because I repealed the Marriage License Laws. Because this is what it's about, isn't it?' She turned back to him. 'Whose future matters? The people here, *now*—or the people who *might* be, beyond?'

'Don't even try,' said Alvar, 'to turn me.'

'I wouldn't insult you by doing that,' Rama said. She walked up to him.

'In fact,' she said, 'I'm not even going to waste time interrogating you.'

She was standing by him now, so that Alvar had to crane his neck to look up at her.

She reached out a hand and withdrew the Heartstone from Alvar's pocket.

'But I will borrow this.'

He jerked forward—and grimaced, as the ropes pulled him up short.

The Heartstone was throbbing in Rama's palms.

'That's Mithila's,' he said, furiously.

'I know.'

'You can't.'

'I have to, Alvar.'

'Then you're just a—a little thief.'

Rama's eyes flashed. 'The last time I let her keep it, she used it to set this City on fire. Enough. This has to end now.'

'We were companions,' Alvar shook his head. 'Friends. We were going to bring down the Wall together. And now, you—'

'And now this, Alvar,' she said, looking straight at him. 'Either you watch me win—and the hope that one day, we can still bring down the Wall, stays alive. Or I lose, they bring *me* down—and then you can watch the dream die, this time for good.'

'You know what?' said Alvar. 'You're just like her sister. Got some power, betrayed your beliefs to keep it, and now you tell yourself it's for the greater good so you can sleep at night. You don't *deserve* her.'

Rama pulled back. For a while she only stood there, in silence, looking at him.

'We're done here,' she said at last, quietly.

She slipped her hand into the pockets of her robe, and pulled out a knife. Alvar flinched as she came close to him, but then the blood rushed back into his hands, as his ropes were cut away.

'You're free to go,' said Rama.

Alvar rubbed his wrists and looked up, scowled, 'Go back and tell Mithila that Rama stole her Heartstone?'

'She'll know soon enough,' Rama said. 'But you can decide which of us gets to tell her. Goodbye, Alvar.'

He watched her leave the room.

He'd walked out of the Eleventh that night with the Heartstone, to draw the Shoortans into a trap. The trap had failed. He had failed. And the Heartstone was gone, lost to Rama, who would destroy the Revolution.

He slumped back in the chair, and let himself cry at last.

Mithila and Mankala raced up the Maliot, heads down, pushing off the ground with their feet, feeling the frame shudder beneath them. As they crossed the Middle Circles, they heard cries from the South, but Maji had done her job for the night. The Maliot was clear.

They passed into the Upper Circles, and into silence. The Council was nowhere to be seen. They flew up the Five, past the dark hulks of the stone mansions. Then they were in the Forum.

Mithila had never seen the Forum Plaza like this before: plunged in darkness, not a single lamp on the paths that connected the towers. The towers themselves seemed abandoned to the night—other than the Citadel, where a single high window held candlelight.

Mankala looked up and sighed in relief. 'She's in.'

They wheeled their chariots to the door of the Citadel. Mankala rapped on it.

There was no response.

'Leader Marwana?' Mankala called out. She rapped again. 'It's me, Mankala. We need your help.'

A long silence fell. Marwana rapped a third time, louder. 'Marwana, we need you now!'

And then Mithila remembered.

'Oh fuck,' she spoke into the night. 'That door's not going to open.'

Mankala turned to her. 'What?'

'Select's Protocol. Absolute neutrality. The door will not open until the Revolution is over, one way or another. She's not coming.'

Denial—and then terror—chased each other across Mankala's face, an expression Mithila had never seen before. 'But she has to—we can't—'

Mithila grimaced. 'You know, there is *one* other way.'

'What?'

'But it's the Council Hall, for one. And we'll need help. I'm not so sure we'll get it.'

'Well, we're not getting it here,' said Mankala.

She turned and led the way across the Forum, to the Council Hall. Mithila hurried to catch her up.

They came to the Elders' stronghold. For a few moments, they stood still at the threshold, listening. From inside, there was no sound.

'Alright then,' said Mankala. 'This or nothing.'

She pushed the door. It creaked open, echoing under her hands.

The passage was pitch-dark, but for a thin line of light beneath a door ahead on their right.

'That's the Great Hall,' Mankala whispered. 'Who's in there?'

'The Elders are all at the Maliot House—can't be them,' Mithila murmured. 'Come on.'

She crept forward along the left side of the passage, feeling her way past each door. Mankala kept inside her shadow. They reached the door of the Great Hall. It was half-open. Light spilt in a dim half-circle into the corridor.

Mithila stopped. Voices came from inside. She felt Mankala's hand on her shoulder. She turned, and put a finger to her lips. Mankala nodded. Mithila crossed to the other side of the corridor and darted past the spill of light. Mankala came behind her. Inside, the voices continued, uninterrupted.

They walked on in darkness, until they reached the doorway on their left. Mithila led the way into the Hall of a Thousand Pillars. The pillars were glowing softly, with their strange, almost imperceptible, blue light.

'Alright,' said Mithila. 'There's a way down from here. But the only people who know it are these two sightless guides.'

'What?'

'That's how I found the Builders last time. I—I found them, and I followed them.'

'Where are these guides?' said Mankala, uncertainly.

Mithila pointed. 'Up the stairs. I saw them when I escaped from here three days ago. I'll go get them. You stay here and watch? In case whoever's in that Hall ...'

Mankala nodded. Mithila jogged to the stairway, and began to climb. The lamps were lit, but far apart, leaving the stairs dim. She counted the steps as she climbed, remembering her last time here, squeezing herself into the side of the stairway as *they* came up, talking to each other—

From behind her, a scream cut through the night.

Mithila stopped dead.

'Mankala?' she whispered.

From the Hall, she heard a thump.

'Mankala!' Mithila turned, and rushed back down the steps, taking two at a time, running back into the Hall. It was silent and empty.

Carefully, she stepped between the pillars, looking around her. The hall stayed quiet.

But halfway across she heard it: a faint sound to her right.

Mithila stopped. She turned and crept towards the sound, suddenly aware of her own footsteps. And then there was something else, an indistinct noise, like a groan—

She came upon her just behind a pillar.

Mankala was lying on her back, her legs crumpled beneath her, unmoving. Her eyes were closed.

Seventeen

Ghada

Mithila rushed forward. She dropped to one knee and grasped Mankala's shoulder, shaking her. Someone had stuffed a rag into her mouth, and tied a strip of cloth over it, tight between her teeth. Her arms were limp, bound.

'Fuck, fuck, fuck,' Mithila whispered. Hands shaking, she touched the cord behind Mankala's head. Just as she began to fumble at the knot, Mankala's eyes flickered open, caught Mithila's—and widened at something beyond.

Running footsteps. Mithila twisted and snatched at her sword, raising it to protect her side. She felt a shock that nearly wrenched her arm from its socket, and threw her back upon the ground. A shadow flew past her.

Mithila rolled away and staggered to her feet, blade out in front. She pushed hair out of her eyes.

Before her stood Minakshi.

For a long moment, Mithila stared at her.

'*Clean* parry, sister,' Minakshi said. 'I see Ba kept your sword sharp.'

'Don't you mean *Savarian*?' said Mithila, a glint in her eye.

'Well, Ananta was a better father than a revolutionary—won't you agree?'

'Take that name out of your mouth,' Mithila said. 'You want to burn down everything he ever believed in.'

'Somebody needed to be grown up in this family.'

'You *Ostracized* me.'

'And I've finished saying sorry for that,' Minakshi said. 'But you know what? I'm not sorry anymore. I'd forgotten that you're willing to see the City fall to have your way. You want to wake Ghada? And *Alora*?'

Behind her, there was a violent movement, as Mankala struggled against her bonds, trying to speak, choking through the gag. Neither Minakshi nor Mithila took their eyes off each other.

'Ah yes,' Minakshi said. 'Your little Tarafian is bad at keeping secrets with a knife at her throat.'

'Why are you here, Minakshi?' said Mithila.

'To stop you.'

'Like you did so brilliantly by the Wall, when you tried to lie about Ba?'

'Back when I still believed you might have a heart.'

'Ha.' Mithila bared her teeth. 'Nice try—but you forget I've always known when you're lying.

Minakshi blinked. 'Enough,' she said. 'Time to finish this.'

'Don't make me hurt you,' said Mithila. 'These blades are—'

Minakshi lunged.

She exploded off her back leg, sword-point aimed at Mithila's chest, covering the distance between them like a streak. Mithila barely got her own blade up in time. The impact jolted into her arm again. Mithila cried out as her wrist twisted. She staggered back.

Minakshi came at her once more. Mithila saw the blade angling towards her throat. Still backing away, she raised her sword to cover her neck, seeing—moments too late—that it was a feint, as Minakshi's blade dropped towards her unprotected chest.

Her backward stumble saved her, a second's worth of distance that allowed her to swipe away the blade with an ugly downward parry, just a hair's-breadth from her chest. Mithila retreated, gasping, disoriented.

Before she could recover, Minakshi lunged a third time, all speed, going straight for her throat. Mithila's own blade was somewhere far away, leaving her defenceless. She threw herself to the side, landing on her knee and rolling away, as Minakshi passed through where she had been. Her sister's blade struck a pillar with an ugly, ringing sound.

They faced each other once more. Mithila felt a shooting pain up her right knee. She grimaced.

'I don't think you *can* hurt me,' Minakshi said, not a beat out of breath.

'You know I always preferred defence,' Mithila said. She could hear her heart throbbing against her chest.

'Defence? Or running away?' Minakshi taunted. 'Ba wouldn't like this.'

Mithila laughed, a bitter sound. 'Ba? Oh, wouldn't he be proud if he could see us now! His daughters, fighting each other.'

Minakshi returned a smile that glinted in the blue light. 'Ba, who wanted to win this City upon the point of a sword? He would not have it any other way.' She advanced on Mithila again, slower this time, more deliberate. 'We are the Malorans, after all.'

Mithila retreated. Minakshi's blade-point, in line with her chest, was tracing little circles in the air, mocking her, asking her to come for it. It sent bolts of tension stabbing through her veins, driving her almost to the edge of panic. She felt her knee throb, but it bore her still. Still backing, Mithila kept Minakshi two blades' length away, watching for that lunge, faster than anything she remembered.

'By the way,' she said, to grasp at something, anything, 'your back foot's rolling again. I thought we'd sorted it out before you left us for your Shoortans.'

Minakshi snorted. 'Nice try,' she said, 'but it turns out Ba was as wrong about that bit of advice as he was about his Revolution.'

And with her words, Mithila remembered something else that Ananta had failed to convince his younger daughter of during their lessons, another point in his map of failures with Minakshi. As her sister continued to advance at her, she kept an eye on her front leg.

Twice Minakshi feinted, teasing a lunge, inviting Mithila to react, to follow Minakshi's blade and leave her side exposed—but each time Mithila saw the planted front leg and did nothing at all, holding her defence, smiling back. And then—the third time—she saw it, the quick half-step forward, predictable, the prelude to the real thing. When Minakshi lunged this time, Mithila was ready, jumping backwards, out of range.

For a moment, her sister was off balance, her sword wavering. Mithila tried to catch it, to beat it away, to move in—but Minakshi was too quick for her, recovering easily, and dancing back out of reach.

Mithila gritted her teeth. It was like duelling a faster version of Maji—only, to the finish.

Minakshi advanced again, moving smoothly. 'You sure you want to go through with this, *Mith*?'

Mithila felt a burst of anger. 'You do not get to call me that.'

'Sorry, should I not have used that word? Does *Mith* belong to Rama now?'

'*Shut up!*' Mithila attacked.

She gave the impression that it was a wild, enraged, careening forward—and Minakshi was fooled. She moved her arm across her body to parry where she thought Mithila's sword would be. But Mithila had already change direction and launched herself at Minakshi's exposed side. Too late her sister realized it, tried to circle back, to deflect the thrust away …

It wasn't enough. The blade took Minakshi's shoulder as Mithila went past her, piercing through cloth and flesh, blood blooming upon her sleeve.

Minakshi cried out in pain and staggered back, clutching her wound. The blood on her robe was spreading, slowly making its way towards the blue circle on her front. She backed up against a pillar, sword arm hanging loose by her side.

Mithila stalked up to her, sword out, breathing hard. 'We can end this now,' she said. 'Walk away. I'll do what I came to.'

Minakshi looked up at her through gritted teeth. Blood had smeared across her cheek, where she'd rubbed her face with her hands

'*Fuck you*,' she whispered, through gritted teeth.

In a flash—so quick that Mithila never quite saw it happen—she switched her sword to her left hand, and launched herself off the pillar. Mithila fell back as Minakshi attacked, her jaw set.

Across the pillars and in the pale light they fought, blade on blade. Her sister pressed her through the hall, forcing her to retreat and retreat, and it was all Mithila could do to keep a silver-swift sword distance between them. But the patch of blood on Minakshi's robe was growing, and after long minutes, there came at last a time when her breath grew ragged, and beads of sweat were visible on her face. Mithila clenched her teeth, hearing her own breath escape her in a whistle, feeling her sword arm burn and her legs cry out in protest.

Minakshi paused, panting. With a final effort Mithila stepped in at last, to close with her. They swatted at each other uselessly, swords locked together, inches from their faces, before Mithila threw herself back against a pillar. Minakshi only stood there, still breathing hard.

Mithila looked up at the ceiling, lost to view far, far above. Everything hurt. Her heart was racing.

'Do we have to do this?' she gasped.

Minakshi knelt on the floor, holding her right arm again. She looked at Mithila, and shook her head. 'Like you said, one of us has to give up everything.'

Mithila felt sadness wash over her. 'You want me to give up the Wall so you can stop trying to kill me?'

'Give up the Wall, and we'll be sisters again.'

She felt a sourness rise to her throat. 'I can't,' Mithila said. 'I—can't.'

'Father's daughters, I suppose,' Minakshi said. 'It's one or the other.'

After a long while, Mithila nodded. 'It is.'

'I'd rather end this now, than spend years fighting each other. At least Sumer can have peace.'

She advanced again, carefully. Mithila realized that she couldn't run any more. She went down into a crouch and waited, balanced on both feet. Minakshi was slower now, but still sure. Two swords' length away—so that the points of their weapons were almost touching—she too stopped, and settled into a crouch.

Eternities passed.

Mithila tried to think. Minakshi's attacks that evening had been—adapting. The feint to the chest and then upwards to the throat was likely—but it could be anything, that blade could go anywhere, so quick, so smooth. She relaxed her arm, trying not to let it stiffen, to hold her blade too tight.

'Come on, sister. One final time,' Mithila murmured.

Minakshi smiled. It didn't reach her eyes. She raised her blade. Her back leg tensed. Mithila watched for the half-step, for the feint, readied herself—

And just then, in mid motion, Minakshi's gaze shifted, to something behind her, and her blade hung in the air, uncertain. It was the only opening Mithila needed. She lunged and caught Minakshi's blade with hers, and before her sister could do anything, she had it locked, and was pressing downwards, feeling Minakshi's elbow give way, watching her eyes widen…

… and Mithila *twisted.*

Minakshi cried out in surprise and pain, as her sword was wrenched from her grasp, and sent clattering down the floor. In a moment, Mithila's own blade was at her throat.

Elmandar stepped out from behind a pillar. 'Am I late?' he said.

Mithila had no time to think. 'Elmandar,' she said, never taking her eyes off Minakshi—who was glaring at her, 'can you untie Mankala? To your left. Behind a pillar.'

'She's what?' There was a moment of silence, and then—

'*Fucking* Builders!' She heard Mankala curse. 'And *ow*. What took you so long? I sent that Messenger *before* the Truce broke.'

'I was in the Great Hall,' Elmandar said sheepishly.

'Oh, it was you in there—hurry up, Builders' sake!' Mithila could tell Elmandar was haplessly pulling at the knots. 'Hold on, were you *playing at being the Elders in there?* I should actually kill you. That's it, I'm going to kill you.'

Mithila smiled—and then looked down, at Minakshi's ugly glare. Mankala appeared beside her, massaging her wrists, looking embarrassed and furious. 'Sorry I let myself get caught so easily—but Builders, Mithila, your sister's a vicious little *unfertilized* shit.'

'Would you like to do the honours?' said Mithila.

'Oh, with pleasure,' Mankala grinned. She took the rope, and—none too gently—flipped Minakshi on her stomach, kneeling on her back. She pulled her arms behind her back, and tied them together with the same rope. Minakshi made no sound.

'We'll put her in the conferral room,' Mankala said. 'Elmandar has the keys.'

She shoved Minakshi ahead of her. Elmandar stepped past, walking up to open the door.

'Hold on,' Mithila said, as they reached. She leaned down and started untying Minakshi's hands.

'What are you doing?' Mankala said. 'She'll get out.'

'We're locking her in,' said Mithila, not looking at Minakshi. 'I'm not a sadist.' She finished, and stepped back.

Mankala pushed Minakshi in, and as she stumbled, nearly falling into the room, she slammed the door shut.

'What?' she said to Mithila, who was staring at her. She took the key and locked the door. 'It's nicer than what she did to me.'

Inside there was silence.

Now Mankala turned to Elmandar. 'We need to talk.'

Elmandar threw up his arms. 'I didn't know you were—' he said, and stopped as Mankala put a single finger on this lips. 'But as your idiocy apparently saved our lives,' she said, her voice softer, 'we'll let it go.' Mithila rolled her eyes. 'Shut up,' Mankala said to her.

'But I didn't even say anything.'

'Are the Hedonists around?' Mankala asked Elmandar.

'In the Great Hall.'

'Can you watch our backs?'

'Yeah, we'll watch' said Elmandar, 'but what are you going down for?'

Mankala smiled at him. 'We're bringing the Builders back. How's that for *good, not great*?'

Elmandar burst out laughing. Then he caught sight of Mankala's face, and stopped abruptly.

'You can't be serious.'

'As a Shoortan,' said Mankala cheerily. 'Just keep watch.' She turned to Mithila. 'Come on, this time you're not leaving me behind.'

Elmandar took a half step forward, and caught her hand. 'Mankala.'

She turned and looked at his face. 'What?'

'Just—be safe. Please?'

She squeezed his hand, and turned again, setting off down the hall. Mithila took a last look at Elmandar, and then ran behind her.

She caught up to Mankala at the stairway. They climbed. The stairs were narrow and steep. Mithila's legs—already tired from the duel—began to protest instantly. Before the first fifty steps, she found herself sweating. She clenched her teeth and forced her legs into a rhythm.

'Okay, slow down,' she panted, around what seemed to be the halfway point.

'We have to go all the way up to the top, no?'

'If you hadn't made me go into battle for you—literally—I'd be in better shape for this!'

Mankala chuckled. 'Fair enough.' She stopped. 'Half a minute.'

'Oh, thanks.' Mithila leaned against the wall, breathing hard. Her calves were on fire. 'She put a knife to your throat, eh?'

'Right after she tied me up. I never had a chance.' Mankala scowled again. 'Still surprised you fought her like that, you know. Felt like you were actually going to kill her at one point.'

Mithila smiled ruefully. 'She could have actually killed me. Thrice. But she didn't. I don't know what would have happened that last time—I guess I never will.'

Mankala grimaced again. 'You give your family way too much credit.'

'Not many of them left, are there?'

Mankala subsided. 'Climb,' she said.

They went on up. Mithila was half-bent now, putting a hand on her knee with every step. The stairs grew narrower, and each breath was laboured. Her back ached.

'We're here!' Mankala gasped at last, pointing up. At the very top, Mithila saw the door.

They struggled up the last few steps. By the time they had reached the top, they were out of breath. They stood on the landing for a minute, panting.

Mithila knocked.

There was no response.

'Oh, *fuck* this,' she muttered, and pushed at the door. It swung open easily.

They entered a tiny, circular room, so small that it could have been a cell. A single, arched window looked out onto a glimmering of stars. The only pieces of furniture were two bare beds placed against each wall, and a small rickety table on which a lonely pitcher stood.

On the beds sat two men, in loose white robes, their heads shaven.

'This is … them?' Mankala whispered.

Mithila nodded. She stepped up close to them. 'Um, hello?'

There was no answer.

'I—er—we need your help,' Mithila said. 'We need to get to the Hall of Kings.'

They answered her with silence. Beside her, she sensed Mankala stiffened. Mithila repeated, louder:

'We need to get to the Hall of Kings. Will you take us, please?'

They stared blankly in her direction, unmoving. They seemed to be at rest, not hearing her at all, not even blinking, almost as if they were—dead. *Maybe they are dead*, a voice whispered in her head. But no—she saw their chests move, and pale though they were, their skin was alive. The beginnings of a thought, cloudy and unformed, began to take shape at the back of her mind.

'Hey!' Mankala said, her voice angry. 'We know you can hear us.'

At that one of them spoke, making them jump. 'We cannot,' he said, his voice grey and gravelly, like the stones at the bottom of the Lake Sumer.

'Cannot? Cannot what?'

'Only One—and no other—can command us. Your voices are not hers. So we cannot.' The words were precise, each syllable separated as though it had been cut with a knife. 'We are the *prayas*. We must obey.'

'I—we're not commanding,' Mankala floundered. 'We *need* to get there. It's important. For Sumer.'

They were silent. Mankala covered her eyes with her palms.

Mithila looked at their sightless eyes. The thought was knocking insistently on a door in her mind that would not open. *What was she missing?*

Mankala looked up hopefully. 'Alright. But can you tell us how to find it? Please?'

A moment of silence. Then:

'We are the *prayas*. We are forbidden.'

From somewhere in the depths of memory, words began to float into Mithila's mind, a song like a heartbeat.

In our hearts and never afar…

Mankala said: 'What do I need to do so you will help us? What can I do?'

This time there was no reply.

But the song gathered pace.

Your eyes are closed, but we won't forget…

Mankala turned to her, and there were tears welling up in her eyes. 'What do we do!'

Your eyes are closed, but we won't forget…

And the song clashed with gravely voice. *We are the prayas.*

Praya. The penance.

Mithila smiled.

She stepped in front of the two men, and in a low, clear voice, began to sing:

Before I gave you my heart,
Oh revolution,
I dipped my brush in the sky
To paint it blue
Blue I dream you
Blue.

She saw them stir. Mithila went on singing.

I ask from the sky its colour,
Oh revolution
To dress you in blue
I ask from the river its wellspring
To bathe you in blue
Blue I dream you
Blue …

Her last note lingered in the air. Both of them were on their feet.

'Maran and Upar,' she said, and her voice rang. 'Twenty-seven years. Did you think we would forget you?'

One of them spoke, slowly, wonderingly: 'Who are you?'

'Know my voice,' said Mithila. 'Savarian has returned. Will you deny his daughter?'

She saw the one who had spoken sink to his knees, his face in his hands. Seconds passed. The other walked slowly up to her, until they stood face to face.

'Savarian's daughter, you say,' he said. 'Tell me, then. What is my name?'

'You are Maran and Upar,' she said automatically. 'The ones who —'

'Yes,' he cut in, voice still soft. 'But which one am I?'

Mithila looked into his unseeing eyes. 'I—don't know?'

'As I thought. You see, Upar? Just like they who cannot tell the Dooma apart are the first to beg for help in the hour of need. You cannot even tell *us* apart, and you ask us to obey in the name of Savarian?'

'H—he gave me this song,' Mithila stammered, suddenly confused. 'My father—he told me, if I ever needed help from the Revolution—'

'And where is he then? If the Revolution has returned, why hasn't *he* come to find us?'

'This is another Revolution—'

'Then find another to make it with you,' Maran turned away. 'We swore to follow Savarian until the end. And we did. We did not swear to follow his children for a Revolution nobody asked us about—song or no song.'

Mithila looked at the floor helplessly.

'It's—we're asking you now,' said Mankala. Her voice rose. 'I don't get you—if you're Maran and Upar, if you fought with Savarian against the Council, *we're supposed to be on the same side!* How can you not—'

Maran stopped dead. Mithila flinched.

Without turning, he said. 'And what happens if your side wins?'

'We'll remake the world.'

'Oh? And you'll let us *see* that world? Do you hear them, Upar?' Suddenly, he began to laugh, a raw, cracked sound, that rang off the walls. Upar rose and came up to him with a sure step, guided by the laughter. Maran collapsed into his open arms, burying his face in his shoulders.

'You come up here,' said Maran softly, 'Savarian's song on your lips, with the memories that have scourged us for twenty-seven years, here, in the darkness, and you tell us that we must obey so you can have *your* new world, a world we'll never see.'

'No!' Mithila almost shouted out. 'It's not like that—it's—'

'I think,' said Upar, 'it's time for you to go.'

Mithila's shoulders slumped. 'We'll go,' she said, her voice small. Mankala whipped her head around to her, opened her mouth, but Mithila silenced her with a look. 'No one will be forced to have faith,' she said, her voice trembling. 'That's what we said. Anyone can decide to leave. And I saw them leave.' She paused. 'I'm—I'm sorry.'

She turned to the door. 'Come on Mankala,' she said. 'We need to find Maji.'

And, just as she turned the door, and the darkness of the stairway came pouring in, she heard the voice, changed utterly.

'*What did you say?*'

They went down to the ramp. Above them, the floor began to close.

'Thank you,' said Mithila.

'Tell her I never forgot,' Upar said.

Mithila looked up at them. 'And she never forgot you. It wasn't just your band of True Marriage that she still wears around her wrist—she even sang you into battle. She'll come back for you. Soon.'

The floor closed. They hurried down the ramp, and into the underground pillared hall.

'Oh, I'm *enraged*,' Mankala spoke at last, through her teeth. 'They took them after the Revolution, blinded them, and had them do this for twenty-seven years? This—*this*—is the sort of thing Maliot's Democracy was built on?'

'How much else,' said Mithila quietly, 'that we don't even know of?'

'Builders' guess,' said Mankala. 'I'm so glad that we're going to tear it all down.'

They ran across the hall, weariness forgotten. Then they were at the wall, with its strangely-drawn figures, and just beside that, the opening with the faintest glimmering of blue.

They stopped at the edge. Mankala breathed in and placed a hand on Mithila's shoulder.

'At the end of all things … you ready, Worldfarer?'

Mithila steadied herself. 'Let's do this.'

They stepped into the hall of the three Kings.

Ghada and Samir were there.

'But do you really think that is … living?'

'What would you have, then?'

'What would any of us have, Ghada?'

'Revenge?'

'Mithila,' said Mankala. 'Go to Ghada's container.'

Mithila tip-toed past Ghada and Samir, to where the three containers were floating in mid-air. There was Ghada's face, visible through the transparent cover, her eyes closed, her right hand holding a Heartstone. Mithila looked back to the Ghada before her, the one with her eyes open and alive.

'All my life, I've only known doubt. But I have made my choice.'

'Mithila!'

Mankala's voice brought her back to life.

'Right side,' Mankala continued, 'go down to the right side.'

Mithila knelt by the container. She saw a wheel protruding outwards from the body. 'I see it,' she called back. She tried to grasp the wheel, but her hands slipped off it, as if it wasn't really there.

'It's not there,' said Mankala. 'Not now, at least.'

'Until the machine stops.'

'Until the machine stops.'

'Keep your hands there,' Mankala said. Watch for my signal. When I say *now*—turn the wheel.'

'But there's no wheel.'

'There will be.'

'There was so much I wanted to show you.' Those words again, the ones that had haunted her ever since she had first heard them. Mithila closed her eyes and let them seep into her, every word a world.

'Red sprites over the troposphere in Tannor. I wanted to show you the Aurora, dancing in the sky, beyond the Reinmar Gate. There was a galaxy, Samir. And now all those dreams will pass, frozen in a suspended future, like so many little beetles in amber … like us.'

Mithila breathed, trying to hold on to the memory of those words, a memory with shape, colour, texture.

'Mithila! *Focus.*'

Her eyes flew open. Ghada and Samir were saying their farewells.

'I still have one of the Stones, and it is charged.'

Mithila's breath quickened. She moved her hands around the side of the container, still feeling them slip off the sides of the wheel.

She turned once. Mankala was rigid. A single bead of sweat trickled down her cheek.

'I love you. Go.'

'I love you. Farewell.'

They walked away.

The light in the chamber *flickered.*

'*Now!*' Mankala screamed.

Like magic, there was something solid in her hands, something real—the wheel. Mithila scrambled and turned it.

It moved smoothly, as though friction was a foreign word. It turned a complete circle—and then stopped.

There was silence in the chamber.

'Did you do it?' Mankala's voice was dry.

'I did.' Mithila stood.

The light in the chamber had gone back to normal. All was still.

Nothing happened. The container was still shut, and Ghada's eyes were still closed.

'Wait, what?' Mankala began to step forward.

A great rumbling shook the chamber. It built up slowly, from a faint noise into something that surrounded them, a movement of everything. As though two worlds were colliding.

Instinctively, Mithila threw out an arm to Ghada's container to balance herself, and stopped as Mankala shouted out: '*Don't touch that.*' She stumbled backwards.

Suddenly, the rumbling stopped.

The cover of Ghada's container began to slide open.

The transparent surface retreated like a veil, like the Rasa flowing over smooth stones, uncovering Ghada's face, and then the rest of her. It withdrew into the body of the container with a small *click*, leaving the front exposed.

The world was still.

Ghada's eyes opened.

Mithila gasped. Ghada turned her face. Their eyes met.

Her eyes were not of Sumer. They were grey, a grey as deep and old as the sea, eyes that spoke all the languages of the stars.

Mithila cried out and tore her gaze away.

Ghada sat up. She raised her arms and examined them, as if to convince herself that she existed. Mithila forced herself to look again. Ghada's eyes were half-closed, her lips slightly parted, a slight puzzlement upon her face.

'Welcome back, Ghada.' Mankala's voice cut through the silence.

Ghada's neck jerked, a quicker movement than before. She turned to Mankala. Mankala did not look away.

Something like understanding dawned in Ghada's eyes.

She rose.

Mithila backed away. Mankala began to step forward. And from somewhere in the darkness of the chamber, an arrow, unerringly aimed, flew through the stillness.

Mithila felt a breath of air, the slightest altering of the shape of the world, the passing of a shadow.

Ghada started, ever so softly. She reached towards her neck. Some thing glistened red. Mithila saw the arrow in the centre of her throat.

Ghada looked to her left, over the head of sleeping Alora, to where Samir lay. Then her head turned—and for the second time, she caught Mithila with her gaze.

This time, Mithila could not look away. Ghada extended her arm towards her, the Heartstone clasped in her hand, an invitation—or a warning.

'Burning glass,' Ghada whispered, the only words they would ever hear from her.

'Gla—*what*?' Mithila croaked.

Ghada's eyes filmed over. Her head slumped to her side. With the quietest of sighs, she fell back into the container.

'*No!*' Mankala shouted. Mithila looked up. Mankala was leaping across the chamber. There was a scrabbling movement in the shadows—a cry that was not Mankala's—and a bamboo bow clattered to the floor. Mankala was grappling with a hooded figure, cloaked in ochre-brown.

Mithila sprinted towards her, but before she could get there, Mankala was hurled against the wall. She hit it hard, and slumped to the ground.

Mithila's blade was out. Iron met iron. For the second time that night, she was fighting for her life.

This time, there was no hesitation. Her body moved in rhythm, a whir of legs and arms, driving her adversary backwards across the chamber. She danced in and out of range, contemptuously swatted away parries, and pressed them towards the far wall. They gave ground, and Mithila, going forward, began to prepare her last attack—

And then, out of nowhere, they switched sword arms, right hand to left hand—and lunged towards her unprotected side.

Again.

Mithila stepped back and flat-parried it away, but the force of the attack sent her stumbling. In an instant, the figure had wheeled around and sprinted away from her, into the tunnel that exited from the chamber. She heard the sound of running footsteps, fading quickly.

Mithila swung around. Mankala had dragged herself over to Ghada's open container, and was leaning over it, her head in her hands.

Mithila walked over to her.

Ghada's eyes were still open. Open—and now unseeing.

There was blood on the container.

'Two thousand years,' Mankala said dully, sitting up against the wall. 'Two thousand years—for this.'

Mithila felt a knot in her chest.

Mankala looked up, and her own eyes were dead.

'We've ended it for everyone. Forever.'

Mithila thought of Maji and the Dooma, and wondered how many had died that night in the Middle Circles.

Mankala's head sank to her chest. Mithila stared at her. Grief was dancing around the edges of her own throat, tightening it, threatening to overwhelm her, except that ...

... there was something else at the back of her mind, clamouring for attention.

She shook Mankala's shoulder. 'Get up,' she whispered.

Mankala rose unwillingly. Mithila turned her around, until they were facing each other. Mankala's cheeks were streaked with tears.

'Mankala,' she murmured, 'I need you to do something.'

'What?'

'Go back up. Find Maji. Tell her to wait for me.'

Mankala screwed her eyes shut. She seemed about to collapse. '*What's the point now?*' she screamed at Mithila. 'It's all over.'

'Mankala,' Mithila said softly, putting an arm around her shoulder. 'Go and find her. I'll be back soon.'

She looked at Ghada's open container, at Ghada herself, no longer sleeping but lifeless—and saw the Heartstone that she had always held in her hand.

It was throbbing gently.

Alive.

Mithila took the Heartstone from Ghada's hand, now used to the tingling one of them sent up her spine. She walked to the end of the chamber, and faced the tunnel. She stepped into the passageway.

Behind her, Ghada and Samir entered the chamber again. As they always had. And now, as they always would.

Third Interlude

From the heights, they watch the fires in the Middle Circles, little dots of light, almost as if they were flame lamps by the Rasa. From the right distance, the Young One thinks, burning buildings can look beautiful. Would you need to watch from the sky to find a burning City beautiful?

'And this is the story,' the Mentor says. 'Thousands upon thousands of years ago, in the Time of the Afternoon, riven humanity turned upon itself in a long, bitter war. In a storm of fire and ash, our ancestors came close to destroying not just themselves, but the world.

'Those who survived gathered together. And they decided. Never again would humanity be allowed to reach a point where it had the power to destroy the world. But left to its own devices, that would *always* happen. It is who we are. And so, there was only one thing to do: turn the clock back. Time after time, every time. Take us to the beginning, to start over. *Apoptosis*. We die to live again.

'And thus did Circular Time enter the world.'

The fires in the Middle Circles seem to be dying out, the battle over. For now.

'But they knew, our ancestors,' the Mentor continues, 'they knew that the choice of when to turn back the clock could not be left to the generations to come. We humans are weak. Our will would crumble. We would persuade ourselves that we weren't quite there—that *this* generation couldn't—or wouldn't—destroy the world, that this time it would be different. They knew. And they were right.

'So they set the time: two thousand and five hundred years. That would be the time allotted to each cycle of humanity. At the end of that: *apoptosis*. We go back to the beginning. Regardless. And that task would be given to a group of us, to pass on the knowledge, generation after generation, in secret, until the time came.

'So it was done. Civilizations rose and fell by this rule, the rule of two thousand five hundred. Each time, unfailingly, we went back, back to the beginning. Afternoon passed into Evening—and the rule held.

'Until the civilization of old Gumfraude. It grew so vast, so powerful, the likes of which had never been seen. The City of Stone, chariots to the stars, a bridge to the galaxy—and they would not go without a fight. And so, after all those thousands of years it was war again, a war that sent our earth shuddering.

'We—our spiritual ancestors—were victorious. The clock was set back. But at what cost: so much death, so much destruction. They were weakened. And so they built this City of Sumer, and the Wall: here we could rest, for the next cycle, with no fear of this happening again. How much could humans do, after all, in a City within a Wall?

'Now the time has come once more. Two thousand five hundred years have passed since Gumfraude fell and the Wall of Sumer came to be. The clock must be set back. And it falls to our generation.

'Because we are *The Select*.'

Moonlight plays upon the faces of Marwana, the Mentor, and the young one—Garuda.

Eighteen
The Citadel

Mithila walked the passageway.

The walls grew uneven. A roaring came to her ears, a sound she remembered. Then it faded, the floor evened, and Mithila made that last slow ascent into the Citadel of the Select.

She entered a room. A man stood there, dressed in plain linen, the ochre belt of the scientists pleated around the waist.

'We've been waiting for you,' he said.

'I know.'

He led her up, through stairways and corridors, climbing, until they stopped before a nondescript door. Through the crack, Mithila saw light. The scientist pushed the door open, and motioned her through.

Mithila entered. The door closed behind her.

Torches blazed in their sconces. There were bookshelves by the walls. A large window looked out onto the Council Hall, the Forum Plaza and the Rasa, a long way below. In front of the window there was a table with two chairs.

Sitting on one of the chairs was Garuda.

Mithila said nothing. She walked to the table and slumped on the chair across from him.

'Hello, sister.'

Garuda's voice had not changed. It brushed her with its gentleness, its laughter, its wry understanding of everything. Mithila blinked, and blinked it away.

'Hello, brother. It's been a while.'

'You don't look surprised.'

Mithila's voice cracked as she laughed. 'The switch of the blade, from right hand to left. Just like Ba taught us. I'd recognise that move in a melee.'

'I was expecting—a little more?' Garuda sounded boyish, bemused. 'It's been two years.'

'Not long enough for this, Garuda,' she said, tired.

'Ah.' Garuda sounded genuinely apologetic. 'I'm sorry. I didn't mean for you to find out this way.'

'What? By murdering Ghada?'

'Wha—oh, no no. That had to be done. No, springing myself upon you like this.'

'*That's* what you're sorry for?' Mithila rubbed her eyes. Her voice sounded dead in her ears.

'Oh. I mean. For much more too.' Garuda extended his arms, palms facing upwards, on the table. 'I know this isn't easy, sister. But here we are now. We can talk. As long as you want. Ask me. I will answer, honestly. I promise.'

She forced herself to straighten. And she forced the words upon her tongue.

'You planned the Pit, knowing we'd be trapped there. You sold us out to the Shoortans. You faked your own death, you let me believe I'd lost you, let me hate myself for it.'

'Yes, but I—'

'Let me finish. You laughed at us from Gumfraude, turning the sky red when you wanted, sending everyone here into a panic—and laughed about it in a fucking *journal*. You kidnapped Dhara, took her there, put her in that—that box. You didn't even leave her her shoes!'

'Mith—'

'And now you've murdered Ghada. She was going to wake the rest, save us, and you killed her. And you're just sitting here, calling me *sister*, as if nothing mattered, none of us mattered.'

Garuda's head was bowed, so that she could only see his shock of black hair. His fingers interlaced.

'Yes,' he said. 'It's true. All of it.'

'*WHY?!*'

Mithila screamed at him from across the world. She slumped again, bent over. Her fists were on the table, supporting her forehead.

'Mithila, I—look at me, please?'

She lifted her head. Garuda's entwined hands were lightly tapping the table, his shoulders rocking back and forth, a movement she remembered from a world ago. It was Garuda desperately wanting you to see what he was seeing.

'Yes?'

'It had to be done,' he said. 'There was a plan, and it needed me out of the picture, presumed dead.'

'I see,' said Mithila. Bleakness descended upon her like a mist. 'And us?'

'It was *critical.* There had to exist a state of heightened conflict between the Shoortans and the Young Tarafians. My death was the catalyst to—escalate things.'

'Could've just stayed dead, then.'

Garuda flinched. 'You really—really think that?'

'Oh Builders, Garuda! Well, you got your wish.'

'Not me—us.' Garuda's voice was still soft. 'And I'd even say that—if you weren't as astonishing as you are—we'd never have to do it at all.'

'We?'

'Can't you guess, Mithila?'

The Great Hall. The Trial. A woman rising, staring down the Council, calm and unafraid.

And that, my friends, is the case for the defence.

'Marwana,' she whispered.

'Yes.'

'All … of you?'

Garuda inclined his head. 'We are the Select.'

The world was whirling. Mithila's head swam.

'We trusted her,' she said. 'She was always there when we needed her. By our side. *On* our side.'

'Yes.' It was the gentleness in Garuda's voice that was so unforgiving. 'As *she* needed to be. So that you could face the Shoortans.' Suddenly, he laughed. 'Until you ruined it all by actually going beyond the Wall, sister! You saw Gumfraude, you saw Geroun. You saw everything. And then you *came back*, fuck the Builders! We had never planned for that. Unforgivable, really.'

'*That* was unforgivable?'

'Ah.' Garuda subsided. 'I hope that you'll soon find that more things can be forgiven than you ever dreamed.'

'Sorry, but my dreams are my own now. And I'm glad I ruined yours.'

'Only for a while,' Garuda said, smiling slightly. 'But then—you set up your own rebellion. Our little sister decided to intervene. And so it did go to plan: the City was riven, and you had to come to us.'

Mithila sat bolt upright. 'The Protocol!'

Garuda laughed once more, delight in his eyes, utterly sure of himself. It reminded her of the time when they were both teenagers, the time when he'd made her see the horizon. Her skin contracted at the memory.

'The Protocol, yes!' said Garuda. 'You gave us control of all the vital installations of the City.'

Mithila put her head in her hands.

'Until you almost spoiled it again. You and that Mankala. Awakening Ghada—the *audacity*. Ghada and Alora weren't going to come back to Sumer, Mithila. Never in eternity were we going to allow that.'

'Tell me something,' said Mithila, dully.

'Ask.'

'Were you and Dhara lovers?'

'Ah.' Garuda dropped his gaze again. His shoulders moved quicker, almost jerking. 'I tried to warn her off—I did, so many times. But she … and I—'

Mithila pointed her finger at him. 'You did *that*—to someone you were in love with? You did that to *her*?'

Garuda's nostrils flared. 'What did you do when you thought that Amrit's daughter might risk your chance at the Wall?'

'I broke up with her,' Mithila snapped. 'Bloody Builders, brother, I didn't put her in a damned box until the end of Circular Time!'

'As if you wouldn't have done *exactly* that, if that had been what it took.'

'It? What "it"? There's no "it" that's worth—'

'Oh, don't fool yourself,' Garuda's voice turned ugly, a cadence she had never known. 'Maloran blood, sister. Our father burned this City in revolution. Our little sister—you don't need me to tell you. We find a cause, Mithila, and we become it. It has always been thus.'

'You're wrong,' said Mithila. Her voice shook unbearably.

'Maybe.' Garuda's voice had grown mild again, the ugliness a memory. 'Does it matter?'

Mithila looked past his shoulder, at the wall. Her mind had begun to work, in bits and pieces.

'Alright,' she said. 'So there we have it. You threw this City into chaos to control its heartbeat, and now you have it. So tell me. *Why*.'

Garuda smiled.

'*Apoptosis*,' he murmured.

'I'm sorry?'

'Do you know what that means?'

'Can't recall it being in any of the imaginary languages you used to invent.'

Garuda didn't react. 'Sometimes,' he said, 'you must die to live again.'

'And then live to die again? Since when did you start talking Shoortan, brother? If you want to kill me—'

Garuda looked genuinely surprised. 'Haven't you figured it out? We want you to join us.'

'Join?'

'We're going, Mithila. We're going into the world, and this time it's forever. Isn't that all you ever wanted?'

'I—'

'Real freedom. No Wall, as someone once said. Never again. Come with us. Mith?'

Her head was spinning again. Mithila clutched at the table for support.

She picked each word.

'I'm not coming anywhere until I know the reason why.'

'Dammit,' said Garuda, with an almost-sigh. 'I was hoping you wouldn't be so predictable. Come then. We're going to the Senate.'

Garuda took her higher into the Citadel, up into a hallway, which yielded to an arched, wooden door. He led her to it, and pushed it upon.

Mithila entered a large circular hall. It was lit by the throbbing glow that she had seen elsewhere in the Forum—in the Hall of a Thousand Pillars, in the Temple, in the Chamber of the Three Kings, a glow that rose from the floor, from the walls, and from the ceiling.

There were chairs arranged in semi-circular arcs, until the back. Each of them was occupied, filling up the latter half of the hall. Mithila saw women and men, even a few children, in the seats, their heads turned towards her. Some, she recognised from their brief forays into the City. Others were unfamiliar.

The Select. Three hundred, the same number as the Council. Gathered here together, all in one place.

The other half of the hall was bare, but for a raised platform at the end. Upon the platform stood Marwana.

She turned as they entered. Her face broke into a brilliant, warm smile.

'Welcome, at last, Mithila,' she said, in a voice that carried to the end of the room. 'Welcome home.'

From the back of the hall, a single, slow clap cut through the air. Swiftly, it was joined by another and then another, and then yet another. By the time Mithila had climbed on to the platform, the entire room was applauding her: steady, rhythmic claps that filled the air, a sound that reminded her of the roar of the sea. Some of the scientists were on their feet.

Marwana bowed to her. Mithila stood there, as the ovation continued. In her ear, she heard Garuda whisper:

'You're a hero here, sister. Get used to it. Nobody else understands you like we do.'

As the applause died down, Marwana's voice rang out once more.

'Companions, here she is. The Worldfarer, they call her. And so will we. She has been beyond the Wall. She has seen Gumfraude and Geroun, she has walked in the footsteps of Alora and of Ghada. She has earned the right to be with us, and to know all that is to be known. Is there anyone here who disagrees? Let them speak now, or be ever silent, until the breaking of the Wall.'

A roar of affirmation answered her.

They all sat back down, and silence fell upon the room. Garuda had slipped away from her side. Out of the corner of her eye, Mithila saw him take a seat at the front. As she faced Marwana, she felt very alone.

'Mithila, Worldfarer,' said Marwana, 'hear me.' Her voice, as always, was mesmeric, rising and falling like the Rasa.

'Everything that you thought you knew about Sumer is a lie. Some of that you understood when you walked within the Stone City. Now know the rest.

'We are the Select. And it is our burden to see Sumer destroyed.'

Mithila clenched her fists and bit her tongue.

'Worldfarer, hear me!' Marwana repeated. 'It is not what it seems. It is not a mindless tearing down. It is *apoptosis*. We die so we may live again. Like the cells of our body that must die to repair a wound. Like the leaves that must drop in the fall, so that spring will come once more. It is … a Circle.'

'And here I thought,' Mithila whispered, 'that it was only the Shoortans that believed in Circles.'

Marwana laughed. 'This is no *system of belief*, Worldfarer. But listen to me. We human beings—we are old. Sumer did not see the birth of humanity. Sumer is the evening of humanity. Before this City, there were other Cities, worlds, *galaxies*. We carry thousands upon thousands of years upon our shoulders. We carry the countless crimes that humans devised in the long morning and the longer afternoon, and we carry benediction.

'Hear me, Worldfarer. Once, in a time out of mind, after endless wars, all of humanity turned upon itself. In that conflagration, most perished. The survivors were left a burnt, barren world, waiting to die. It was then that the living came together and said: *never again*. But they were wise, our ancestors, and they knew how easily *never again* becomes *until next time*. So, if *never again* was to mean anything, there was only one solution: *apoptosis*. We die to live again.'

'But wait!' Mithila interrupted. 'Who in Sumer has the power to destroy the world?'

'Thankfully,' said Marwana, 'Nobody. *Yet*.'

'Then why—'

'Why indeed, Worldfarer. Remember Gumfraude. Remember that City of Stone. Do you think—even now—if I was to tell you to go set it on fire, you could do it? For an idea? Now imagine that world was built by your own hands. Would you not tell yourself, Worldfarer, that *you* are different, that *your* civilization is different, that *you* are better than *them*, that *you* will always find a way to pull back from the brink, to stop at that last, last moment before you used your power to destroy the world? Isn't that human, Worldfarer—only too human?'

Mithila was silent.

'And what do you do, Worldfarer, when you know that if you had the choice, you would choose wrongly?

'You take away that choice, of course.'

'Of course,' Mithila echoed.

Marwana was speaking to her, but the story was meant for every ear in the room. Mithila wondered how many times it had been told and retold.

'And so it came to be,' said Marwana, 'that two thousand five hundred years was the time allotted to a span of human civilization. An arbitrary number? Yes. Would there be civilizations that did not rise so far, so fast? Yes. Would that be unfair upon the generation that saw the final year? Yes. Do not believe, Worldfarer, that our ancestors did not think about these questions, that they were not tormented by them. But in the end, there was only one way.'

Her voice rolled like a coin on a bare floor.

'How many?' said Mithila quietly.

'What was that?' said Marwana.

'How many times have the Select destroyed a civilization?'

'That we do not know. Is it not enough that we bear responsibility for our own time?'

'Marwana,' Mithila cut in, trying to think, to fashion words. 'We have spent these two thousand five hundred years within a Wall! You can't hold any one of those lives responsible for what happened before. There must be another way—perhaps we can find it. Perhaps you can skip one cycle, perhaps we can reconsider this next time…'

Marwana's voice grew reflective. 'Do you know something, Worldfarer? Gumfraude—the last civilization before Sumer, the most powerful of them all—was a riven and broken world. Its splendour reached the stars and its people died in agony. You, who stood there in the ruined City, and found that statue of black stone—what do you think *that* was about?'

'It was a man,' said Mithila, unwillingly. 'He had wings. They were burning—'

'So that another could fly,' Marwana finished. 'This is what they were, Worldfarer. They discovered how to harness the light of the sun and build a bridge to the stars, but the—eruption—of energy they needed had to pass through a human body, burn it up, burn it out, every time, and they said *so be it.* That was where Samati was born. Because they used people as fuel, to be burned up if need be. Imagine a world built on that?'

'That world has more than just people in it,' Mithila said. 'I've seen it. It has the sea—it has the forest—'

'And do you know what else it had? Other beings that lived, like we do. You saw their remains by the sea, you even brought one back. They destroyed it all, and then—in their regret—they tried to recreate it all, with the science they knew. So it was, "*for our garden, we grew a forest.*"'

Mithila started, as she heard the lines from the Book of Alora.

'Once, the word for world was forest,' said Marwana, 'and in their hands it became a garden. Worldfarer, the world you walked in was an artificial creation born out of guilt. It is as dead as the ruined City, as dead as Gumfraude. It only ever lived in their imagination.'

Mithila remembered another line from the Book of Alora. '*The winged myth we brought to life.*'

'Yes,' said Marwana. 'They created the garudas out of their own fantasies. And sometimes a fantasy outlives its makers.'

'And then?' Mithila said, suddenly fascinated, in spite of herself.

'And then, at the end of all things, the great philosophers of Gumfraude were summoned to answer for this contradiction. Why was there such suffering in a world that had built a bridge to the galaxy? Where had they gone wrong? The consensus was that it was too big. They said, these philosophers, that justice was only possible in a bounded world. A world built on the logic of perpetual expansion would always need fuel to burn—even if, in the end, it had to burn people. But of course, those philosophers were driven away, because Gumfraude had long made a song out of murder and called it *sacrifice*.

'And so, when the time came for *apoptosis*, for Gumfraude to fall, we decided that the next world would be a world within a Wall. A bounded world where we'd find justice.'

'Did it work?' Mithila asked, automatically.

Marwana's voice, when she replied, was suddenly, intensely bitter.

'Of course not. We put you within a Wall, and you cut yourselves into circles. We gave you enough stone to go around, but of course, some of you took it all for yourselves, and left mud-brick for the rest. We gave you farmland in common, and you created wage-labourers—and you won't even pay them properly! We gave you *every* condition to make an equal society, but you couldn't wait to bring power into the world.'

'*We* never—'

'And you lurched from one misbegotten form of government to another—kings to Shoortans to Oligarchies to tyrants, each one needing to be overthrown in blood when it got too much to bear, just like it used to happen in every damned Cycle before, until you got to the Elders. Democracy, but you managed to ruin even that. Might as well never have had the Wall, except that it protected the world *from* you.'

Marwana stopped, her fists clenched.

'Are you done?' said Mithila.

'Yes.'

'You accuse Sumer, you accuse us,' Mitihla said. 'But what did *you* do? You watched. You, with the memory of the Morning and the Afternoon, you who knew how it had happened before, you stood by and watched the same mistakes repeated again. We are human. We have an excuse. What's yours?'

Marwana pursed her thin lips. 'Ours is not to interfere. That would have been to play Builders—the Builders that the City believes in, but never existed. We *never* interfere.'

'You're interfering now!'

'No,' said Marwana, 'This is not interference. We are the end.'

Mithila said nothing.

'Worldfarer. The time is here. Sumer has run its course. But humanity hasn't. All your life, you've longed to go beyond the Wall. We are offering you that chance now. Come with us. We're going beyond. Forever. To begin again.'

'After you've broken the world?'

Marwana smiled faintly. 'Don't you remember what someone once said, not so very long ago? *Not every broken thing deserves to be put back together.*'

Mithila's knees almost buckled at hearing her own words spoken to her, and for a suspended instant in time, she felt herself waver.

'Isn't this all you've ever wanted?' Marwana said softly.

Some of us know how to burn. And some of us, to make sure they burned for something.

'Not like this!' She wavered no more, but stepped forward to the edge of the platform, to face the Select. Unlike the Elders, there were no stony faces: just faces alive with curiosity.

'Can I just say one thing?' she said.

'You can say anything you want,' said Marwana, 'for as long as you want. That has always been our way: the way of reason.'

'Alright,' said Mithila. She took a deep breath. 'Think about it this way.' She was making things up as she went along, scarcely knowing what the next word would be.

'Think about our lives. From babes in arms to dotage, every moment slowly new, even in this City within the Wall. My father used to say, *you can never read the same book twice, because the book is the same, but you are new.* Think about that babe in arms, growing. The first step. The first word. The first sight of the river, the first taste of *khire*. And then to look into its eyes, and stop that life, send it back, over and over again. The word unsaid, the step untaken, the world unseen, untasted. Is that what you want?'

Did she fancy that she saw faces change, doubt creep into eyes, a few furrowed brows?

'Such newfound affection for life in Sumer?' Marwana smiled.

The moment shattered.

'An elegant analogy,' said the scientist, 'but a flawed one. Let me reframe it. Imagine that we know human beings will die at the age of thirty. At twenty-nine, we send them back to be reborn. Isn't it better by far?'

'But we *don't* die at thirty!' Mithila shouted.

'But civilizations *do* die in the afternoon. And sometimes they take the world with them.'

'They could, but they don't *have* to. Civilizations don't die—people kill them. And people can choose not to. Don't you keep telling us to use our own reason? And yet—' again, she found herself running out of words.

'You like images, Worldfarer,' Marwana mused. 'That image of the cave that you gave to the City that night in the Maidan, and now this. Let me give you one too. In the morning of humanity, there was a story much beloved of people, a story they passed down through the Cycles, until it was lost—but not to us. Indeed, you, a singer—' Marwana smiled again, 'will appreciate this.

'Remember the sea, Worldfarer? There were these people—or so the story goes—who lived in the sea, and who sang with such unbearable beauty, that anyone travelling upon the sea, who passed by, would go to them—and to their doom. Many thought they were immune, many risked it. None survived. Then along came a traveller, who found an answer. As he travelled the sea, he asked his companions to close their ears, so that they would not hear; and he bound himself, so that no force in the world would be able to move him. And as they travelled past the fated place, the music came over the air; the travellers' companions could hear nothing, and carried on. The traveller himself was driven near-mad by the music, but he could not move to go to it. And thus they passed by in safety.

'Worldfarer. Sumer is not the cave of Taraf's imagination, or the child of yours. Sumer is us. We have bound ourselves, so that we *can't* make this choice. Apoptosis will happen, without corrupted sentiment clouding our judgment.'

'But you do have a choice,' said Mithila.

'We made it a long time ago. Our choice was to stop, forever, the risk of choices.'

Mithila knew that her next answer would only take them in a circle, from which there was no escape. The faces around her were settling back into polite interest. They must have heard these arguments a thousand times. It was folly to think that she could convince them out of it in a single night.

'Tell me something,' said Mithila, 'how are you going to carry on with so few of you … beyond the Wall? Don't you need to take people from the City with you? How will you tell them? Who will you choose?'

Marwana laughed. 'We know what we need. And there is enough of it, kept in Gumfraude all these long years, for us to start over.'

'You mean,' Mithila whispered, 'that everyone in Sumer—'

'Sumer will be destroyed, yes,' Marwana affirmed. 'We will save some. And if there is anyone *you* wish to save, we—'

'But so many will die!' Mithila cried out.

'And so many will live again' Marwana replied, 'in a new world.'

Mithila slumped. 'There's always a time to change,' she said quietly. 'If not now, then when?'

Marwana looked at her with sympathy. 'If only you knew all that we know. You have seen those dreams that do not die. You have seen fire and water. What if I told you that there was a time the water turned black, and anyone who drank it would die? What if I told you about fires that ravaged the soil, so that nothing could ever grow again? What if I told you that every breath of air tore through our blood like a blunt blade? What if I told you that once you know what we can do, you would live your days in terror for the world if we were ever able to do it again?'

Mithila did not speak.

'Truth be told, Worldfarer,' Marwana said gently, 'It is hard to accept this in one night. We spend months and years, from childhood, reconciling ourselves to this, piece by piece. I would have done this gently. But there is no time. The end of the cycle approaches.

'But here is what I can do,' she continued, and there was a ring of finality in her voice, 'a night of grace. You will stay as our guest here tonight, Mithila, Worldfarer. You and one other may join us. Or you may stay in Sumer. Tell us your decision in the morning. Whatever it is, we will accept your choice.'

'Is it a choice?' said Mithila. 'What if I tell Sumer what you've just told me?'

Marwana's smile was utterly without doubt.

'You could, Worldfarer. But who will believe you?'

Garuda led her back through the Citadel, and into a small room. There was a bed at one end, and a high window that let in the night. Two flame lamps provided a little light.

She turned to face him, as he stood framed in the doorway.

'Well, goodnight brother,' she said.

Garuda breathed softly. It might have been a sigh. 'Can I come in?'

Mithila hesitated, then stood aside. He walked into the room, and sat upon the edge of the bed. Mithila closed the door. They sat side by side for a while, in silence.

'Do you remember,' said Garuda, 'all those years of trying to get people to see?'

'It was two years,' said Mithila, 'after you pulled that trick of yours in the Pit.'

'Two years,' Garuda said. 'Or twenty. Or two hundred. It would have made no difference. You know this.'

Mithila stared at the wall.

'You had to *fly* out of the City in secret, at Wallrise,' Garuda went on. 'You were alone. You've always been alone. Alone, Mith, in needing to see. Alone in burning up because you couldn't. You were never of this City. Why do you care about leaving it behind?'

'That's not true,' Mithila whispered.

'But it is,' Garuda murmured. 'We don't need to lie to each other, sister. We never have.'

'I'm not lying,' Mithila felt wildness at the edge of her throat. 'But you have, all our lives!'

'Never about the things that matter.'

'*How?*'

'Remember that day by the lake, when you saw the horizon for the first time? Was that a lie?'

Mithila said nothing.

'I've looked for ways of seeing, Mith, as long as you have. And where did it get you? You could never make them see. Even now, they don't want you. They just need you for a while. None of them really wants to see the horizon. None of them wants to leave. Not the Dooma, they just want the Shoortans overthrown. Not the Union, they're happy with better wages. They'll discard you the moment you've served your purpose. Is *that* a lie?'

'What do you know of Sumer, Garuda, you who can't wait to burn it down?'

'I can't understand what—whom—you're fighting for!' Garuda's voice rose, and he checked it with an effort. 'I'm—we are—giving you the world, the same world you just had a taste of, what you've always wanted—we're giving you a chance to come and find the horizon—with *us*, to whom you never have to explain what it means. You'll never need to look for words with us, Mith, we already have them.'

'I think, Garuda,' Mithila said through clenched teeth, 'it's time for you to get out.'

Garuda stood. 'They *Ostracized* you and nobody said a word. I can't believe I have to convince you of this. You wanted it all your life, but you won't take it when it's being given to you!'

'*Shut up*, brother,' Mithila hissed.

Garuda nodded, and walked away. At the threshold, he paused and turned back. Mithila looked past him.

'Anyone you want,' Garuda said, 'can be saved.' One final time, he paused.

'Rama can be saved.'

Mithila's head jerked up, but the door had already closed.

She closed her eyes. Darkness was around her, and in that darkness, she heard a sound, and it was the sound of the Sumer harp, playing inside her head.

It played the dream-song of Taraf.

Upon the map an empty space …

The tune that Garuda had taught her to sing to, while he played the harp in all those endless evenings by the fireside, dreaming of new words and empty spaces on the map, and every note was a memory, a memory of Garuda in a world that had not yet known betrayal.

She pressed her hands to her ears. '*Leave me alone*,' she whispered, but the sound was inside her, and it rose into the crescendo of the last lines, a pitch that heightened, shuddering through her body, the words of Taraf and the music of Garuda accompanying each other, until she was at the sea, beneath another blazing sunset, sand between her toes and the spiral in her hand, and then the music died down and she heard Garuda's voice saying, '*wasn't it good to be saved!*'

'*Shut up*!' Mithila screamed into the emptiness. She opened her eyes. In front of her was the wall, that wall of the Forum's white stone, so smooth, so cold, so—attractive.

Mithila rose on unsteady legs. She walked to the far wall. She drew in a breath, and punched it.

She pulled the punch at the last moment. Her knuckles hit the wall flatly, stinging at the skin. Mithila gritted her teeth. She pulled her hand back, leaned her body into it, and punched the wall again. The shock of pain burst through her hand and radiated into her arm. Her elbow shuddered. She breathed a sob. She pulled back and punched a third time, all she could give. Her skin cracked open. Mithila laughed—and kept laughing—gasping—as her knuckles bled.

She punched until her skin on her right hand was raw, until her arm felt like it was on fire, and blood was smeared on the pure-white wall. There was pain, only pain, crowding away all thoughts of Garuda, of the world. Whimpering, Mithila stumbled back to the bed. She collapsed upon it and buried her face in the pillow (*so soft!*), letting the spasms surging through her hand overwhelm her. She reached out to shift her pillow. Her body screamed out when her knuckles grazed the sheet. Gingerly, she brought her hand to her stomach. With the dull, throbbing pain in her hand that left no room for thoughts or dreams, Mithila sank slowly into a dark, aching sleep.

She awoke to a knocking upon the door, and a shock of pain in her fingers. The grey light of Wallrise was streaming into the room.

Mithila rose. She sat on the bed for a while, rubbing her eyes with one hand. Everything ached. Her right hand was on fire, knuckles bruised and caked with dried blood.

The knocking came again.

Mithila went to the door, and opened it.

Garuda stood outside.

'Have you decided?'

Mithila took a deep breath. 'Yes.'

'And?'

'Fuck you. And fuck the Select. Let me go.'

Garuda started. 'You're making a mistake.'

'I'm not helping you play Builders. I'm out.'

Garuda's eyes glinted. 'How funny,' he said, 'you accusing anyone of playing the Builders.'

'I'm not the one planning on killing thousands of people and grinning about it.'

'Ah.' He turned. 'Come, then.'

He led her in silence down to the main stairway, and into the Hall of a Thousand Pillars. She heard dim sounds from the interiors of the Citadel—a slow, rhythmic, muffled noise—as though someone was sawing wood. And then they were out into the Forum Plaza, the cold morning air sudden and sharp upon their faces.

'I have two questions,' Mithila said.

Garuda looked at her, vague hope flickering in his eyes. 'Go on.'

'Taraf,' said Mithila. 'One of you, wasn't he?'

'He was. He rebelled. Didn't have the stomach for it.'

'And you destroyed him.'

Garuda shrugged. 'Not enough, clearly.'

'And you also destroyed,' said Mithila, 'your second rebel?'

'Ah, Tefnakth?' Garuda said. 'Yes. We killed him.'

'Thought as much,' said Mithila.

'There's still a chance, Mith,' Garuda looked at her. 'If you change your mind, come back here. We'll be waiting for you. But not for long.'

'You know something, Garuda?' she held his gaze.

'Yes, Mith?'

'I wish you'd stayed dead. And let me have the version of you that I had built up in my head.'

Garuda flinched. Mithila turned and walked away from him, away from the Citadel.

She stood at the edge of the First Mandala, her arms raised, palms outwards. The Watch approached her, warily at first, suspecting a trap. They grew bolder when they seized her, and nothing happened. Mithila was dragged, unresisting, to The Maliot House. There they left her, their footsteps receding through the passageway. Mithila was alone.

Grey morning light struggled in through the windows, into a room that recalled a squandered beauty. Denuded of Prasanna's hanging tapestries, the walls showed her their cold, stone faces. Cracked lines ran through the roof, shorn of the hanging lamps that had once lit up the room with an impossibly soft light. The round tables with their lace-cloths and little *diyas* were gone, replaced by piles of weapons tossed upon the hard floor. In the centre of the room, there was one long table, with an unrolled map of Sumer. Chairs crowded around it. The rest of *The Maliot House* had been stripped bare.

Except for one thing.

Her heart careened.

At the far end of the room, by a circular window that she remembered well, two chairs, carefully arranged, faced each other across a round table.

As if they had never left.

As if it was still the night of the harpist and the song.

Mithila closed her eyes.

When she opened them, the chairs and the table were still there.

Mithila stepped around the long table, past the map of Sumer, and walked to the window. She pulled up the chair that she'd sat on that night, an eternity ago. She put her arms on the table, closed her eyes, and let her head drop into the crook they made.

After many forevers, footsteps sounded from above.

Mithila looked up. They were coming from where the harpist used to sit.

From the shadows, Rama walked into the room.

She was clad in a loose-sleeved white tunic. It was dirty, almost grey in patches. Upon her hands she wore blue gloves.

Mithila stood. Her eyes met Rama's. She saw her own weariness reflected in them.

'You came … through the lines?' Mithila saw her body tense, expecting an attack.

'Hm? Oh no,' she said. 'From the Forum.'

Rama relaxed. She approached Mithila, still walking cautiously. Mithila held up her hands. 'I'm not here to fight,' she said.

Rama started back. 'What happened to your hand?'

Mithila snatched her right hand away, out of sight, feeling her face flush. 'Accident,' she muttered.

Rama's eyes grew wide. 'You stay right here.' She swung around and passed back into the shadows.

Mithila sat, blinking back sudden tears of shame. Bringing her closed fist to her mouth, she sucked at her knuckles. The metallic taste of blood trickled into her mouth.

She was still sucking at her knuckles when she heard Rama's voice again.

'*Don't* do that.'

Mithila hadn't heard her return. But now Rama was standing in front of her, holding a bowl of water in one hand, a wooden container in the other, and a roll of linen tucked under her arm.

Rama placed it all on the table. She pulled up the other chair, until she was next to Mithila.

'Hand.'

'Er—'

'Give it to me, Mith.'

She held it out obediently. Rama took it lightly between hers.

'You may want to take your gloves off,' Mithila said.

'I didn't even think of that.'

Mithila reached across with her free hand. Gently, she pulled the tip of each finger, and when it was loose, slid it off Rama's skin.

Their hands lay bare across the bowl.

'Thank you,' Rama said. She took Mithila's hand in hers, and lowered it into the bowl.

The water was mildly warm. It stung her raw skin. Mithila gasped and raised her head to the ceiling, screwing her eyes shut.

'Sorry, sorry …' Rama murmured. She held Mithila's hand under the water. Her touch felt unbearably light, a presence as quiet and essential as breath.

Mithila let out a long, shuddering breath, keeping pain at bay. '*Warm* water?' She raised an eyebrow.

'It was for my bath. I can do without a bowl-full.'

'Ah yes,' Mithila looked down into the water, at their fingers, at the sliver of her skin that was touching Rama's.

'Better?' said Rama.

'It hurt a little less when you braided my hair,' said Mithila, 'but it'll do.'

She thought she saw a shadow of a smile at the edge of Rama's lips. 'Did you punch someone, Mith?'

'Just a wall.'

Now Rama did smile. 'Really? You never went that hard against *the* Wall.'

'Needed to stop thinking. Pain's good for that.'

Rama withdrew their hands from the water. She took up her gloves from the table absently, and dabbed at Mithila's skin. Mithila shivered once, but Rama moved the fabric against her knuckles with a leaf-like touch, until her hand was dry.

'This is going to hurt,' Rama said, 'I'm sorry.'

She reached across the table to the container and withdrew a wooden spatula, its surface smeared with a pale paste.

What is it?' Mithila said, closing her eyes.

'Paste of sugarcane. Should keep it from getting infected.' Rama scooped a bit of it onto her finger, and began to dab it onto Mithila's knuckles.

'Sugar? But we never—' Mithila was cut off by a wave of pain.

She clenched her teeth to keep from screaming. She grasped the back of her chair with her other hand until her arm ached. She bent her head and let herself whimper.

'*It's over, it's over*,' Rama was holding her hand tightly between hers. 'Don't move,' she said.

Mithila trembled. She watched Rama get to work on the linen, tearing away an untidy strip with her teeth. Then her hand was back in Rama's, as she covered her knuckles with a cotton swab, and wrapped the bandage around it.

'The good part about battle,' said Rama, 'is that medical supplies are always nearby.'

Mithila felt her hand throb, but it was less painful now. 'Even for the enemy?' she said.

Rama looked down at her hands, wrapped around Mithila's own. Neither of them had withdrawn. 'You sure you want to provoke me in this position, Mith?'

Mithila moved her thumb delicately across the tender skin at Rama's wrist, tracing the lines along her right palm. 'Always,' she murmured.

'*Builders*,' Rama whispered. 'I've missed you.'

Mithila dropped her gaze, to where their fingers were entwined. From the window, light from a sun risen high over the Wall poured down on them in a blaze.

Rama sighed. 'Why've you come, Mithila?'

Her hand still in Rama's, Mithila said: 'To surrender.'

Nineteen

The Alliance

'*Worldfarer!* Worldfarer is back!'

They pulled her over the barricade. Mithila winced as her bandaged hand hit a splinter. Holding her throbbing right arm by her side, she whispered: 'can someone help me down please?'

There were hands around her shoulders, supporting her, gently guiding her down the barricade. Mithila stumbled twice, but they held her up, and set her upon the Maliot.

Prana stood there, streaks of dirt and blood upon his face.

'Is—are you fine, Worldfarer?' he said.

'Yes, I just—' she took in the emptiness around him, the barren Maliot Road, the silent houses. 'Where is everyone?'

'Those who remain—Konar Hall.'

'I'll get there.' She turned—and then stopped, remembering. 'Prana, will you do something for me?'

'Yes, Worldfarer?'

She leaned over and whispered in his ear. Prana's brow furrowed. 'Yes,' he said. 'I'll go now.'

She walked away from the barricade. Down the tributary, she saw nobody—not even a signalman—until she reached Konar Hall, and pushed open the door.

A sharp, pungent smell hit her nostrils. The front part of the hall had been turned into a makeshift hospital. There were two rows of wooden beds on either side, hastily arranged. People moved quickly between them, talking in low voices. The first few beds were occupied, although she could not see anything more serious than splints and bandages. As she walked beyond the beds, she saw people sitting with their backs up against the wall.

'Worldfarer!' Maji said, from the long table. She rose. Mithila saw a long, fresh wound running down the side of her face, down to her collarbone. 'Yes,' she said, as she saw Mithila's eyes on it. 'It stings.'

Around the table, Mithila saw Carina and the Union Members, looking at her. 'I'm sorry,' she said. 'I was detained—'

'We know,' said Maji. 'Your friend told us what happened. Did you catch them? The ones who killed Ghada?'

Mithila stared at the floor. 'No. They got away. I'm sorry.'

'Oh.' Maji sighed. 'So this is the end, then.'

Mithila looked up at her. 'Last night … did you—were you—'

'Worldfarer.' Maji held her gaze, and there was something unbearably gentle in her voice. 'There is something you need to know.'

Mithila looked back at her.

'Your father's dead.'

Blue, I dream you, blue…

Mithila walked slowly to the table. She pulled up a chair, and lowered herself into it. Her legs had lost all feeling.

'So now I am alone,' she said to the empty air.

'Worldfarer?' said Maji.

She didn't turn. 'Go on.'

'We were ambushed,' said Maji. 'They drove us back to the Eleventh. They were going to crush us. And then he came. Unasked. But he came. Brand and blade, upon the barricade, it was the Blue Revolution all over again. Everyone remembered. And the Shoortans doubted. We saw the moment they stopped believing. He turned it, Worldfarer. They broke themselves upon us. And then he led us to attack.'

Mithila stared at the door at the end of the Hall, which she had closed upon Ananta two days ago. 'And then?'

'An arrow in the back,' said Carina. 'I saw him fall.'

'Shoortans?'

'Council,' said Maji. 'They were hidden in the Ninth. Waiting. Just when the Shoortans broke and ran, when we stood with our wounds and our shattered weapons, they came upon us. And *he* faced them again, just like it was in the old days. He gave us cover to fall back here. He saved us. But he could not save your Revolution.'

Mithila let her head sink to her chest. 'Ba,' she whispered, 'had you guessed? Did you decide it was better to leave now, than stay to know—*this*?'

'What was that?' said Maji.

Mithila's head jerked up. Maji was giving her a strange look.

'I'm sorry,' she said to the table. 'I am not myself. Will you give me a little time to be—alone?'

Maji exchanged a glance with Carina.

'Take all the time you need,' she said, her voice raw. 'There is nothing left for us here, but wait to surrender.'

A knock upon the door.

Mithila, kneeling upon the floor, arms on the surface of the bed, looked up. Soft evening light floated in through the window.

'Come in,' she said.

Alvar and Mankala entered. Mithila tried to rise. 'I—'

'Hush,' Alvar said. 'You don't always have to look for words.'

They came and sat beside her, as they had the evening before, when it had still seemed that there was a world to remake. Somewhere beyond, the sun began to decline beyond the Wall.

'I had so much to say,' Mithila said, at last. 'But like every other time, I came too late to say it.'

'He would've understood,' said Alvar. 'Didn't he always?'

'I just don't want the last time to be how I remember him. Asking me for something I couldn't give. But that's all I have to remember him by.'

'Oh, Mith,' said Alvar. 'You have a lifetime of memories.'

'Do I?'

And some of us to make sure that they burned for something.

She remembered. A journey in the dark, the Heartstone in her hands, counting how many had become Samatis to her Garuda, and now there was one more, Ananta, who had walked off the stage to give her a few hours of grace in a dying world.

'Will you stay with me,' she said quietly, 'while I sleep a little?'

They put their arms around her, and Mithila let her head drop to Alvar's shoulders.

Running footsteps cut through her dreams. Mithila's eyes flickered open. Outside, the light had grown grey.

'What's that?' said Alvar, as the footsteps reached the door, and a loud knock sounded in their ears. Without waiting for an answer, the door burst open, and a man entered. 'Worldfarer,' he panted. 'It happened just like you said. We were watching—just after Wallset—'

Mithila rose to her feet, her fists clenched, her teeth set. 'Well done,' she said. 'Well done. You've taken them to the barricade?'

'Yes, as you asked.'

'Good. Summon the POUM. Bring Maji. Tell them it's an emergency.'

'Mithila,' said Mankala, also standing. 'What's happening?'

She turned to them. 'You'll know,' she said. 'Now.'

The two scientists of the Select stood at the banks of the Rasa, hands tied behind their back.

'*Oh!*' Mithila heard Mankala gasp. The Select turned their eyes up. Mithila saw murder in their gaze. She shivered.

'Well,' she said, stopping a few feet from them. 'How goes *apoptosis*?'

Neither of them reacted.

'May we know,' said one of them instead, in a voice that dripped deadly politeness, 'the purpose of this outrage?'

'You know already,' Mithila's voice matched his. 'But I'll just remind you.'

Footsteps sounded. Maji came hurrying from the tributary road. Behind her, Mithila saw Carina, Prana and the POUM.

'An emergency?' Maji panted, as she reached the Maliot. 'What—' Then she saw the two scientists. 'What's going on?'

'Commander,' the older one stepped forward. 'I am Kanu of the Select, and I must register my displeasure at this—'

'*Be quiet*,' snapped Mithila. She pointed at Kanu's chest. 'You'll get to speak soon, *Kanu of the Select*. Let everyone hear you this time.' She breathed hard, and then turned to the man who had come up to their room. 'Please,' she said, 'tell us what you saw.'

'Uh, alright.' The man cleared his throat. Behind them, Mithila saw more people gather around, coming up from the Eleventh.

'I am Lahar-Fourteen. Today afternoon, on the Worldfarer's instructions, Prana-Eleven asked me to go to the sewage chamber of the Eleventh. He told us to watch the Select and seize them if they stopped standing guard, and did anything else. We kept watch from the terraces. At Wallset we saw these two enter the ground and start to dig into the sewage chamber. That's when we came down and seized them. They had dug a full hole, and—' Lahar drew something from his robe, and dropped a dark, opaque cylinder, half an arm's length, on the ground. 'They were lowering this in.'

Silence descended upon the Maliot.

'Well,' said Mithila. 'Kanu of the Select. Mind telling us why you were digging into the sewage chamber? *Apoptosis*, maybe?'

Kanu looked unperturbed. 'I am unaware of this word,' he said to her. Then he turned to Maji, as though Mithila didn't exist. 'Commander, this is highly irregular. My companion and I were guarding the sewage chamber, under the Protocol. Just as we began our periodic disinfecting of the chamber, we were rudely grabbed by your men here.'

'Do you normally disinfect in the dark?' Mithila said.

Kanu waved her words away. 'We can do it any time of the day—or night,' he said, still looking at Maji. The crowd around them had grown denser. 'This is the regular maintenance work we've been doing for *centuries*.'

'And your lies have grown smoother in that time,' Mithila said. She stepped in front of the Select, and faced Maji. Her breath came quickly. 'Do you know what I found last night, after Ghada was killed? I found out who it was that stayed back in Sumer to see we never got out.' She pointed at Kanu, shaking. 'Two thousand five hundred years, measuring the harvest, keeping the sewage chambers, the Towers of Rebirth, to ensure we live here, and in that life, not have to seek a new one. And now …' She paused. 'They want to destroy even that, they want to destroy us.'

Kanu looked at her, almost pitying. 'Do you hear this?' He spread out his arms. 'We, the Select. We, who have never sought power. We, who have only ever pursued reason for its own sake. We are women and men of science. And now you say we want to destroy Sumer. The Sumer we are standing in? Now?' His voice lowered, and he spoke gently. 'Revolution is stressful. I understand that. But this—*this*, Citizens—is paranoia. You can't indulge this.'

There was a low muttering in the air. Then Maji spoke, and her voice was racked with doubt.

'Worldfarer,' she said, 'this is a serious accusation. The Select? Really?'

'I met them last night,' said Mithila. 'They told me. They tried to convince me to join them.' The pitch of her voice rose. She tried to calm it. 'I did not tell you when I came back, for just this reason. That you wouldn't believe me without proof. Because *they are the Select*. Now we have this—digging up the sewage chamber, Maji. At night. There is no reason why anyone would do that.'

'Digging is … it's just digging, Worldfarer,' Prana said. 'And he's explained it.'

'If we, the Select, were planning to destroy Sumer,' Kanu added, 'do you think we would just tell people about it? Are we that stupid?'

'Shut up,' Mithila said. She turnd to Maji. 'This is exactly what Marwana—yes, Marwana—told me last night: *go and tell, if you want. Who will believe you?*

But Maji's face was unchanged, skeptical, almost kind. And as Mithila turned, she saw other faces looking back at her, embarrassed, even pained.

As if to confirm it, Maji said gently: 'Why would the Select destroy their own City, Worldfarer? When they're all here with us?'

'*Because they've been able to go beyond the Wall this whole time!* And because they think that we'd destroy the world if they didn't destroy us first!' Even as she said that, she realized how ridiculous it sounded.

'Worldfarer,' said Maji, now firm. 'Savar—Ananta has just died. You may be—'

'Maji, what are you suggesting?' Mithila interrupted, her voice very soft. 'That my father's death may have made me lose my judgment? That I can't think straight anymore?'

Maji flinched. 'No no, it's just—'

'Let us go,' Kanu's voice cut through the air, crisp and clear. 'Things happen in conflict—people snap—we understand that. We will not hold this against you. We can even protect you.'

And now Mithila saw the expressions around her change once more, into cold calculation. She felt as if she was falling back, backwards into the Rasa, into the cold waters that would take her forever, that would become the sea—

Maji stepped forward. 'Untie them,' she said, firmly.

'No ...' Mithila whispered.

Mithila heard the bonds snap. Maji picked up the cylinder, walked up to the Select, and returned it to Kanu. 'Our apologies. We will see that she gets help.'

'Think nothing of it,' Kanu said graciously. 'And if we can to anything for her—'

'Yes, yes of course.' Maji turned to Mithila. 'Worldfarer—let's go home. We need to talk about this. I have seen this before—sometimes things become too much. There's no shame in needing help.'

Maji made the slightest of gestures with her fingers. Out of the corner of her eye, Mithila saw two of her men move to position themselves behind her, on either side. She stepped back, her body thrumming, tense—the crowd was around her, closing off the road—

'One moment, please.'

Mankala's voice seemed to come from very, very far away.

'What is it?' Maji said, irritated.

Mankala ignored her. She spoke directly to Kanu. 'This is to disinfect the sewage chambers, yes?'

'Yes,' Kanu said easily.

'How does it work, exactly?'

'Wood-pulp, boiled down to speed up the decomposition of the rahi-lined walls.'

'Ah,' said Mankala. 'Then you won't mind a little experiment.'

She spun around to one of Maji's men, who was holding a flame lamp in his hand, and before he could react, seized it from him.

Kanu staggered back, his arms up, shielding his face. The cylinder dropped to the ground.

Mankala darted forward and picked it up. 'Oh dear,' she said. 'Scared of fire? For a disinfectant?' She flicked open the lid of the cylinder, and—tearing a strip off the hem of her shirt—stuffed it into its mouth.

'*NO!*' Kanu screamed.

'Yes,' Mankala answered, and set the cloth alight.

Kanu screamed once again, but Mankala had turned to the Rasa, taken a short run-up and hurled the cylinder across the river as far as she could throw it. It swung in the air, a flaming arc, and landed on the other shore, on the bank before the fields.

For around three seconds, they saw the flickering light of the flame.

The explosion ripped through the Sumerian night.

The noise was nothing like Mithila had ever heard, a punch to the gut, and then a roaring wave, consuming everything. She was hurled off her feet and thrown backwards, with everyone around her.

Across the river, the fields had begun to burn.

Mankala staggered to her knees and pointed at Kanu, who was coughing on the ground.

'*Fucking* disinfectant, is it? Just like you disinfected my house?' she shouted, hoarse, and turned to the people. 'They were going to burn the City down. They've done it before. The *great fire*, they called it—oh yes, I see, some of you have heard about this. And they were going to do it again. I bet they've started planting these all over the City, the moment they got control from the Protocol.'

Her voice died down to silence.

Maji stepped up to Kanu, who was struggling to his feet. Moonlight glinted off a knife-blade. And then the blade was hovering around Kanu's neck.

'Listen, Select,' Maji said, as the flames rose across the river. 'There are many ways a man can die. Some are more painful than others. What will it be?'

Without a word, Kanu threw himself backwards into the Rasa.

There were shouts from the road, as his body hit the water. Mithila ran to the shore. The ripples were already widening out into nothingness. They did not see him rise to the surface.

'Oh no you don't.' Maji groaned.

'Maji!' Mithila grasped her shoulder and shouted. 'We have no time! Citadel. Now. Before they kill us all.'

Maji snapped into action. 'DOOMA!' she called, and her voice carried. 'POUM. To the Citadel. Now. *Now!*' She turned to Mithila. 'But, Worldfarer, the Council! They're in the way.'

Mithila held up a hand. 'The Council will not interfere as long as we stay on the Maliot.' As Maji looked at her doubtfully, Mithila drew herself up. 'This time you *will* do what I say.'

Maji nodded. Then she was amongst the people, moving, talking, calling, summoning.

Mithila turned to Mankala. 'I'm sorry.'

Mankala looked into the river. 'Oh, Marwana …'

They did not march up the Maliot. They ran.

Maji was at the head of the column, alongside Mithila, Prana, and Mankala. Behind them, no longer in formation, holding flame lamps in one hand and blades in the other, came the women and men of the Dooma and the POUM.

Sumer had not seen this before: a stream of flame lamps up the Maliot, heading towards the Forum. Maji set the pace, a steady, rhythmic cycle, a relentless speed that had them panting as they entered the Upper Circles.

For a few moments, Mithila was afraid. Afraid that she had a made a mistake, that the Council would find them too soft a target to resist. She clutched the piece of paper in her pocket, on which she had secretly signed away her banner, thrown away her allies, and dropped her claims to going beyond the Wall, from the morning to come, for all time.

A surrender for one night of non-interference, Rama. And then you can start the world over, in whatever shape it's in, from the morning after.

Her betrayal of the Revolution, of herself, to save Sumer. The other copy was with Rama.

Her eyes flicked to roof and ground, for arrows and swords. There was nothing.

They entered the Forum Plaza at a run. It was dark and unlit.

As they approached the Citadel, Mithila hesitated. Maji didn't. She hurled herself against the wooden doors, shoulder-first. They gave way, and Maji careened into the hall of a thousand pillars, Mithila behind her.

Throbbing blue light surrounded them.

The hall was empty.

'The Senate' Mithila gasped. 'That's where they assemble. Straight up the stairs, in the dome.'

'Marwana could be in her office,' Mankala offered. 'I know where it is.'

Maji turned around and barked quick orders. Her fighters fanned out, some behind Mankala. Maji turned to Mithila. 'You coming?'

But that uneasy feeling in her head was back, the feeling of things out of place. 'Carry on,' said Mithila. 'I'll just join you.'

She heard the receding sound of their footsteps, sprinting towards the stairway, leaving silence behind.

Silence?

And Mithila realized what was wrong. That faint, sawing noise she had heard in the Citadel was gone. There was nothing.

There was nobody.

'*Shit!*' Mithila whispered.

She ran. She ran like she'd never run before, through the hall and into the descending corridor, through the empty rooms, through the hidden passageway, and then down at last, into that last room, whose door was open, ever so slightly, and a flickering light came through …

Mithila burst inside.

The room was bare, but for a table and a chair set against the wall.

Garuda sat there, head bent, arms folded

Mithila came to an astonished halt.

Garuda looked up. His eyes were tired.

'So it's my turn to ask,' he said, 'will you kill me, Mithila?'

Mithila covered the distance between them in seconds. She seized Garuda's collar and smashed him against the wall, her blade at his throat. Garuda went limp, unresisting.

'Ow,' he said.

'Give me one reason,' she said, '*one* reason why I shouldn't.'

'I haven't got one.' Garuda's eyes flickered. 'I won't blame you if you did. Just. Make it quick.'

'Quick? *Quick*? Is death by burning quick, brother?' Mithila whispered. 'How do you think fire feels upon the skin? Smoke in your throat? Your flesh charring like paper, your bones cracking like kindling? Quick?'

Garuda flinched. He turned his neck until the vein was touching the tip of the blade. 'I have no defence. Bleed me out if you want. I don't deserve anything else.'

'Not yet.' She did not let the blade waver. 'Where are the fucking Select?'

'Gone.'

'*What?*'

'Gone,' Garuda repeated. 'You stopped them before all the devices had been planted. They knew the game was up when they heard the explosion. They're in the world now.'

'Then what are you doing here?'

Garuda smiled, a strange feeble smile that she had never seen before. 'Can't you guess?'

'Don't play games with me. Are you the one to set us on fire?'

'What? No—I—there's no fire now,' he said. 'It's over.'

'*Then why are you still here?*' She pressed the knife, watched a fine red line well at its edge. Garuda made no move. Mithila felt a hysterical laugh bubbling at the back of her throat.

'Because they Ostracized me,' Garuda said.

Now the blade wavered—wildly. For a moment, her grip on his collar slackened. Garuda slumped.

'Lies,' Mithila trembled. 'Again.'

'They Ostracized me because I refused to let them burn this damned place to the ground with you still in it. They despise weakness. They always have.'

'I don't believe you,' said Mithila. 'Why should I believe you?'

Garuda looked at her wonderingly. 'Do you remember that night in the Pit? You and me and that mud wall between?'

'Garuda, if you're going to try—'

'I told you of a Sumer beneath our feet.'

'From where the Rasa flows,' Mithila completed automatically. She had played that night in her mind for two years. Even now, she recalled every word, every moment.

'I was trying to tell you—'

'You told me nothing but lies, brother, and I am so tired. What, you were playing some double-double-double agent game? Fuck you.

You could've told me. I would have done anything for you.' Her voice cracked. 'I have no brother.'

'Or father now,' he murmured.

'*What*?'

'Did they tell you who did it?'

Disoriented, she looked at him. 'How do you know he died?'

'So they didn't, then. I'm not surprised.' He turned his face up, and for the first time that night, looked her in the eye. 'It was Rama.'

Mithila staggered back. 'You're out of your mind.'

'The Council at their backs, perfectly placed,' he said gently. 'The President whose rule he could have destroyed. But more than that—the daughter whose father he sent into a deathless sleep.'

'No,' she whispered. 'No, no, no, no …'

'Yes,' Garuda said softly. 'I'm sorry. I'm sorry.'

Her blade arm almost dropped from Garuda's throat. It was all she could do to keep it there. He must have known that he could've brushed it away. But Garuda didn't move.

'Stop changing the subject,' Mithila said.

'I thought you needed to know,' Garuda said. 'But, Mith. I promise you. I was never convinced by *apoptosis*. I never wanted it. But if I'd let it show, they would have killed me for my weakness.'

Mithila felt tears trickling down her cheeks.

'You're either lying or a coward,' she said, fighting to keep her voice steady. 'Pick one.'

'A coward, if you must,' Garuda said. 'But every choice I made was for you. I couldn't save the City. I didn't have that power. But I could save you.'

'Save?'

'I gave you the horizon, and I hoped you'd come and find it. How I hoped, Mith, it was my only reason to live. I watched you for two years, waiting. And you did. I can't tell you what joy it was to see you there.'

'What?'

'The overground City. The courtyard and the pillars. You, watching from the high dome. You ducked.'

'That was you, in blue?' Mithila choked out.

Garuda inclined his head.

'See, Mithila. I couldn't make this up. I saw you in there. I opened that door, I left you a trail of *rahi*, I hoped you'd come back home. To save it where I couldn't.

'And you did.'

Garuda closed his eyes and turned his face upwards. His entire throat was exposed to the blade, but Mithila's hand had begun to shake uncontrollably.

'I betrayed Sumer because I could not die,' Garuda said softly, 'and I betrayed the Select because I could not believe. Now the Select are gone, and Sumer is saved. History can judge me. I have done.'

Garuda opened his eyes.

'You were worth the wait.'

Mithila withdrew the blade from his throat.

Garuda's eyes widened.

There was a rush of air beside Mithila, a rustle of cloth, and a knife-hilt sticking out of Garuda's side.

Garuda looked down at the dark-red stain upon his Select's tunic, bewildered.

He slumped to the ground, his back against the wall.

'He nearly fucking had you *all over again*,' Minakshi said.

'Wha—what?' Mithila whirled around. 'What are you—you stabbed our *brother*.'

Minakshi—a bandage around her arm—seized Mithila's shoulders. 'Mithila. *You came here for the passage*.'

'Oh my—Builders!' Mithila's eyes widened. She turned and ran down the passage, Minakshi at her heels.

The fire from their torches cast the walls in a jagged, leaping light. They went on down, and into the subterranean corridor that connected the Citadel to the chamber of the Three Kings.

Minakshi stopped, panting. 'Your move, sister. Where's the way out—the way to Gumfraude? The way you came back?'

'Ten paces down,' said Mithila. 'There's a trapdoor in the wall, on the right—which opens into the road to Gumfraude.'

'Go on.'

Mithila counted the paces. She faced the wall. She ran her hands along the smooth surface, looking for that slight bump, the bump she had been careful to fix in her mind when she'd come out from the passageway.

There it was.

Mithila pressed.

The wall parted.

She heard Minakshi gasp.

In front of her, there was no passageway that led into the far darkness, and into the world.

There was only a gleaming, black, featureless, block of stone.

Mithila extended her index finger, and brought it to touch the stone.

It was smooth, and utterly cold.

It was the material of the Wall.

'They've escaped,' said Minakshi. 'And closed the passage. We cannot follow.'

Mithila ran her palm along the wall.

'If I had called for help,' she said quietly, 'instead of talking to Garuda …'

'Every time he hurts you, you blame yourself.' Minakshi's voice was so unexpectedly gentle, that it stung. 'They were probably long gone.'

Mithila put her forehead against the cold stone.

'How does it feel,' Minakshi said, 'to have saved our Sumer?'

They didn't say anything as they walked slowly into the Forum Plaza. Mithila winced at the light, a thousand torches gathered and burning, waiting on a command. She heard the murmurs begin as the swelling crowd realised who she was, and whom she was with.

'Why were you here,' Mithila whispered. 'Why did you even come after me?'

Minakshi's eyes were fixed into the distance. She raised her hand to her brow, cutting off the light falling brightly onto her. 'Someone has to,' she said. 'Besides. You're all that's left.'

Mithila faced them, lamplight dancing in their eyes, as they turned to her.

'The Select have fled,' she said, her voice resounding in the Plaza. 'They have closed the way out beyond the Wall. Forever.'

She let it fall.

Maji came running out of the Citadel. 'Worldfarer, what is—'

'It's over, Maji,' Mithila said. 'There's no way out. We lost. But ...' She paused. 'At least we saved ourselves.' She looked back at the people.

'Tomorrow we can remake Sumer.'

Twenty

The Shattered Three

They sat by the riverbank, warmed by the late-morning sun. The grass felt soft and springy. The Rasa was laughing. The white stone of the Forum, towering above them, glinted in the light.

'I still can't quite understand,' said Mithila. 'About Ghada.'

'Oh, it just—you had to be there,' said Mankala. 'That moment when Samir says *it's too hot*, I understood we weren't looking at memories or dreams, but at real people, real *in their world*. They were there, in that moment. Alive. And then, Alora's words: *come walk between the worlds once more.* But I wouldn't have known it, Mithila, had you not seen what you saw in Gumfraude. Water flowing up, water flowing down, two planes that could not exist in the same world. They didn't change the laws of reality. They just had two realities.'

Mithila grinned. 'What were the odds that I'd see exactly what *you* needed—to solve this two thousand five hundred year-old problem?'

'These people didn't do coincidences, Mithila.' Mankala shook her head. 'You were meant to see that. It was a message they left for whoever would come looking for them: *this is how you wake us.* It must have been their last act, when they knew Gumfraude would fall, when they knew their own fate, an endless sleep, and all they could do was to leave us messages, in the words Ghada and Samir spoke to each other, in Alora's song, in Gumfraude—hoping that someday, we would have the eyes to see, and then *they* would live again.'

'They deserved a much better ending than this,' said Alvar.

'So did we,' said Mankala, looking into the water. 'So did we. I wish you'd actually had a chance to draw the horizon, Alvar. From life.'

'A horizon line without a horizon. Forever.' Alvar hugged his knees. 'Because stories never end the way you want them to.'

'Everyone got what they wanted, though,' Mithila said. 'Everyone but us.'

'Oh, I don't know,' Mankala said. 'Seems the Select lost pretty badly as well.'

'They've left us here with no way of getting out.' Mithila leaned back. 'I know, I know—we could've died. But the world's gone. So what was it for?'

'Did you ever think Marwana was right?' Mankala said. 'Just for a moment?'

'About *apoptosis*?' Mithila stared fixedly at the ground. 'I don't know. And now it doesn't matter.'

A horizon line without a horizon.

'Ah well.' Mankala turned her gaze up to the silent Citadel. 'I don't want to ever think of Marwana again, if I can help it. At least my dad wouldn't have to go to the fields anymore. That's something. He always wanted to be with the babies.' She smiled. 'All thanks to the Banner, to the Revolution. *And* you'll be here for Lamon's wedding.'

'Speaking of which, ready for today's Ceremony?' Alvar said.

Mithila laughed shortly. 'No. So not ready.'

'Rama?' Alvar asked, his voice hesitant.

'Not ready for that either,' Mithila said, tired. 'But it's over. It died with Ba.'

'Ah.' Alvar searched for words. 'Your sister—'

'Now *there's* a long way back.' Mithila laughed carelessly. 'You know what we agreed to do? Immediately after the Ceremony, we're going to go off together. We're going do the Round Walk, the full circle of Sumer, by the Wall. We'll fill our six lost years into six days. Just the two of us.'

Alvar grimaced. 'I can think of a thousand ways in which that can go wrong.'

Mithila smiled. 'What I'd give if we could just fight as *sisters* again.'

'But what *is* her story?' Mankala broke in. 'You never told us.'

'Oh.' Mithila shook her head. 'She's so … ah, I guess I can just about see her side. Six years ago, she was on the roof when Marwana paid Ba a surprise visit. She heard Marwana tell Ba they'd expose him as Savarian unless he agreed to reveal himself on an appointed day, and then the Select would protect him. Minakshi—she wanted to save Ba, but she also figured this was much bigger, that the Select were dangerous, and there was only one way in this City to fight them. She agonized about it for a long time, but then made her choice. And once she was with the Shoortans—it was all in …'

'You believe that?' Mankala asked.

'It's very much in-character.'

'Malorans, huh?' Mankala said.

'That too.' Mithila chuckled. 'Yes—yes I guess I want to believe her. She really is all that's left.'

'Wait,' said Alvar, 'does that mean that the afternoon in the Maidan, when Ananta became Savarian—that was a set up?'

'I'll never know,' Mithila said. She ran her hands through her hair. 'I'm choosing to believe that he turned them down, and what happened in the Maidan was just—he couldn't help himself. Ba doing the right thing.'

'All threads tied, then,' Alvar said.

'Except Garuda,' Mithila said. 'I don't know if he stayed for me. Or if he was just buying time for them.'

Alvar put an arm around her shoulder and squeezed it gently. Mithila sighed.

Mankala was frowning at the Rasa. 'I don't like loose threads either.'

'What?' Alvar said.

Slowly, softly, Mankala began to chant.

The stars are out.
The Builders will not stay.
But we remain. There was a time, before

And there will be a time to come
Who will remake the broken world?

No more enough, the word.
Where yesterday
We bound into our will the sum of all
Now and today, the bound are we
Who will remake the broken world?

They will not come.
The earth is riven now.
The stones lie scattered. In the coming dusk
Who will put back the shattered three?
Who will remake the broken world?

Hear me.
Upon the dying of the day
Will you renew Samati's sacrifice?
When light from light shall come again
Will you remake the broken world?

Mithila shivered.

'I thought the shattered three were the three Kings,' Mankala said. 'Bound, here, within the Wall. The Wall cuts off the sun. The world is broken by the Wall. It makes sense. But then, who is the *they* who will not come?'

Behind them, they heard a bustle in the Forum Plaza.

Alvar looked up. 'Well, the people have come, at least.'

'Ah, I should go.' Mithila sat up. 'Maybe I can learn to love this City.'

'You're actually doing it?' Mankala said. 'Giving up the Heartstone to the City?'

'That's what we agreed,' Mithila said. She drew out the Heartstone that she had taken from Ghada's hand. 'Can't make a Revolution out of this anymore.'

Mankala reached out, cupped her hands around the Heartstone, and stiffened as she felt the crackling run up her arm. 'This one too—alive?'

'All of them,' said Mithila. 'The one in the Temple is the most intense.'

'It seems to be some form of energy,' Mankala said.

'Ghada said *burning glass*,' said Mithila. 'Does that mean anything to you?'

'Burning—what?' said Alvar.

'Glass?' Mithila shrugged.

'I don't know who Glass is. But burning always puts me in the mind of Samati,' said Mankala. She withdrew her hand from the Heartstone. 'Guess we're never going to find out now.'

'And here I thought that all we needed to remake the world were the words for it,' said Mithila. 'Oh well. Let me get this over with.'

She stood. Before her, in the Forum Plaza, she saw the gathered crowd. Mithila took a deep breath.

'You can do this,' said Alvar.

She nodded, and walked forward, on slow steps. As she approached the crowd, she saw three sets of people, standing slightly apart. There was Rama and the Council; Minakshi and the Shoortans; and Maji, with Carina and Prana. Mithila walked across the empty circle, sensing the peoples' eyes on her, and stood beside Maji.

'You're late,' Maji muttered.

'I'm here now,' Mithila said, looking into the crowd. The sun hit her eyes. She could not now raise a hand to block it out. Mithila squinted, feeling her eyes fill with tears. In the sharp daylight, little bits of the Forum seemed to be melting away in a haze, like the last remnants of a dream.

Their dream.

Somebody had brought out a table, and placed it at an equal distance from all of them. There was paper on it, and a pen.

Rama stepped forward. Mithila turned her eyes to the ground.

Rama addressed the crowd.

'I am glad to tell you,' she said, 'that the State of Emergency was revoked this morning. The Council has met. The New Settlement has been unanimously ratified.'

Behind them, there was a pattering of applause from Hansa and the Councillors.

'Let me remind you what it says. *First*—the marriage license laws are abolished. No more licenses for lovers.'

No applause from the Councillors, but a smattering of cheers from the people.

'*Second*: no woman or man in this City is bound to their Circles anymore.'

The cheers grew louder, and spread.

'And *third*: the Farmers' Circles will have a voice in all decisions to do with the farmlands. We will soon extend this to all other forms of production.' Rama's voice grew serious. 'In fact, we need to. Because to those of you who have not heard, I must tell you this: the Select left us last night.'

There was an instant, shocked silence, followed by a low hum of chatter. Rama went on speaking before it could rise.

'Last night we discovered that the Select were going to set Sumer on fire. Burn us all. If you were wondering why the fields around the Maliot are scorched, now you know. It would have been the Great Fire all over again '—Rama gestured at Mithila—'but for the Worldfarer and her companions.'

She knew Rama was looking at her, but Mithila kept her eyes firmly fixed on the ground.

'The Select told us how to keep this City alive,' Rama continued. 'Now we know how they knew. And we also know why they never shared what they knew. Why they kept science hidden from us. It was knowledge they held over us, the idea that the world was too complex for anyone but them to understand. Well, they are gone, and we have no choice: we are on our own.' Her voice rose. 'And Select or no Select, we will prevail. *We will survive.*'

There it was. The moment was coming. Mithila readied herself.

'Until last night,' Rama said, 'we were a riven City. Now that is over. The Revolution is over. We are going to go forward together. A more equal Sumer. As a sign of good faith, I call the Matriarch and the Worldfarer to sign this Charter with me'—she held up the paper—'where we all agree to forgive the past, endorse amnesty for prior crimes, and pledge our future to the New Settlement.'

Minakshi joined her in the middle of the circle. Still looking at the ground, Mithila walked up to them.

Rama and Minakshi signed. Her sister passed her the pen. Mithila scratched her name below theirs.

'And as a further sign of our binding ourselves to each other'—Mithila flinched at the words—'we yield up to the City our Heartstones. The Heartstones will belong to all, and to no one: each Mandala will have them for a month, and then will pass them on to the next. So they will travel in the City, a reminder of the day this Revolution died, and a new world was born.

'To mark the new beginning of a more equal Sumer, we begin with the Fifteenth Mandala.'

Rama took out her Heartstone and held it high above her head. Mithila and Minakshi followed, until their hands were almost touching, and the white, throbbing light had multiplied threefold.

This time, the cheers were resounding.

And from the river, Mankala watched the three stones come together.

'*Oh,*' she whispered.

Maji stepped into the semi-circle, and came up to them. In her hands there was a box of wood, crafted cunningly—so cunningly that it took Mithila back to a little house in the Seventh, and the smell of wood-shavings in a sculptor's workshop.

'To an ending and a beginning,' said Maji.

The corners of her lips quirked at Mithila, the smallest and saddest of smiles, telling her, *I know*. The tears in Mithila's eyes were no longer of the sun. She surrendered her Heartstone, the crackling feeling leaving her, the hairs on her skin slowly settling. Alongside hers, the other two Heartstones went into the box. Maji shut the lid upon the glowing white light. She inclined her head to them, her scar livid in the morning sunlight, and carried the stones away.

'To a new Sumer,' Rama said. 'We *will* remake the broken world.'

Her words opened something, like a river-lock upon the Rasa letting the water through. With a great bustle, and to the sound of cheers and clamour, the crowd entered the circle, milling around them. Mithila felt her back thumped by—she recognised Kodali—and her hands shaken, by women and men from the Dooma and the POUM, and even her old Circle, the Seventh. She was dimly aware of the glazed smile plastered to her face, the words that came unthinking, meaningless, and the words themselves collapsing into ambient noise—

A pressure at her elbow. 'Come on, sister,' she heard Minakshi whisper into her ear. She let her sister steer her away from the centre of the Forum Plaza, and into a corner, away from the people.

'Wait here, Mithila?' said Minakshi. 'I'll get my things. And don't worry about going back to the Seventh, I'll bring food and clothes for you too. See you in half an hour?'

Mithila nodded. She saw Minakshi set off towards the Temple. She remained standing at the edge of the Plaza, watching the crowd diminish, thin, and melt away into the afternoon, until only Rama was there, alone in the Plaza, as though she had lost something.

In the great shadows of the Forum's towers, across the swaying grass, they looked at each other. At last, Rama let her gaze drop. She turned and walked away, back into the Council Hall.

Mithila was left alone.

The winter sun had climbed into the sky. She suddenly realized that her throat was parched. Mithila took her flask out of her bag—the one she'd carried to the world and back—and shook it. It was empty.

She cursed. She walked across the Plaza and to the tributary of the First Mandala. Bending down, Mithila scooped water into the flask. Straightening again, she took a swig.

The water tasted ... different.

Mithila stopped. There was a tinge, nameless, something sharp, gnawingly familiar.

Mithila closed her eyes and drank again.

Memories came rushing into her. Of a *sun*set, a horizon, rain, and sheets of moving water before her.

A taste like tears.

'*Fuck.*'

Mithila ran.

She sprinted back across the Plaza to where Mankala and Alvar sat by the river.

'They've sent in the sea!' she shouted as she reached them, the wind tearing her words away.

Mankala stood. 'What?'

Mithila thrust her flask at Mankala. 'The water—taste it.'

'But water doesn't taste …'

'*Taste* it.'

Mankala took a drink. She made a face. 'What in Sumer … ?'

'That's the taste of the sea,' Mithila gasped. 'Remember, the sea? Endless water. Beyond the Wall.'

'Mithila,' said Alvar, slowly, 'is it just me, or has the water come up?'

Mithila swung around. By the smallest of degrees—almost unnoticeable—the Rasa appeared to have risen.

A look of horror crossed Mankala's face. 'Tefnakth,' she whispered. '*The end will reflect the beginning*. Oh, what a fool I was. The beginning was *fire*. Reflect …' her head snapped up. 'They're going to drown us!'

'What—we can't—*where do we go?*' Alvar said.

The waters of the Rasa lapped their quiet journey Wallwards.

Mankala's eyes were squeezed shut, her fists against her forehead, her head bowed. Mithila looked at Alvar. 'I was so fucking stupid,' she whispered. 'As if the Select were just going to flee, after planning this for two thousand five hundred years.'

Mankala's eyes flew open.

'We need to move,' she said.

'*Where?*'

'Council Hall. *Now.*' She whirled around and began to run. They sprinted after her.

In the conferral room, Rama stood up in surprise, as they burst in. 'What?'

Mithila's heart lurched, but this time she forced herself to look.

'President,' Mankala panted.

'Yes?'

'You need to—need to—order—'

'What? Mankala, make sense—what's going on?'

'Everyone to come to the Wall, where the Rasa turns.'

'*Will you just tell me what is happening!*'

Mankala recovered her breath. 'Rama,' she said. 'The Select—they're trying to kill us. This isn't over. You have to listen to me. They're going to kill us.'

'How?'

'They're sending in the sea,' Mithila said quickly. 'They'll drown us.'

Rama's face changed. 'But—but—why the Wall then? We need to find higher ground!'

'There's going to be no ground, Rama!' Mithila shouted. 'The sea doesn't end. We are—Sumer is like a bowl, and they're filling it.'

Rama's eyes widened. '*No.*'

'Rama!' Mankala said sharply. She walked up to her and looked her in the eye. 'We do not have time for this. Listen to me. Issue the order.'

'Now?' said Rama, faintly.

'*Now*!'

Rama gave her a nod, gathered herself, and strode out of the room.

Mankala breathed. She turned to Alvar. 'Alvar, Tenth Mandala. You have to get the children out.' Her voice lowered. 'Get your parents, and mine.'

Alvar nodded, and dashed from the room.

'Mithila,' Mankala said to her. 'Boats.'

'Go' said Mankala. 'To the Dooma.'

The current of the rising river felt rougher, choppier. It took them faster than ever before, flying Wallwards. Mithila struggled with the paddles, unable to steer, helplessly holding on.

'*Who will put back the shattered three?*' Mankala muttered. '*Who will remake the broken world?*'

'Mankala, some help here?' Mithila gasped.

'*The stones lie scattered*,' Mankala chanted. Her hands were tracing little, frantic circles in the air. '*In the coming dusk*.'

'Mankala, the paddles!' Mithila cried out.

Their boat careened down the Rasa, and the Circles fell away. Upon the Maliot, traffic was back, the morning after the Revolution.

'*Mithila—hey!*'

She heard the voice as they passed the Tenth, and she knew it to be Kodali's. 'Kodali!' she shouted back, 'No time. Get to the Wall!'

'*What!*' she heard his surprised cry, but they were long past. Sumer sped by, glistening under the noonday sun, and all she had was a moment to think about how there was no time for a last look.

She dipped her fingers in the water once, and tasted it. Still tears. A shadow. There.

The Wall appeared ahead of them, a dim outline in the distance, growing clearer and sharper, and now they were drawing up to the Fifteenth—

'Stop!' said Mankala.

The boat swung violently in the river, as Mithila fought to bring it to shore. She felt it slam against the side of the bank, just as Mankala threw out the rope, catching the dock. Water splashed them, cold and teary. The second impact sent them tumbling out upon the Maliot, and into a crowd of people staring into the river.

'Worldfarer—what—'

Mankala struggled to her feet. 'No time!' she gasped. 'Maji. We need to get to Maji.'

'Now!' said Mithila.

The crowd parted, and a man stepped forward. 'Come.'

They left the sound of rising voices behind them and ran into the Fifteenth, once again through passageways and ladders, a remembered journey, and at last through a familiar stairway, before a door, bursting in—

Maji rose. 'Worldfarer?'

Mithila gestured to Mankala. Mankala stepped forward. 'Maji,' she said, 'you—all of you—everyone needs to come to the Wall, to where the Rasa branches. With the Heartstones.'

'What—why—?'

'The Select are flooding the City. We need to get to the Wall.'

'But why the Wall? Shouldn't we—'

'*Please,*' Mankala cut in. 'We have no time.'

Maji looked at Mithila, an eyebrow raised. Mithila nodded.

'Charu, you heard her,' said Maji. 'See it done.' She looked at Mithila. 'Let's go.'

Maji took them up to the terraces. They ran across the roofs, leaping between the smaller gaps and crawling over ladders. Very soon the Fifteenth Mandala ended, yielding to the fields. Maji turned North, to the Maliot and the Rasa.

As they reached the Rasa, Mithila saw it.

A stream of people moving upon the Maliot, upon the farmlands, and in the streets adjoining the Maliot, moving Wallwards. There were children, walking in lines of two, harried Carers guiding them. At the Wall, there was already a crowd.

'They've come,' Mithila whispered.

'Not enough,' Mankala said. 'Mithila, there's not enough.'

'More are coming,' said Maji. Sure enough, the line of people stretched out into the distance.

'To the Wall,' said Mankala.

As they hurried to the Wall, they could hear a low, muffled noise over the air, a noise that Mithila remembered. It was the sound she had heard in the tunnel between the chamber of the Three Kings and the Citadel, that beating sound against the walls. Only now it was in the air, all around them, in Sumer.

'What's that?' Mankala asked, just as Maji said: 'Look at the river.'

The Rasa had burst its banks. Water flowed out over the Maliot, into the fields, into the farmlands. From the distance, it seemed to be creeping upon them.

'*Fuck*,' said Maji.

'*Move!*' shouted Mankala, as others around them saw the Rasa, as the first murmurings filled the air, as astonishment—and then fear—descended upon Sumer like a blanket.

People cleared a way for them. Mithila was seen, recognised. 'Worldfarer,' someone shouted, 'what's happening?'

'The Select!' Mithila called back, realizing how stupid she sounded as soon as the words left her mouth. 'We're—get everyone here. *Now*.'

In the distance, she saw boats, lifted upon the river, keeling over, falling sideways on the ground. The water approached them.

'They're going to panic,' said Maji, 'they're going to run.' Mithila already saw some people at the edge of the fields turn back, as others pushed forward to the Wall. Voices began to rise.

'*Stay!*'

The word cracked through the air, calm, assured, carrying authority.

Rama was standing by the Wall, her palms up. 'You will stay,' she called again, her voice even. 'There is a plan. *Do not panic*.'

They were almost at the Wall now. Beneath their feet, the ground had grown moist, and there were small puddles forming in uneven parts of the fields.

Rama looked at them. 'Well?' she whispered. 'What *is* the plan?'

'Maji,' said Mankala calmly, 'give me the Heartstones.' Maji drew out the wooden box, sprung it open, and placed it on the ground.

Around her, there was sudden silence. Everyone was looking at them. From the distance, Mithila heard the noise rise.

The ground beneath her was slush, and there was water in her sandals; she saw people begin to slip as they came towards the Wall, saw a man fall and pick himself up, his face streaked with wet dirt, and she forced herself to look away, to ignore the dampness in her feet, to look at Mankala—

Smoothly, Mankala bent and picked up the first of the Heartstones. 'Were you the shattered Three?' she said softly.

That throbbing, that crackling of sudden energy, that gasp as the warmth entered Mankala's body. The Heartstone, again, had disappeared into its outlines, as though there was nothing within the frame but the core of a small sun.

'*Will you renew Samati's sacrifice?*' Mankala bent again. She picked up the second Heartstone.

Slowly, as if she was handling something fragile, she brought it to the first, and pressed. Mithila started. The second stone was almost *sucked* into the first, their boundaries blurring. Where there should have been two, there was only one, a burning light.

The crackling grew, and sharpened. Mithila saw triumph in Mankala's eyes.

'*The stones lie scattered in the coming dusk.*' She stuck out her hand, eyes fixed on the Heartstones, beckoning. Maji moved quickest, scooping up the third stone and putting it into her hand. This time, there was no hesitation. Mithila saw her standing there, her face lit by the throbbing ball of white light in her hands.

'Mankala,' she whispered. Something was wrong. There was something—nagging—that she should have been thinking of.

The water lapped at her ankles, cold, clammy, as though it was gripping her.

Mankala spun around, and for a moment, she stared at Mithila, uncomprehending. Then her eyes widened. '*Of course! Light shall come from light.*'

She lifted her palms high above her head, beneath the noonday sun.

For a few moments more, nothing happened.

The Heartstones throbbed violently.

Bolts of radiance began to dart and shoot around the edges of the light, turning it golden, translucent. A spear of light hit the water. It glowed molten. Before Mankala the crowd turned their gazes, shielding their eyes from the sudden brilliance. In the centre, the throbbing increased in pace, in depth, in fierceness, until even Mithila had to look away.

'Mith …' Mankala cried out. Mithila saw that her arms were rock-steady, but the rest of her body seemed to convulse. 'It's getting hotter.'

'*What!* Drop it!' Mithila shouted. Mankala shook her head. Mithila leapt at her, but the ground gripped her ankles and then let go, sending her feet sliding. Mithila pitched forward face-first, throwing out her arms to break her fall, and screamed as her injured hand hit the ground. There was wet mud in her eyes, in her nose, in her mouth. She struggled to her knees, spitting out the water, to see—

Mankala's veins had turned golden. A liquid light was running through her arms, and up her neck. Her hair was standing up.

'Mankala, what's happening?' she screamed.

'Mith, it's burning,' Mankala's voice was hoarse. 'I'm burning. I can't …'

But her hands were never moved.

A curtain of light flowed from the sun to the light in Mankala's hands, joining with the Heartstones that throbbed there.

And Mithila remembered Samati, his veins liquid, his black face carved into stone in a ruined world, holding up the Heartstone to the sun, a silent City his due, *if you want to fly …*

Around them, the muffled sound of the water was growing into a roar, a roar that went through all Sumer, from Wall to Wall.

Mithila staggered to her feet, stumbled towards Mankala, reached a hand to touch her—and fell back with a cry as a bolt passed through her skin, almost stilling her heart.

A halo appeared around Mankala's face. Mithila saw her eyes raised to the sky, screwed shut, her teeth clenched. She heard her breath, coming in ragged quick gasps, long, short, long, and then a sob.

They used people for fuel.

Suddenly, Mankala's eyes opened, and her gaze met Mithila's. She smiled.

'Don't worry, Mith,' she said. 'It doesn't hurt too much. The world—'

A burst of pure energy shot through the Heartstones, blinding them. Whiteness filled the air, a whiteness to begin the world, or to end it. People screamed. Mithila threw herself forward one last time, reaching out with her hand towards that curtain of white light, and now her own fingers were burning up, curling in fire, and—

A shock, like a burst of flaming wind, threw her back on her knees, into the water.

And the world exploded in brilliance, forcing her to shield her eyes, to look down into the muck and the water.

When Mithila looked up, Mankala was gone.

A giant hole had burned through the Wall.

Outside, she saw the forest.

The fingers of her right hand were charred.

'Mankala ...' Mithila whimpered. Pain shot through her hand.

'*Move!*' Rama roared, her voice cutting through the air. 'Through the gap. It can take five—*don't fucking crowd it.* Mithila, get out of here, go, you've been out there—tell them what to do.'

Mithila stumbled forwards through knee-deep water. The hole began just above her waist. She lifted herself up, and swung across. She was out.

She stood on the other side, as people began to come out. 'South!' she shouted, pointing, her voice choked. 'Don't crowd here, go South. Make space. *South.*'

They spilled out, and on the other side she heard cries, instructions, snatched commands—'*line, line, line!*'—Rama's voice, and then others—'*pick up the children!*', '*Carers—can we get them here?*', '*Time—no time!*' There were people at the gap, she saw children passed through, wails rending the air.

Behind her, she felt a crowd form. She swung around. '*What are you waiting for!*' she screamed. '*Move! There's more coming!*'

In Sumer, the water had risen to waist height, and had begun to pour out into the forest. *That will keep the level constant for a while*, a voice in her head, bizarrely calm, whispered. It drove the crowd behind her into panic, and she heard them retreat, move back, away from the creeping water.

Through the gap the people came in droves, a crunch, stumbling and falling through, now almost a stampede—before someone on the other side did something, and the crush thinned into a line between order and chaos.

'*South … keep going …*'

The people blurred into a heaving mass, that she saw through blurry eyes, coming through, pitching into the forest, the world, a rumbling in the background shot through with a clattering of voices, *yes,* her mind shouted at her, *yes, Sumer will live, yes, fuck apoptosis, yes—*

'Mith!'

Alvar's voice pierced her. He was at her side. They could hear the roaring from inside the City.

'What?' Mithila shouted over it.

'Look at the gap!'

She saw it. Little tendrils of stone were creeping around the edges—slowly, ever so slowly, but ever so surely.

The Wall was healing itself.

She leapt to the gap. '*Move, move, move!*' she screamed. 'It's closing!'

The fields were almost empty, Rama directing the last of the people through the gap, as the waters rose. But in the far distance, at the edge of the Fifteenth Mandala, she saw a figures half-wading, half-swimming towards the Wall.

A kilometre away.

Too far.

The stone moved like a living thing, finding emptiness, creeping to fill it, weaving itself together, the gap now like a window from the world into the City, like a wound that was scabbing before her eyes, and—

Rama came through, flailing upon the current, expelled by the water.

The gap closed behind her, and Sumer was gone forever.

High on a terrace in the Dooma, he watches the waters rise.

The roaring has subsided. There is quietness now. Just the sound of the water, lapping against the walls.

There is something beautiful about it, he thinks. The cleanest of all ends.

He sees things float upon the water: chairs, boards, furniture. Bodies. It is taking on a muddy, opaque look, as it swirls beneath him.

Footsteps.

He turns and smiles.

'I knew I'd find you here,' she says.

'Ah, the oldest of my foes—and the oldest of my friends,' he says.

'Are foes still foes, at the end of all things?'

She comes to stand beside him. Together, they lean upon the parapet.

'So you couldn't leave,' she says. It is not a question.

'I would not,' he says. It has only ever been Sumer—or nothing.'

'The history of Sumer is the history of struggle,' she quotes him.

He laughs, delighted. 'Twenty-seven years. You remember.'

She is silent, looking into the City. His eyes grow soft.

'Seems we ran out of time.' she shakes her head. 'In another world, perhaps. But not in this one.'

'We'll find each other there,' he says softly. 'Did you say your goodbyes?'

'I had no one left. Did you?'

'Some goodbyes are best left unsaid.'

'But now we're here. Shall we?'

He nods. And he remembers, for the last time, the little note he had tucked into the pocket of the Dooma boy that he had caught running towards the Wall, saying: 'By the love you bear me, find Mithila and give this to her.' The note, which said:

Dearest Love,

They will tell you I died upon the barricades, by the hand of the President. But I didn't stay alive this long just to be killed by the same story. I have stayed behind, Ila. I will die with my City. Don't let a lie spoil your love.

Farewell.

'Shall we?' he echoes. 'How much do you think it will hurt?'

She smiles. 'It won't.' She takes out a little box from her pocket, opens it, and hands him a little white pellet.

'We'll lose consciousness within the minute.'

'Together?' he says.

'Together,' she replies.

They swallow their pellets.

She looks at him, and for the first time, he reaches for her, and holds her hand. Her breath catches. She turns, and looks into the water before them. Her hair is flying around her face in the wind.

They climb upon the parapet.

'Goodbye,' she whispers.

'Until we meet again,' he says.

Hand in hand, Savarian Maloran and Councillor Malati leap into the water.

The last thing he sees is a path of blue. A clear, beautiful blue.

The blue of revolution.

Epilogue

By evening, they reach the sea.

Mithila calls for a halt.

'There's a river here,' she says, 'you can drink.'

She watches them rush on weary feet to the river, to slake their parched throats. She turns to the sea. 'Hello again,' she says.

'Mith.'

Alvar is at her side.

She rubs her eyes. 'How many do we have?'

'A lot,' he whispers. 'And we lost many. And there are others in the forest—we need to go find them. First, we'll have to put ourselves back together and then we'll know whom we left … behind. But tomorrow, we'll do a first count.'

'You can do that?'

'I'll have help,' he says, his voice raw.

'We'll name each and every one of them,' she says. 'Starting with Bhavi. Like I promised. But for now … do you have …?'

'It's ready.'

'Let's see it?'

A wooden board, salvaged from the City, that Mithila had begged off someone on their march to the sea. Alvar has chiselled the letters upon it, as neatly as he could.

MANKALA, WHO REMADE THE BROKEN WORLD THE YOUNG TARAFIANS

'It's perfect,' she says.

They walk to where the river meets the sea, where Taraf's memory-stone lies. With their fingers, they scoop out the mud, sand and earth around it, grainy beneath their nails. It gives way easily. They set it up, and pat the earth back into place.

There are two memory-stones now.

'It'll have to do for now,' Mithila says. 'We'll come back.'

They kneel. A light rain begins to fall again. The people have spread themselves out upon the beach, a scattered mass along the sea-line as far as she can see, far too many to count, still bewildered beyond comprehension. From the forest, she sees figures emerge, long lines, ghostly in the dark.

'What will happen now?' Alvar says.

'This is just the beginning,' Mithila says. 'Sooner or later, the Select will know. They'll come after us. We need to run. But we also need to get ready.'

'Worldfarer.'

'We are all Worldfarers,' she says, as she turns, still kneeling. It is a small boy, standing across from her. 'What is it?'

'There's a note for you.' He holds out his hand.

'Oh?' She says. 'Thank you.' She takes it and stuffs it into a pocket. 'I'll see about this later.' She nods at him. He vanishes into the dusk.

She turns back to Alvar.

'Will you lead?' he asks.

She smiles and shakes her head. 'Never my thing,' she says. 'Rama will. She'll know what to do. Minakshi will help, I'm sure. Maji's there. They'll sort it out. They don't need me.'

'What are you going to do, Mith?' he asks.

And Mithila thinks about Gumfraude, the old City of Stone, and the pool of Geroun.

'I'm going to go find Dhara,' she says. 'And then we're going to bring the Select down. No more *apoptosis*. No more cycles. The next time we don't fight to escape, we fight to win. All that matters ...' Her voice breaks. 'All that matters is that there be a next time.'

They stand up. They hug each other. 'See you soon, Alvar,' she says.

Alvar smiles. 'There will always be a world to discover. With you.'

She gives him the reverse circle salute. The last of the Young Tarafians.

Mithila turns and walks away from the sea, into the rain and the night.

Appendix

Sometimes, writing feels little more than simply re-organising the fragments of everything you've ever read. In writing *The Wall* and *The Horizon*, I drew upon a host of influences that have come to form a part of my own interior mental landscape. This Appendix is by way of a (very) incomplete tribute.

The Songs and the Poems

Savarian's revolutionary song, *Blue, I Dream You Blue*, is inspired by the radical Spanish poet and playwright Federico Garcia Lorca's *Verde, Que Te Quiero Verde*. YouTube has many excellent renditions of the poem. My personal favourite is the one sung by Manzanita and Ana Belen. Lorca was gone too soon, murdered by the fascists, but his work lives on. Speaking of radicals, Maji's song to Maran and Upar, '*Here's to you …*' follows the structure and metre of *Here's To You, Nicola and Bart*, Joan Baez's tribute to Sacco and Vanzetti, the two Italian-American labour organizers who were executed by electric chair during the First Red Scare. A poignant and haunting song, I suggest listening to the YouTube version that has scenes from the black-and-white film on Sacco and Vanzetti.

Still on the subject of radicals, Carina's poem-fragment in Chapter 1 of *The Horizon* ('… for in the shadow of the Wall/ we look for sap to grow/ we thirst for sunlight') is inspired by the Nigerian poet, Christopher Okigbo ('for he was a shrub among poplars/needing more roots/more sap to grow to sunlight/thirsting for sunlight …'). The phrase 'thirsting for sunlight' gives its name to a beautiful biography of Okigbo by Obi Nwakanma, which brings to life the literary firmament of post-colonial Nigeria.

Staying with radicals (clearly a theme!), Carina's song-fragment ('when power by power confronted …') riffs off Satan's exhortation to the rebel angels in Book 1 of Milton's *Paradise Lost*: 'his utmost power by adverse power oppos'd/ in dubious battels by the Plains of Heav'n/and shook his throne. What though the field be lost/ all is not lost.' There is, of course, a long tradition of fantasy writers finding inspiration in Milton (*His Dark Materials*, a childhood favourite of mine), and I firmly place myself in that meta-tradition.

Within the same symbolic universe, Vidusha's invocation of bardic independence at the end of Chapter Seven of *The Horizon* follows the form and structure of Jesus' response in the *Simon Zealots* song of the rock opera, *Jesus Christ Superstar* ('neither you, Simon, nor the fifty thousand/nor the Romans, nor the Jews/ nor Judas, nor the Twelve, nor the priests, nor the scribes/ understand what power is/ understand what glory is/ understand at all'). *Jesus Christ Superstar* is one of the most deliciously subversive pieces of musical performance I've come across, and to put a version of its lines in the mouth of irreverent musicians seemed particularly apt.

Finally, a pure indulgence: the song of the Wall, sung at the night of the Carnival, follows the metrical patterns of Mervyn Peake's *Linger now with me, thou beauty*, in the classic novel *Titus Groan*. Peake is one of those genre-defining writers whom everyone, I think, writes with or against, whether or not they know it.

The rest of the songs and poems in *The Wall* and *The Horizon* are my own, although readers will probably see echoes of *The Lord of the Rings* in them. After reading Tolkien, fantasy without songs cannot but feel incomplete.

The Legends and the Stories

The story of Samati and Garuda, that underpins *The Horizon*, is—of course—the story of Sampati and Jatayu from *The Ramayana*. It can also be read as adjacent to the story of Icarus and Dadaelus (the similarities between the two are a source of endless fascination for me). The myth of Malan will be broadly recognizable as an inversion of Lakshman's injunction to Sita not to cross the *Lakshman Rekha.* I hardly need to point out that Sita was also called Mythili because she belonged to the kingdom of *Mithila.*

The myth of Alora is Promethean in its inspiration. Mithila's own vision of Alora towards the end of *The Wall* is inspired by a scene in Ismail Kadare's *The Siege*, which captures more poignantly than anything else the role of competing origin stories in constructing contemporary reality. More generally, the Shoortan insistence on oral history, and the conflict between the oral and the written is a theme that Ismail Kadare explores in multiple novels, most notably, *The File on H* (which, itself, was inspired by the real-life quest to find the origins of *The Iliad*, chronicled by Milman Parry and Albert Lord in *The Singer of Tales.*)

Mithila's debate with Minakshi in the Maidan in *The Wall* involves a direct reference to the parable of the Cave in Plato's *Republic.* Keeping with the general theme of mythic inversion, I was interested in exploring whether the Platonic parable could be put to the service of emancipation or liberation, rather than in the service of order. Similarly, Maji's parable in the Senate (*The Horizon*, Ch. 18) is easily recognizable as an inversion of the story of Odysseus and the Sirens.

The People and the Events

The story of *The Wall* and *The Horizon* takes place in the shadow of one revolution, and in the course of another. In writing both revolutions, I drew on a rich history of our own world, where people have, so many times, risen up with dreams of building a better world. The refrain—*we can remake the world*—is a tip of the hat to that remarkable revolutionary thinker, Tom Paine's 'we have it in our power to begin the world over again.'

Savarian's exhortation to the Rebel in *The Wall* is based upon Sergei Necheyev's *Revolutioniary Catechism*, as is Savarian's ability to repeatedly escape his pursuers—although I hope that, by the end, Savarian is a somewhat more sympathetic character than the hard-to-love Necheyev.

Mithila receiving loyalty with a knife held to her palm (*The Horizon*, Ch. 12) echoes a scene described in Leopold Infeld's *Whom The Gods Love*, a beautiful and haunting (fictional) biography of the French mathematician and republican revolutionary, Evariste Galois, who was killed at the age of twenty-one. At a banquet in honour of King Louis Philippe, Galois raised a toast to the Emperor—and then held a knife against the glass. At his trial, the defence turned upon whether he had said '*if he betrays*' under his breath while doing so. *Whom The Gods Love* is worth reading just for this scene alone, although it's also worth reading for everything else as well.

Mithila watching the Eleventh abandon her to the sound of *Blue, I Dream You Blue* riffs off a famous poem by the Greek-Egyptian poet, Konstantin Cavafy, titled 'The God Abandons Antony'. Itself based upon an incident in Plutarch's *Lives*, the poem recounts how, on the eve of his decisive battle against Octavian, Antony—holed up in Alexandria—hears the sound of music outside his window, and realizes that his protector-God Bacchus is leaving him. 'The God Abandons Antony' was set to music by Leonard Cohen ('Alexandra Leaving'), and there's a particularly beautiful rendition of it by Sharon Robinson, on YouTube.

Barricade battles in *The Horizon* draw upon the centuries-long history of the barricade in urban insurgencies across Europe. This history is admirably chronicled in Mark Traugott's *The Insurgent Barricade*, which was the main scholarly source I referred to while writing the barricade chapters. Mithila's invention of the V-shaped barricade is 'real' in the sense that V-shaped barricades were used as defences against artillery fire, and the physics behind their design is accurate. Unfortunately, I doubt that they were invented in similarly memorable circumstances, and—of course—trebuchets were not historically used in urban combat.

The farmers' movement in *The Wall*—for a third share of the harvest—that eventually leads to their joining the revolution in *The*

Horizon carries echoes of the heroic—and ultimately tragic—*Tebhaga* movement in undivided Bengal on the eve of Indian independence. A wonderful account of the movement, written from the perspective of feminist oral history, can be found in Kavita Punjabi's *Unclaimed Harvest*. I couldn't resist smuggling in a *Tebhaga* reference into the revolution: Savarian/Ananta referring to Mithila as 'Ila' is a tip of the hat to Ila Mitra, one of the most memorable leaders of *Tebhaga*.

Even though the Tebhaga movement was crushed, its legacy was a history of land reforms in post-Independence West Bengal. These land reforms were driven by the communist politician Hare Krishna Konar, from whom we get Konar Hall, the farmers' meeting place in the Eleventh Mandala.

Historically-minded readers would also be quick to recall that one of the leading protagonists in the Spanish Civil War, on the side of the republic, was the Workers' Party of Marxist Unification. Its Spanish name was the *Partido Obrero de Unificacion Marxista*, which is shortened to POUM. George Orwell happened to serve with the POUM during the Spanish Civil War, and *Homage to Catalonia* chronicles his experiences with those brave, but doomed, idealists.

The revolution in *The Horizon* is accelerated by the Council's refusal to accept Sanchika's Social Law, and his eventual murder, in *The Wall*. The events around Sanchika's death are very loosely modelled on the murder of Gaius Gracchus, a fiery land reformer in the Roman Republic, who met a similar end for daring to be too radical. *Sanchika* itself was the pen-name of E.M.S. Namboodiripad, India's first elected Communist Chief Minister, whose own land reforms—happily—succeeded, at least to a substantial degree.

The Concepts and the Ideas

The political arrangements in Sumer do not borrow from any one thinker or historical example, but are perhaps most closely inspired by James Harrington, the Seventeenth-century English philosopher and early Utopian thinker. The two-thirds rule for altering property arrangements, however, has a distinctly contemporary flavour: it echoes

Pinochet's military Constitution in Chile, which sought to 'lock in' unequal economic arrangements against any popular, egalitarian upsurge, and to ensure that someone like Salvador Allende—the democratically elected socialist President whom Pinochet overthrew in an American-assisted coup—would never be able to govern again. Pinochet's Constitution—that codified gross inequality—was itself finally overthrown in 2020 in a popular referendum following months of street protests, defined by the slogan '*neoliberalism was born in Chile, and here it will die.*' Perhaps Rama was on to something!

The Towers of Rebirth—where corpses are gradually allowed to decompose and eventually become fertilizers for the soil—are necessary for Sumer, where the question of disposing of corpses is of prime importance. They are also drawn from a real-life example: that of the American Urban Death Project. Perhaps unsurprisingly, that idea hasn't yet caught on in our world.

There are two pieces of science-fantasy that underlie the story. The first—the Builders' ability to have a projection of reality upon actual reality—owes its origins to the Argentine author Adolfo Bioy Casares, and his legendary novel *The Invention of Morel* (I have, of course, adapted the idea). Mithila's glimpse of water flowing simultaneously up and down in Gumfraude—which allows Mankala to deduce what is going on—is my imagination of what Escher's lithograph, *Waterfall*, would look like if it was brought to life. The connection between Escher and Bioy Casares is my own, although I would like to believe that there exists an elective affinity between Bioy Casares' two realities and Escher's two-dimensional bending of the laws of physics in his lithographs.

The Heartstones—and what they do—are the second piece of science fantasy. The Heartstones are imaginary, but it *is* interesting to note that not only was amber one of the earliest conducting materials that human being discovered, but the word 'amber', in the original Greek, is etymologically related to the phrase 'beaming sun'. Perhaps the ancients knew something we don't! The phrase 'burning glass'—Ghada's last words, and also in the Book of Alora—refers to the use of convex mirrors to concentrate sunlight and generate a very high degree of heat (although, of course, glass does not exist in Sumer, and the phrase, therefore, remains opaque to Mithila and Mankala).

Language

Smara, in the original Sanskrit, means 'memory' (unsurprisingly). *Praya* is drawn from the Sanskrit word for 'penance', and *prala* is a riff off 'apocalypse'.

Mithila's journey beyond the Wall introduces her to a set of sensations that she doesn't have words for, and needs to find. In Chapter Four, she searches for a description for the smell of rain in the soil, and settles upon 'it runs like the blood in your veins.' This refers to the etymology of the word *petrichor*, which originally meant 'the fluid that flows in the veins of the gods'. In Chapter Eight, looking down on Gumfraude, Mithila has a dizzy feeling that she names 'sky-turn'; this tracks the etymology of the word 'vertigo', which means 'to turn'/ 'whirling'.

Other Indulgences

Alvar's invention of perspective art in *The Horizon,* unfortunately, bears no resemblance to the historical discovery of perspective by Renaissance artists; I did find it a happy coincidence, however, that the 'horizon lines' are *actually* called horizon lines, and the same phrase—'vanishing point'—is used both in drawing perspective, and in the mathematical operation Mankala describes in Chapter Seven.

Speaking of Alvar, his unpublished and unsuccessful play, *The Necessity of the Breach*, owes its title to Shelley's *The Necessity of Atheism*, which had him expelled from University (Alvar, happily, escaped expulsion and was only mocked). Shelley's enigmatic poet/revolutionary figure was the inspiration—in small part—for Alvar.

Palestine and Palestinian writing has been a formative influence upon me. The legendary Garuda's desire to 'be dangerous … even if for a moment' (*The Wall*, Ch. 2) recalls Jean Genet's *Prisoner of Love*. Maji's query to Rama about the sword coming to talk to the neck (*The Horizon*, Ch. 9)—a personal favourite—is drawn from a famous interview given by the Palestinian writer Ghassan Kanafani, when he was asked why he refused to negotiate with Israel. Kanafani also features in Garuda's conversation with Mithila in Chapter Eighteen of *The Horizon*: 'we find a cause and become it' echoes the incredibly powerful line, 'a man is a cause', that Israeli and Palestinian characters say to each other in *Returning to Haifa.*

Garuda's idea of a language that is free (*The Wall,* Ch. 2) recalls Colm Toibin's dream of a language untouched by exploitation, in his book of essays, *Love in A Dark Time.* Whether that is possible in a world riven by hierarchies is another question. Toibin makes another appearance in Mithila's diary entry (*The Horizon, Ch. 2*), when she compares being in the world to having the memory of language, now lost. Describing Bacon's painting, *Three Studies for Figures at the Base of a Crucifixion,* Toibin writes: 'there is a sense of overwhelming pain here, but experienced by a creature who has known language, howling out a word rather than a cry, or a cry that has the memory of a word.' The idea of a 'cry that has the memory of a word'—the thought of knowing language and then having it stripped from you—has always haunted me.

Mithila's desire to give time a 'little push' (*The Wall*, Ch. 2) is drawn from Yuri Trifonov's description of the *narodnik* revolutionaries in 1880s Russia, who felt that history moved too slowly, and needed a push. Milton makes a reappearance, with the Samati's fall 'from noon to dusk' recalling the description of Lucifer's fall in *Paradise Lost.* Rana's exhortation to Malan to have courage to use his reason (*The Wall*, Ch. 4) is an inversion of Kant's exhortation, that eventually became a slogan of the Enlightenment. Mankala telling Alvar that 'life is elsewhere' (*The Wall*, Ch. 6) is a nod to Milan Kundera's identically-named novel, which also happens to be about revolution and poetry. Rastogi's critique of writing being a form of exclusion by definition (*The Wall*, Ch. 7) echoes the Latin American philosopher Ortega y Gasset, who once wrote '*to define is to exclude.*'

Rama and Mithila's tug-of-war about 'something of equality is yet to come' (*The Wall*, Ch. 13; *The Horizon*, Ch. 14) echoes the words of the

Nineteenth-century American labour leader Ira Steward, speaking after the Civil War, and remains one of the most damning indictments of how incremantalism is used to suppress popular aspirations: 'something of slavery still remains, something of freedom is yet to come.' Ghada's wistful conversation with Samir—'there was so much I wanted to show you' (Ch. 17, *The Wall*)—is, of course, a tip of the hat to the iconic *tears in the rain* scene in *Blade Runner*.

Mithila's encounter with the fireflies in Ch. 2, and her thinking of them as a net of stars, is my one—mandatory—tribute to J.R.R. Tolkien. It refers to *remnirath*, the constellation whose name translates to 'netted stars.' Speaking of mandatory tributes, Marwana's invocation 'the word for world was forest' (*The Horizon*, Ch. 18), is of course a hat-tip to the writer who has had the greatest influence upon the ideas explored in both books, Ursula Le Guin.

Mithila's feelings at the grave of Taraf (*The Horizon*, Ch. 4), in particular 'his words, like messengers', recall James Elroy Flecker's musing on the power of words in 'To a Poet A Thousand Years Hence.' Indeed, Flecker's poem speaks to various themes in the books, especially his second paragraph: 'I care not if you bridge the seas/ Or ride secure the cruel sky/ Or build consummate palaces/ Of metal or of masonry.'

The game of *treys* played by the Bards (*The Horizon*, Ch. 7) is a little in-genre tip of the hat to Guy Gavriel Kay's *The Last Light of the Sun*, and the game of triads. In the next scene Minakshi's recollection of Ananta's words to Alvar, comparing Sumer to a melody where if there's '*one note out of place, and everything falls*' (*The Horizon*, Ch. 7) echoes Antonio Salieri describing the perfection of Mozart's music, in the film *Amadeus*: 'displace one note, and there would be diminishment; displace one phrase, and the structure would fall.' This remains one of the most memorable expositions of unattainable beauty that I have come across.

'*We'll still chase the sun*' was graffiti on a wall in Padua that I saw in 2013, and never forgot.

Acknowledgments

To all those who beta-read *The Horizon*—through its multiple iterations in a pandemic-infested year—Vakasha, Vidushi, Didon, Vinita, Sanya, Abhilasha, Nishkala, Tania, Samit, Pritesh, Prashanth, Pranavi, Asawari: thank you. You were incredibly generous with your friendship and your time. Some of you were inflicted with a raw first draft of *The Wall* in 2018, and inexplicably agreed to come back for a second round with *The Horizon* in 2020: special thanks to you.

Special thanks, also, to Abhilasha for some truly dazzling book art, and to members of the Kosambi Research and Analaysis Circle who allowed me to eavesdrop while they dissected the plot and characters of *The Wall.*

To Indra, for a detailed and granular alpha-read: thank you.

To The Musketeers—Pritesh, Prashanth, Lavanya, and Chaitanya—for writing sprints, query rants, and comradeship as we all began to navigate the SFF writing life together: thank you.

To Samit, fellow-conspirator: thank you.

To the crew at *Strange Horizons*, for just about everything: thank you.

To Prerna, my editor at HarperCollins, and all the staff at HarperCollins, for letting me run with this idea for two books; for giving me the freedom to imagine something that was not a deep-frozen, microwaved, 'India-inspired' fantasyland from a 'South Asian writer' for the sake of marketability; and for overseeing my work from draft to duology: thank you.

To Naomi, for all the lost ellipsis, for the 'Ctrl+F your *and thens*', for the '*where are the fireflies and the shells and the bees?*', for being alpha, beta, gamma, and theta reader, and for breathing life into Sumer: thank you.

About the Author

Gautam Bhatia is a science-fiction writer, reviewer, and an editor of the award-winning *Strange Horizons* magazine. *The Wall*, his first novel, was critically acclaimed in places such as *Locus*, *Interzone* and *The Hindu*, and was shortlisted for the 2020 Valley of Words Award in the English fiction category. *The Horizon* is the sequel to *The Wall*.